T0144267

The Life and Adventures of Peter Wilkins

The Life and Adventures of Peter Wilkins

Robert Paltock

MINT EDITIONS

The Life and Adventures of Peter Wilkins was first published in 1751.

This edition published by Mint Editions 2021.

ISBN 9781513218427 | E-ISBN 9781513217420

Published by Mint Editions®

 MINT EDITIONS

minteditionbooks.com

Publishing Director: Jennifer Newens
Design & Production: Rachel Lopez Metzger
Project Manager: Micaela Clark
Typesetting: Westchester Publishing Services

CONTENTS

Volume II

Preface

In one of those bright racy essays at which modern dulness delights to sneer, Hazlitt discussed the question whether the desire of posthumous fame is a legitimate aspiration; and the conclusion at which he arrived was that there is "something of egotism and even of pedantry in this sentiment." It is a true saying in literature as in morality that "he that seeketh his life shall lose it." The world cares most for those who have cared least for the world's applause. A nameless minstrel of the North Country sings a ballad that shall stir men's hearts from age to age with haunting melody; Southey, toiling at his epics, is excluded from Parnassus. Some there are who have knocked at the door of the Temple of Fame, and have been admitted at once and forever. When Thucydides announced that he intended his history to be a "possession for all time," there was no mistaking the tone of authority. But to be enthroned in state, to receive the homage of the admiring multitude, and then to be rejected as a pretender,—that is indeed a sorry fate, and one that may well make us pause before envying literary despots their titles. The more closely a writer shrouds himself from view, the more eager are his readers to get a sight of him. The loss of an arm or a leg would be a slight price for a genuine student to pay if only he could discover one new fact about Shakespeare's history. I will not attempt to impose on the reader's credulity by professing myself eager to acquire information about the author of "Peter Wilkins" at such a sacrifice; but it would have been a sincere pleasure to me if I could have brought to light some particulars about one whose personality must have possessed a more than ordinary charm. The delightful *voyage imaginaire* here presented to the reader was first published in 1751.*

An edition appeared immediately afterwards at Dublin; so the book must have had some sale. The introduction and the dedication to the Countess of Northumberland (to whom it will be remembered Percy dedicated his "Reliques" and Goldsmith the first printed copy of his "Edwin and Angelina") are signed with the initials "R. P.;" and for many years the author's full name was unknown. In 1835, Nicol, the printer, sold by auction a number of books and manuscripts in his possession,

---

* Some copies are said to be dated 1750. It appears on the list of new books announced in the "Gentleman's Magazine" for November 1750.

which had once belonged to Dodsley, the publisher; and when these were being catalogued, the original agreement* for the sale of the MS. of "Peter Wilkins" was brought to light.

From this document it appeared that the author was Robert Paltock of Clement's Inn, and that he received for the copyright 20L., twelve copies of the book, and "the cuts of the first impression" (proof impressions of the illustrations). The writer's name shows him to have been, like his hero, of Cornish origin; but the authors of the admirable and exhaustive "Bibliotheca Cornubiensis" could discover nothing about him beyond the fact that he was not a bencher of Clement's Inn. That Paltock should have chosen Clement's Inn as a place of residence is not surprising. It still keeps something of its pristine repose. The sun-dial is still supported by the negro; the grass has not lost its verdure, and on August evenings the plane-trees' leaves glint golden in the sun. One may still hear the chimes at midnight as Falstaff and Justice Shallow heard them of old. Here, where only a muffled murmur comes from the work-a-day world, a man in the last century might have dreamed away his life, lonely as Peter Wilkins on the island. One can imagine the amiable recluse composing his homely romance amid such surroundings. Perhaps it was the one labour of his life. He may have come to the Inn originally with the aspiration of making fame and money; and then the spirit of cloistered calm turned him from such vulgar paths, and instead of losing his fine feelings and swelling the ranks of the plutocrats, he gave us a charming romance for our fireside. With the literary men of his day he seems to have had no intercourse. Not a single mention of him is to be found among his contemporaries, and we may be sure that he cut no brilliant figure at the club-houses. No chorus of reviewers chimed the praises of "Peter Wilkins." So far as I can discover, the "Monthly Review" was the only journal in which the book was noticed, and such criticism as the following can hardly be termed laudatory:—"Here is a very strange performance indeed. It seems to be the illegitimate offspring of no very natural conjunction, like 'Gulliver's Travels' and 'Robinson

---

* It is now in the collection, shortly to be dispersed, of the late Mr. James Crossley of Manchester, a gentleman who was esteemed throughout his long life not less for unfailing courtesy than for rare scholarship. Mr. Crossley promised to search for the document and send me a transcript of it; but his kind intention was frustrated by his death. Paltock's name is sometimes written Pultock or Poltock. There is no ground for identifying the author of "Peter Wilkins" with the "R. P., Gent.," who published in 1751 "Memoirs of the Life of Parnese, a Spanish Lady, Translated from the Spanish MS."

Crusoe;' but much inferior to the manner of these two performances as to entertainment or utility. It has all that is impossible in the one or impossible in the other, without the wit and spirit of the first, or the just strokes of nature and useful lessons of morality in the second. However, if the invention of wings for mankind to fly with is sufficient amends for all the dulness and unmeaning extravagance of the author, we are willing to allow that his book has some merit, and that he deserves some encouragement at least as an able mechanic, if not as a good author." But the book was not forgotten. A new edition appeared in 1783, and again in the following year. It was included in Weber's "Popular Romances," 1812, and published separately, with some charming plates by Stothard, in 1816. Within the last fifty years it has been frequently issued, entire or mutilated, in a popular form. A drama founded on the romance was acted at Covent Garden on April 16, 1827; and more than once of late years "Peter Wilkins" has afforded material for pantomimes. In 1763 a French translation (by Philippe Florent de Puisieux) appeared under the title of "Les Hommes Volants, ou les Aventures de Pierre Wilkins," which was included in vols. xxii–xxiii. of DePerthe's "Voyages Imaginaires" (1788–89). A German translation was published in 1767, having for title "Die fliegenden Menschen, oder wunderbare Begebenheiten Peter Wilkins." Whether the author lived to see the translations of this work cannot be ascertained. A Robert Paltock was buried at Ryme Intrinseca Church, Dorset, in 1767, aged seventy (Hutchin's "Dorset," iv. 493–494, third edition), but it is very doubtful whether he was the author of the romance.

Paltock's fame may be said to be firmly established. An American writer, it is true, in a recent "History of Fiction," says not a word about "Peter Wilkins;" but, we must remember, another American wrote a "History of Caricature" without mentioning Rowlandson. Coleridge admired the book, and is reported to have said: "Peter Wilkins is, to my mind, a work of uncommon beauty. . . I believe that 'Robinson Crusoe' and 'Peter Wilkins' could only have been written by islanders. No continentalist could have conceived either tale. . . It would require a very peculiar genius to add another tale *ejusdem generis* to 'Robinson Crusoe' and 'Peter Wilkins.' I once projected such a thing, but the difficulty of the preoccupied ground stopped me. Perhaps La Motte Fouqué might effect something; but I should fear that neither he nor any other German could entirely understand what may be called the *desert island* feeling. I would try the marvellous line of 'Peter Wilkins' if I attempted it rather than the real fiction of 'Robinson Crusoe'" ("Table-Talk," 1851, pp. 331–332). Southey, in a note on a passage of the "Curse of Kehama," went so far as to say that Paltock's winged people "are the most beautiful creatures of imagination that ever were devised," and added that Sir Walter Scott was a warm admirer of the book. With Charles Lamb at Christ's Hospital the story was a favourite. "We had classics of our own," he says, "without being beholden to 'insolent Greece or haughty Rome,' that passed current among us—'Peter Wilkins,' the 'Adventures of the Hon. Captain Robert Boyle,' the 'Fortunate Blue-Coat Boy,' and the like." But nobody loved the old romance with such devotion as Leigh Hunt. He was never tired of discoursing about its beauties, and he wrote with such thorough appreciation of his subject that he left little or nothing for another to add. "It is interesting," he writes in one place, "to fancy R. P., or 'Mr. Robert Paltock of Clement's Inn,' a gentle lover of books, not successful enough, perhaps, as a barrister to lead a public or profitable life, but eking out a little employment or a bit of a patrimony with literature congenial to him, and looking oftener to 'Purchase Pilgrims' on his shelves than to 'Coke on Littleton.' We picture him to ourselves with 'Robinson Crusoe' on one side of him and 'Gaudentio di Lucca' on the other, hearing the pen go over his paper in one of those quiet rooms in Clement's Inn that look out of its old-fashioned buildings into the little garden with the dial in it held by the negro: one of the prettiest corners in London, and extremely fit for a sequestered fancy that cannot get any further. There he sits, the unknown, ingenious, and amiable Mr. Robert Paltock, thinking of an imaginary beauty for want of a better, and creating her for the delight of posterity, though his contemporaries were to know little or nothing of her. We shall never go through the place again without regarding him as its crowning interest. . . Now a sweeter creature [than Youwarkee] is not to be found in books; and she does him immortal honour. She is all tenderness and vivacity; all born good taste and blessed companionship. Her pleasure consists but in his; she prevents all his wishes; has neither prudery nor immodesty; sheds not a tear but from right feeling; is the good of his home and the grace of his fancy. It has been well observed that the author has not made his flying women in general light and airy enough. . . And it may be said, on the other hand, that the kind of wing, the graundee, or elastic drapery which opens and shuts at pleasure, however ingeniously and even beautifully contrived, would necessitate creatures whose modifications of humanity, bodily and mental, though never so good after their kind, might have startled the inventor had he been more of a naturalist; might have developed a being very different from the feminine, sympathising, and lovely Youwarkee. Muscles and nerves not human must have been associated with inhuman wants and feelings; probably have necessitated talons and a beak! At best the woman would have been wilder, more elvish, capricious, and unaccountable. She would have ruffled her whalebones when angry; been horribly intimate, perhaps, with birds' nests and fights with eagles; and frightened Wilkins out of his wits with dashing betwixt rocks and pulling the noses of seals and gulls. ("Book for a Corner," 1868, i. 68, &c.) Could criticism be more delightful? But in the "London Journal," November 5, 1834, the genial essayist's fancy dallied even more daintily with the theme: "A peacock with his plumage displayed, full of 'rainbows and starry eyes,' is a fine object, but think of a lovely woman set in front of an ethereal shell and wafted about like a Venus. . . We are to picture to ourselves a nymph in a vest of the finest texture and most delicate carnation. On a sudden this drapery parts in two and flies back, stretched from head to foot like an oval fan or an umbrella; and the lady is in front of it, preparing to sweep blushing away from us and 'winnow the buxom air.'"

For many of us the conduct of life is becoming evermore a thing of greater perplexity. It is wearisome to be rudely jostling one another for the world's prizes, while myriads are toiling round us in an Egyptian bondage unlit by one ray of sunshine from the cradle to the grave. Some have attained to Lucretian heights of philosophy, whence they look with indifference over the tossing world-wide sea of human misery; but others are fain to avert their eyes, to clean forget for a season the actual world and lose themselves in the mazes of romance. In moments of despondency there is no greater relief to a fretted spirit than to turn to the "Odyssey" or Mr. Payne's exquisite translation of the "Arabian Nights." Great should be our gratitude to Mr. Morris for teaching us in golden verse that "Love is Enough," and for spreading wide the gates of his "Earthly Paradise." Lucian's "True History," that carries us over unknown seas beyond the Atlantic bounds to enchanted islands in the west, is one of those books which we do not half appreciate. And among the world's benefactors Robert Paltock deserves a place. An idle hour could not be spent in a much pleasanter way than in watching Peter Wilkins go a-field with his gun or haul up the beast-fish at the lonely creek. What can be more delightful than the description how, wakened from dreams of home by the noise of strange voices overhead, he sees fallen at his door the lovely winged woman Youwarkee! Prudish people may be scandalised at the unreserved frankness shown in the account of the consummation of Wilkins' marriage with this fair creature; but the editor was unwilling to mutilate the book in the interests of such refined readers. A man or a woman who can find anything to shock his or her feelings in the description of Youwarkee's bridal night deserves the commiseration of sensible people. Very charming is the picture of the children sitting round the fire on the long winter evenings listening wide-eyed to the ever-fresh story of their father's marvellous adventures. The wholesome morality, the charitableness and homely piety apparent throughout, give the narrative a charm denied to many works of greater literary pretension. When Peter Wilkins leaves his solitary home to live among the winged people, the interest of the story, it must be confessed, is somewhat diminished. The author's obligations to Swift in the latter part of the book are considerable; and of course in describing how Peter Wilkins ordered his life on the lonely island, he was largely indebted to Defoe. But the creation of the winged beings is Paltock's own. It has been suggested that he named his hero after John Wilkins, Bishop of Chester, who, among other curious theories, had seriously discussed the question whether men could acquire the art of flying. In the second part of his "Mathematical Magick," the Bishop writes: "Those things that seem very difficult and fearfull at the first may grow very facil after frequent trial and exercise: And therefore he that would effect anything in this kind must be brought up to the constant practice of it from his Youth; trying first only to use his wings in running on the ground, as an Estrich or tame geese will do, touching the earth with his toes; and so by degrees learn to rise higher till he shall attain unto skill and confidence. I have heard it from credible testimony that one of our nation hath proceeded so far in this experiment that he was able by the help of wings to skip constantly ten yards at a time." Youwarkee spread wide her graundee, and in an instant was lost in the clouds. Had the author given her the motion of a goose, or even of an ostrich—bah! the thought is too dreadful.

Judicious reader, the long winter evenings have come round, and you have now abundance of leisure. Let the poets stand idle on the shelves till the return of spring, unless perchance you would fain resume acquaintance with the "Seasons," which you have not read since a boy, or would divert yourself with Prior or be grave with Crabbe. Now is the time to feel once more the charm of Lamb's peerless and unique essays; now is the time to listen to the honied voice of Leigh Hunt discoursing daintily of men and books. So you will pass from Charles Lamb and Leigh Hunt to the books they loved to praise. Exult in the full-blooded, bracing life which pulses in the pages of Fielding; and if Smollett's mirth is occasionally too riotous and his taste too coarse, yet confess that all faults must be pardoned to the author of "Humphry Clinker." Many a long evening you will spend pleasantly with Defoe; and then, perchance, after a fresh reading of the thrice and four times wonderful adventures of Robinson Crusoe, you will turn to the romance of "Peter Wilkins." So may rheums and catarrhs be far from you, and may your hearth be crowned with content!

A. H. B.
5 Willow Road, Hampstead, November 1883

A Cornish Man:
Relating particularly,
    His Shipwreck near the South Pole; his wonderful Passage thro' a subterraneous Cavern into a kind of new World; his there meeting with a Gawry or flying woman, whose Life he preserv'd, and afterwards married her; his extraordinary Conveyance to the Country of Glums and Gawrys, or Men and Women that fly. Likewise a Description of this strange Country, with the Laws, Customs, and Manners of its Inhabitants, and the Author's remarkable Transactions among them.
    Taken from his own Mouth, in his Passage to England from off Cape Horn in America, in the ship Hector,
    With an Introduction, giving an Account of the surprizing Manner of his coming on board that Vessel, and his Death on his landing at Plymouth in the Year 1739.
    Illustrated with several Cuts, clearly and distinctly representing the Structure and Mechanism of the Wings of the Glums and Gawrys, and the Manner in which they use them either to swim or fly.

To the Right Honourable
Elizabeth,
Countess of Northumberland, Madam,
    Few Authors, I believe, who write in my Way (whatever View they may set out with) can, in the Prosecution of their

Works, forbear to dress their fictitious Characters in the real Ornaments themselves have been most delighted with.

THIS, I confess, hath been my Case, in the Person of *Youwarkee*, in the following Sheets; for having formed her Body, I found myself at an inexpressible Loss how to adorn her Mind in the masterly Sentiments I coveted to endue her with; 'till I recollected the most aim[i]able Pattern in your Ladyship; a single View of which, at a Time of the utmost fatigue to his Lordship, hath charmed my Imagination ever since.

If a Participater of the Cares of Life in general, alleviates the Concerns of Man; what an invaluable Blessing must that Lady prove, to the Softness of whose Sex Nature hath conjoined an Aptitude for Council, an Application, Zeal, and Dispatch but too rarely found in his own!

Had my Situation in Life been so happy as to have presented me with Opportunities of more frequent and minuter Remarks upon your Ladyship's Conduct, I might have defy'd the whole *British* Fair to have outshone my southern Gawry: For if, to a majestic Form and extensive Capacity, I had been qualified to have copied that natural Sweetness of Disposition, that maternal Tenderness, that Cheerfulness, that Complacency, Condescension, Affability, and unaffected Benevolence, which so apparently distinguish the Countess of *Northumberland*; I had exhibited in my *Youwarkee* a Standard for future Generations.

Madam, I am the more sensible of my Speaking but the Truth from the late Instance of your Benignity, which entitles me to the Honour of subscribing myself,

Madam, Your Ladyship's
most obliged and
most obedient Servant,
R. P.

VOLUME I

The Introduction

I t might be looked upon as impertinent in me, who am about to give the life of another, to trouble the reader with any of my own concerns, or the affairs that led me into the South Seas. Therefore I shall only acquaint him, that in my return on board the "Hector," as a passenger, round Cape Horn, for England, full late in the season, the wind and currents setting strong against us, our ship drove more southernly, by several degrees, than the usual course, even to the latitude of 75 or 76; when the wind chopping about, we began to resume our intended way. It was about the middle of June, when the days are there at the shortest, on a very starry and moonlight night, that we observed at some distance a very black cloud, but seemingly of no extraordinary size or height, moving very fast towards us, and seeming to follow the ship, which then made great way. Everyone on deck was very curious in observing its motions; and perceiving it frequently to divide, and presently to close again, and not to continue long in any determined shape, our captain, who had never before been so far to the southward as he then found himself, had many conjectures what this phenomenon might portend; and everyone offering his own opinion, it seemed at last to be generally agreed that there might possibly be a storm gathering in the air, of which this was the prognostic; and by its following, and nearly keeping pace with us, we were in great fear lest it should break upon and overwhelm us, if not carefully avoided. Our commander, therefore, as it approached nearer and nearer, ordered one of the ship's guns to be fired, to try if the percussion of the air would disperse it. This was no sooner done than we heard a prodigious flounce in the water, at but a small distance from the ship, on the weather-quarter; and after a violent noise, or cry in the air, the cloud, that upon our firing dissipated, seemed to return again, but by degrees disappeared. Whilst we were all very much surprised at this unexpected accident, I, being naturally very curious and inquisitive into the causes of all unusual incidents, begged the captain to send the boat to see, if possible, what it was that had fallen from the cloud, and offered myself to make one in her. He was much against this at first, as it would retard his voyage, now we were going so smoothly before the wind. But in the midst of our debate, we plainly heard a voice calling out for help, in our own tongue, like a person in great distress. I then insisted on going, and not suffering a fellow-creature to perish for the sake of a trifling delay. In compliance with my resolute demand, he slackened sail; and hoisting out the boat, myself and seven others made to the cry, and soon found it to come from an elderly man, labouring for life, with his arms across several long poles, of equal size at both ends, very light, and tied to each other in a very odd manner. The sailors at first were very fearful of assisting or coming near him, crying to each other, "He must be a monster!" and perhaps might overset the boat and destroy them; but hearing him speak English, I was very angry with them for their foolish apprehensions, and caused them to clap their oars under him, and at length we got him into the boat. He had an extravagant beard, and also long blackish hair upon his head. As soon as he could speak (for he was almost spent), he very familiarly took me by the hand, I having set myself close by him to observe him, and squeezing it, thanked me very kindly for my civility to him, and likewise thanked all the sailors. I then asked him by what possible accident he came there; but he shook his head, declining to satisfy my curiosity. Hereupon reflecting that it might just then be troublesome for him to speak, and that we should have leisure enough in our voyage for him to relate, and me to hear, his story (which, from the surprising manner of his falling amongst us, I could not but believe would contain something very remarkable), I waived any farther speech with him at that time.

We had him to the ship, and taking off his wet clothes, put him to bed in my cabin; and I having a large provision of stores on board, and no concern in the ship, grew very fond of him, and supplied him with everything he wanted. In our frequent discourses together, he had several times dropped loose hints of his past transactions, which but the more inflamed me with impatience to hear the whole of them. About this time, having just begun to double the Cape, our captain thought of watering at the first convenient place; and finding the stranger had no money to pay his passage, and that he had been from England no less than thirty-five years, despairing of his reward for conducting him thither, he intimated to him that he must expect to be put on shore to shift for himself, when we put in for water. This entirely sunk the stranger's spirits, and gave me great concern, insomuch that I fully resolved, if the captain should really prove such a brute, to take the payment of his passage on myself.

As we came nearer to the destined watering, the captain spoke the plainer of his intentions (for I had not yet hinted my design to him or anyone else); and one morning the stranger came into my cabin, with tears in his eyes, telling me he verily believed the captain would be as good as his word, and set him on shore, which he very much dreaded. I did not choose to tell him immediately what I designed in his favour, but asked him if he could think of no way of satisfying the captain, or anyone else, who might thereupon be induced to engage for him; and farther, how he expected to live when he should get to England, a man quite forgotten and penniless. Hereupon he told me he had, ever since his being on board, considering his destitute condition, entertained a thought of having his adventures written; which, as there was something so uncommon in them, he was sure the world would be glad to know; and he had flattered himself with hopes of raising somewhat by the sale of them to put him in a way of living; but as it was plain now he should never see England without my assistance, if I would answer for his passage, and write his life, he would communicate to me a faithful narrative thereof, which he believed would pay me to the full any charge I might be at on his account. I was very well pleased with this overture, not from the prospect of gain by the copy, but from the expectation I had of being fully satisfied in what I had so long desired to know; so I told him I would make him easy in that respect. This quite transported him: he caressed me, and called me his deliverer, and was then going open-mouthed to the captain to tell him so. But I put a stop to that: For, says I, though I insist upon hearing your story, the captain may yet relent of his purpose, and not leave you on shore; and if that should prove the case, I shall neither part with my money for you, nor you with your interest in your adventures to me. Whereupon he agreed I was right, and desisted.

When we had taken in best part of our water, and the boat was going its last turn, the captain ordered up the strange man, as they called him, and told him he must go on board the boat, which was to leave him on shore with some few provisions. I happening to hear nothing of these orders, they were so sudden, the poor man was afraid, after all, he should have been hurried to land without my knowledge: but begging very hard of the captain only for leave to speak with me before he went, I was called (though with some reluctance, for the captain disliked me for the liberties I frequently took with him, on account of his brutal behaviour). I expostulated with the cruel wretch on the inhumanity of the action he was about; telling him, if he had resolved the poor man should perish, it would have been better to have suffered him to do so when he was at the last extremity, than to expose him afresh, by this means, to a death as certain, in a more lingering and miserable way. But the savage being resolved, and nothing moved by what I said, I paid him part of the passage down, and agreed to pay the rest at our arrival in England.

Thus having reprieved the poor man, the next thing was to enter upon my new employ of amanuensis: and having a long space of time before us, we allotted two hours every morning for the purpose of writing down his life from his own mouth; and frequently, when wind and weather kept us below, we spent sometime of an afternoon in the same exercise, till we had quite completed it. But then there were somethings in it so indescribable by words, that if I had not had some knowledge in drawing, our history had been very incomplete. Thus it must have been, especially in the description of the *Glumms* and *Gawrys* therein mentioned. In order to gain (that so I might communicate) a clear idea of these, I made several drawings of them from his discourses and accounts; and, at length, after divers trials, I made such exact delineations, that he declared they could not have been more perfect resemblances if I had drawn them from the life. Upon a survey, he confessed the very persons themselves could not have been more exact. I also drew with my pencil the figure of an aerial engagement, which, having likewise had his approbation, I have given a draught of, plate the sixth.

Then, having finished the work to our mutual satisfaction, I locked it up, in order to peruse it at leisure, intending to have presented it to him at our arrival in England, to dispose of as he pleased, in such a way as might have conduced most to his profit; for I resolved, notwithstanding our agreement, and the obligations he was under to me, that the whole of that should be his own. But he, having been in a declining state sometime before we reached shore, died the very night we landed; and his funeral falling upon me, I thought I had the greatest right to the manuscript, which, however, I had no design to have parted with; but showing it to some judicious friends, I have by them been prevailed with not to conceal from the world what may prove so very entertaining, and perhaps useful.

R. P.
A Genuine Account
of the
Life of Peter Wilkins

I

GIVING AN ACCOUNT OF THE AUTHOR'S BIRTH AND FAMILY—
THE FONDNESS OF HIS MOTHER—HIS BEING PUT TO AN
ACADEMY AT SIXTEEN BY THE ADVICE OF HIS FRIEND—
HIS THOUGHTS OF HIS OWN ILLITERATURE

I was born at Penhale, in the county of Cornwall, on the 21st day of December 1685, about four months after my father, Peter Wilkins, who was a zealous Protestant of the Church of England, had been executed by Jeffreys, in Somersetshire, for joining in the design of raising the Duke of Monmouth to the British throne. I was named, after my father and grandfather, Peter, and was my father's only child by Alice his wife, the daughter of John Capert, a clergyman in a neighbouring village. My grandfather was a shopkeeper at Newport, who, by great frugality and extraordinary application, had raised a fortune of about £160 a year in lands, and a considerable sum of ready money, all which at his death devolved upon my father, as his only child; who, being no less parsimonious than my grandfather, and living upon his own estate, had much improved it in value before his marriage with my mother; but he coming to that unhappy end, my mother, after my birth, placed all her affection upon me (her growing hope, as she called me), and used every method, in my minority, of increasing the store for my benefit.

In this manner she went on, till I grew too big, as I thought, for confinement at the apron-string, being then about fourteen years of age; and having met with so much indulgence from her, for that reason found very little or no contradiction from anybody else; so I looked on myself as a person of some consequence, and began to take all opportunities of enjoying the company of my neighbours, who hinted frequently that the restraint I was under was too great a curb upon an inclination like mine of seeing the world; but my mother, still impatient of any little absence, by excessive fondness, and encouraging every inclination I seemed to have, when she could be a partaker with me, kept me within bounds of restraint till I arrived at my sixteenth year.

About this time I got acquainted with a country gentleman, of a small paternal estate, which had been never the better for being in his hands, and had some uneasy demands upon it. He soon grew very fond of me, hoping, as I had reason afterwards to believe, by a union with my mother to set himself free from his entanglements. She was then about thirty-five years old, and still continued my father's widow, out of particular regard to me, as I have all the reason in the world to believe. She was really a beautiful woman, and of a sanguine complexion, but had always carried herself with so much reserve, and given so little encouragement to any of the other sex, that she had passed her widowhood with very few solicitations to alter her way of life. This gentleman observing my mother's conduct, in order to ingratiate himself with her, had shown numberless instances of regard for me; and, as he told my mother, had observed many things in my discourse, actions, and turn of mind, that presaged wonderful expectations from me, if my genius was but properly cultivated.

This discourse, from a man of very good parts, and esteemed by everybody an accomplished gentleman, by degrees wrought upon my mother, and more and more inflamed her with a desire of adding what lustre she could to my applauded abilities, and influenced her so far as to ask his advice in what manner most properly to proceed with me. My gentleman then had his desire, for he feared not the widow, could he but properly dispose of her charge; so having desired a little time to consider of a matter of such importance, he soon after told her he thought the most useful method of establishing me would be at an academy, kept by a very worthy and judicious gentleman, about thirty, or more, miles from us, in Somersetshire; where, if I could but be admitted, the master taking in but a stated number of students at a time, he did not in the least doubt but I should fully answer the character he had given her of me, and outshine most of my contemporaries.

My mother, over-anxious for my good, seeming to listen to this proposal, my friend (as I call him) proposed taking a journey himself to the academy, to see if any place was vacant for my reception, and learn the terms of my admission; and in three days' time returned with an engaging account of the place, the master, the regularity of the scholars, of an apartment secured for my reception, and, in short, whatever else might captivate my mother's opinion in favour of his scheme; and indeed, though he acted principally from another motive, as was plain afterwards, I cannot help thinking he believed it to be the best way of disposing of a lad sixteen years old, born to a pretty fortune, and who, at that age, could but just read a chapter in the Testament; for he had before beat my mother quite out of her inclination to a grammar-school in the neighbourhood, from a contempt, he said, it would bring upon me from lads much my juniors in years, by being placed in the first rudiments of learning with them.

Well, the whole concern of my mother's little family was now employed in fitting me out for my expedition; and as my friend had been so instrumental in bringing it about, he never missed a day inquiring how preparations went on; and during the process, by humouring me, ingratiated himself more and more with my mother, but without seeming in the least to aim at it. In short, the hour of my departure arrived; and though I had never been master of above a sixpence at one time, unless at a fair or so, for immediate spending, my mother, thinking to make my heart easy at our separation (which, had it appeared otherwise, would have broke hers, and spoiled all), gave me a double pistole in gold, and a little silver in my pocket to prevent my changing it.

Thus I (the coach waiting for us at the door), having been preached into a good liking of the scheme by my friend, who now insisted upon making one of our company to introduce us, mounted the carriage with more alacrity than could be expected for one who had never before been beyond the smoke of his mother's chimney; but the thoughts I had conceived, from my friend's discourse, of liberty in the academic way, and the weight of so much money in my pocket, as I then imagined would scarce ever be exhausted, were prevailing cordials to keep my spirits on the wing. We lay at an inn that night, near the master's house, and the next day I was initiated; and, at parting with me, my friend presented me with a guinea. When I found myself thus rich, I must say I heartily wished they were all fairly at home again, that I might have time to count my cash, and dispose of such part of it as I had already appropriated to several uses then in embryo.

The next morning left me master of my wishes, for my mother came and took her last (though she little thought it) leave of me, and smothering me with her caresses and prayers for my well-doing, in the height of her ardour put into my hand another guinea, promising to see me again quickly; and desiring me, in the meantime, to be a very good husband, which I have since taken to be a sort of prophetic speech, she bid me farewell.

I shall not trouble you with the reception I met from my master, or his scholars, or tell you how soon I made friends of all my companions, by some trifling largesses which my stock enabled me to bestow as occasion required; but I must inform you that, after sixteen years of idleness at home, I had but little heart to my nouns and pronouns, which now began to be crammed upon me; and being the eldest lad in the house, I sometimes regretted the loss of the time past, and at other times despaired of ever making a scholar at my years; and was ashamed to stand like a great lubber, declining of *hæc mulier* a woman, whilst my schoolfellows, and juniors by five years, were engaged in the love stories of Ovid, or the luscious songs of Horace. I own these thoughts almost overcame me, and threw me into a deep melancholy, of which I soon after, by letter, informed my mother; who (by the advice, as I suppose, of my friend, by this time her suitor) sent me word to mind my studies, and I should want for nothing.

II

I had now been passing my time for about three months in this melancholy way, and, you may imagine, under that disadvantage, had made but little progress in my learning, when one of our maids, taking notice one day of my uneasiness, as I sat musing in my chamber, according to my custom, began to rally me that I was certainly in love, I was so sad. Indeed I never had a thought of love before, but the good-natured girl seeming to pity me, and seriously asking me the cause, I fairly opened my heart to her; and for fear my master should know it, gave her half-a-crown to be silent. This last engagement fixed her my devotee, and from that time we had frequent conferences in confidence together, till at length inclination, framed by opportunity, produced the date of a world of concern to me; for about six months after my arrival at the academy, instead of proving my parts by my scholarship, I had proved my manhood by being the destined father of an infant which my female correspondent then assured me would soon be my own.

We nevertheless held on our frequent intercourse; nor was I so alarmed at the news as I ought to have been, till about two months after, when Patty (for that was the only name I then knew her by) explained herself to me in the following terms:—"You know, Mr. Peter, how matters are with me: I should be very sorry, for your sake, and my own too, to reveal my shame, but in spite of us both nature will show itself; and truly I think some care should be taken, and some method proposed, to preserve the infant, and avoid, as far as may be, the inconveniences that may attend us, for here is now no room for delay." This speech, I own, gave me the first reflection I ever had in my life, and locked up all my faculties for a long time; nor was I able, for the variety of ideas that crowded my brain, to make a word of answer, but stood like an image of stone, till Patty, seeing my confusion, desired me to recollect my reason; for as it was too late to undo what had been done, it remained now only to act with that prudence and caution which the nature of the case required; and that, for her part, she would concur in every reasonable measure I should approve of; but I must remember she was only a servant, and had very little due to her for wages, and not a penny besides that; and that there must necessarily be a preparation made for the reception of the infant when time should produce it. I now began to see the absolute necessity of all she said, but how to accomplish it was not in me to comprehend. My own small matter of money was gone, and had been so a long time; we therefore agreed I should write to my mother for a fresh supply. I did so; and to my great confusion was answered by my former friend in the following words:—

Son Peter,

Your mother and I are much surprised you should write for money, having so amply provided for you; but as it is not many months to Christmas, when possibly we may send for you home, you must make yourself easy till then; as a school-boy, with all necessaries found him, cannot have much occasion for money.

Your loving father,
J. G.

Imagine, if it is possible, my consternation at the receipt of this letter. I began to think I should be tricked out of what my father and grandfather had with so much pains and industry for many years been, heaping up for me, and had a thousand thoughts all together jostling out each other, so could resolve on nothing. I then showed Patty the letter, and we both condoled my hard fortune, but saw no remedy. Time wore away, and nothing done, or like to be, as I could see. For my part, I was like one distracted, and no more able to assist or counsel what should be done than a child in arms. At length poor Patty, who had sat thinking sometime, began with telling me she had formed a scheme which in some measure might help us; but fearing it might be disagreeable to me, she durst not mention it till I should assure her, whatever I thought of that, I would think no worse of her for proposing it. This preparatory introduction startled me a great deal; for it darted into my head she waited for my concurrence to destroy the child, to which I could never have consented. But upon my assuring her I would not think the worse of her for whatever she should propose, but freely give her my opinion upon it, she told me, as she could see no other way before us but what tended to our disgrace and ruin, if I would marry her she would immediately quit her place and return to her aunt, who had brought her up from a child, and had enough prettily to live upon, who, she did not doubt, would entertain her as my wife; but she was assured, upon any other score, or under any other name, would prove her most inveterate enemy. When Patty had made an end, I was glad to find it no worse; and revolving matters a little in my mind, both as to affairs at home and the requested marriage, I concluded upon this latter, and had a great inclination to acquaint my mother of it, but was diverted from that, by suspecting it might prove a good handle for my new father to work with my mother some mischief against me; so determined to marry forthwith, send Patty to her aunt's, and remain still at the academy myself till I should see what turn things would take at home. Accordingly, the next day good part of Patty's wages went to tie the connubial knot, and to the honest parson for a bribe to antedate the certificate; and she very soon after took up the rest to defray her journey to her aunt's.

Though Patty was within two months of her time, she had so managed that no one perceived it; and getting safe to her aunt's, was delivered of a daughter, of which she wrote me word, and said she hoped to see me at the end of her month. How, thought I, can she expect to see me; money I have none! and then I despaired of leave for a journey if I had it; and to go without leave would only arm J. G. against me, as I perceived plainly his interest and mine were very remote things; so I resolved to quit all thoughts of a journey, and wait till opportunity better served for seeing my wife and child, and our good aunt to whom we were so much obliged. While these and such-like cogitations engrossed my whole attention, I was most pleasingly surprised one day, upon my return-from a musing walk by the river-side at the end of our garden, where I frequently got my tasks, to find Patty sitting in the kitchen with my old mistress, my master's mother, who managed his house, he having been a widower many years. The sight of her almost overcame me, as I had bolted into the kitchen, and was seen by my old mistress before I had seen Patty was with her. The old lady, perceiving me discomposed, inquired into the cause, which I directly imputed to the symptoms of an ague that I told her I had felt upon me best part of the morning. She, a good motherly woman, feeling my pulse, and satisfying herself of its disorder, immediately ran to her closet to bring me a cordial, which she assured me had done wonders in the like cases; so that I had but just time to embrace Patty and inquire after our aunt and daughter before madam returned with the cordial. Having drank it, and given thanks, I was going to withdraw, but she would not part with me so; for nothing less than my knowledge that this cordial was of her own making, from whence she had the receipt, and an exact catalogue of the several cures it had done, would serve her turn; which, taking up full three-quarters of an hour, gave room to Patty and me to enjoy each other's glances for that time, to our mutual satisfaction. At last the old prattlebox having made a short pause to recover breath from the narrative of the cordial, "Mr. Peter," says she, "you look as if you did not know poor Patty; she has not left me so long that you should forget her; she is a good tight wench, and I was sorry to part with her; but she is out of place, she says, and as that dirty creature Nan is gone, I think to take her again." I told her I well knew she was judge of a good servant, and I did not doubt Patty was such, if she thought so; and then I made my exit, lighter in heart by a pound than I came.

I shall not tire you any farther with the amours between self and Patty; but to let you know she quitted her place again seven months after, upon the same score.

III

Minds his studies—Informs his master of his mother's
marriage, and usage of him—Hears of her death—
Makes his master his guardian—Goes with him to take
possession of his estate—Is informed all is given to his
father-in-law—Moral reflections on his condition,
and on his father's crimes.

I was now near nineteen years of age; and though I had so much more
in my head than my school-learning, I know not how it happened,
but ever since the commencement of my amour with Patty, having
somebody to disburden my mind to, and to participate in my concerns,
I had been much easier, and had kept true tally with my book, with
more than usual delight; and being arrived to an age to comprehend
what I heard and read, I could, from the general idea I had of things,
form a pretty regular piece of Latin, without being able to repeat the
very rules it was done by; so that I had the acknowledgment of my
master for the best capacity he ever had under his tuition: this, he not
sparing frequently to mention it before me, was the acutest spur he
could have applied to my industry; and now, having his good will, I
began to disuse set hours of exercise, but at my conveniency applied
myself to my studies as I best pleased, being always sure to perform as
much, or more, than he ever enjoined me; till I grew exceedingly in his
confidence, and by reason of my age (though I was but small, yet manly)
I became rather his companion upon parties than his direct pupil.

It was upon one of these parties I took the opportunity to declare the
dissatisfaction I had at my mother's second marriage. "Sir," says I, "surely
I was of age to have known it first, especially considering the affection
my mother had always shown to me, and my never once having done
the least thing to disoblige her; but, sir," said I, "something else, I fear, is
intended by my mother's silence to me; for I have never received above
three letters from her since I came here, which is now, you know, three
years, and those were within the first three months. I then showed him
the fore-mentioned letter I received from my new father-in-law, and
assured him that gave me the first hint of this second marriage."

I found, by the attention my master gave to my relation, he seemed
to suspect this marriage would prove detrimental to me; but not on the

sudden knowing what to say to it, he told me he would consider of it; and, by all means, advised me to write a very obliging letter to my new father, with my humble request that he would please to order me home the next recess of our learning. I did so under my master's dictation; and not long after received an answer to the following effect:—

Son Peter,
    Your mother has been dead a good while; and as to your request, it will be only expensive, and of little use; for a person who must live by his studies can't apply to them too closely.

This letter, if I had a little hope left, quite subdued my fortitude, and well-nigh reduced me to clay. However, with tears in my eyes, I showed it to my master, who, good man! wishing me well, "Peter," says he, "what can this mean? here is some mystery concealed in it; here is some ill design on foot!" Then taking the letter into his hand, "A person who must live by his studies," says he; "here is more meant than we can think for. Why, have not you a pretty estate to live upon, when it comes to your hands? Peter," says he, "I would advise you to go to your father and inquire how your affairs are left; but I am afraid to let you go alone, and will, when my students depart at Christmas, accompany you myself with all my heart; for you must know I have advised on your affair already, and find you are of age to choose yourself a guardian, who may be any relation or friend you can confide in; and may see you have justice done you." I immediately thanked him for the hint, and begged him to accept of the trust, as my only friend, having very few, if any, near relations: this he with great readiness complied with, and was admitted accordingly.

So soon as our scholars were gone home, my master lending me a horse, we set out together to possess ourselves of all my father's real estate, and such part of the personal as he had been advised would belong to me. Well, we arrived at the old house, but were not received with such extraordinary tokens of friendship as would give the least room to suppose we were welcome. For my part, all I said, or could say, was that I was very sorry for my mother's death. My father replied so was he. Here we paused, and might have sat silent till this time for me, if my master, a grave man, who had seen the world, and was unwilling any part of our time there, which we guessed would be short, should be lost, had not broke silence. "Mr. G." says he, "I see the loss of Master Wilkins's mother puts him under some confusion; so that you will excuse me, as his preceptor and friend, in making some inquiry how his affairs stand, and how his effects are disposed, as I don't doubt you have taken care to schedule everything that will be coming to him; and though he is not yet of the necessary age for taking upon himself the management of his estate, he is nevertheless of capacity to understand the nature and quantum of it, and to show his approbation of the disposition of it, as if he was a year or two older." During this discourse, Mr. G. turned pale, then reddened, was going to interrupt, then checked himself; but however kept silence till my master had done; when, with a sneer, he replied, "Sir, I must own myself a great stranger to your discourse; nor can I, for my life, imagine what your harangue tends to; but sure I am, I know of no estate, real or personal, or anything else belonging to young Mr. Wilkins, to make a schedule of, as you call it: but this I know, his mother had an estate in land, near two hundred a year, and also a good sum of money when I married her; but the estate she settled on me before her marriage, to dispose of after her decease as I saw fit; and her money and goods are all come to my sole use, as her husband." I was just ready to drop while Mr. G. gave this relation, and was not able to reply a word; but my master, though sufficiently shocked at what he had heard, replied, "Sir, I am informed the estate, and also the money you mention, was Mr. Wilkins's father's at his death; and I am surprised to think anyone should have a better title to them than my pupil, his only child."—"Sir," says Mr. G., "you are deceived; and though what you say seems plausible enough, and is in some part true, as that the late Mr. Wilkins had such estate, and some hundreds—I may say thousands—at his death; yet you seem ignorant that he made a deed, just before entering into the fatal rebellion, by which he gave my late wife both the estate, money, and everything else he had, absolutely, without any conditions whatsoever; all which, on his unhappy execution, she enjoyed, and now of right, as I told you before, belongs to me. However, as I have no child, if Peter behaves well under your direction, I have thoughts of paying another year's board for him, and then he must shift for himself."—"Oh!" cried I, "for the mercy of some savage beast to devour me! Is this what I have been cockered up for? Why was I not placed out to some laborious craft, where I might have drudged for bread in my proper station? But I fear it is too late to inquire into what is past, and must submit."

My master, good man! was thunderstruck at what he had heard; and finding our business done there, we took our leaves; after Mr. G. had again repeated, that if I behaved well, my preceptor should keep me another year, which was all I must expect from him; and at my departure he gave me a crown-piece, which I then durst not refuse, for fear of offending my master.

We made the best of our way home again to my tutor's, where I stayed but a week to consider what I should do for myself. In this time he did all he could to comfort me; telling me if I would stay with him and become his usher, he would complete my learning for nothing, and allow me a salary for my trouble. But my heart was too lofty to think of becoming an usher within so little way from mine own estate in other hands. However, since I had not a penny of money to endeavour at recovering my right with, I told my master I would consider of his proposal.

During my stay with him he used all methods to make me as easy as possible; and frequently moralised with so much effect, that I was almost convinced I ought to submit and be content. Amongst the rest of his discourse, he endeavoured to show me (one day after I had been loudly condemning my cruel fortune, and saying I was born to be unhappy) that I was mistaken if I thought or imagined it was chance or accident that had been against me when I complained of fortune. "For," says he, "Peter, there is nothing done below but is at least foreknown, if not decreed, above; and our business in life is to believe so: not that I would have such belief make us careless, and think it to no purpose to strive, as some do; who, being persuaded that our actions are not in our own choice, but that, being pressed by an irresistible decree, we are forced to act this or that, fancy we must be necessarily happy or miserable hereafter; or, as others, who, for fear of falling upon that shocking principle, would even deprive the Almighty of foreknowledge, lest it should consequentially amount to a decree: for, say they, what is foreknown, will and must be. But I would have you act so as that, let either of these tenets be true, you may still be sure of making yourself easy and happy; and for that purpose let me recommend to you a uniform life of justice and piety; always choosing the good rather than the bad side of every action: for this, say they what they will to the contrary, is not above the power of a reasonable being to practise: and doing so, you may without scruple say,—If there is foreknowledge of my actions, or they are decreed, I then am one who is foreknown or decreed to be happy. And this, without farther speculation, you will find the only means always to keep you so; for all men, of all denominations, fully allow this happy effect to follow good actions. Again, Peter, a person acting in a vicious course, with such an opinion in his head as above, must surely be very miserable, as his very actions themselves must pronounce the decree against him: whilst, therefore, we have not heard the decree read, you see we may easily give sentence whether it be for good or evil to us, by the tenor and course of our own actions.

"You are not now to learn, Peter, that the crimes of the father are often punished in the children, often in the father himself, sometimes in both, and not seldom in neither, in this life; and though, at first, one should think the future punishment annexed to bad actions was sufficient, still it is necessary some should suffer here also for an example to others; we being much more affected with what the eye sees, than what the heart only meditates upon.

"Now, to bring it to our own case; your father, Peter, rose against the lawful magistrate, to deprive him (it matters not that he was a bad one) of his lawful power. Your father's policy was such, and his design so well laid, as he thought, that upon any ill success to himself, he had secured his estate to go in the way of all others he could wish to have it, and sits down very well contented that, happen what would, he should bite the Government in preventing the forfeiture. But lo! his policy is as a wall of sand blown down with a puff! for it is to you it ought, even himself being umpire, to have come, as no one would think he would prize any before you, his own child. Now, could he look from the grave, and know what passes here, and see Mr. G. in possession of all he fancied he had secured for you, what a weak and short-sighted creature would he find himself! If it be said he did not know he should have a child, then herein appears God's policy beyond man's; for He knew it, and has so ordered that that child should be disinherited; for, by the way, Peter, take this for a maxim, wherever the first principle of an action is ill, no good consequence can possibly ever be an attendant on it. Could he, as I said before, but look up and see you, his only child, undone by the very instrument he designed for your security, how pungent would be his anxiety! I say, Peter, though there is something so unaccountable to human wisdom in such events of things, yet there is something therein so reasonable and just withal, that by a prying eye, the Supreme Hand may very visibly be seen in them. Now, this being plainly the case before us, and herein the glory of the Almighty exalted, rest content under it, and let not this disappointment, befallen you for your father's faults, be attended with others sent down for your own; but remember this, the Hand that depresses a man is no less able to exalt and establish him."

IV

Departs secretly from his master—Travels to
Bristol—Religious thoughts by the way—Enters on
shipboard, and is made captain's steward

I seemed to be very well satisfied whilst my master was speaking; but though I thought he talked like an angel, my former uneasiness seized me at parting with him. In short, without more consideration, I rose in the morning early and marched off, having first wrote to my wife at her aunt's, relating the state of the case to her, with my resolution to leave England the first opportunity, giving her what comfort I could, assuring her if I ever was a gainer in life she should not fail to be a partaker, and promising also to let her know where I settled. I walked at a great rate, for fear my master's kindness should prompt him to send after me; and taking the bye-ways, I reached by dark night a little village, where I resolved to halt. Upon inquiry I found myself thirty-five miles from my master's. I had eaten nothing all day, and was very hungry and weary, but my crown-piece was as yet whole; however I fed very sparingly, being over-pressed with the distress of my affairs and the confusion of my thoughts. I slept that night tolerably, but the morning brought its face of horror with it. I had inquired over-night where I was, and been informed that I was not above sixteen miles from Bristol, for which place I then resolved.

At my setting out in the morning, after I had walked about three miles, and had recollected a little my master's last discourse, I found by degrees my spirit grew calmer than it had been since I left Mr. G. at my house (as I shall ever call it), and looking into myself for the cause, found another set of thoughts were preparing a passage into my mind, which did not carry half the dread and terror with them that their predecessors had; for I began to cast aside the difficulties and apprehensions I before felt in my way, and encouraging the present motions, soon became sensible of the benefit of a virtuous education; and though what I had hitherto done in the immediate service of God, I must own had been performed from force, custom, and habit, and without the least attention to the object of the duty; yet, as under my mother at home, and my master at the academy, I had been always used to say my prayers, as they called it, morning and night: I began, with a sort of superstitious reflection, to accuse myself of having omitted that duty the night before, and also at my setting out in the morning, and very much to blame myself for it, and, at the same instant, even wondered at myself for that blame. What, says I, is the real use of this praying; and to whom or to what do we pray? I see no one to pray to; neither have I ever thought that my prayers would be answered. It is true they are worded as if we prayed to God: but He is in heaven; does He concern Himself with us who can do Him no service? Can I think all my prayers that I have said, from day to day, so many years, have been heard by Him? No, sure; if they had, I should scarce have sustained this hard fate in my fortune. But hold, how have I prayed to Him? Have I earnestly prayed to Him, as I used to petition my mother for anything when I wanted it against her inclination? No, I can't say I have. And would my mother have granted me such things, if she had not thought I had from my heart desired them, when I used to be so earnest with her? No, surely; I can't say she had any reason for it. But I had her indeed before me; now I have not God in my view: He is in heaven. Yet, let me see; my master (and I can't help thinking he must know) used to say that God is a spirit, and not confined by the incumbrance of a body, as we are; now, if it is so, why may He not virtually be present with me, though I don't perceive Him? Why may He not be at once in heaven and elsewhere? For if He consists not in parts, nothing can circumscribe Him: and, truly, I believe it must be so; for if He is of that supreme power as He is represented, He could never act in so unconfined a capacity, under the restraint of place; but if He is an operative and purely spiritual Being, then I can see no reason why His virtual essence should not be diffused through all nature; and then (which I begin to think most likely) why should I not suppose Him ever present with me, and able to hear me? And why should not I, when I pray, have a full idea of the Being, though not of any corporeal parts or form of God, and so have actually somewhat to be intent upon in my prayers, and not do as I have hitherto done, say so many words only upon my knees; which I cannot help thinking may be as well without either sense or meaning in themselves, as without a proper object in my mind to direct them unto?

These thoughts agitated me at least two miles, working stronger and stronger in me; till at length, bursting into tears, Have I been doing nothing, says I, in the sight of God, under the name of prayers, for so many years? Yes, it is certainly so. Well, by the grace of God, it shall be so no longer; I will try somewhat more. So looking round about me, to see if I was quite alone, I stepped into an adjoining copse, and could scarce refrain falling on my knees, till I came to a proper place for kneeling in. I then poured forth my whole soul and spirit to God; and all my strength, and every member, every faculty was to the utmost employed, for a considerable time, in the most agreeable as well as useful duty. I would indeed have begun with my accustomed prayers, and had repeated some words of them; when, as though against and contrary to my design, I was carried away by such rapturous effusions that, to this hour, when I reflect thereon, I cannot believe but I was moved to them by a much more than human impulse. However, this ecstasy did not last above a quarter of an hour; but it was considerably longer before my spirits subsided to their usual frame. When I had a little composed myself, how was I altered! how did I condemn myself for all my past disquiet! what calm thanks did I return for the ease and satisfaction of mind I then enjoyed! And coming to a small rivulet, I drank a hearty draught of water and contentedly proceeded on my journey. I reached Bristol about four o'clock in the afternoon. Having refreshed myself, I went the same evening to the quay to inquire what ships were in the river, whither bound, and when they would depart. My business was with the sailors, of whom there were at that time great numbers there; but I could meet with no employ, though I gave out I would gladly enter myself before the mast. After I had done the best I could, but without success, I returned to the little house I had dined at, and went to bed very pensive. I did not forget my prayers; but I could by no means be roused to such devotion as I felt in the morning. Next day I walked again to the quay, asking all I met, who looked like seafaring men, for employment; but could hear of none, there being many waiting for berths; and I feared my appearance (which was not so mean as most of that sort of gentry is) would prove no small disappointment to my preferment that way. At last, being out of heart with my frequent repulses, I went to a landing-place just by, and as I asked some sailors, who were putting two gentlemen on shore, if they wanted a hand on board their ship, one of the gentlemen, whom I afterwards found to be the master of a vessel bound to the coast of Africa, turned back and looking earnestly on me, "Young man," says he, "do you want employment on board?" I immediately made him a bow, and answered, "Yes, sir." Said he, "There is no talking in this weather (for it then blew almost a storm), but step into that tavern," pointing to the place, "and I will be with you presently." I went thither, and not long after came my future master. He asked me many questions, but the first was, whether I had been at sea. I told him no; but I did not doubt soon to learn the duty of a sailor. He then looked on my hand, and shaking his head, told me it would not do, for I had too soft a hand. I told him I was determined for the sea, and that my hand and heart should go together; and I hoped my hand would soon harden, though not my heart. He then told me it was a pity to take such a pretty young fellow before the mast; but if I understood accounts tolerably, and could write a good hand, he would make me his steward, and make it worth my while. I answered in the affirmative, joyfully accepting his offer; but on his asking me where my chest was (for, says he, if the wind had not been so strong against me, I had fallen down the river this morning), I looked very blank, and plainly told him I had no other stores than I carried on my back. The captain smiled. Says he, "Young man, I see you are a novice; why, the meanest sailor in my ship has a chest, at least, and perhaps something in it. Come," says he, "my lad, I like your looks; be diligent and honest; I will let you have a little money to set you out, and deduct it in your pay." He was then pulling out his purse, when I begged him, as he seemed to show me so great a kindness, that he would order somebody to buy what necessaries he knew I should want for me, or I should be under as great a difficulty to know what to get, and where to buy them, as I should have been at for want of them. He commended my prudence, and said he would buy them and send them on board himself; so bid me trouble myself no more about them, but go to the ship in the return of his boat, and stay there till he came; giving me a ticket to the boat's crew to take me in. When I came to the shore, the boat was gone off and at a good distance; but I hailed them, and showing my ticket, they put back and took me safe to the ship; heartily glad that I was entered upon my new service.

V

His first entertainment on board—Sets sail—
His sickness—Engagement with a French privateer—
Is taken and laid in irons—Twenty-one prisoners turned
adrift in a small boat with only two days' provision

Being once on board and in pay, I thought I was a man for myself, and set about considering how to behave; and nobody knowing, as yet, upon what footing I came on board, they took me for a passenger, as my dress did not at all bespeak me a sailor; so everyone, as I sauntered about, had something to say to me. By and by comes a pert young fellow up: "Sir," says he, "your servant; what, I see our captain has picked up a passenger at last."—"Passenger?" says I; "you are pleased to be merry, sir; I am no passenger."—"Why, pray," says he, "what may you be then?"—"Sir," says I, "the captain's steward."—"You impertinent puppy," says he, "what an answer you give me; you the captain's steward! No, sir, that place, I can assure you, is in better hands!" and away he turned. I knew not what to think of it, but was terribly afraid I should draw myself into some scrape. By and by others asked me, someone thing, some another, and I was very cautious what answers I made them, for fear of offence: till a gravish sailor came and sat down by me; and after talking of the weather and other indifferent matters, "Pray," says I, "sir, who is that gentleman that was so affronted at me soon after I came on board?"—"Oh," says he, "a proud, insignificant fellow, the captain's steward; but don't mind him," says he; "he uses the captain himself as bad; they have had high words just before the captain went on shore; and had he used me as he did him, I should have made no ceremony of tipping him overboard—a rascal!" Says I, "You surprise me; for the captain sent me on board to be his steward, and agreed with me about it this afternoon."—"Hush," says he, "I see how it will go; the captain, if that's the case, will discharge him when he comes on board; and indeed I believe he would not have kept him so long, but we have waited for a wind, and he could not provide himself."

The captain came on board at night; and the first thing he did was to demand the keys of Mr. Steward, which he gave to me, and ordered him on shore.

The next morning the captain went on shore himself; but the wind chopping about and standing fair about noon, he returned then with my chest, and before night we were got into sailing order, and before the wind with a brisk gale.

What happened the first fourteen days of our passage I know not, having been all that time so sick and weak I could scarcely keep life and soul together; but after grew better and better. We prosecuted our voyage, touching for about a week at the Madeiras in our way. The captain grew very fond of me, and never put me to hard duty, and I passed my time, under his favour, very pleasantly. One evening, being within sixty leagues of the Cape of Palms, calm weather, but the little wind we had against us, one of our men spied a sail, and gave the captain notice of it He, not suspecting danger, minded it little, and we made what way the wind would permit, but night coming on, and the calm continuing, about peep of day we perceived we were infallibly fallen in with a French privateer, who, hoisting French colours, called out to us to strike. Our captain had scarce time to consider what to do, they were so near us; but as he had twenty-two men on board, and eight guns he could bring to, he called all hands upon deck, and telling them the consequence of a surrender, asked them if they would stand by him. One and all swore they would fight the ship to the bottom, rather than fall into the privateer's hands. The captain immediately gave the word for a clear deck, prepared his firearms, and begged them to be active and obey orders; and perceiving the privateer out-numbered our hands by abundance, he commanded all the small arms to be brought upon deck loaded, and to run out as many of the ship's guns as she could bring to on one side, and to charge them all with small shot, then stand to till he gave directions. The privateer being a light ship, and a small breeze arising, run up close to us, first firing one gun, then another, still calling out to us to strike, but we neither returned fire nor answer, till he came almost within pistol-shot of us, and seeing us a small vessel, thought to board us directly; but then our captain ordered a broadside, and immediately all hands to come on deck; himself standing there at the time of our first fire with his fusee in his hand, and near him I stood with another. We killed eight men and wounded several others. The privateer then fired a broadside through and through us. By this time our hands were all on deck, and the privateer pushing, in hopes to grapple and board us, we gave them a volley from thence, that did good execution; and then all hands to the ship's guns again, except four, who were left along with me to charge the small arms. It is incredible how soon they had fired the great guns and were on deck again. This last fire, being with ball, raked the privateer miserably. Then we fired the small arms, and away to the ship's guns. This we did three times successively without loss of a man, and I believe if we could have held it once more, and no assistance had come to the privateer, she had sheered quite off: but our captain spying a sail at some distance behind the privateer, who lay to windward of us, and seeing by his glass it was a Frenchman, was almost dismayed; the same sight put courage into our enemies, who thereupon redoubled the attack, and the first volley of their small arms shot our captain in the breast, upon which he dropped dead without stirring. I need not say that sight shocked me exceedingly. Indeed it disconcerted the whole action; and though our mate, a man of good courage and experience, did all that a brave man could do to animate the men, they apparently drooped, and the loss of the ship became inevitable; so we struck, and the Frenchman boarded us.

During the latter part of the engagement we had two men killed and five wounded, who died afterwards of their wounds. We, who were alive, were all ordered on board the Frenchman, who, after rifling us, chained us two and two and turned us into the hold. Our vessel was then ransacked; and the other privateer, who had suffered much the day before in an engagement with an English twenty-gun ship of war, coming up, the prize was sent by her into port, where she herself was to refit. In this condition did I and fourteen of our crew lie for six weeks, till the fetters on our legs had almost eaten to the bone, and the stench of the place had well-nigh suffocated us.

The "Glorieux" (for that was the name of the privateer who took us) saw nothing farther in five weeks worth her notice, which very much discouraged the men; and consulting together, it was agreed to cruise more northward, between Sierra Leone and Cape de Verde; but about noon next day they spied a sail coming west-north-west with a fresh gale. The captain thereupon ordered all to be ready, and lie by for her. But though she discerned us, she kept her way, bearing only more southward; when the wind shifting to northeast, she ran for it, full before the wind, and we after her, with all the sail we could crowd; and though she was a very good sailer, we gained upon her, being laden, and before night came pretty well up with her; but being a large ship, and the evening hazy, we did not choose to engage her till morning. The next morning we found she was slunk away; but we fetched her up, and hoisting French colours, fired a shot, which she not answering, our captain run alongside of her and fired a broadside; then slackening upon her, a hard engagement ensued; the shot thumping so against our ship, that we prisoners, who had nothing to do in the action, expected death, one or other of us, every moment. The merchantman was so heavy loaded, and drew so much water, that she was very unwieldy in action; so after a fight of two hours, when most of her rigging and masts were cut and wounded, she struck. Twelve men were sent on board her, and her captain and several officers were ordered on board us.

There were thirty-eight persons in her, including passengers; all of whom, except five, and the like number which had been killed in the action, were sent chained into the hold to us, who had lain there almost six weeks. This prize put Monsieur into good heart, and determined him to return home with her. But in two days' time his new acquisition was found to have leaked so fast near the bottom, that before they were aware of it the water was risen some feet. Several hands were employed to find out the leak; but all asserted it was too low to be come at; and as the pumps, with all the labour the prisoners, who were the persons put to it, could use, would not reduce it, but it still increased, they removed what goods they could into the privateer; and before they could unload it the prize sunk.

The next thing they consulted upon was what to do with the prisoners, who, by the loss of the prize, were now grown too numerous to be trusted in the privateer; fearing, too, as they were now so far out at sea, by the great addition of mouths, they might soon be brought to short. allowance, it was, on both accounts, resolved to give us the prize's boat, which they had saved, and turn us adrift to shift for ourselves. There were in all forty-three of us; but the privateer having lost several of their own men in the two engagements, they looked us over, and picking out two-and-twenty of us, who were the most likely fellows for their purpose, the remaining one-and-twenty were committed to the boat, with about two days' provision and a small matter of ammunition, and turned out.

VI

THE BOAT, TWO HUNDRED LEAGUES FROM LAND, MAKES NO
WAY, BUT DRIVES MORE TO SEA BY THE WIND—THE PEOPLE
LIVE NINE DAYS AT QUARTER ALLOWANCE—FOUR DIE WITH
HUNGER THE TWELFTH DAY—FIVE MORE THE FOURTEENTH
DAY—ON THE FIFTEENTH THEY EAT ONE JUST DEAD—WANT
OF WATER EXCESSIVE—SPY A SAIL—ARE TAKEN UP—WORK
THEIR PASSAGE TO THE AFRICAN SHORE—ARE SENT ON A
SECRET EXPEDITION—ARE WAYLAID, TAKEN SLAVES, AND
SENT UP THE COUNTRY.

When we, who were in the boat, came to reflect on our condition, the prospect before us appeared very melancholy; though we had at first readily enough embraced the offer, rather than perish in so much misery as we suffered in our loathsome confinement. We now judged we were above two hundred leagues from land, in about eight degrees north latitude; and it blowing north-east, a pretty stiff gale, we could make no way, but rather lost, for we aimed at some port in Africa, having neither sail, compass, nor any other instrument to direct us; so that all the observation we could make was by the sun for running southward, or as the wind carried us, for we had lost the North Pole. As we had little above two days' provisions, we perceived a necessity of almost starving voluntarily, to avoid doing it quite, seeing it must be many days before we could reach shore, if ever we did, having visibly driven a great deal more southward than we were; nay, unless a sudden change happened, we were sure of perishing, unless delivered by some ship that Providence might send in our way. In short, the ninth day came, but no relief with it; and though we had lived at quarter allowance, and but just saved life, our food, except a little water, was all gone, and this caused us quite to despair. On the twelfth day four of our company died with hunger in a very miserable way; and yet the survivors had not strength left to move them to pity their fellows. In truth, we had sat still, attempting nothing in several days; as we found that, unless the wind shifted, we only consumed the little strength we had left to no manner of purpose. On the fourteenth day, and in the night, five more died, and a sixth was near expiring; and yet we, the survivors, were so indolent, we would scarce lend a hand to throw them overboard. On the fifteenth day, in the morning, our carpenter, weak as he was, started up, and as the sixth man was just dead, cut his throat, and whilst warm let out what blood would flow; then pulling off his old jacket, invited us to dinner, and cutting a large slice of the corpse, devoured it with as much seeming relish as if it had been ox-beef. His example prevailed with the rest of us, one after another, to taste and eat; and as there had been a heavy dew or rain in the night, and we had spread out everything we had of linen and woollen to receive it, we were a little refreshed by wringing our clothes and sipping what came from them; after which we covered them up from the sun, stowing them all close together to keep in the moisture, which served us to suck at for two days after, a little and a little at a time; for now we were in greater distress for water than for meat. It has surprised me, many times since, to think how we could make so light a thing of eating our fellow creature just dead before our eyes; but I will assure you, when we had once tasted, we looked on the blessing to be so great, that we cut and eat with as little remorse as we should have had for feeding on the best meat in an English market; and most certainly, when this corpse had failed, if another had not dropped by fair means, we should have used foul by murdering one of our number as a supply for the rest.

Water, as I said before, to moisten our mouths, was now our greatest hardship, for every man had so often drank his own, that we voided scarce anything but blood, and that but a few drops at a time; our mouths and tongues were quite flayed with drought, and our teeth just fallen from our jaws; for though we had tried, by placing all the dead men's jackets and shirts one over another, to strain some of the sea-water through them by small quantities, yet that would not deprive it of its pernicious qualities; and though it refreshed a little in going down, we were so sick, and strained ourselves so much after it, that it came up again, and made us more miserable than before. Our corpse now stunk so, what was left of it, that we could no longer bear it on board, and every man began to look with an evil eye on his fellow, to think whose turn it would be next; for the carpenter had started the question, and preached us into the necessity of it; and we had agreed, the next morning, to put it to the lot who should be the sacrifice. In this distress of thought it was so ordered by good Providence, that on the twenty-first day we thought we spied a sail coming from the north-west, which caused us to delay our lots till we should see whether it would discover us or not: we hung up some jackets upon our oars, to be seen as far off as we could, but had so little strength left we could make no way towards it; however, it happened to direct its course so much to our relief, that an hour before sunset it was within a league of us, but seemed to bear away more eastward, and our fear was that they should not know our distress, for we were not able to make any noise from our throats that might be heard fifty yards; but the carpenter, who was still the best man amongst us, with much ado getting one of the guns to go off, in less than half-an-hour she came up with us, and seeing our deplorable condition, took us all on board, to the number of eleven. Though no methods were un-essayed for our recovery, four more of us died in as many days. When the remaining seven of us came a little to ourselves, we found our deliverers were Portuguese, bound for Saint Salvadore. We told the captain we begged he would let us work our passage with him, be it where it would, to shore; and then, if we could be of no further service to him, we did not doubt getting into Europe again: but in the voyage, as we did him all the service in our power, we pleased him so well that he engaged us to stay with him to work the ship home again, he having lost some hands by fever soon after his setting sail.

We arrived safe in port; and in a few days the captain, who had a secret enterprise to take in hand, hired a country coasting vessel, and sent her seventeen leagues farther on the coast for orders from some factory or settlement there. I was one of the nine men who were destined to conduct her; but not understanding Portuguese, I knew little of the business we went upon. We were to coast it all the way; but on the tenth day, just at sunrise, we fell in with a fleet of boats which had waylaid us, and were taken prisoners. Being carried ashore, we were conducted a long way up the country, where we were imprisoned, and almost starved, though I never knew the meaning of it; nor did any of us, unless the mate, who, we heard, was carried up the country much farther, to Angola; but we never heard more of him, though we were told he would be sent back to us.

Here we remained under confinement almost three months, at the end of which time our keeper told us we were to be removed; and coupling us two and two together, sent a guard with us to Angola; when, crossing a large river, we were set to work in removing the rubbish and stones of a castle or fortress, which had been lately demolished by an earthquake and lightning. Here we continued about five months, being very sparingly dieted, and locked up every night.

This place, however, I thought a paradise to our former dungeon; and as we were not overworked, we made our lives comfortable enough,

ROBERT PALTOCK

having the air all day to refresh us from the heat, and not wanting for company; for there were at least three hundred of us about the whole work; and I often fancied myself at the tower of Babel, each labourer almost speaking in a language of his own.

Towards the latter end of our work our keepers grew more and more remiss in their care of us. At my first coming thither, I had contracted a familiarity with one of the natives, but of a different kingdom, who was then a slave with me; and he and I being able tolerably to understand each other, he hinted to me, one day, the desire he had of seeing his own country and family, who neither knew whether he was dead or alive, or where he was, since he had left them, seven years before, to make war in this kingdom; and insinuated that as he had taken a great liking to me, if I would endeavour to escape with him, and we succeeded, he would provide for me. "For," says he, "you see, now our work is almost over, we are but slightly guarded; and if we stay till this job is once finished, we may be commanded to some new works at the other end of the kingdom, for aught we know, so that our labours will only cease with our lives: and for my part, immediate death in the attempt of liberty is to me preferable to a lingering life of slavery."

These, and such-like arguments, prevailed on me to accompany him, as he had told me he had travelled most of the country before in the wars of the different nations; so having taken our resolution, the following evening, soon after our day's work, and before the time came for locking up, we withdrew from the rest, but within hearing, thinking if we should then be missed and called, we would appear and make some excuse for our absence, but if not, we should have the whole night before us.

When we were first put upon this work, we were called over singly, by name, morning and evening, to be let out and in, and were very narrowly observed in our motions; but not one of us having been ever absent, our actions were at length much less minded than before, and the ceremony of calling us over was frequently omitted; so that we concluded if we got away unobserved the first night, we should be out of the reach of pursuers by the next; which was the soonest it was possible for them to overtake us, as we proposed to travel the first part of our journey with the utmost despatch.

VII

Having now set out with all possible speed, we seemed to each other as joyful as we could; though it cannot be supposed we had no fears in our minds the first part of our journey, for we had many; but as our way advanced our fears subsided; and having, with scarce any delay, pushed forwards for the first twenty-four hours, nature then began to have two very pressing demands upon us, food and rest; but as one of them was absolutely out of our power to comply with, she contented herself with the other till we should be better able to supply her, and gave a farther time till the next day.

The next morning found us very empty and sharp-set, though a very sound night's rest had contributed its utmost to refresh us. But what added much to our discomfort was, that though our whole subsistence must come from fruits, there was not a tree to be found at a less distance than twelve leagues, in the open rocky country we were then in; but a good draught of excellent water we met with did us extraordinary service, and sent us with much better courage to the woods, though they were quite out of the way of our route: there, by divers kinds of fruits, which, though my companion knew very well, I was quite a stranger to, we satisfied our hunger for the present, and took a moderate supply for another opportunity. This retarded our journey very much, for in so hard travel every pound weighed six before night.

I cannot say this journey, though bad enough, would have been so discouraging, but for the trouble of fetching our provisions so far; and then, if we meant not to lose half the next day in the same manner, we must double load ourselves, and delay our progress by that means; but we still went on, and in about eight days got quite clear of Angola.

On the eighth day, my companion, whose name was Glanlepze, told me we were very near the confines of Congo, but there was one little village still in Angola by which we must pass within half a league; and if I would agree to it, he would go see what might be got here to supply ourselves with. I told him I was in an unknown world, and would follow wherever he should lead me; but asked him if he was not afraid of the people, as he was not of that country. He told me as there had been wars between them and his country for assisting their neighbours of Congo, he was not concerned for any mischief he should do them, or they him. "But," says he, "you have a knife in your pocket, and with that we will cut two stout clubs, and then follow me and fear nothing."

We soon cut our clubs, and marching on, in the midst of some small shrubs and a few scattering trees, we saw a little hovel, larger indeed, but worse contrived, than an English hog-stye, to which we boldly advanced; and Glanlepze entering first, saluted an old man who was lying on a parcel of rushes. The man attempted to run away, but Glanlepze stopped him, and we tied his hands and feet He then set up such a hideous howl, that had not Glanlepze threatened to murder him, and prepared to do it, he would have raised the whole village upon us; but we quieted him, and rummaging to find provision, which was all we wanted, we by good luck spied best part of a goat hanging up behind a large mat at the farther end of the room. By this time in comes a woman with two children, very small. This was the old man's daughter, of about five-and-twenty. Glanlepze bound her also, and laid her by the old man; but the two children we suffered to lie untied. We then examined her, who told us the old man was her father, and that her husband, having killed a goat that morning, was gone to carry part of it to his sister; that they had little or no corn; and finding we wanted victuals, she told us there was an earthen pot we might boil some of the goat in if we pleased.

Having now seen all that was to be had, we were going to make up our bundle, when a muletto very gently put his head into the doorway: him Glanlepze immediately seized; and bidding me fetch the great mat and the goat's flesh, he in the meantime put a long rope he found there about the beast's neck, and laying the mat upon him, we packed up the goat's flesh and a little corn in a calabash-shell; and then turning up the mat round about, skewered it together, and over all we tied the earthen pot; Glanlepze crying out at everything we loaded, "It is no hurt to plunder an enemy!" and so we marched off.

I own I had greater apprehensions from this adventure than from anything before. "For," says I, "if the woman's husband returns soon, or if she or her father can release themselves, they will raise the whole village upon us, and we are undone." But Glanlepze laughed at me, saying we had not an hour's walk out of the Angola dominions, and that the king of Congo was at war with them in helping the king of Loango, whose subject himself was; and that the Angolans durst not be seen out of their bounds on that side the kingdom; for there was a much larger village of Congovians in our way, who would certainly rise and destroy them, if they came in any numbers amongst them; and though the war being carried on near the sea, the borders were quiet, yet, upon the least stir, the whole country would be in arms, whilst we might retire through the woods very safely.

Well, we marched on as fast as we could all the remainder of that day till moonlight, close by the skirt of a long wood, that we might take shelter therein, if there should be occasion $ and my eyes were the best part of the way behind me; but neither hearing nor seeing anything to annoy us, and finding by the declivity of the ground we should soon be in some plain or bottom, and have a chance of water for us all, and pasture for our muletto, which was now become one of us, we would not halt till we found a bottom to the hill, which in half an hour more we came to, and in some minutes after to a rivulet of fine clear water, where we resolved to spend the night. Here we fastened our muletto by his cord to a stake in the ground; but perceiving him not to have sufficient range to fill his belly in before morning, we, under Glanlepze's direction, cut several long slips from the mat, and soaking them well in water, twisted them into a very strong cord, of sufficient length for the purpose. And now, having each of us brought a bundle of dry fallen sticks from the wood with us, and gathered two or three flints as we came along, we struck fire on my knife upon some rotten wood, and boiled a good piece of our goat's flesh; and having made such a meal as we had neither of us made for many months before, we laid us down and slept heartily till morning.

As soon as day broke we packed up our goods, and filling our calabash with water, we loaded our muletto, and got forward very pleasantly that day and several others following, and had tolerable lodgings.

About noon, one day, travelling with great glee, we met an adventure which very much daunted me, and had almost put a stop to my hopes of ever getting where I intended. We came to a great river whose name I have now forgot, near a league over, but full, and especially about the shores, of large trees that had fallen from the mountains and been rolled down with the floods, and lodged there in a shocking manner. This river,

Glanlepze told me, we must pass: for my part, I shrunk at the sight of it, and told him if he could get over, I would not desire to prevent his meeting with his family; but as for my share, I had rather take my chance in the woods on this side than plunge myself into such a stream only for the sake of drowning. "Oh!" says Glanlepze, "then you can't swim?"—"No," says I; "there's my misfortune."—"Well," says the kind Glanlepze, "be of good heart; I'll have you over." He then bade me go cut an armful of the tallest of the reeds that grew there near the shore, whilst he pulled up another where he then was, and bring them to him. The side of the river sloped for a good way with an easy descent, so that it was very shallow where the reeds grew, and they stood very close together upon a large compass of ground. I had no sooner entered the reeds a few yards, to cut some of the longest, but (being about knee-deep in the water and mud, and every step raising my feet very high to keep them clear of the roots, which were matted together) I thought I had trod upon a trunk of one of the trees, of which, as I said, there was such plenty thereabouts; and raising my other foot to get that also upon the tree, as I fancied it, I found it move along with me; upon which I roared out, when Glanlepze, who was not far from me, imagining what was the matter, cried out, "Leap off, and run to shore to the right!" I knew not yet what was the case, but did what I was bid, and gained the shore. Looking back, I perceived the reeds shake and rustle all the way to the shore, by degrees after me. I was terribly frightened, and ran to Glanlepze, who then told me the danger I had escaped, and that what I took for a tree was certainly a large alligator or crocodile.

My blood ran chill within me at hearing the name of such a dangerous creature; but he had no sooner told me what it was, than out came the most hideous monster I had ever seen. Glanlepze ran to secure the muletto; and then taking the cord which had fastened him, and tying it to each end of a broken arm of a tree that lay on the shore, he marched up to the crocodile without the least dismay, and beginning near the tail, with one leg on one side, and the other on the other side, he straddled over him, still mending his pace as the beast crept forward, till he came to his fore-feet; then throwing the great log before his mouth, he, by the cord in his hand, bobbed it against the creature's nose, till he gaped wide enough to have taken in the muletto; then of a sudden, jerking the wood between his jaws with all his force by the cord, he gagged the beast, with his jaws wide open up to his throat, so that he could neither make use of his teeth nor shut his mouth; he then threw one, end of the cord upon the ground, just before the creature's under-jaw, which, as he by degrees crept along over it, came out behind his fore-legs on the contrary side; and serving the other end of it in the same manner, he took up those ends and tied them over the creature's back, just within his forelegs, which kept the gag firm in his mouth; and then calling out to me (for I stood at a good distance), "Peter," says he, "bring me your knife!" I trembled at going so near, for the crocodile was turning his head this way and that very uneasy, and wanting to get to the river again, but yet I carried it, keeping as much behind him as I could, still eyeing him which way he moved, and at length tossed my knife so near that Glanlepze could reach it; and he, just keeping behind the beast's forefeet, and leaning forward, first darted the knife into one eye, and then into the other; and immediately leaping from his back, came running to me. "So, Peter," says he, "I have done the business."—"Aye! business enough, I think," says I, "and more than I would have done to have been king of Congo."—"Why, Peter," says he, "there is nothing but a man may compass by resolution, if he takes both ends of a thing in his view at once, and fairly deliberates on both sides what may be given and taken from end to end. What you have seen me perform is only from a thorough notion I have of this beast and of myself, how far each of us hath power to act and counteract upon the other, and duly applying the means. But,", says he, "this talk will not carry us across the river; come, here are the reeds I have pulled up, which I believe will be sufficient without anymore, for I would not overload the muletto."—"Why," says I, "is the muletto to carry them?"—"No, they are to carry you," says he.—"I can never ride upon these," says I.—"Hush!" says he, "I'll not lose you, never fear. Come, cut me a good tough stick, the length of these reeds."—"Well," says I, "this is all conjuration; but I don't see a step towards my getting over the river yet, unless I am to ride the muletto upon these reeds, and guide myself with the stick."

"I must own, Peter," says he, "you have a bright guess." So taking an armful of the reeds, and laying them on the ground, "Now, Peter," says he, "lay that stick upon those reeds and tie them tight at both ends." I did so. "Now, Peter," says he, "lay yourself down upon them." I then laying myself on my back, lengthwise, upon the reeds, Glanlepze laughed heartily at me, and turning me about, brought my breast upon the reeds at the height of my arm-pits; and then taking a handful of the reeds he had reserved by themselves, he laid them on my back, tying them to the bundle close at my shoulders, and again at the ends. "Now,

ROBERT PALTOCK

Peter," says he, "stand up;" which I did, but it was full as much as I could do. I then seeing Glanlepze laughing at the figure I cut, desired him to be serious, and not put me upon losing my life for a joke; for I could not think what he would do next with me. He bid me never fear; and looking more soberly, ordered me to walk to the river, and so stand just within the bank till he came; then leading the muletto to me, he tied me to her, about a yard from the tail, and taking the cord in his hand, led the muletto and me into the water. We had not gone far before my guide began to swim, then the muletto and I were presently chin-deep, and I expected nothing but drowning every moment: however, having gone so far, I was ashamed to cry out; when getting out of my depth, and my reeds coming to their bearing, up I mounted, and was carried on with all the ease imaginable; my conductor guiding us between the trees so dexterously, that not one accident happened to either of us all the way, and we arrived safe on the opposite shore.

We had now got into a very low, close, swampy country, and our goat's flesh began to be very stale through the heat, not only of the sun, but the muletto's back: however, we pleased ourselves we should have one more meal of it before it was too bad to eat; so, having travelled about three miles from the river, we took up our lodging on a little rising, and tied our muletto in a valley about half a furlong below us, where he made as good a meal in his way as we did in ours.

We had but just supped, and were sauntering about to find the easiest spot to sleep on, when we heard a rustling and a grumbling noise in a small thicket just on our right, which seeming to approach nearer and nearer, Glanlepze roused himself, and was on his legs just time enough to see a lioness and a small whelp which accompanied her, within thirty yards of us, making towards us, as we afterwards guessed, for the sake of our goat's flesh, which now smelt very strong. Glanlepze whipped on the contrary side of the fire to that where the goat's flesh lay, and fell to kicking the fire about at a great rate, which being made of dry wood, caused innumerable sparks to fly about us; but the beasts still approaching in a couchant manner, and seizing the ribs of the goat and other bones (for we had only cut the flesh off), and grumbling and cracking them like rotten twigs, Glanlepze snatched up a fire-brand, flaming, in each hand, and made towards them; which sight so terrified the creatures that they fled with great precipitation to the thicket again.

Glanlepze was a little uneasy at the thoughts of quitting so good a lodging as we had found, but yet held it best to move farther; for as the lions had left the bones behind them, we must expect another visit if we stayed there, and could hope for no rest; and, above all, we might possibly lose our muletto; so we removed our quarters two miles farther, where we slept with great tranquillity.

Reflections on the nature of mankind have often astonished me. I told you at first my thoughts concerning prayer in my journey to Bristol, and of the benefit I received from it, and how fully I was convinced of the necessity of it; which one would think was a sufficient motive to a reasonable creature to be constant in it; and yet, it is too true that, notwithstanding the difficulties I had laboured under, and hardships I had undergone, and the danger of starving at sea or being murdered for food by my fellows, when there was as urgent a necessity of begging Divine assistance as can be conceived, I never once thought of it, nor of the Object of it, nor returned thanks for my being delivered, till the lioness had just left me; and then I felt near the same force urging me to return thanks for my escape, as I had impelling me to prayer before; and I think I did so with great sincerity.

I shall not trouble you with a relation of the common accidents of our journey, which lasted two months and better, nor with the different methods we used to get subsistence, but shall at once conduct you to Quamis; only mentioning that we were sometimes obliged to go about, and were once stopped by a cut that my guide and companion received by a ragged stone in his foot, which growing very bad, almost deprived me of the hopes of his life; but by rest and constant sucking and licking it, which was the only remedy we had to apply, except green leaves chewed, that I laid to it by his direction, to supple and cool it, he soon began to be able to ride upon the muletto, and sometimes to walk a little.

I say we arrived at Quamis, a small place on a river of that name, where Glanlepze had a neat dwelling, and left a wife and five children when he went out to the wars. We were very near the town when the day closed; and as it is soon dark there after sunset, you could but just see your hand at our entrance into it We met nobody in the way, but I went directly to Glanlepze's door, by his direction, and struck two or three strokes hard against it with my stick. On this there came a woman to it stark-naked. I asked her, in her own language, if she knew one Glanlepze. She told me, with a deep sigh, that once she did. I asked then where he was. She said, with their ancestors, she hoped, for he was the greatest warrior in the world; but if he was not dead, he was in slavery. Now you must know Glanlepze had a mind to hear how his wife took his death or slavery, and had put me upon asking these questions before he discovered himself. I proceeded then to tell her I brought some news of Glanlepze, and was lately come from him, and by his order. "And does my dear Glanlepze live!" says she, flying upon my neck, and almost smothering me with caresses, till I begged her to forbear, or she would strangle me, and I had a great deal more to tell her; then ringing for a light, when she saw I was a white man she seemed in the utmost confusion at her own nakedness; and immediately retiring, she threw a cloth round her waist and came to me again. I then repeated to her that her husband was alive and well, but wanted a ransom to redeem himself, and had sent me to see what she could anyways raise for that purpose. She told me she and her children had lived very hardly ever since he went from her, and she had nothing to sell, or make money of, but her five children; that as this was the time for the slaving-trade, she would see what she could raise by them, and if that would not do, she would sell herself and send him the money, if he would let her know how to do it.

Glanlepze, who heard every word that passed, finding so strong a proof of his wife's affection, could hold out no longer, but bursting into the room, clasped her in his arms, crying, "No, Zulika! (for that was her name) I am free; there will be no occasion for your or my dear children's slavery, and rather than have purchased my freedom at that rate, I would willingly have died a slave myself. But my own ears have heard the tender sentiments my Zulika has for me." Then, drowned in tears of joy, they embraced each other so close and so long, that I thought it impertinent to be seen with them till their first transports were over. So I retired without the house, till Glanlepze called me in, which was not less than full half an hour. I admired at the love and constancy of the person I had just left behind me; and, Good Heaven, thinks I to myself, with a sigh, how happy has this our escape rendered Glanlepze and his wife! what a mutual felicity do they feel! And what is the cause of all this? Is it that he has brought home great treasures from the wars? Nothing like it; he is come naked. Is it that, having escaped slavery and poverty, he is returned to an opulent wife, abounding with the good things of life? No such thing. What, then, can be the cause of this excess of satisfaction, this alternate joy, that Patty and I could not have been as happy with each other? Why, it was my pride that interposed and prevented it. But what am I like to get by it, and by all this travel and these hazards? Is this the way to make a fortune, to get an estate? No, surely the very contrary. I could not, forsooth, labour for Patty and her children where I was known; but am I any better for labouring here where I am not known, where I have nobody to assist me, than I could have been where I am known, and where there would have been my friends about me, at least, if they could have afforded no great assistance? I have been deceived, then, and have travelled so many thousand miles, and undergone so many dangers, only to know at last I had been happier at home; and have doubled my misery for want of consideration—that very consideration which, impartially taken, would have convinced me I ought to have made the best of my bad circumstances, and to have laid hold of every commendable method of improving them. Did I come hither to avoid daily labour or voluntary servitude at home? I have had it in abundance. Did I come hither to avoid poverty or contempt? Here I have met with them tenfold And now, after all, was I to return home empty and naked, as Glanlepze has done, should I meet a wife, as bare as myself, so ready to die in my embraces, and to be a slave herself, with her children, for my sake only? I fear not.

These and the like reflections had taken possession of me when Glanlepze called me in; where I found his wife, in her manner, preparing our supper, with all that cheerfulness which gives a true lustre to innocence.

The bustle we made had by this time awakened the children; who, stark-naked as they were born, both boys and girls, came crawling out, black as jet, from behind a curtain at the farther end of the room, which was very long. The father as yet had only inquired after them; but upon sight of them he fell into an ecstasy, kissing one, stroking another, dandling a third, for the eldest was scarce fourteen; but not one of them knew him, for seven years makes a great chasm in young memories. The more I saw of this sport, the stronger impression Patty and my own children made upon me. My mind had been so much employed on my own distresses, that those dear ideas were almost effaced; but this moving scene introduced them afresh, and imprinted them deeply on my imagination, which cherished the sweet remembrance.

VIII

How the author passed his time with Glanlepze—His acquaintance with some English prisoners—They project an escape—He joins them—They seize a Portuguese ship and get off.—Make a long run from land—Want water—They anchor at a desert island—The boat goes on shore for water—They lose their anchor in a storm—The author and one Adams drove to sea—A miraculous passage to a rock—Adams drowned there—The author's miserable condition.

I passed my time with Glanlepze and his wife, who both really loved me, with sufficient bodily quiet, for about two years: my business was chiefly, in company with my patron, to cultivate a spot of ground wherein we had planted grain and necessaries for the family; and once or twice a week we went a fishing, and sometimes hunted and shot venison. These were our chief employments; for as to excursions for slaves, which is a practice in many of those countries, and what the natives get money by, since our own slavery, Glanlepze and I could not endure it.

Though I was tolerably easy in my external circumstances, yet my mind hankering after England made my life still: unhappy; and that infelicity daily increased as I saw the less probability of attaining my desire. At length, hearing of some European sailors who were under confinement for contraband trade at a Portuguese fort about two miles from Quamis, I resolved to go to see them; and if any of them should be English, at least to inquire after my native country. I went and found two Dutchmen who had been sailors in British pay several years, three Scotchmen, an Irishman, and five Englishmen, but all had been long in English merchants' service. They were taken, as they told me, by a Portuguese vessel, together with their ship, as a Dutch prize under pretence of contraband trade. The captain was known to be a Dutchman, though he spoke good English, and was then in English pay and his vessel English; therefore they would have it that he was a Dutch trader, and so seized his ship in the harbour, with the prisoners in it The captain, who was on shore with several of his men, was threatened to be laid in irons if he was taken, which obliged him and his men to abscond, and fly overland to an English factory for assistance to recover his ship and cargo; being afraid to appear and claim it amongst so many enemies without an additional force. They had been in confinement two months, and their ship confiscated and sold. In this miserable condition I left them, but returned once or twice a week for a fortnight or three weeks to visit them. These instances of regard, as they thought them, created some confidence in me, so that they conversed with me very freely. Amongst other discourse, they told me one day that one of their crew who went with the captain had been taken ill on the way, and being unable to proceed, was returned; but as he talked good Portuguese, he was not suspected to belong to them; and that he had been to visit them, and would be there again that day. I had a mind to see him, so stayed longer than I intended, and in about an hour's time he came. After he was seated he asked who I was, and (privately) if I might be trusted. Being satisfied I might, for that I was a Cornish man, he began as follows, looking narrowly about to see he was not overheard: "My lads," says he, "be of good courage; I have hopes for you; be but men and we shall see better days yet." I wondered to what this preface tended, when he told us that since his return from the captain, as he spoke good Portuguese and had sailed on board Portuguese traders several years, he mixed among that people, and particularly among the crew of the "Del Cruz," the ship which had taken them; that that ship had partly unloaded, and was taking in other goods for a future voyage; that he had informed himself of their strength, and that very seldom more than three men and two boys lay on board; that he had hired himself to the captain, and was to go on board the very next day. "Now," says he, "my lads, if you can break prison any night after tomorrow, and come directly to the ship (telling them how she lay, for, says he, you cannot mistake, you will find two or three boats moored in the gut against the church), I will be ready to receive you, and we will get off with her in lieu of our ship they have taken from us, for there is nothing ready to follow us."

The prisoners listened to this discourse very attentively; but scratched their heads, fearing the difficulty of it, and severer usage if they miscarried, and made several objections; but at last they all swore to attempt it the night but one following. Upon which the sailor went away to prepare for their reception on board. After he was gone, I surveyed his scheme attentively in my own mind, and found it not so difficult as I first imagined, if the prisoners could but escape cleverly. So before I went away I told them I approved of their purpose; and as I was their countryman, I was resolved, with their leaves, to risk my fortune with them. At this they seemed much pleased, and all embraced me. We then fixed the peremptory night, and I was to wait at the water-side and get the boats in readiness.

The prison they were in was a Portuguese fort, which had been deserted ever since the building a much better on the other side of the river, a gunshot lower. It was built with walls too thick for naked men to storm; the captives were securely locked up every night; and two soldiers, or sentinels, kept watch in an outer-room, who were relieved from the main-guard in the body of the building.

The expected night arrived, and a little before midnight, as had been concerted, one of the prisoners cried out he was so parched up he was on fire, he was on fire! The sentinels were both asleep, but the first that waked called at the door to know what was the matter. The prisoner still crying out, "I am on fire!" the rest begged the sentinel to bring a bowl of water for him, for they knew not what ailed him.

The good-natured fellow, without waking his companion, brought the water, and having a lamp in the guard-room, opened the door; when the prisoners seizing his arms, and commanding him to silence, bound his hands behind him, and his feet together; then serving the other in the same manner, who was now just awake, and taking from them their swords and muskets, they made the best of their way over the fort wall; which being built with buttresses on the inside was easily surmounted. Being got out, they were not long in finding me, who had before this time made the boats ready and was impatiently waiting for them; so in we all got and made good speed to the ship, where we were welcomed by our companion ready to receive us.

Under pretence of being a new-entered sailor, he had carried some Madeira wine on board, and treated the men and boys so freely that he had thrown them into a dead sleep, which was a wise precaution. There being now, therefore, no fear of disturbance or interruption, we drew up the two boats and set all hands at work to put the ship under way; and plied it so closely, the wind favouring us, that by eleven o'clock the next morning we were out of sight of land; but we set the men and boys adrift, in one of the boats, nigh the mouth of the river.

The first thing we did after we had made a long run from shore was to consult what course to steer. Now, as there was a valuable loading on board of goods from Portugal and others taken in since, some gave their opinion for sailing directly for India, selling the ship and cargo there and returning by some English vessel; but that was rejected; for we did not doubt but notice would be given of our escape along the coast, and if we should fall into the Portuguese's hands, we could expect no mercy; besides, we had not people sufficient for such an enterprise. Others, again, were for sailing the directest course for England; but I told them, as our opinions were different, and no time was to be lost, my advice was to stretch southward till we might be quite out of fear of pursuit, and then, whatever course we took, by keeping clear of all coasts, we might hope to come safe off.

My proposal seemed to please the whole crew; so crowding all the sail we could, we pushed southwards very briskly before the wind for several days. We now went upon examining our stores, and found we had flour enough, plenty of fish and salt provisions, but were scant of water and wood; of the first whereof there was not half a ton, and but very little of the latter. This made us very uneasy, and being none of us expert in navigation farther than the common working of the ship, and having no chart on board that might direct us to the nearest land, we were almost at our wits' end, and came to a short allowance of liquor. That we must get water if we could was indisputable; but where to do it puzzled us, as we had determined not to get in with the African shore on any account whatever.

In this perplexity, and under the guidance of different opinions (for we were all captains now), we sometimes steered eastward, and sometimes westward, for about nine days, when we espied a little bluish cloud-like appearance to the southwest; this continuing, we hoped it might be land, and therefore made to it. Upon our nearer approach we found it to be, as we judged, an island; but not knowing its name or whether it was inhabited, we coasted round it two days to satisfy ourselves as to this last particular. Seeing no living creature on it during that time, and the shore being very broken, we came to an anchor about two miles from it, and sent ten of our crew in our best boat with some casks to get water and cut wood. The boat returned at night with six men and the casks filled, having left four behind to go on with the cutting of wood against next day. Accordingly next morning the boat went off again and made two turns with water and wood ere night, which was repeated for two or three days after. On the sixth she went off for wood only, leaving none but me and one John Adams on board.

The boat had scarce reached the island this last turn before the day overcast, and there arose such a storm of wind, thunder, lightning, and hail as I had never before seen. At last our cable broke close to the anchor, and away we went with the wind full southward by west; and not having strength to keep the ship upon a side wind, we were forced to set her head right before it and let her drive. Our hope was, every hour, the storm would abate; but it continued with equal violence for many days, during all which time neither Adams nor I had any rest, for one or other of us was forced, and sometimes both, to keep her right before the wind, or she would certainly have overset. When the storm abated, as it did by degrees, neither Adams nor I could tell where we were, or in what part of the world.

I was sorry I had no better a sailor with me, for neither Adams nor myself had ever made more than one voyage till now, so that we were both unacquainted with the latitude, and scarce knew the use of the compass to any purpose; and being out of all hope of ever reaching the island to our companions, we neither knew which way to steer, nor what to do; and indeed had we known where we were, we two only could not have been able to navigate the ship to any part we desired, or ever to get to the island, unless such a wind as we had before would of itself have driven us thither.

Whilst we were considering, day after day, what to do, though the sea was now very calm and smooth, the ship seemed to sail at as great a rate as before, which we attributed to the velocity she had acquired by the storm, or to currents that had set that way by the violence of the winds. Contenting ourselves with this, we expected all soon to be right again; and as we had no prospect of ever seeing our companions, we kept the best look-out we could to see for any vessel coming that course which might take us in, and resolved to rest all our hopes upon that.

When we had sailed a good while after this manner, we knew not whither, Adams called out, "I see land!" My heart leapt within me for joy, and we hoped the current that seemed to carry us so fast set in for some islands or rivers that lay before us. But still we were exceedingly puzzled at the ship's making such way, and the nearer we approached the land, which was now very visible, the more speed the ship made, though there was no wind stirring. We had but just time to think on this unexpected phenomenon, when we found that what we had taken for land was a rock of an extraordinary height, to which, as we advanced nearer, the ship increased its motion, and all our strength could not make her answer her rudder any other way. This put us under the apprehension of being dashed to pieces immediately, and in less than half an hour I verily thought my fears had not been groundless.

Poor Adams told me he would try when the ship struck if he could leap upon the rock, and ran to the head for that purpose; but I was so fearful of seeing my danger that I ran under hatches, resolving to sink in the ship. We had no sooner parted but I felt so violent a shock that I verily thought the ship had brought down the whole rock upon her, and been thereby dashed to pieces, so that I never more expected to see the light.

I lay under this terror for at least half an hour, waiting the ship's either filling with water or bulging every moment. But finding neither motion in her nor any water rise, nor the least noise whatsoever, I ventured with an aching heart from my retreat, and stole up the hatchway as if an enemy had been on deck, peeping first one way then another. Here nothing presented but confusion, the rock hung over the hatchway at about twenty feet above my head, our foremast lay by the board, the mainmast yard-arm was down, and great part of the mainmast snapped off with it, and almost everything upon deck was displaced. This sight shocked me extremely; and calling for Adams, in whom I hoped to find some comfort, I was too soon convinced I had lost him.

IX

WILKINS THINKS OF DESTROYING HIMSELF—HIS SOLILOQUY—
STRANGE ACCIDENT IN THE HOLD—HIS SURPRISE—CANNOT
CLIMB THE ROCK—HIS METHOD TO SWEETEN HIS WATER—
LIVES MANY MONTHS ON BOARD—VENTURES TO SEA IN HIS
BOAT SEVERAL TIMES, AND TAKES MANY FISH—ALMOST
OVERCOME BY AN EEL.

After I had stood a while in the utmost confusion of thought, and my spirits began to be a little composed, I was resolved to see what damage the hull of the ship had received. Accordingly I looked narrowly, but could find none, only she was immovably fixed in a cleft of the rock, like a large archway, and there stuck so fast, that though upon fathoming I could find no bottom, she never moved in the least by the working of the water.

I now began to look upon Adams as a happy man, being delivered by an immediate death from such an inextricable scene of distress, and wished myself with him a thousand times. I had a great mind to have followed him into the other world; yet I know not how it is, there is something so abhorrent to human nature in self-murder, be one's condition what it will, that I was soon determined on the contrary side. Now again I perceived that the Almighty had given me a large field to expatiate in upon the trial of His creatures, by bringing them into imminent dangers ready to overwhelm them, and at the same time, as it were, hanging out the flag of truce and mercy to them. These thoughts brought me to my knees, and I poured out my soul to God in a strain of humiliation, resignation to His will, and earnest petitions for deliverance or support in this distress. Having finished, I found myself in a more composed frame; so having eaten a biscuit and drank a can of water, and not seeing anything to be done whereby I could better my condition, I sat me down upon the deck, and fell into the following soliloquy—

Peter, says I, what have you to do here?—Alas! replied I to myself, I am fixed against my will in this dismal mansion, destined, as rats might be, to devour the provisions only, and having eaten all up, to perish with hunger for want of a supply.—Then, says I, of what use are you in the world, Peter?—Truly, answered I, of no other use that I can see but to be an object of misery for Divine vengeance to work upon, and to show what a deplorable state human nature can be reduced to; for I cannot think anyone else can be so wretched.—And again, Peter, says I, what have you been doing ever since you came into the world?—I am afraid, says I, I can answer no better to this question than to either of the former; for if only reasonable actions are to be reckoned among my doings, I am sure I have done little worth recording; for let me see what it all amounts to. I spent my first sixteen years in making a fool of my mother; my three next in letting her make a fool of me, and in being fool enough myself to get me a wife and two children before I was twenty. The next year was spent in finding out the misery of slavery from experience. Two years more I repined at the happiness of my benefactor, and at finding it was not my lot to enjoy the same. This year is not yet spent, and how many more are to come, and where they may be passed, and what they may produce, requires a better head than mine even to guess at; but certainly my present situation seems to promise nothing beside woe and misery.—But hold a little, says I, and let me clearly state my own wretchedness. I am here, it is true; but for any good I have ever done or any advantage I have reaped in other places, I am as well here as anywhere. I have no present want of food or unjust or cruel enemy to annoy me; so as long as the ship continues entire and provisions last, I shall do tolerably. Then why should I grieve or terrify myself about what may come? What my frighted imagination suggests may perhaps never happen. Deliverance, though not to be looked for, is yet possible; and my future fate may be as different from my present condition as this is from the hopes with which I lately flattered myself. And why, after all, may I not die a natural death here as well as anywhere? All mankind die, and then there is an end of all——An end of all! did I say? No, there is something within that gives me the lie when I say so. Let me see; Death, my master used to say, is not an end, but a beginning of real life: and may it not be so? May I not as well undergo a change from this to a different state of life when I leave this world, as be born into it I know not from whence? Who sent me into this world? Who framed me of two natures so unlike, that death cannot destroy but one of them? It must be the Almighty God. But all God's works tend to some end; and if He has given me an immortal nature, it must be His intention that I should live somewhere and somehow forever. May not this stage of being then be only an introduction to a preparative for another? There is nothing in this supposition repugnant to reason. Upon the whole, if God is the author of my being, He only has a right to dispose of it, and

I may not put an end thereto without His leave. It is no less true that my continuing therein during His pleasure, and because it is so, may turn vastly to my advantage in His good time; it may be the means of my becoming happy for even when it is His will that I go hence. It is no less probable that, dismal as my present circumstances appear, I may be even now the object of a kind Providence: God may be leading me by affliction to repentance of former crimes; destroying those sensual affections that have all my days kept me from loving and serving Him. I will therefore submit myself to His will, and hope for His mercy.

These thoughts, and many others I then had, composed me very much, and by degrees reconciled me to my destined solitude. I walked my ship, of which I was now both master and owner, and employed myself in searching how it was fastened to the rock, and where it rested; but all to no purpose as to that particular. I then struck a light and went into the hold, to see what I could find useful, for we had never searched the ship since we took her.

In the hold I found abundance of long iron bars, which I suppose were brought out to be trafficked with the blacks. I observed they lay all with one end close to the head of the ship, which I presumed was occasioned by the violent shock they received when she struck against the rock; but seeing one short bar lying out beyond the rest, though touching at the end of one of the long bars, I thought to take it up, and lay it on the heap with the others; but the moment I had raised the end next the other bars, it flew out of my hand with such violence, against the head of the ship, and with such a noise, as greatly surprised me, and put me in fear it had broke through the plank.

I just stayed to see no harm was done, and ran upon deck with my hair stiff on my head; nor could I conceive less than that some subtle spirit had done this prank merely to terrify me.

It ran in my pate several days, and I durst upon no account have gone into the hold again, though my whole support had lain there; nay, it even spoiled my rest, for fear something tragical should befall me, of which this amazing incident was an omen.

About a week after, as I was shifting myself (for I had not taken my clothes off since I came there), and putting on a new pair of shoes which I found on board, my own being very bad, taking out my iron buckles, I laid one of them upon a broken piece of the mast that I sat upon; when to my astonishment, it was no sooner out of my hand but up it flew to the rock and stuck there. I could not tell what to make of it, but was sorry the devil had got above deck. I then held several other things one after another in my hand, and laid them down where I laid the buckle, but nothing stirred till I took out the fellow of that from the shoes; when letting it go away, it jumped also to the rock.

I mused on these phenomena for sometime, and could not forbear calling upon God to protect me from the devil; who must, as I imagined, have a hand in such unaccountable things as they then seemed to me. But at length reason got the better of these foolish apprehensions, and I began to think there might be some natural cause of them, and next to be very desirous of finding it out In order to this I set about making experiments to try what would run to the rock and what would not. I went into the captain's cabin, and opening a cupboard, of which the key was in the door, I took out a pipe, a bottle, a pocket-book, a silver spoon, a tea-cup, &c, and laid them successively near the rock; when none of them answered, but the key which I had brought out of the cupboard on my finger dropping off while I was thus employed, no sooner was it disengaged but away it went to it. After that I tried several other pieces of iron-ware with the like success. Upon this, and the needle of my compass standing stiff to the rock, I concluded that this same rock contained great quantity of loadstone, or was itself one vast magnet, and that our lading of iron was the cause of the ship's violent course thereto, which I mentioned before.

This quite satisfied me as to my notions of spirits, and gave me a more undisturbed night's rest than I had had before, so that now, having nothing to affright me, I passed the time tolerably well in my solitude, as it grew by degrees familiar to me.

I had often wished it had been possible for me to climb the rock, but it was so smooth in many places and craggy in others, and over-hanging, continuing just the same to the right and left of me as far as ever I could see, that from the impossibility of it, I discharged all thoughts of such an attempt.

I had now lived on board three months, and perceived the days grow shorter and shorter, till, having lost the sun for a little time, they were quite dark: that is, there was no absolute daylight, or indeed visible distinction between day and night; though it was never so dark but I could see well enough upon deck to go about.

What now concerned me the most was my water, which began to grow very bad (though I had plenty of it) and unsavoury, so that I could scarce drink it, but had no prospect of better. Now and then indeed it snowed a little, which I made some use of, but this was far from contenting me. Hereupon I began to contrive; and having nothing else to do, I set two open vessels upon deck, and drawing water from the hold I filled one of my vessels, and letting it stand a day and a night I poured it into the other, and so shifted it every twenty-four hours; this, I found, though it did not bring it to the primitive taste and render it altogether palatable, was nevertheless a great help to it, by incorporating the fresh air with it, so that it became very potable, and this method I constantly used with my drinking-water, so long as I stayed on board the ship.

It had now been sharp weather for sometime, and the cold still increasing, this put me upon rummaging the ship farther than ever I thought to do before; when opening a little cabin under deck, I found a large cargo of fine French brandy, a great many bottles, and some small casks of Madeira wine, with divers cordial waters. Having tasted these, and taken out a bottle or two of brandy, and some Madeira, I locked up my door and looked no farther that time.

The next day I inquired into my provisions, and some of my flesh having soaked out the pickle, I made fresh pickle and closed it up again. I that day also found several cheeses cased up in lead, one of which I then opened and dined upon: but what time of day or night it was when I eat this meal I could not tell. I found a great many chests well filled, and one or two of tools which some years after stood me in a very good stead, though I did not expect they would ever be of that service when I first met with them.

In this manner I spent my time till I began to see broad daylight again, which cheered me greatly. I had been often put in hopes during the dark season that ships were coming towards me, and that I should once more have the conversation of mankind, for I had by the small glimmering seen many large bodies (to my thinking) move at a little distance from me, and particularly toward the reappearing of the light, but though I hallooed as loud as I could, and often fired my gun, I never received an answer.

When the light returned, my days increased in proportion as they had before decreased; and gathering comfort from that, I determined to launch my small boat and to coast along the island, as I judged it, to see if it was inhabited and by whom; I determined also to make me some lines for fishing, and carry my gun to try for other game, if I found a place for landing; for though I had never, since my arrival, seen a single living creature but my cat, except insects, of which there were many in the water and in the air before the dark weather, and then began to appear again, yet I could not but think there were both birds and beasts to be met with.

Upon launching my boat I perceived she was very leaky, so I let her fill and continue thus a week or more to stop her cracks, then getting down the side of my ship I scooped her quite dry and found her very fit for use; so putting on board my gun, lines, brandy bottles, and clothes chest for a seat, with some little water and provisions for a week, I once more committed myself to the sea, having taken all the observation I could to gain my ship again if any accident should happen, though I resolved upon no account to quit sight of the rock willingly.

I had not rowed very long before I thought I saw an island to my right about a league distant, to which I inclined to steer my course, the sea being very calm; but upon surveying it nearer, I found it only a great cake of ice, about forty yards high above the water and a mile or two in length. I then concluded that what I had before taken for ships were only these lumps of ice. Being thus disappointed as to my island, I made what haste I could back to the rock again and coasted part of its circumference; but though I had gone two or three leagues of its circuit, the prospect it afforded was just the same.

I then tried my lines by fastening several very long ones, made of the log-line, to the side of the boat, baiting them with several different baits, but took only one fish of about four pounds weight, very much resembling a haddock, part of which I dressed for my supper after my return to the ship, and it proved very good. Towards evening I returned to my home, as I may call it.

The next day I made a voyage on the other side of the rock, though but to a small distance from the ship, with intent only to fish, but took nothing. I had then a mind to victual my boat or little cruiser, and prepare myself for a voyage of two or three days, which I thought I might safely undertake, as I had never seen a troubled sea since I came to the island; for though I heard the wind often roaring over my head, yet it coming always from the land-side, it never disturbed the water near the shore. I set out the same way I went at first, designing to sail two or three days out and as many home again, and resolved if possible to fathom the depth as I went. With this view I prepared a very long line with a large shot tied in a rag at the end of it, by way of plummet, but I felt no ground till the second night. The next morning I came into thirty fathom water, then twenty, then sixteen. In both tours I could perceive no abatement in the height or steepness of the rock.

In about fourteen fathom water I dropped my lines, and lay by for an hour or two. Feeling several jars as I sat on my chest in the boat, I was sure I had caught somewhat, so pulling up my lines successively, I brought first a large eel near six feet long and almost as thick as my thigh, whose mouth, throat, and fins, were of a fine scarlet, and the belly as white as snow: he was so strong while in the water, and weighty, I had much ado to get him into the boat, and then had a harder job to kill him; for though, having a hatchet with me to cut wood in case I met with any landing-place, I chopped off his head the moment I had him on board, yet he had several times after that have like to have broken my legs and beat me overboard before I had quite taken his life from him, and had I not whipped off his tail and also divided his body into two or three pieces, I could not have mastered him. The next I pulled up was a thick fish like a tench, but of another colour and much bigger. I drew up several others, flat and long fish, till I was tired with the sport; and then I set out for the ship again, which I reached the third day.

During this whole time, I had but one shot, and that was as I came homewards, at a creature I saw upon a high crag of the rock, which I fired at with ball, fearing that my small shot would not reach it The animal, being mortally wounded, bounded up, and came tumbling down the rock, very near me. I picked it up, and found it to be a creature not much unlike our rabbits, but with shorter ears, a longer tail, and hoofed like a kid, though it had the perfect fluck of a rabbit I put it into my boat, to contemplate on when I arrived at the ship; and, plying my oars, got safe, as I said, on the third day.

I made me a fire to cook with as soon as I had got my cargo out of the boat into my ship, but was under debate which of my dainties to begin upon. I had sometimes a mind to have broiled my rabbit, as I called it, and boiled some of my fish; but being tired, I hung up my flesh till the next day, and boiled two or three sorts of my fish, to try which was best. I knew not the nature of most of them, so I boiled a piece of my eel, to be sure, judging that, however I might like the others, I should certainly be able to make a good meal of that. This variety being ready, I took a little of my oil out of the hold for sauce, and sat down to my meal, as satisfied as an emperor. But upon tasting my several messes, though the eel was rather richer than the smaller fishes, yet the others were all so good, I gave them the preference for that time, and laid by the rest of the eel, and of the other fish, till the next day, when I salted them for future use.

I kept now a whole week or more at home, to look farther into the contents of the ship, bottle off a cask of Madeira, which I found leaking, and to consume my new stores of fish and flesh, which, being somewhat stale when first salted, I thought would not keep so well as the old ones that were on board. I added also some fresh bread to my provision, and sweetened more water by the aforementioned method; and when my necessary domestic affairs were brought under, I then projected a new voyage.

X

I had for a long time wanted to see the other side of the rock, and at last resolved to try if I could not coast it quite round; for, as I reasoned with myself, I might possibly find some landing-places, and perhaps a convenient habitation on shore. But as I was very uncertain what time that might take up, I determined on having provisions, instruments of divers kinds, and necessary utensils in plenty, to guard against accidents as well as I could. I therefore took another sea-chest out of the hold of the ship, and letting it into my boat, replenished it with a stock of wine, brandy, oil, bread, and the like, sufficient for a considerable voyage. I also filled a large cask with water, and took a good quantity of salt to cure what fish I should take by the way. I carried two guns, two brace of pistols, and other arms, with ammunition proportionable; also an axe or two, a saw to cut wood if I should see any, and a few other tools, which might be highly serviceable if I could land. To all these I added an old sail, to make a covering for my goods and artillery against the weather. Thus furnished and equipped, having secured my hatches on board, and everything that might spoil by wet, I set out, with a God's speed, on my expedition, committing myself once more to Providence and the main ocean, and proceeding the same way I went the first time.

I did not sail extraordinary fast, but frequently fished in proper places, and caught a great deal, salting and drying the best of what I took. For three weeks' time and more, I saw no entrance into the island, as I call it, nor anything but the same unscalable rock. This uniform prospect gave me so little hopes of landing, that I was almost of a mind to have returned again. But, on mature deliberation, resolving to go forward a day or two more, I had not proceeded twenty-four hours, when, just as it was becoming dark, I heard a great noise, as of a fall of water, whereupon I proposed to lie by and wait for day, to see what it was; but the stream insensibly drawing me on, I soon found myself in an eddy; and the boat drawing forward beyond all my power to resist it, I was quickly sucked under a low arch, where, if I had not fallen flat in my boat, having barely light enough to see my danger, I had undoubtedly been crushed to pieces or driven overboard. I could perceive the boat to fall with incredible violence, as I thought, down a precipice, and suddenly whirled round and round with me, the water roaring on all sides, and dashing against the rock with a most amazing noise.

I expected every moment my poor little vessel would be staved against the rock, and I overwhelmed with waters; and for that reason never once attempted to rise up, or look upon my peril, till after the commotion had in some measure ceased. At length, finding the perturbation of the water abate, and as if by degrees I came into a smoother stream, I took courage just to lift up my affrighted head; but guess, if you can, the horror which seized me, on finding myself in the blackest of darkness, unable to perceive the smallest glimmer of light.

However, as my boat seemed to glide easily, I roused myself and struck a light; but if I had my terrors before, what must I have now! I was quite stupefied at the tremendous view of an immense arch over my head, to which I could see no bounds; the stream itself, as I judged, was about thirty yards broad, but in some places wider, in some narrower. It was well for me I happened to have a tinder-box, or, though I had escaped hitherto, I must have at lust perished; for in the narrower parts of the stream, where it ran swiftest, there were frequently such crags stood out from the rock, by reason of the turnings and windings, and such sets of the current against them, as, could I not have seen to manage my boat, which I took great care to keep in the middle of the stream, must have thrown me on them, to my inevitable destruction.

Happy it was for me, also, I was so well victualled, and that I had taken with me two bottles of oil (as I supposed, for I did not imagine I had anymore), or I had certainly been lost, not only through hunger, for I was, to my guess, five weeks in the vault or cavern, but for want of light, which the oil furnished, and without which all other conveniences could have been of no avail to me. I was forced to keep my lamp always burning; so, not knowing how long my residence was to be in that place, or when I should get my discharge from it, if ever, I was obliged to husband my oil with the utmost frugality; and notwithstanding all my caution, it grew low, and was just spent, in little above half the time I stayed there.

I had now cut a piece of my shirt for a wick to my last drop of oil, which I twisted and lighted. I burnt the oil in my brass tobacco-box, which I had fitted pretty well to answer the purpose Sitting down, I had many black thoughts of what must follow the loss of my light, which I considered as near expiring, and that, I feared, forever. I am here, thought I, like a poor condemned criminal, who knows his execution is fixed for such a day, nay, such an hour, and dies over and over in imagination, and by the torture of his mind, till that hour comes: that hour, which he so much dreads! and yet that very hour which releases him from all farther dread! Thus do I—my last wick is kindled—my last drop of fuel is consuming!—and I am every moment apprehending the shocks of the rock, the suffocation of the water; and, in short, thinking over my dying thoughts, till the snuff of my lamp throws up its last curling, expiring flame, and then my quietus will be presently signed, and I released from my tormenting anxiety! Happy minute! Come then; I only wait for thee! My spirits grew so low and feeble upon this, that I had recourse to my brandy bottle to raise them; but, as I was just going to take a sip, I reflected that would only increase thirst, and, therefore, it were better to take a little of my white Madeira; so, putting my dram-bottle again into the chest, I held up one of Madeira, as I fancied, to the lamp, and seeing it was white (for I had red too) I clapped it eagerly to my mouth, when the first gulp gave me a greater refreshment, and more cheered my heart, than all the other liquors I had put together could have done; insomuch, as I had almost leaped over the boat's side for joy. "It is oil!" cried I aloud, "it is oil!" I set it down carefully, with inexpressible pleasure; and examining the rest of the bottles I had taken for white Madeira, I found two more of those to be filled with oil. "Now," says I, "here is the counterpart of my condemned prisoner! For let but a pardon come, though at the gallows, how soon does he forget he has been an unhappy villain! And I, too, have scarce a notion now, how a man, in my case, could feel such sorrow as I have for want of a little oil."

After my first transport, I found myself grow serious, reflecting upon the vigilance of Providence over us poor creatures, and the various instances wherein it interposes to save or relieve us in cases of the deepest distress, where our own foresight, wisdom, and power have utterly failed, and when, looking all around, we could discover no means of deliverance. And I saw a train of circumstances leading to the incident I have just mentioned, which obliged me to acknowledge the superintendence of Heaven over even my affairs; and as the goodness of God had cared for me thus far, and manifested itself to me now, in rescuing me, as it were, from being swallowed up in darkness, I had ground to hope He intended a complete deliverance of me out of that dismal abyss, and would cause me yet to praise Him in the full brightness of day.

A series of these meditations brought me (at the end of five weeks, as nearly as I could compute it by my lamp) to a prodigious lake of water, bordered with a grassy down, about half a mile wide, of the finest verdure I had ever seen: this again was flanked with a wood or grove, rising like an amphitheatre, of about the same breadth; and behind, and above all, appeared the naked rock to an immense height.

XI

His joy on his arrival at land—A description of the place—No inhabitants—Wants fresh water—Resides in a grotto—Finds water—Views the country— Carries his things to the grotto.

I t is impossible to express my joy at the sight of day once more. I got on the land as soon as possible after my dismission from the cavern, and, kneeling on the ground, returned hearty thanks to God for my deliverance, begging, at the same time, grace to improve His mercies, and that I might continue under His protection, whatever should hereafter befall me, and at last die on my native soil.

I unloaded my vessel as well as I could, and hauled her up on the shore; and, turning her upside down, made her a covering for my arms and baggage. I then sat down to contemplate the place, and eat a most delightful meal on the grass, being quite a new thing to me.

I walked over the greensward to the wood, with my gun in my hand, a brace of pistols in my girdle, and my cutlass hanging before me; but, when I was just entering the wood, looking behind me and all around the plain, "Is it possible," says I, "that so much art (for I did not then believe it was natural) could have been bestowed upon this place, and no inhabitant in it? Here are neither buildings, huts, castle, nor any living creature to be seen! It cannot be," says I, "that this place was made for nothing!"

I then went a considerable way into the wood, and inclined to have gone much farther, it being very beautiful, but, on second thoughts, judged it best to content myself at present with only looking out a safe retreat for that night; for, however agreeable the place then seemed, darkness was at hand, when everything about me would have more or less of horror in it.

The wood, at its first entrance, was composed of the most charming flowering shrubs that can be imagined; each growing upon its own stem, at so convenient a distance from the other, that you might fairly pass between them anyway without the least incommodity. Behind them grew numberless trees, somewhat taller, of the greatest variety of shapes, forms, and verdures the eye ever beheld; each, also, so far asunder as was necessary for the spreading of their several branches and the growth of their delicious fruits, without a bush, briar, or shrub amongst them.

Behind these, and still on the higher ground, grew an infinite number of very large, tall trees, much loftier than the former, but intermixed with some underwood, which grew thicker and closer the nearer you approached the rock. I made a shift to force my way through these as far as the rock, which rose as perpendicular as a regular building, having only here and there some crags and unevennesses. There was, I observed, a space all the way between the underwood and the rock, wide enough to drive a cart in; and, indeed, I thought it had been left for that purpose.

I walked along this passage a good way, having tied a rag of the lining of my jacket at the place of my entrance, to know it again at my coming back, which I intended to be ere it grew dark; but I found so much pleasure in the walk, and surveying a small natural grotto which was in the rock, that the daylight forsook me unawares: whereupon I resolved to put off my return unto the boat till next morning, and to take up my lodging for that night in the cave.

I cut down a large bundle of underwood with my cutlass, sufficient to stop up the mouth of the grotto, and laying me down to rest, slept as sound as if I had been on board my ship; for I never had one hour's rest together since I shot the gulf till this. Nature, indeed, could not have supported itself thus long under much labour; but as I had nothing to do but only keep the middle stream, I began to be as used to guide myself in it with my eyes almost closed, and my senses retired, as a higgler is to drive his cart to market in his sleep.

The next morning I awaked sweetly refreshed; and, by the sign of my rag, found the way again through the underwood to my boat I raised that up a little, took out some bread and cheese, and, having eat pretty heartily, laid me down to drink at the lake, which looked as clear as crystal, expecting a most delicious draught; but I had forgot it brought me from the sea, and my first gulp almost poisoned me. This was a sore disappointment, for I knew my water-cask was nigh emptied; and, indeed, turning up my boat again, I drew out all that remained, and drank it, for I was much athirst.

However, I did not despair; I was now so used to God's providence, and had a sense of its operations so riveted in my mind, that though the vast lake of salt water was surrounded by an impenetrable rock or barrier of stone, I rested satisfied that I should rather find even that yield me a fresh and living stream, than that I should perish for want of it.

With this easy mind did I travel five or six miles on the side of the lake, and sometimes stepped into the wood, and walked a little there, till

I had gone almost half the diameter of the lake, which lay in a circular or rather an oval figure. I had then thoughts of walking back, to be near my boat and lodging, for fear I should be again benighted if I went much farther; but, considering I had come past no water, and possibly I might yet find some if I went quite round the lake, I rather chose to take up with a new lodging that night, than to return; and I did not want for a supper, having brought out with me more bread and cheese than had served for dinner, the remainder of which was in the lining of my jacket. When it grew darkish, I had some thoughts of eating; but I considered, as I was then neither very hungry nor dry, if I should eat it would but occasion drought, and I had nothing to allay that with; so I contented myself for that night to lay me down supperless.

In the morning I set forward again upon my water search, and hoped to compass the whole lake that day. I had gone about seven miles more, when, at a little distance before me, I perceived a small hollow or cut in the grass from the wood to the lake; thither I hasted with all speed, and blessed God for the supply of a fine fresh rill, which, distilling from several small clefts in the rock, had collected itself into one stream, and cut its way through the green sod to the lake.

I lay down with infinite pleasure, and swallowed a most cheering draught of the precious liquid; and, sitting on the brink, made a good meal of what I had with me, and then drank again. I had now got five-sixths of the lake's circumference to go back again to my boat, for I did not suspect any passage over the cavern's mouth where I came into the lake; and I could not, without much trouble, consider that, if I would have this water for a constant supply, I must either come a long way for it, or fix my habitation near it. I was just going back again, revolving these uneasy thoughts in my breast, when this rose suddenly in my mind, that, if I could possibly get over the mouth of the cavern, I should not have above three miles from my grotto to the water. Now, as I could not get home that night otherwise than by crossing it, and as, if I lost my labour, I should be but where I was, whereas if I should get over it, it would very much shorten my journey, I resolved to try whether the thing was practicable, first, however, looking out for a resting-place somewhere near my water, if I should meet with a disappointment.

I then walked into the wood, where, meeting with no place of retreat to my liking, I went to my rill, and taking another sup, determined not to leave that side of the lake till morning; but having sometime to spare, I walked about two miles to view the inlet of the lake, and was agreeably surprised, just over the mouth of the cavern, to see a large stone arch like a bridge, as if it had been cut out of the rock, quite across the opening: this cheered me vastly, and, pushing over it, I found a path that brought me to my boat before night.

I then went up to my grotto for the third night in this most delightful place; and the next morning early I launched my boat, and taking my water-cask and a small dipping bucket with me, I rowed away for the rill, and returned highly pleased with a sufficiency of water, whereof I carried a bucket and a copper kettle full up with me to the grotto. Indeed, it was not the least part of my satisfaction that I had this kettle with me; for though I was in hopes, in my last voyage, I should have come to some shore, where I could have landed and enjoyed myself over some of my fish, and for that reason had taken it, notwithstanding things did not turn out just as I had schemed, yet my kettle proved the most useful piece of furniture I had.

Having now acquainted myself with the circumference of the lake, and settled a communication with my rill, I began to think of commencing housekeeper. In order thereunto, I set about removing my goods up to the grotto. By constant application, in a few days I had gotten all thither but my two great chests and my water-cask; and how to drag or drive any of those to it, I was entirely at a loss. My water-cask was of the utmost importance to me, and I had thoughts sometimes of stopping it close, and rolling it to the place; but the ascent through the wood to the grotto was so steep, that, besides the fear of staving it, which would have been an irreparable loss, I judged it impossible to accomplish it by my strength; so with a good deal of discontent, I determined to remit both that and the chests to future consideration.

ROBERT PALTOCK

XII

Having come to a full resolution of fixing my residence at the grotto, and making that my capital seat, it is proper to give you some description of it.

This grotto, then, was a full mile from the lake, in the rock which encompassed the wood. The entrance was scarcely two feet wide, and about nine feet high, rising from the height of seven feet upward to a point in the middle. The cavity was about fifteen feet long within, and about five wide. Being obliged to lie lengthwise in it, full six feet of it were taken up at the farther end for my lodging only, as nothing could stand on the side of my bed that would leave me room to come at it. The remaining nine feet of the cave's length were taken up, first, by my fireplace, which was the deepest side of the doorway, ranging with my bed (which I had set close to the rock on one side), and took up near three feet in length; and my furniture and provisions, of one sort or other, so filled up the rest, that I had much ado to creep between them into my bed.

In the chest which I had taken for a seat in the boat, as aforesaid, upon breaking it open by the water-side, I found a mattress, some shirts, shoes, stockings, and several other useful things; a small case of bottles with cordials in them, some instruments of surgery, plasters and salves; all which, together with a large quantity of fish that I had salted, I carried to the grotto.

My habitation being thus already overcharged, and as I could not, however, bear the thoughts of quitting it, or of having any of my goods exposed to the weather on the outside, I was naturally bent on contriving how I should increase my accommodations. As I had no prospect of enlarging the grotto itself, I could conceive no other way of effecting my desire but by the addition of an outer room. This thought pleased me very much, so that the next day I set myself to plan out the building, and trace the foundation of it.

I told you before there was about the space of a cart-way between the wood and the rock clear; but this breadth, as I was building for life (so I imagined), not appearing to me spacious enough for my new apartment, I considered how I should extend its bounds into the wood. Hereupon I set myself to observe what trees stood at a proper distance from my grotto, that might serve as they stood, with a little management of hewing and the like, to compose a noble doorway, posts, and supporters; and I found, that upon cutting down three of the nearest trees, I should answer my purpose in this respect; and there were several others, about twenty feet from the grotto, and running parallel with the rock, the situation of which was so happily adapted to my intention, that I could make them become, as I fancied, an out-fence or wall; so I took my axe and cut down my nearest trees, but as I was going to strike, a somewhat different scheme presented itself to my imagination that altered my resolution.

In conformity with this new plan, I fixed the height of my intended ceiling, and sawed off my nearest trees to that, sloping from the sides to the middle, to support cross-beams for the roof to rest on, and left the trunks standing, by way of pillars, both for the use and ornament of the structure. In short, I worked hard everyday upon my building for a month, in which time I had cut all my timber into their proper lengths for my outworks and covering, but was at a great stand how to fix my side-posts, having no spade or mattock, and the ground almost as hard as flint, for to be sure it had never been stirred since the creation. I then thought I had the worst part of my job to get over; however, I went on, and having contrived, in most of my upright side-quarters, to take the tops of trees, and leave on the lower parts their cleft, where they began to branch out and divide from the main stem, I set one of them upright against the rock, then laid one end of my long ceiling-pieces upon the cleft of it, and laid the other end upon a tree on the same side, whose top I had also sawed off with a proper cleft I then went and did the same on the other side; after this I laid on a proper number of cross-beams, and tied all very firmly together with the bark of young trees stripped off in long thongs, which answered that purpose very well. Thus I proceeded, crossing, joining, and fastening all together, till the whole roof was so strong and firm that there was no stirring any part of it I then spread it over with small lop wood, on which I raised a ridge of dried grass and weeds, very thick, and thatched over the whole with the leaves of a tree very much resembling those of a palm, but much thicker, and not quite so broad; the entire surface, I might say, was as smooth as a die, and so ordered, by a gentle declivity every way, as to carry off the wet.

Having covered in my building, I was next to finish and close the walls of it; the skeleton of these was composed of sticks, crossing one another checker-wise and tied together; to fill up the voids, I wove upon them the longest and most pliable twigs of the underwood I could find, leaving only a doorway on one side, between two stems of a tree which, dividing in the trunk at about two feet from the ground, grew from thence, for the rest of its height, as if the branches were a couple of trees a little distance from one another, which made a sort of stile-way to my room. When this was all done, I tempered up some earth by the lake-side, and mixing it to a due consistence with mud, which I took from the lake, applied it as a plastering in this manner: I divided it into pieces, which I rolled up of the size of a foot-ball; these lumps I stuck close by one another on the lattice, pressing them very hard with my hands, which forced part of them quite through the small twigs, and then I smoothed both sides with the back of my saw, to about the thickness of five or six inches; so that by this means I had a wall round my new apartment a foot thick. This plaster-work cost me sometime and a great deal of labour, as I had a full mile to go to the lake for every load of stuff, and could carry but little at once, it was so heavy; but there was neither water for tempering, nor proper earth to make it with any nearer. At last, however, I completed my building in every respect but a door, and for this I was forced to use the lid of my sea chest; which indeed I would have chosen not to apply that way, but I had nothing else that would, do; and there was, however, this conveniency, that it had hinges ready fixed thereon.

I now began to enjoy myself in my new habitation, like the absolute and sole lord of the country, for I had neither seen man nor beast since my arrival, save a few animals in the trees like our squirrels, and some water-rats about the lake; but there were several strange kinds of birds I had never before seen, both on the lake and in the woods.

That which now troubled me most was how to get my water nearer to me than the lake, for I had no lesser vessel than the cask, which held above twenty gallons, and to bring that up was a fatigue intolerable. My next contrivance, therefore, was this: I told you I had taken my chest-lid to make a door for my ante-chamber, as I now began to call it; so I resolved to apply the body of the chest also to a purpose different from that it originally answered. In order to this, I went to the lake where the body of the chest lay, and sawed it through within about three inches of the bottom. Of the two ends, having rounded them as well as I could, I made two wheels; and with one of the sides I made two more. I burnt a hole through the middle of each; then preparing two axle-trees, I fastened them, after putting on the wheels, to the bottom of the chest with the nails I had drawn out, of it. Having finished this machine, on which I bestowed no small labour, I was hugely pleased with it, and only wished I had a beast, if it were but an ass, to draw it; however, that task I was satisfied to perform myself, since there was no help for it; so I made a good strong cord out of my fishing-lines, and fixed that to drag it by. When all was thus in readiness, filling my water-cask, I bound it thereon, and so brought it to the grotto with such ease, comparatively, as quite charmed me. Having succeeded so well in the first essay, I no sooner unloaded but down went I again with my cart, or truckle rather, to the lake, and brought from thence on it my other chest, which I had left entire.

I had now nothing remaining near the lake but my boat, and had half a mind to try to bring that up too; but having so frequent occasion for her to get my water in, which I used in greater abundance now than I had done at first, a great part going to supply my domestic uses, as well as for drinking, I resolved against that, and sought out for a convenient dock to stow it in as a preservative against wind and weather, which I soon after effected; for having pitched upon a swampy place, overgrown with a sort of long flags or reeds, I soon cut a trench from the lake, with a sort of spade or board that I had chopped and sharpened for that use.

Thus having stowed my boat and looked over all my goods and sorted them, and taken a survey of my provisions, I found I must soon be in want of the last if I did not forthwith procure a supply; for though I had victualled so well at setting out, and had been very sparing ever since, yet had it not been for a great quantity of fish I took and salted in my passage to the gulf, I had been to seek for food much sooner. Hereupon I thought it highly prudent to look out before I really wanted.

With this resolution I accoutred myself, as in my first walk, with my instruments and arms; but instead of travelling the lake-side, I went along the wood, and therein found great plenty of divers kinds of

ROBERT PALTOCK

fruits \ though I could scarce persuade myself to taste or try the effects of them, being so much unlike our own, or any I had seen elsewhere. I observed amongst the shrubs abundance of a fruit, or whatever else you may call it, which grew like a ram's-horn; sharp at the point next the twig it was fastened to, and circling round and round, one fold upon another, which gradually increased to the size of my wrist in the middle, and then as gradually decreased till it terminated in a point again at the contrary extreme; all which spiral, if it were fairly extended in length, might be a yard or an ell long. I surveyed this strange vegetable very attentively; it had a rind, or crust, which I could not break with my hand, but taking my knife and making an opening therewith in the shell, there issued out a sort of milky liquor in great quantity, to at least a pint and half, which having tasted, I found as sweet as honey, and very pleasant: however, I could not persuade myself anymore than just to taste it. I then found on the large trees several kinds of fruit, like pears or quinces, but most of them exceeding hard and rough, and quite disagreeable; so I quitted my hopes of them.

About three miles from my grotto I met with a large space of ground full of a low plant, growing only with a single woody stalk half a foot high, and from thence issued a round head, about a foot or ten inches diameter, but quite flat, about three-quarters of an inch thick, and just like a cream-cheese standing upon its edge: these grew so close together, that upon the least wind stirring, their heads rattled against each other very musically; for though the stalks were so very strong that they would not easily either bend or break, yet the fanning of the wind upon the broad heads twisting the stalks, so as to let the heads strike each other, they made a most agreeable sound.

I stood sometime admiring this shrub, and then cutting up one of them, I found it weighed about two pounds; they had a tough green rind or covering, very smooth, and the inside full of a stringy pulp, quite white. In short, I made divers other trials of berries, roots, herbs, and what else I could find, but received little satisfaction from any of them for fear of bad qualities. I returned back ruminating on what things I had seen, resolving to take my cart the next walk, and bring it home loaded with different kinds of them, in order to make my trials thereof at leisure: but my cart being too flat and wanting sides, I considered it would carry very little, and that what it would otherwise bear, on that account, must tumble and roll off, so I made a fire and turned smith; for with a great deal to do breaking off the wards of a large key I had, and making it red-hot, I by degrees fashioned it into a kind of spindle, and therewith making holes quite round the bottom of my cart, in them I stuck up sticks about two feet high that I had tapered at the end to fit them.

Having thus qualified my cart for a load, I proceeded with it to the wood, and cutting a small quantity of each species of green, berry, fruit, and flower that I could find, and packing them severally in parcels, I returned at night heavy-laden, and held a council with myself what use they could most properly be applied to.

I had amongst my goods, as I said, a copper-kettle which held about a gallon: this I set over my fire and boiled something by turns of every sort in it, watching all the while, and with a stick stirring and raising up one thing and then another, to feel when they were boiled tender: but of upwards of twenty greens which I thus dressed, only one proved eatable, all the rest becoming more stringy, tough, and insipid for the cooking. The one I have excepted was a round, thick, woolly-leafed plant, which boiled tender and tasted as well as spinach; I therefore preserved some leaves of this to know it again by; and for distinction called it by the name of that herb.

I then began upon my fruits of the pear and quince kind, at least eight different sorts; but I found I could make nothing of them, for they were most of them as rough and crabbed after stewing as before, so I laid them all aside. Lastly, I boiled my ram's-horn and cream-cheese, as I called them, together. Upon tasting the latter of these, it was become so watery and insipid, I laid it aside as useless. I then cut the other and tasted the juice, which proved so exceeding pleasant that I took a large gulp or two of it, and tossed it into the kettle again.

Having now gone through the several kinds of my exotics, I had a mind to re-examine them after cooling, but could make nothing of any of my greens but the spinach. I tried several berries and nuts too, but, save a few sort of nuts, they were all very tasteless. Then I began to review the fruits, and could find but two sorts that I had any the least hopes from. I then laid the best by and threw the others away. After this process, which took me up near a whole day, and clearing my house of good-for-nothings, I returned to reexamine my cheese, that was grown cold, and was now so dry and hard I could not get my teeth into it; upon which I was going to skim it away out of my grotto, saying, "Go, thou worthless!" (for I always spoke aloud my thoughts to myself)—I say I was just despatching it when I checked my hands, and as I could make no impression with my teeth, had a mind to try what my knife would do. Accordingly I began at the edge of the quarter, for I had boiled but a quarter of it, but the rind was grown so hard and brittle that my knife slipping and raking along the cut edge of it, scratched off some powder as white as possible; I then scraped it backward and forward sometime, till I found it would all scrape away in this powder, except the rind, upon which I laid it aside again for farther experiment.

During this review my kettle and ram's-horn had been boiling, till hearing it blubber very loud, and seeing there was but little liquor in it, I whipped it off the fire, for fear of burning its bottom, but took no further notice of it till about two hours after; when returning to the grotto, I went to wash out my kettle, but could scarce get my ram's-horn from the bottom; and when I did, it brought up with it a sort of pitchy substance, though not so black, and several gummy threads hanging to it, drawn out to a great length. I wondered at this, and thought the shell of the ram's-horn had melted, or some such thing, till, venturing to put a little of the stuff on my tongue, it proved to my thinking as good treacle as I had ever tasted.

This new discovery pleased me very much. I scraped all the sweet thing up, and laid it near my grotto in a large leaf of one of the trees (about two feet long, and broad in proportion) to prevent its running about. In getting this curiosity out of my kettle, I found in it a small piece of my cheese, which I suppose had been broke off in stirring; and biting it (for it was soft enough) I think it was the most luscious and delicate morsel I ever put into my lips. This unexpected good fortune put me on trying the best of my pears again; so setting on my kettle, with very little water, and putting some of my treacle into it, and two of the best pears quartered, I found, upon a little boiling, they also became an excellent dainty.

Having succeeded so well, I was quite ripe for another journey with my cart; which I accordingly undertook, taking my route over the stone bridge, to see what the other side of the lake produced. In travelling through the trees, I met, amongst other things, with abundance of large gourds, which, climbing the trees, displayed their fruit to the height of twenty or thirty feet above the ground. I cut a great many of these, and some very large ones of different hues and forms; which of themselves making a great load, with some few new sorts of berries and greens, were the gathering of that day. But I must tell you I was almost foiled in getting them home; for coming to my stone bridge, it rose so steep, and was so much ruggeder than the grass or wood ground, that I was at a set upon the first entrance and terribly afraid that I should either break my wheels or pull off my axle-trees. Hereupon I was forced to unload, and carry my cargo over in my arms to the other side of the bridge; whither having then, with less fear but much caution, drawn my cart, I loaded again and got safe home.

I was mightily pleased with the acquisitions of this journey; for now, thought I, I shall have several convenient family utensils; so spent the next day or two in scooping my gourds and cleaning away the pulp. When I had done this, finding the rinds to be very weak and yielding, I made a good fire, and setting them round it at a moderate distance to dry, I went about something else without doors: but, alas! my hopes were ill founded; for coming home to turn my gourds and see how dry they were, I found them all warped and turned into a variety of uncouth shapes. This put me to a stand; but, however, I recovered some pieces of them for use, as the bottom parts of most of them, after paring away the sides, would hold something, though they by no means answered my first purpose.

Well, thought I, what if I have lost my gourds, I have gained experience. I will dry them next time with the guts in, and having stiffened their rinds in their proper dimensions, then try to cleanse them. So next morning (for I was very eager at it) I set out with my cart for another load; and having handed them over the bridge, got safe with them to the grotto. These by proper management proved exceedingly valuable to me, answering, in one way or other, the several uses of plates, bottles, pans, and divers other vessels.

I now got a large quantity of the vegetable ram's-horn, and filled a great many of the gourds with the treacle it yielded; I also boiled and dried a large parcel of my cheeses, and hung them up for use, for I had now for sometime made all my bread of the latter, scraping and bruising the flour, and mixing it with my treacle and water; and this indeed made such a sweet and nourishing bread, that I could even have lived wholly upon it; but I afterwards very much improved it by putting the milky juice of the ram's-horn, unboiled, to my flour in a small quantity, and then baking it on the hearth, covered over with embers. This detracted nothing from the sweetness and mellowness of my bread, but made it much lighter than the treacle alone would have done.

Finding there was no fear of starving, but so far from it, that from day to day I found out something new to add to my repast, either in substantials or by way of dessert, I set me down very well contented with my condition. I had nothing to do but to lay up store against sickness and the dark weather, which last I expected would soon be upon me, as the days were now exceeding short. Indeed, though I had now been here six months, I had never seen the sun since I first entered the gulf; and though there was very little rain, and but few clouds, yet the brightest daylight never exceeded that of half an hour after sunset in the summer-time in England, and little more than just reddened the sky. For the first part of my time here, there was but little if any difference between day and night; but afterwards, what I might call the night, or lesser degree of light, took up more hours than the greater, and went on gradually increasing as to time, so that I perceived total darkness approached, such as I had on board my ship the year before.

XIII

I had now well stored my grotto with all sorts of winter provisions, and feeling the weather grow very cold, I expected and waited patiently for the total darkness. I went little abroad, and employed myself within doors endeavouring to fence against the approaching extremity of the cold. For this purpose I prepared a quantity of rushes, which being very dry, I spread them smoothly on the floor of my bed-chamber a good thickness, and over them I laid my mattress. Then I made a double sheet of the boat's awning or sail, that I had brought to cover my goods; and having skewered together several of the jackets and clothes I found in the chest, of them I made a coverlid; so that I lay very commodiously, and made very long nights of it now the dark season was set in.

As I lay awake one night, or day, I know not which, I very plainly heard the sound of several human voices, and sometimes very loud; but though I could easily distinguish the articulations, I could not understand the least word that was said; nor did the voices seem at all to me like such as I had anywhere heard before, but much softer and more musical. This startled me, and I rose immediately, slipping on my clothes and taking my gun in my hand (which I always kept charged, being my constant travelling companion) and my cutlass. Thus equipped, I walked into my ante-chamber, where I heard the voices much plainer, till after some little time they by degrees died quite away. After watching here, and hearkening a good while, hearing nothing, I walked back into the grotto, and laid me down again on my bed. I was inclined to open the door of my ante-chamber, but I own I was afraid; besides, I considered that if I did, I could discover nothing at any distance by reason of the thick and gloomy wood that enclosed me.

ROBERT PALTOCK

I had a thousand different surmises about the meaning of this odd incident; and could not conceive how any human creatures should be in my kingdom (as I called it) but myself, and I never yet see them, or any trace of their habitation. But then again I reflected, that though I had surrounded the whole lake, yet I had not traced the out-bounds of the wood next the rock, where there might be innumerable grottoes like mine; nay, perhaps some as spacious as that I had sailed through to the lake; and that though I had not perceived it, yet this beautiful spot might be very well peopled. But, says I again, if there be any such beings as I am fancying here, surely they don't skulk in their dens, like savage beasts, by daylight, and only patrole for prey by night; if so, I shall probably become a delicious morsel for them ere long, if they meet with me. This kept me still more within doors than before, and I hardly ever stirred out but for water or firing. At length, hearing no more voices, nor seeing anyone, I began to be more composed in my mind, and at last grew persuaded it was all a mere delusion, and only a fancy of mine, without any real foundation; and sometimes, though I was sure I was fully awake when I heard them, I persuaded myself I had rose in my sleep, upon a dream of voices, and recollected with myself the various stories I had heard when a boy of walking in one's sleep, and the surprising effects of it; so the whole notion was now blown over.

I had not enjoyed my tranquillity above a week, before my fears were roused afresh, hearing the same sound of voices twice the same night, but not many minutes at a time. What gave me most pain was that they were at such a distance, as I judged by the languor of the sound, that if I had opened my door I could not have seen the utterers through the trees, and I was resolved not to venture out; but then I determined, if they should come again anything near my grotto, to open the door, see who they were, and stand upon my defence, whatever came of it: For, says I, my entrance is so narrow and high that more than one cannot come at a time; and I can with ease despatch twenty of them before they can secure me, if they should be savages; but if they prove sensible human creatures, it will be a great benefit to me to join myself to their society. Thus had I formed my scheme, but I heard no more of them for a great while; so that at length beginning to grow ashamed of my fears, I became tranquil again.

The day now returning, and with it my labours, I applied to my usual callings; but my mind ran strangely upon viewing the rock quite round, that is, the whole circuit of my dominions; for, thinks I, there may possibly be an outlet through the rock into someother country, from whence the persons I heard may come. As soon therefore as the days grew towards the longest, I prepared for my progress. Having lived so well at home since my settlement, I did not care to trust only to what I could pick up in the woods for my subsistence during this journey, which would not only take up time in procuring, but perhaps not agree with me; so I resolved to carry a supply with me, proportionate to the length of my perambulation. Hereupon considering that though my walk round the lake was finished in two days, yet as I now intended to go round by the rock, the way would be much longer and perhaps more troublesome than that was; remembering also my journey with Glanlepze in Africa, and how much I complained of the fruits we carried for our subsistence; these circumstances, I say, laying together, I resolved to load the cart with a variety of food, bread and fruits especially, and draw that with me.

Thus provided, I sallied forth with great cheerfulness, and proceeded in the main easily; though in some places I was forced to make way with my hatchet, the ground was so over-run with underwood. I very narrowly viewed the rock as I went, bottom and sides, all the way, but could see nothing like a passage through it, or indeed anymore than one opening, or inlet, which I entered for about thirty yards, but it was not above three feet wide, and terminated in the solid rock.

After some days' travel (making all the observations I could on the several plants, shrubs, and trees which I met with, particularly where any of these occurred to me entirely new), finding myself a little faintish, I had a mind for a sup of ram's-horn juice; so I cut me one, but upon opening it found therein only a pithy pulp, and noways fit to taste. I supposed by this I was too early for the milk, it being three months later the last year when I cut them. Hereon, seeing one upon another shrub, which by its rusty colour I judged might have hung all the winter, I opened that, and found it full of milk; but putting some of it into my mouth, it was as sour as any vinegar I ever tasted in my life. So, thinks I (and said so too; for, as I told you before, I always spoke out), here's sauce for something when I want it; and this gave me a hint to store myself with these gourds, to hang by for vinegar the next winter.

By this time I had come almost to my rill, when I entered upon a large plat of ground miserably over-run with weeds, matted together very thick. These choked up my wheels in such a manner that I could neither free them with my hands, nor get either backwards or forwards, they binding my cart down like so many cords; so that I was obliged to cut my way back again with my hatchet, and take a sweep round in the wood, on the outside of these weeds.

In all my life I never saw anything of its size, for it was no thicker than a whipcord, so strong as this weed; and what raised my wonder was the length of it, for I drew out pieces of it near fifty feet long, and even they were broken at the end, so that it might be as long again for aught I know, for it was so matted and twisted together, that it was a great trial of patience to untangle it; but that which was driest, and to me looked the rottenest and weakest, I found to be much the strongest. Upon examination of its parts, I discovered it to be composed of an infinite number of small threads, spirally overlaying and enfolding one another.

As I saw but few things that I could not find a use for, so this I perceived would serve all the common purposes of packthread; a thing I was often in want of. This inclined me to take a load of it home with me. Indeed the difficulty of getting a quantity in the condition I desired it, puzzled me a little; for, says I, if I cut up a good deal of it with my hatchet, as I first designed, I shall only have small lengths, good for little, and to get it in pieces of any considerable length, so as to be of service, will require much time and labour. But reflecting how much I needed it, and of what benefit it would be, I resolved to make a trial of what I could do; so, without more hesitation, I went to work, and cutting a fibre close to its root, I extricated that thread from all its windings, just as one does an entangled whipcord. When I had thus disengaged a sufficient length, I cut that off, and repeating the like operation, in about three hours' time, but with no little toil, I made up my load of different lengths just to my liking. Having finished this task, I filled the gourd, brought for that purpose, with water; and having first viewed the whole remaining part of the rock, I returned over the stone bridge home again.

This journey, though it took me up several days, and was attended with some fatigue, had yet given me great satisfaction; for now I was persuaded I could not have one rival or enemy to fear in my whole dominions. And from the impossibility, as I supposed, of there being any, or of the ingress of any, unless by the same passage I entered at, and by which I was well assured they could never return, I grew contented, and blamed myself for the folly of my imaginary voices, as I called them then, and took it for a distemper of the fancy only.

The next day I looked over my load of matweed, having given it that name, and separated the different lengths from each other. I then found I had several pieces between forty and fifty feet long, of which I resolved to get a good number more, to make me a drag-net that I might try for some fish in the lake. A day or two after, therefore, I brought home another load of it Then I picked out a smooth level spot upon the greensward, and having prepared a great number of short wooden pegs, I strained a line of the matweed about ten feet long, tying it at each end to a peg, and stuck a row of pegs along by that line, about two inches asunder; I next strained another line of the same length, parallel to that, at the distance of forty feet from it, and stuck pegs thereby, corresponding to the former row; and from each peg on one side, to the opposite peg on the other, I tied a like length of my mat-line, quite through the whole number of pegs; when the work looked like the inside of a harpsichord. I afterwards drove pegs in like manner along the whole length of the two outermost longer lines, and tied shorter lines to them, so that the whole affair then represented the squares of a racket; the corners of each of which squares I tied very tight with smaller pieces of the line, till I had formed a complete net of forty feet long and ten wide.

When I had finished my net, as I thought, I wrapped several stones in rags, and fastened them to the bottom to sink it, and some of the smallest unscooped dry gourds to the top, to keep that part buoyant. I now longed to begin my new trade, and carried the net to my boat with that intention; but after two or three hauls I found it would not answer for want of length (though by chance I caught a blackish fish without scales, a little bigger than whiting, but much longer, which stuck by the gills in it); so I left the net in the boat, resolving to make an addition to it with all speed; and returning to my grotto, I supped on the fish I had taken and considered how to pursue my enterprise with better effect.

I provided me with another large parcel of line; and having brought two more lengths to perfection, I joined all together, and fixing one end on shore, by a pole I had cut for that purpose, I launched my boat, with the other end in it, taking a sweep the length of my net round to my stick again, and getting on shore, hauled up my net by both ends together. I found now I had mended my instrument, and taken a proper way of applying it; for by this means, in five hauls, I caught about sixteen fish of three or four different sorts, and one shell-fish, almost like a lobster, but without great claws, and with a very small short tail; which made me think, as the body was thrice as long as a lobster's in proportion, that it did not swim backwards, like that creature, but only crawled forwards (it having lobsterlike legs, but much shorter and stronger), and that the legs all standing so forward, its tail was, by its motion, to keep the hinder part of the body from dragging upon the ground, as I observed it did when the creature walked on land, it then frequently flacking its short tail.

These fish made me rich in provisions. Some of them I ate fresh, and the remainder I salted down. But of all the kinds, my lobster was the most delicious food, and made me almost three meals.

Thus finding there were fish to be had, though my present tackle seemed suitable enough to my family, yet could I not rest till I had improved my fishery by enlarging my net; for as it was, even with my late addition, I must either sweep little or no compass of ground, or it would have no bag behind me. Upon this I set to work and shortly doubled the dimensions of it. I had then a mind to try it at the mouth of my rill; so taking it with me the next time I crossed the lake for water, and fastening it to my pole, close by the right side of the rill, I swept a long compass round to the left, and closing the ends, attempted to draw it up in the hollow cut of the rill. But by the time I had gathered up two-thirds of the net, I felt a resistance that quite amazed me. In short, I was not able to stand against the force I felt. Whereupon sitting down in the rill, and clapping my feet to the two sides of it, I exerted all my strength, till finally I became conqueror, and brought up so shocking a monster, that I was just rising to run for my life on the sight of it. But recollecting that the creature was hampered, and could not make so much resistance on the land as in the water, I ventured to drag the net up as far from the rill as my strength and breath would permit me; and then running to the boat for my gun, I returned to the net to examine my prize. Indeed, I had not instantly resolution enough to survey it, and when at length I assumed courage enough to do so, I could not perfectly distinguish the parts, they were so discomposed; but taking hold of one end of the net, I endeavoured to disentangle the thing, and then drawing the net away, a most surprising sight presented itself: the creature reared upright, about three feet high, covered all over with long, black shaggy hair, like a bear, which hung down from his head and neck quite along his back and sides. He had two fins, very broad and large, which, as he stood erect, looked like arms, and these he waved and whirled about with incredible velocity; and though I wondered at first at it, I found afterwards it was the motion of these fins that kept him upright; for I perceived when they ceased their motion he fell flat on his belly. He had two very large feet, which he stood upon, but could not run, and but barely walk on them, which made me in the less haste to despatch him; and after he had stood upon his feet about four minutes, clapping his fins to his sides, he fell upon his belly.

When I found he could not attack me, I was moving closer to him; but upon sight of my stirring, up he rose again, and whirled his fins about as before so long as he stood. And now I viewed him round, and found he had no tail at all, and that his hinder fins, or feet, very much resembled a large frog's, but were at least ten inches broad, and eighteen long, from heel to toe; and his legs were so short that when he stood upright his breech bore upon the ground. His belly, which he kept towards me, was of an ash-colour, and very broad, as also was his breast His eyes were small and blue, with a large black sight in the middle, and rather of an oval than round make. He had a long snout like a boar, and vast teeth. Thus having surveyed him near half an hour living, I made him rise up once more and shot him in the breast. He fell, and giving a loud howl, or groan, expired.

I had then time to see what else I had caught; and turning over the net, found a few of the same fish I had taken before, and someothers of a flat-tish make, and one little lump of flesh unformed; which last, by all I could make of it, seemed to be either a spawn or young one of that I had shot.

The great creature was so heavy, I was afraid I must have cut him in pieces to get him to the boat; but with much ado, having stowed the rest, I tumbled him on board. I then filled my water-cask and rowed homewards. Being got to land, I was obliged to bring down my cart, to carry my great beast-fish, as I termed him, up to the grotto. When I had got him thither, I had a notion of first tasting, and then, if I liked his flesh, of salting him down and drying him; so, having flayed him and taken out the guts and entrails, I boiled a piece of him; but it made such a blaze that most of the fat ran into the fire, and the flesh proved so dry and rank that I could no ways endure it.

I then began to be sorry I had taken so much pains for no profit, and had endangered my net into the bargain (for that had got a crack or two in the scuffle), and was thinking to throw away my large but worthless acquisition.

However, as I was now prone to weighing all things, before I threw it away I resolved to consider a little; whereupon I changed my mind.

Says I, Here is a good warm skin, which, when dry, will make me a rare cushion. Again, I have for a long while had no light beside that of the day; but now as this beast's fat makes such a blaze in the fire, and issues in so great a quantity from such a small piece as I broiled, why may not I boil a good tallow or oil out of it? and if I can, I have not made so bad a hand of my time as I thought for.

In short, I went immediately to work upon this subject (for I never let a project cool after I had once started it), and boiled as much of the flesh as the kettle would hold, and letting it stand to cool, I found it turned out very good oil for burning; though I confess I thought it would rather have made tallow. This success quickened my industry; and I repeated the operation till I got about ten quarts of this stuff, which very well rewarded my labour. After I had extracted as much oil as I could from the beast-fish, the creature having strongly impressed my imagination, I conceived a new fancy in relation to it; and that was, having heard him make a deep, howling groan at his death, I endeavoured to persuade myself, and at last verily believed, that the voices I had so often heard in the dark weather proceeded from numbers of these creatures, diverting themselves in the lake, or sporting together on the shore; and this thought, in its turn, contributed to ease my apprehensions in that respect.

XIV

I passed the summer (though I had never yet seen the sun's body) very much to my satisfaction: partly in the work I have been describing (for I had taken two more of the beast-fish, and had a great quantity of oil from them); partly in building me a chimney in my ante-chamber of mud and earth burnt on my own hearth into a sort of brick; in making a window at one end of the abovesaid chamber, to let in what little light would come through the trees when I did not choose to open my door; in moulding an earthen lamp for my oil; and, finally, in providing and laying in stores, fresh and salt (for I had now cured and dried many more fish), against winter. These, I say, were my summer employments at home, intermixed with many agreeable excursions. But now the winter coming on, and the days growing very short, or indeed there being no day properly speaking, but a kind of twilight, I kept mostly in my habitation, though not so much as I had done the winter before, when I had no light within doors, and slept, or at least lay still, great part of my time; for now my lamp was never out. I also turned two of my beast-fish skins into a rug to cover my bed, and the third into a cushion, which I always sat upon, and a very soft and warm cushion it made. All this together rendered my life very easy, yea, even comfortable.

An indifferent person would now be apt to ask, What would this man desire more than he had? To this I answer, that I was contented while my condition was such as I have been describing; but a little while after the darkness or twilight came on, I frequently heard the voices again; sometimes a few only at a time, as it seemed, and then again in great numbers. This threw me into new fears, and I became as uneasy as ever, even to the degree of growing quite melancholy; though, otherwise, I never received the least injury from anything. I foolishly attempted several times, by looking out of my window, to discover what these odd sounds proceeded from, though I knew it was too dark to see anything there.

I was now fully convinced, by a more deliberate attention to them, that they could not be uttered by the beast-fish, as I had afore conjectured, but only by beings capable of articulate speech; but then, what or where they were, it galled me to be ignorant of.

At length, one night or day, I cannot say which, hearing the voices very distinctly, and praying very earnestly to be either delivered from the uncertainty they had put me under, or to have them removed from me, I took courage, and arming myself with gun, pistols, and cutlass, I went out of my grotto and crept down the wood. I then heard them plainer than before, and was able to judge from what point of the compass they proceeded. Hereupon I went forward towards the sound, till I came to the verge of the wood, where I could see the lake very well by the dazzle of the water. Thereon, as I thought, I beheld a fleet of boats, covering a large compass, and not far from the bridge. I was shocked hereat beyond expression. I could not conceive where they came from, or whither they would go; but supposed there must be someother passage to the lake than I had found in my voyage through the cavern, and that for certain they came that way, and from some place of which as yet I had no manner of knowledge.

Whilst I was entertaining myself with this speculation, I heard the people in the boats laughing and talking very merrily, though I was too distant to distinguish the words. I discerned soon after all the boats (as I still supposed 'em) draw up, and push for the bridge; presently after, though I was sure no boat entered the arch, I saw a multitude of people on the opposite shore all marching towards the bridge; and what was the strangest of all, there was not the least sign of a boat now left upon the whole lake. I then was in a greater consternation than before; but was still much more so when I saw the whole posse of people, that as I have just said were marching towards the bridge, coming over it to my side of the lake. At this my heart failed, and I was just going to run to my grotto for shelter; but taking one look more, I plainly discovered that the people, leaping one after another from the top of the bridge, as if into the water, and then rising again, flew in a long train over the lake, the lengthways of it, quite out of my sight, laughing, hallooing, and sporting together; so that looking back again to the bridge and on the lake, I could neither see person nor boat, nor anything else, nor hear the least noise or stir afterwards for that time.

I returned to my grotto brimful of this amazing adventure, bemoaning my misfortune in being at a place where I was like to remain ignorant of what was doing about me. For, says I, if I am in a land of spirits, as now I have little room to doubt, there is no guarding against them. I am never safe, even in my grotto; for that can be no security against such beings as can sail on the water in no boats, and fly in the air on no wings, as the case now appears to me, who can be here and there and wherever they please. What a miserable state, I say, am I fallen to! I should have been glad to have had human converse, and to have found inhabitants in this place; but there being none, as I supposed hitherto, I contented myself with thinking that I was at least safe from all those evils mankind in society are obnoxious to. But now, what may be the consequence of the next hour I know not; nay, I am not able to say but whilst I speak, and show my discontent, they may at a distance conceive my thoughts, and be hatching revenge against me for my dislike of them.

The pressure of my spirits inclining me to repose, I laid me down, but could get no rest; nor could all my most serious thoughts, even of the Almighty Providence, give me relief under my present anxiety: and all this was only from my state of uncertainty concerning the reality of what I had heard and seen, and from the earnestness with which I coveted a satisfactory knowledge of those beings who had just taken their flight from me.

I really believe the fiercest wild beast, or the most savage of mankind that had met me, and put me upon my defence, would not have given me half the trouble that then lay upon me; and the more, for that I had no seeming possibility of ever being rid of my apprehensions: so finding I could not sleep, I got up again; but as I could not fly from myself, all the art I could use with myself was but in vain to obtain me any quiet.

In the height of my distress I had recourse to prayer, with no small benefit; begging that if it pleased not the Almighty Power to remove the object of my fears, at least to resolve my doubts about them, and to render them rather helpful than hurtful to me. I hereupon, as I always did on such occasions, found myself much more placid and easy, and began to hope the best, till I had almost persuaded myself that I was out of danger; and then laying myself down, I rested very sweetly till I was awakened by the impulse of the following dream.

Methought I was in Cornwall, at my wife's aunt's; and inquiring after her and my children, the old gentlewoman informed me, both my wife and children had been dead sometime, and that my wife, before her departure, desired her (that is, her aunt) immediately upon my arrival to tell me she was only gone to the lake, where I should be sure to see her, and be happy with her ever after. I then, as I fancied, ran to the lake to find her. In my passage she stopped me, crying, "Whither so fast, Peter? I am your wife, your Patty." Methought I did not know her, she was so altered; but observing her voice, and looking more wistfully at her, she appeared to me as the most beautiful creature I ever beheld. I then went to seize her in my arms; but the hurry of my spirits awakened me.

When I got up, I kept at home, not caring even to look out at my door. My dream ran strangely in my head, and I had now nothing but Patty in my mind. "Oh!" cries I, "how happy could I be with her, though I had only her in this solitude. Oh! that this was but a reality, and not a dream." And indeed, though it was but a dream, I could scarce refrain from running to the lake to meet my Patty. But then I checked my folly, and reasoned myself into some degree of temper again. However, I could not forbear crying out, "What, nobody to converse with! Nobody to assist, comfort, or counsel me! This is a melancholy situation indeed." Thus I ran on lamenting till I was almost weary, when on a sudden I again heard the voices. "Hark!" says I, "here they come again. Well, I am now resolved to face them, come life, come death! It is not to be alone I thus dread; but to have company about me, and not know who or what, is death to me worse than I can suffer from them, be they who or what they will."

During my soliloquy the voices increased, and then by degrees diminished as usual; but I had scarce got my gun in my hand, to pursue my resolution of showing myself to those who uttered them, when I felt such a thump upon the roof of my ante-chamber as shook the whole fabric and set me all over into a tremor. I then heard a sort of shriek, and a rustle near the door of my apartment; all which together seemed very terrible. But I, having before determined to see what and who it was, resolutely opened my door and leaped out I saw nobody; all was quite silent, and nothing that I could perceive but my own fears amoving. I went then softly to the corner of the building, and there looking down, by the glimmer of my lamp which stood in the window, I saw something in human shape lying at my feet. I gave the word, "Who is there?" Still no one answered. My heart was ready to force a way through my side. I was for a while fixed to the earth like a statue. At length, recovering, I stepped in, fetched my lamp, and returning saw the very beautiful face my Patty appeared under in my dream; and not considering that it was only a dream, I verily thought I had my Patty before me; but she seemed to be stone dead. Upon viewing her other parts (for I had never yet removed my eyes from her face), I found she had a sort of brown chaplet, like lace, round her head, under and about which her hair was tucked up and twined; and she seemed to me to be clothed in a thin hair-coloured silk garment, which, upon trying to raise her, I found to be quite warm, and therefore hoped there was life in the body it contained. I then took her into my arms, and treading a step backwards with her, I put out my lamp; however, having her in my arms, I conveyed her through the doorway in the dark into my grotto; here I laid her upon my bed, and then ran out for my lamp.

This, thinks I, is an amazing adventure. How could Patty come here, and dressed in silk and whalebone too? Sure that is not the reigning fashion in England now? But my dream said she was dead. Why, truly, says I, so she seems to be. But be it so; she is warm. Whether this is the place for persons to inhabit after death or not, I can't tell (for I see there are people here, though I don't know them); but be it as it will, she feels as flesh and blood; and if I can but bring her to stir and act again as my wife, what matters it to me what she is? It will be a great blessing and comfort to me; for she never would have come to this very spot but for my good.

Top-full of these thoughts, I re-entered my grotto, shut my door and lighted my lamp; when going to my Patty (as I delighted to fancy her), I thought I saw her eyes stir a little. I then set the lamp farther off for fear of offending them if she should look up; and warming the last glass I had reserved of my Madeira, I carried it to her, but she never stirred. I now supposed the fall had absolutely killed her, and was prodigiously grieved; when laying my hand on her breast I perceived the fountain of life had some motion. This gave me infinite pleasure; so, not despairing, I dipped my finger in the wine and moistened her lips with it two or three times, and I imagined they opened a little. Upon this I bethought me, and taking a teaspoon, I gently poured a few drops of the wine by that means into her mouth. Finding she swallowed it, I poured in another spoonful, and another, till I brought her to herself so well as to be able to sit up. All this I did by a glimmering light which the lamp afforded from a distant part of the room, where I had placed it, as I have said, out of her sight.

I then spoke to her, and asked divers questions, as if she had really been Patty and understood me; in return of which she uttered a language I had no idea of, though in the most musical tone, and with the sweetest accent I ever heard. It grieved me I could not understand her. However, thinking she might like to be on her feet, I went to lift her off the bed, when she felt to my touch in the oddest manner imaginable; for while in one respect it was as though she had been cased up in whalebone it was at the same time as soft and warm as if she had been naked.

I then took her in my arms and carried her into my ante-chamber again, where I would fain have entered into conversation, but found she and I could make nothing of it together, unless we could understand one another's speech. It is very strange my dream should have prepossessed me so of Patty, and of the alteration of her countenance, that I could by no means persuade myself the person I had with me was not she; though, upon a deliberate comparison, Patty, as pleasing as she always was to my taste, would no more come up to this fair creature than a coarse ale-wife would to Venus herself.

You may imagine we stared heartily at each other, and I doubted not but she wondered as much as I by what means we came so near each other. I offered her everything in my grotto which I thought might please her; some of which she gratefully received, as appeared by her looks and behaviour. But she avoided my lamp, and always placed her back toward it. I observing that, and ascribing it to her modesty in my company, let her have her will, and took care to set it in such a position myself as seemed agreeable to her, though it deprived me of a prospect I very much admired.

After we had sat a good while, now and then, I may say, chattering to one another, she got up and took a turn or two about the room. When I saw her in that attitude, her grace and motion perfectly charmed me, and her shape was incomparable; but the strangeness of her dress put me to my trumps to conceive either what it was, or how it was put on.

Well, we supped together, and I set the best of everything I had before her, nor could either of us forbear speaking in our own tongue, though we were sensible neither of us understood the other. After supper I gave her some of my cordials, for which she showed great tokens of thankfulness, and often in her way, by signs and gestures, which were very far from being insignificant, expressed her gratitude for my kindness. When supper had been sometime over, I showed her my bed and made signs for her to go to it; but she seemed very shy of that, till I showed her where I meant to lie myself, by pointing to myself, then to that, and again pointing to her and to my bed. When at length I had made this matter intelligible to her, she lay down very composedly;

and after I had taken care of my fire, and set the things I had been using for supper in their places, I laid myself down too; for I could have no suspicious thoughts or fear of danger from a form so excellent.

I treated her for sometime with all the respect imaginable, and never suffered her to do the least part of my work. It was very inconvenient to both of us only to know each other's meaning by signs; but I could not be otherwise than pleased to see that she endeavoured all in her power to learn to talk like me. Indeed I was not behindhand with her in that respect, striving all I could to imitate her. What I all the while wondered at was, she never showed the least disquiet at her confinement; for I kept my door shut at first, through fear of losing her, thinking she would have taken an opportunity to run away from me; for little did I then think she could fly.

XV

WILKIN IS AFRAID OF LOSING HIS NEW MISTRESS—THEY LIVE
TOGETHER ALL WINTER—A REMARK ON THAT—THEY BEGIN
TO KNOW EACH OTHERS LANGUAGE—A LONG DISCOURSE
BETWEEN THEM AT CROSS PURPOSES—SHE FLIES—THEY
ENGAGE TO BE MAN AND WIFE.

After my new love had been with me a fortnight, finding my water run low, I was greatly troubled at the thought of quitting her anytime to go for more; and having hinted it to her, with seeming uneasiness, she could not for a while fathom my meaning; but when she saw me much confused, she came at length, by the many signs I made, to imagine it was my concern for her which made me so; whereupon she expressively enough signified I might be easy, for she did not fear anything happening to her in my absence. On this, as well as I could declare my meaning, I entreated her not to go away before my return. As soon as she understood what I signified to her by actions, she sat down, with her arms across, leaning her head against the wall to assure me she would not stir. However, as I had before nailed a cord to the outside of the door, I tied that for caution's sake to the tree, for fear of the worst: but I believe she had not the least design of removing.

I took my boat, net, and water-cask, as usual, desirous of bringing her home a fresh fish dinner, and succeeded so well as to catch enough for several good meals, and to spare. What remained I salted, and found she liked that better than the fresh, after a few days' salting; though she did not so well approve of that I had formerly pickled and dried. As my salt grew very low, though I had been as sparing of it as possible, I now resolved to try making some; and the next summer I effected it.

Thus we spent the remainder of the winter together, till the days began to be light enough for me to walk abroad a little in the middle of them; for I was now under no apprehensions of her leaving me, as she had before this time had so many opportunities of doing so, but never once attempted it.

I must here make one reflection upon our conduct, which you will almost think incredible, viz., that we two, of different sexes, not wanting our peculiar desires, fully inflamed with love to each other, and no outward obstacle to prevent our wishes, should have been together, under the same roof alone for five months, conversing together from morning to night (for by this time she pretty well understood English, and I her language), and yet I should never have clasped her in my arms, or have shown any further amorous desires to her than what the deference I all along paid her could give her room to surmise. Nay, I can affirm that I did not even then know that the covering she wore was not the work of art, but the work of nature, for I really took it for silk; though it must be premised that I had never seen it by any other light than of my lamp. Indeed the modesty of her carriage and sweetness of her behaviour to me had struck into me such a dread of offending her, that though nothing upon earth could be more capable of exciting passion than her charms, I could have died rather than have attempted only to salute her without actual invitation.

When the weather cleared up a little by the lengthening of daylight, I took courage one afternoon to invite her to walk with me to the lake; but she sweetly excused herself from it, whilst there was such a frightful glare of light, as she said; but looking out at the door, told me, if I would not go out of the wood she would accompany me: so we agreed to take a turn only there. I first went myself over the stile of the door, and thinking it rather too high for her, I took her in my arms and lifted her over. But even when I had her in this manner, I knew not what to make of her clothing, it sat so true and close; but seeing by a steadier and truer light in the grove, though a heavy gloomy one, than my lamp had afforded, I begged she would let me know of what silk or other composition her garment was made. She smiled, and asked me if mine was not the same under my jacket "No, lady," says I, "I have nothing but my skin under my clothes."—"Why, what do you mean?" replies she, somewhat tartly; "but indeed I was afraid that something was the matter by that nasty covering you wear, that you might not be seen. Are you not a glumm?"*—"Yes," says I, "fair creature." (Here, though you may conceive she spoke part English, part her own tongue, and I the same, as we best understood each other, yet I shall give you our discourse, word for word, in plain English.) "Then," says she, "I am afraid you must have been a very bad man, and have been crashee,† which I should be very sorry to hear."

I told her I believed we were none of us so good as we might be, but I hoped my faults had not at most exceeded other men's; but I had

---

* A man.
† Slit.

suffered abundance of hardships in my time; and that at last Providence having settled me in this spot, from whence I had no prospect of ever departing, it was none of the least of its mercies to bring to my knowledge and company the most exquisite piece of all His works, in her, which I should acknowledge as long as I lived. She was surprised at this discourse, and asked me (if I did not mean to impose upon her, and was indeed an ingcrashee* glumm) why I should tell her I had no prospect of departing hence. "Have not you," says she, "the same prospect that I or any other person has of departing? Sir," added she, "you don't do well, and really I fear you are slit, or you would not wear this nasty cumbersome coat (taking hold of my jacket-sleeve), if you were not afraid of showing the signs of a bad life upon your natural clothing."

I could not for my heart imagine what way there was to get out of my dominions. But certainly, thought I, there must be some way or other, or she would not be so peremptory. And as to my jacket, and showing myself in my natural clothing, I profess she made me blush; and but for shame, I would have stripped to my skin to have satisfied her. "But, madam," says I, "pray pardon me, for you are really mistaken; I have examined every nook and corner of this new world in which we now are, and can find no possible outlet; nay, even by the same way I came in, I am sure it is impossible to get out again."—"Why," says she, "what outlets have you searched for, or what way can you expect out but the way you came in? And why is that impossible to return by again? If you are not slit, is not the air open to you? Will not the sky admit you to patrole in it, as well as other people? I tell you, sir, I fear you have been slit for your crimes; and though you have been so good to me, that I can't help loving of you heartily for it, yet if I thought you had been slit, I would not, nay, could not, stay a moment longer with you; no, though it should break my heart to leave you."

I found myself now in a strange quandary, longing to know what she meant by being slit, and had a hundred strange notions in my head whether I was slit or not; for though I knew what the word naturally signified well enough, yet in what manner or by what figure of speech she applied it to me, I had no idea of. But seeing her look a little angrily upon me, "Pray, madam," says I, "don't be offended, if I take the liberty to ask you what you mean by the word crashee* so often repeated by you;

---

* Unslit.

for I am an utter stranger to what you mean by it."—"Sir," says she, "pray answer me first how you came here?"—"Madam," replied I, "will you please to take a walk to the verge of the wood, I will show you the very passage."—"Sir," says she, "I perfectly know the range of the rocks all round, and by the least description, without going to see them, can tell from which you descended."—"In truth," said I, "most charming lady, I descended from no rock at all; nor would I for a thousand worlds attempt what could not be accomplished but by my destruction."—"Sir," says she, in some anger, "it is false, and you impose upon me."—"I declare to you," says I, "madam, what I tell you is strictly true; I never was near the summit of any of the surrounding rocks, or anything like it; but as you are not far from the verge of the wood, be so good as to step a little farther and I will show you my entrance in hither."—"Well," says she, "now this odious dazzle of light is lessened, I don't care if I do go with you."

When we came far enough to see the bridge, "There, madam," says I, "there is my entrance, where the sea pours into this lake from yonder cavern."—"It is not possible," says she; "this is another untruth; and as I see you would deceive me, and are not to be believed, farewell; I must be gone. But, hold," says she, "let me ask you one thing more; that is, by what means did you come through that cavern? You could not have used to have come over the rock?"—"Bless me, madam!" says I, "do you think I and my boat could fly? Come over the rock, did you say? No, madam; I sailed from the great sea, the main ocean, in my boat, through that cavern into this very lake here."—"What do you mean by your boat?" says she. "You seem to make two things of your boat you say you sailed with and yourself."—"I do so," replied I; "for, madam, I take myself to be good flesh and blood, but my boat is made of wood and other materials."—"Is it so?" says she. "And, pray, where is this boat that is made of wood and other materials?—under your jacket?"—"Lord, madam!" says I, "you put me in fear that you were angry; but now I hope you only joke with me. What, put a boat under my jacket! No, madam; my boat is in the lake."—"What, more untruths?" says she.— "No, madam," I replied; "if you would be satisfied of what I say (every word of which is as true as that my boat now is in the lake), pray walk with me thither and make your own eyes judges what sincerity I speak with." To this she agreed, it growing dusky; but assured me, if I did not give her good satisfaction, I should see her no more.

We arrived at the lake; and going to my wet-dock, "Now, madam," says I, "pray satisfy yourself whether I spake true or no." She looked at my boat, but could not yet frame a proper notion of it. Says I, "Madam, in this very boat I sailed from the main ocean through that cavern into this lake; and shall at last think myself the happiest of all men if you continue with me, love me, and credit me; and I promise you I'll never deceive you, but think my life happily spent in your service." I found she was hardly content yet to believe what I told her of my boat to be true; till I stepped into it, and pushing from the shore, took my oars in my hand, and sailed along the lake by her, as she walked on the shore. At last she seemed so well reconciled to me and my boat, that she desired I would take her in. I immediately did so, and we sailed a good way; and as we returned to my dock I described to her how I procured the water we drank, and brought it to shore in that vessel.

"Well," says she, "I have sailed, as you call it, many a mile in my lifetime, but never in such a thing as this. I own it will serve very well where one has a great many things to carry from place to place; but to be labouring thus at an oar when one intends pleasure in sailing, is in my mind a most ridiculous piece of slavery."—"Why, pray, madam, how would you have me sail? for getting into the boat only will not carry us this way or that without using some force."—"But," says she, "pray, where did you get this boat, as you call it?"—"O madam!" says I, "that is too long and fatal a story to begin upon now; this boat was made many thousand miles from hence, among a people coal-black, a quite different sort from us; and, when I first had it, I little thought of seeing this country; but I will make a faithful relation of all to you when we come home." Indeed, I began to wish heartily we were there, for it grew into the night; and having strolled so far without my gun, I was afraid of what I had before seen and heard, and hinted our return; but I found my motion was disagreeable to her, and so I dropped it.

I now perceived and wondered at it, that the later it grew the more agreeable it seemed to her; and as I had now brought her into good-humour again by seeing and sailing in my boat, I was not willing to prevent its increase. I told her, if she pleased, we would land, and when I had docked my boat, I would accompany her where and as long as she liked. As we talked and walked by the lake, she made a little run before me and sprung into it Perceiving this, I cried out, whereupon she merrily called on me to follow her. The light was then so dim, as prevented my having more than a confused sight of her when she jumped in; and looking earnestly after her, I could discern nothing more than a small boat in the water, which skimmed along at so great a rate that I almost lost sight of it presently; but running along the shore for fear of losing her, I met her gravely walking to meet me, and then had entirely lost sight of the boat upon the lake. "This," says she, accosting me with a smile, "is my way of sailing, which, I perceive, by the fright you were in, you are altogether unacquainted with; and, as you tell me you came from so many thousand miles off, it is possible you may be made differently from me: but, surely we are the part of the creation which has had most care bestowed upon it; and I suspect, from all your discourse, to which I have been very attentive, it is possible you may no more be able to fly than to sail as I do."—"No, charming creature," says I, "that I cannot, I'll assure you." She then, stepping to the edge of the lake, for the advantage of a descent before her, sprung up into the air, and away she went farther than my eyes could follow her.

I was quite astonished. "So," says I, "then all is over! all a delusion which I have so long been in! a mere phantom! Better had it been for me never to have seen her, than thus to lose her again! But what could I expect had she stayed? For it is plain she is no human composition. But," says I, "she felt like flesh, too, when I lifted her out at the door!" I had but very little time for reflection; for, in about ten minutes after she had left me in this mixture of grief and amazement, she alighted just by me on her feet.

Her return, as she plainly saw, filled me with a transport not to be concealed; and which, as she afterwards told me, was very agreeable to her. Indeed, I was some moments in such an agitation of mind from these unparalleled incidents, that I was like one thunder-struck; but coming presently to myself, and clasping her in my arms with as much love and passion as I was capable of expressing, and for the first time with any desire,—"Are you returned again, kind angel," said I, "to bless a wretch who can only be happy in adoring you? Can it be, that you, who have so many advantages over me, should quit all the pleasures that nature has formed you for, and all your friends and relations, to take an asylum in my arms? But I here make you a tender of all I am able to bestow—my love and constancy."—"Come, come," says she, "no more raptures; I find you are a worthier man than I thought I had reason to take you for, and I beg your pardon for my distrust whilst I was ignorant of your imperfections; but now I verily believe all you have said is true; and I promise you, as you have seemed so much to delight in me, I will never quit you till death, or other as fatal accident shall part us. But we will now, if you choose, go home; for I know you have been sometime

ROBERT PALTOCK

uneasy in this gloom, though agreeable to me: for, giving my eyes the pleasure of looking eagerly on you, it conceals my blushes from your sight."

In this manner, exchanging mutual endearments and soft speeches, hand in hand, we arrived at the grotto; where we that night consummated our nuptials, without farther ceremony than mutual solemn engagements to each other; which are, in truth, the essence of marriage, and all that was there and then in our power.

XVI

Every calm is succeeded by a storm, as is every storm by its calm; for, after supper, in order to give my bride the opportunity of undressing alone, which I thought might be most agreeable the first night, I withdrew into the antechamber till I thought she was laid; and then, having first disposed of my lamp, I moved softly towards her, and stepped into bed too; when, on my nearer approach to her, I imagined she had her clothes on. This struck a thorough damp over me; and asking her the reason of it, not being able to touch the least bit of her flesh but her face and hands, she burst out a-laugh-ing; and, running her hand along my naked side, soon perceived the difference she before had made such doubt of between herself and me. Upon which she fairly told me, that neither she, nor any person she had ever seen before, had any other covering than what they were born with, and which they would not willingly part with but with their lives. This shocked me terribly; not from the horror of the thing itself, or any distaste I had to this covering (for it was quite smooth, warm, and softer than velvet or the finest skin imaginable), but from an apprehension of her being so wholly encased in it, that, though I had so fine a companion, and now a wife, yet I should have no conjugal benefit from her, either to my own gratification, or the increase of our species.

In the height of my impatience I made divers essays for unfolding this covering, but unsuccessfully. Surely, says I, there must be some way of coming at my wishes, or why should she seem so shy of me at first, and now we are under engagements to each other, meet me half way with such a yielding compliance? I could, if I had had time to spare, have gone on, starting objections and answering them, in my own breast, a great while longer (for I now knew not what to make of it); but being prompted to act as well as think, and feeling, as tenderly as possible, upon her bosom, for the folds or plaits of her garment, she lying perfectly still, and perceiving divers flat broad ledges, like whale-bone, seemingly under her covering, which closely enfolded her body, I thought it might be all laced on together somewhat like stays, and felt behind for the lacing.

At length, perceiving me so puzzled, and beyond conception vexed at my disappointment, of a sudden, lest I should grow outrageous (which I was almost come to), she threw down all those seeming ribs flat to her side so imperceptibly to me, that I knew nothing of the matter, though I lay close to her; till putting forth my hand again to her bosom, the softest skin, and most delightful body, free from all impediment, presented itself to my wishes, and gave itself up to my embraces.

I slept very soundly till morning, and so did she; but at waking I was very solicitous to find out what sort of being I had had in my arms, and with what qualities her garment was endued, or how contrived that, notwithstanding all my fruitless attempts to uncover her, she herself could so instantaneously dispose of it undiscerned by me. Well, thought I, she is my wife, I will be satisfied in everything; for surely she will not now refuse to gratify my curiosity.

We rose with the light; but surely no two were ever more amorous, or more delighted with each other. I, being up first, lighted the fire, and prepared breakfast of some fish soup, thickened with my cream-cheese; and then calling her, I kept my eye towards the bed to see how she dressed herself; but throwing aside the clothes, she stepped out ready dressed, and came to me. When I had kissed her, and wished her a good day, we sat down to breakfast; which being soon over, I told her I hoped every minute of our lives would prove as happy as those we so lately passed together; which she seemed to wish with equal ardour. I then told her, now she was my wife, I thought proper to know her name, which I had never before asked, for fear of giving uneasiness; for, as I added, I did not doubt she had observed in my behaviour, ever since I first saw her, a peculiar tenderness for her, and a sedulous concern not to offend, which had obliged me hitherto to stifle several questions I had to ask her whenever they would be agreeable to her. She then bid me begin; for as she was now my wife, whilst I was speaking it became her to be all attention, and to give me the utmost satisfaction she could in all I should require, as she herself should have so great an interest in everything for the future which would oblige me.

Compliments (if, in compliance with old custom, I may call them so, for they were by us delivered from the heart) being a little over on both sides, I first desired to know what name she went by before I found her: "For," says I, "having only hitherto called you madam, and my lady, besides the future expression of my love to you in the word dear, I would know your original name, that so I might join it with that tender epithet."—"That you shall," says she, "and also my family at another opportunity; but as my name will not take up long time to repeat at present, it is Youwarkee. And pray," says she, "now gratify me with the knowledge of yours."—"My dear Youwarkee," says I, "my name was Peter Wilkins when I heard it last; but that is so long ago, I had almost forgot it. And now," says I, "there is another thing you can give me a pleasure in."—"You need, then, only mention it, my dear Peter," says she.—"That is," says I, "only to tell me if you did not, by some accident, fall from the top of the rock over my habitation, upon the roof of it, when I first took you in here; and whether you are of the country upon the rocks?"—She, softly smiling, answered, "My dear Peter, you run your questions too thick. As to my country, which is not on the rocks, as you suppose, but at a vast distance from hence, I shall leave that till I may hereafter, at more leisure, speak of my family, as I promised you before; but as to how I came into this grotto, I knew not at first, but soon perceived your humanity had brought me in, to take care of me, after a terrible fall I had; not from the rock, as you suppose, for then I must not now have been living to enjoy you, but from a far less considerable height in the air. I'll tell you how it happened. A parcel of us young people were upon a merry *swangean** round this *arkoe*,[†] which we usually divert ourselves with at set times of the year, chasing and pursuing one another, sometimes soaring to an extravagant height, and then shooting down again with surprising precipitancy, till we even touch the trees; when of a sudden we mount again and away."

"I say, being of this party, and pursued by one of my comrades, I descended down to the very trees, and she after me; but as I mounted, she over-shooting me, brushed so stiffly against the upper part of my *graundee*[‡] that I lost my bearing; and being so near the branches before I could recover it again, I sunk into the tree, and rendered my graundee useless to me; so that down I came, and that with so much force, that I but just felt my fall, and lost my senses. Whether I cried out or no upon my coming to the ground, I cannot say; but if I did, my companion was too far gone by that time to hear or take notice of me; as she, probably,

---

* Flight.
† Water surrounded with a wood.
‡ The covering and wings of skin they flew with.

ROBERT PALTOCK

in so swift a flight, saw not my fall. As to the condition I was in, or what happened immediately afterwards, I must be obliged to you for a relation of that; but one thing I was quickly sensible of, and never can forget, viz., that I owe my life to your care and kindness to me."

I told her she should have that part of her story from me another time. "But," says I, "there is something so amazing in these flights, or swangeans, as you call them, that I must, as the questions for this day, beg you would let me know what is the method of them. What is the nature of your covering, which was at first such an obstacle to my wishes? How you put it on? And how you use it in your swangean?"

"Surely, my dearest Peter," says she, "but that I can deny you nothing, since you are my *barkatt** which you seem so passionately to desire, the latter of your questions would not be answered, for it must put me to the blush. As to our method of flight, you saw somewhat of that last night, though in a light hardly sufficient for you; and for the nature of my covering, you perceive that now; but to show you how it is put on, as you call it, I am afraid it will be necessary, as far as I can, to put it off, before I can make you comprehend that; which having done, the whole will be no farther a mystery. But, not to be tedious, is it your command that I uncover? Lay that upon me, it shall be done."

Here I was at a plunge whether to proceed or drop the question. Thinks I, if my curiosity should be fatal to me, as I may see something I can never bear hereafter, I am undone. She waits the command! Why so? I know not the consequence! What shall I do? At last, somewhat resolutely, I asked her whether her answer either way to my command would cause her to leave me, or me to love her less? She, seeing my hesitation, and perceiving the cause, was so pleased, that she cried out— "No, my dear Peter, not that, nor all the force on earth, shall ever part me from you. But I conceive you are afraid you shall discover something in me you may not like. I fear not that; but an immodest appearance before you I cannot suffer myself to be guilty of, but under your own command."—"My lovely Youwarkee," says I, "delay then my desires no longer; and since you require a warrant from me, I do command you to do it." Immediately her graundee flew open (discovering her naked body just to the hip, and round the rim of her belly) and, expanding itself, was near six feet wide. Here my love and curiosity had a hard conflict; the one to gain my attention to the graundee, and the other to retain

---

* Husband.

my eyes and thoughts on her lovely body, which I had never beheld so much of before. Though I was very unwilling to keep her uncovered too long, I could not easily dismiss so charming a sight I attentively viewed her lovely flesh, and examined the case that enshrined it; but as I shall give you a full description of the graundee hereafter, in a more proper place, I will mention it no farther here, than to tell you that when I had narrowly surveyed the upper part of it, she in a moment contracted it round her so close that the nicest eye could not perceive the joining of the parts. "Indeed, my dear Youwarkee," says I, "you had the best of reasons for saying you was not fearful I should discover anything in you displeasing; for if my bosom glowed with love before, you have now therein raised an ardent flame, which neither time, nor aught else, will ever be able to extinguish. I now almost conceive how you fly; though yet I am at a loss to know how you extend and make use of the lower part of your graundee, which rises up and meets the upper; but I will rather guess at that by what I have seen, than raise the colour higher in those fair cheeks, which are, however, adorned with blushes." Then running to her, and taking her in my arms, I called her the dearest gift of Heaven; and left off further interrogatories till another opportunity.

XVII

Youwarkee and I having no other company than one another's, we talked together almost from morn to night, in order to learn each other's dialect. But how compilable soever she was in all other respects, I could not persuade her to go out with me to fetch water, or to the lake, in the day-time. It being now the light season, I wanted her to be more abroad; but she excused herself, telling me her people never came into those luminous parts of the country during the false glare, as they called it, but kept altogether at home, where their light was more moderate and steadier; and that the place where I resided was not frequented by them for half the year, and at other times only upon parties of pleasure, it not being worth while to settle habitations where they could not abide always. She said Normnbdsgrsutt was the finest region in the world, where her king's court was, and a vast kingdom. I asked her twice or thrice more to name the country to me, but not all the art we could use, hers in dictating, and mine in endeavouring to pronounce it, would render me conqueror of that her monosyllable (for as such it sounded from her sweet lips); so I relinquished the name to her, telling her whenever she had anymore occasion to mention the place, I desired it might be under the style of Doorpt Swangeanti, which she promised; but wondered, as she could speak the other so glibly, as she called it, I could not do so too.

I told her that the light of my native country was far stronger than any I had seen since my arrival at Graundevolet (for that, I found by her, was the name my dominions went by); and that we had a sun, or ball of fire, which rolled over our heads everyday, with such a light, and such a heat, that it would sometimes almost scorch one, it was so hot, and was of such brightness that the eye could not look at it without danger of blindness. She was heartily glad, she said, she was not born in so wretched a land; and she did not believe there was any other so good as her own. I thought no benefit could arise from my combating these innocent prejudices, so I let them alone.

She had often lamented to me the difference of our eyesight, and the trouble it was to her that she could not at all times go about with me, till it gave me a good deal of uneasiness to see her concern. At last I told her, that though I believed it would be impossible to reduce my sight to the standard of hers, yet I was persuaded I could bring hers to bear the strongest light I had ever seen in this country. She was mightily pleased with the thought of that, and said she wished I might, for she was sensible of no grief like being obliged to stay at home when I went abroad on my business, and was resolved to try my experiment if I pleased, and in the meantime should heartily pray for the success. I hit on the following invention.

I rummaged over all my old things, and by good luck found an old crape hatband. This I tried myself, single, before my own eyes, in the strongest light we had; but believing I had not yet obscured it enough, I doubled it, and then thought it might do; but for fear it should not I trebled it, and then it seemed too dark for eyes like mine to discover objects through it, and so I judged it would suit hers; for I was determined to produce something, if possible, that would do at first, without repetition of trial, which I thought would only deject her more, by making her look on the matter as impracticable. I now only wanted a proper method for fixing it on her, and this I thought would be easily effected, but had much more difficulty in it than I imagined. A first I purposed to tie the crape over her eyes, but trying it myself, I found it very rough and fretting: I then designed fixing it to an old crown of a hat that held my fish-hooks and lines, and so let it hang down before her face; but that also had its inconveniences, as it would slap her eyes in windy weather, and would be not only useless, but very troublesome in flight; so that I was scarce ever more puzzled before. At last I thought of a method that answered exceedingly well, the hint of which I took from somewhat I had seen with my master when I was at school, which he called goggles, and which he used to tie round his head to screen his eyes in riding. The thing I made upon that plan was composed of old hat, pieces of rams-horn, and the above-mentioned crape.

When I had finished the whole apparatus, I tried it first upon myself, and finding great reason to believe it would perfectly answer the intention, I ran directly to Youwarkee. "Come," says I, "my dear, will you go with me to the water-rill; for I must fetch some this morning?" She shook her head, and, with tears in her eyes, wished she could. "But," says she, "let me see how light it is abroad."—"No," says I, "my love, you must not look out till you go."—"Indeed," says she, "if it did not affect my eyes and head you should not ask me twice."—"Well," says I, "my

Youwarkee, I am now come to take you with me; and that you may not suffer by it, turn about, and let me apply the remedy I told you of for your sight" She wanted much to see first what it was, but I begged her to forbear till she tried whether it would be useful or not She told me she would absolutely submit to my direction, so I adjusted the thing to her head. "Now," says I, "you have it on, let us go out and try it, and let me know the moment you find the light offensive, and take particular notice how you are affected." Hereupon away we marched, and I heard no complaint in all our walk to the lake.

"Now, my dear Youwarkee," says I, when we got there, "what do you think of my contrivance? Can you see at all?"—"Yes, very well," says she. "But, my dear Peter, you have taken the advantage of the twilight, I know, to deceive me; and I had rather have stayed at home than have subjected you to return in the night for the sake of my company." I then assured her it was mid-day, and no later, which pleased her mightily; and, to satisfy her, I untied the string behind, and just let her be convinced it was so. When I had fixed the shade on her head again, she put up her hands and felt the several materials of which it consisted; and after expressing her admiration of it, "So, my dear Peter," says she, "you have now encumbered yourself with a wife indeed, for since I can come abroad in a glaring light with so much ease, you will never henceforward be without my company."

Youwarkee being thus in spirits, we launched the boat, watered, took a draught of fish, and returned; passing the night at home, in talking of the spectacles (for that was the name I told her they must go by) and of the fishing, for that exercise delighted her to a great degree. But, above all, the spectacles were her chief theme; she handled them and looked at them again and again, and asked several rational questions about them; as, how they could have that effect on her eyes, enabling her to see, and the like. She ventured out with them next day by herself; and, as she threatened, was as good as her word, for she scarcely afterwards let me go abroad by myself, but accompanied me everywhere freely, and with delight.

XVIII

About three months after we were married, as we called it, Youwarkee told me she believed she was breeding, and I was mightily pleased with it, for though I had had two children before by Patty, yet I had never seen either of them, so that I longed to be a father. I sometimes amused myself with whimsical conjectures, as, whether the child would have a graundee or not; which of us it would be most like; how we should do without a midwife; and what must become of the infant, as we had not milk, in case Youwarkee could not suckle it. Indeed, I had leisure enough for indulging such reveries; for, having laid in our winter stores, my wife and I had nothing to do but enjoy ourselves over a good fire, prattling and toying together, making as good cheer as we could; and truly that was none of the worst, for we had as fine bread as need to be eaten; we had pears preserved; all sorts of dried fish; and once a fortnight, for two or three days together, had fresh fish; we had vinegar, and a biting herb which I had found, for pepper; and several sorts of nuts; so there was no want.

It was at this time, after my return from watering one day, where Youwarkee had been with me, that, having taken several fish, and amongst them some I had not before seen, I asked her, as we were preparing and salting some of them, how they managed fish in her country, and what variety they had of them there. She told me she neither ever saw nor heard of a fish in her life till she came to me. "How!" says I, "no fish amongst you? Why, you want one of the greatest dainties that can be set upon a table. Do you wholly eat flesh," says I, "at Doorpt Swangeanti?"—"Flesh," says she laughingly, "of what?"—"Nay," says I, "you know best what the beasts of your own country are. We have in England, where I was born and bred, oxen, very large hogs, sheep, lambs, and calves; these make our ordinary dishes: then we have deer, hares, rabbits, and these are reckoned dainties; besides numberless kinds of poultry, and fish without stint"—"I never heard of any of these things in my life," says Youwarkee, "nor did I ever eat anything but fruits and herbs, and what is made from them, at Normnbdsgrsutt."—"You will speak that crabbed word," says I, "again."—"I beg your pardon, my dear," says she; "at Doorpt Swangeanti, I say; nor I, nor anyone else, to my knowledge, ever ate any such thing; but seeing you eat fish, as you call them, I made no scruple of doing so too, and like them very well, especially the salted ones, for I never tasted what you call salt neither till I came here."—"I cannot think," says I, "what sort of a country yours is, or how you all live there."—"Oh," says she, "there is no want; I wish you and I were there." I was afraid I had talked too much of her country already, so we called a new cause.

Soon after winter had set in, as we were in bed one night, I heard the voices again; and though my wife had told me of her countryfolk's swangeans in that place, I, being frighted a little, waked her; and she hearing them too, cried out, "There they are! it is ten to one but my sister or some of our family are there. Hark! I believe I hear her voice." I myself hearkened very attentively; and by this time understanding a great deal of their language, I not only could distinguish different speakers, but knew the meaning of several of the words they pronounced.

I would have had Youwarkee have gotten up and called to them. "Not for the world," says she; "have you a mind to part with me? Though I have no intent to leave you, as I am with child, if they should try to force me away without my consent, I may receive some injury, to the danger of my own life, or at least of the child's." This reason perfectly satisfying me, endeared the loving creature to me ten times more, if possible, than ever.

The next summer brought me a yawm,* as fair as alabaster.

My wife was delivered without the usual assistance, and had as favourable a labour as could be. The first thing I did, after giving her some fish-soup, made as skilfully as I was able, and a little cordial, was to see if my yawm had the graundee or not. Finding it had—"So," says I to Youwarkee, "you have brought me a legitimate heir to my dominions, whose title sure cannot be disputed, being one of you." Though I spoke this with as much pleasure, and in as endearing a way as ever I spoke in my life, and quite innocently, the poor Youwarkee burst into tears to such excess there was no pacifying her. I asked her the reason of her grief, begged and entreated

---

* Man-child.

her to let me know what disturbed her, but all in vain; till, seeing me in a violent passion, such as I had never before appeared to be in, she told me she was very sorry I should question her fidelity to me. She surprised me in saying this, as I never had any such apprehension. "No, my dearest wife," says I, "I never had any such suspicion as you charge me with, I can safely affirm; nor can I comprehend your meaning by imputing such a thing to me."—"Oh!" says she, "I am sure you have no cause for it; but you said the poor child was one of us; as much as to intimate that had it been your own, it would have been born as you were, without the graundee, which thought I cannot bear, and if you continue to think so it must end me; therefore take away my life now, rather than let me live to see my farther misery."

I was heartily sorry for what I had said, when I saw the effects of it, though I did not imagine it could have been perverted to such a contrary meaning. But considering her to be the faithful-lest and most loving creature upon earth, and that true love cannot bear anything that touches upon or can be applied (though with ever so forced a construction) to an opprobrious or contemptuous meaning, I attributed her groundless resentment to her excess of fondness only for me; and falling upon the bed by her, and bathing her face in my tears, I assured her the interpretation she had put on my words was altogether foreign from the view they were spoken with; professing to her that I never had, nor ever could have, the least cause of jealousy. On my confirming this absolute confidence in her virtue by the strongest asseverations, she grew fully convinced of her error, and acknowledged she had been too rash in censuring me; and growing pleased at my fresh professions of love to her, we presently were reconciled, and became again very good friends.

When Youwarkee had gathered strength again, she proved an excellent nurse to my Pedro (for that was the name I gave him), so that he soon grew a charming child, able to go in his twelvemonth, and spoke in his twentieth. This and two other lovely boys I had by her in three years, everyone of which she brought up with the breast, and they thrived delicately.

I don't mention the little intervening occurrences which happened during this period; they consisted chiefly of the old rota of fishing, watering, providing in the summer for the winter, and in managing my salt-work; which altogether kept me at full employment, comfortably to maintain an increasing family.

In this time I had found out several new sorts of eatables. I had observed, as I said before, abundance of birds about the wood and lake in the summer months. These, by firing at them two or three times on my first coming, I had almost caused to desert my dominions. But as I had for the last two or three years given no disturbance at all to them, they were now in as great plenty as ever; and I made great profit of them by the peace they enjoyed; and yet my table never wanted a supply, fresh in the summer, or salted and pickled in winter.

I took notice it was about October these birds used to come; and most of the month of November they were busy in laying their eggs, which I used at that time to find in great plenty along the banks of the lake in the reeds, and made great collections of them; I used also to find a great many in the woods amongst the shrubs and underwood. These furnished our table various ways; for with my cream-cheese flour, and a little mixture of ram's-horn juice, I had taught my wife to make excellent puddings of them; abundance of them also we ate boiled or fried alone, and often as sauce to our fish. As for the birds themselves, having long omitted to fire at them, I had an effectual means of taking them otherwise by nets, which I set between the trees, and also very large pitfall nets, with which I used to catch all sorts, even from the size of a thrush to that of a turkey. But as I shall say more of these when I come to speak of my ward by and by, and of my poultry, I shall omit any further mention of them here.

You may perhaps wonder how I could keep an account of my time so precisely, as to talk of the particular months. I will tell you. At my coming from America, I was then exact; for we set sail the fourteenth of November, and struck the first or second day of February. So far I kept perfect reckoning; but after that I was not so exact, though I kept it as well as my perplexity would admit even then, till the days shortening upon me, prevented it.

Hereupon I set about making a year for myself. I found the duration of the comparative darkness, or what might with me be termed night, in the course of the twenty-four hours, or day, gradually increased for six months; after which it decreased reciprocally for an equal time, and the lighter part of the day took its turn, as in our parts of the world, only inversely: so that as the light's decrease became sensible about the middle of March, it was at the greatest pitch the latter end of August, or beginning of September; and from thence, on the contrary, went on decreasing to the close of February, when I had the longest portion of light. Hereupon, dividing my year into two seasons only, I began the winter half in March, and the summer half in September. Thus my winter was the spring and summer quarters in Europe, and my summer those of our autumn and winter.

From my settling this matter, I kept little account of days or weeks, but only reckoned my time by summer and winter, so that I am pretty right as to the revolutions of these; though the years, as to their notation, I kept no account of, nor do I know what year of the Lord it now is.

XIX

As my boy Pedro grew up, though, as I said before, he had the graundee, yet it was of less dimensions than it ought to have been to be useful to him, so that it was visible he could never fly; for it would scarce meet before, whereas it ought to have reached from side to side both ways. This pleased my wife to the heart; for now she was sure, whatever I had done before, I could not suspect her. Be that as it will, the boy's graundee not being a sufficient vestment for him, it became necessary he should be clothed.

I turned over my hoard, but could find nothing that would do; or, at least, that we knew how to fit him with. I had described my own country vest for lads to Youwarkee, and she formed a tolerable idea of it, but we had no tackle to alter anything with. "Oh, my dear," says I, "had I but been born with the graundee, I need not be now racking my brains to get my child clothes."—"What do you mean by that?" says she.—"Why," says I, "I would have flown to my ship (for I had long before related to her all my sea adventures, till the vessel's coming to the magnetical rock), and have brought some such things from thence, as you, not wanting them in this country, can have no notion of." She seemed mighty inquisitive to understand how a ship was made, what it was most like to, how a person who never saw one might know it only by the description, and how one might get into it; with abundance of the like questions. She then inquired what sort of things those needles and several other utensils were, which I had at times been speaking of; and in what part of a ship they usually kept such articles. And I, to gratify her curiosity, as I perceived she took a pleasure in hearing me, answered all her questions to a scruple; not then conceiving the secret purpose of all this inquisitiveness.

About two days after this, having been out two or three hours in the morning, to cut wood, at coming home I found Pedro crying, ready to break his heart, and his little brother Tommy hanging to him and crawling about the floor after him: the youngest pretty baby was fast asleep upon one of the beast-fish skins, in a corner of the room. I asked Pedro for his mother; but the poor infant had nothing farther to say to the matter, than "Mammy run away, I cry! mammy run away, I cry!" I wondered where she was gone, never before missing her from our habitation. However, I waited patiently till bed-time, but no wife. I grew very uneasy then; yet, as my children were tired and sleepy, I thought I had best go to bed with them, and make quiet; so, giving all three their suppers, we lay down together. They slept; but my mind was too full to permit the closure of my eyes. A thousand different chimeras swam in my imagination relating to my wife. One while I fancied her carried away by her kinsfolks; then, that she was gone of her own accord to make peace with her father. But that thought would not fix, being put aside by her constant tenderness to her children and regard to me, whom I was sure she would not have left without notice. "But alas!" says I, "she may even now be near me, but taken so ill she cannot get home, or she may have died suddenly in the wood." I lay tumbling and tossing in great anxiety, not able to find out any excusable occasion she could have of so long absence. And then, thinks I, if she should either be dead, or have quite left me, which will be of equally bad consequence to me, what can I do with three poor helpless infants? If they were a little more grown up, they might be helpful to me and to each other; but at their age how shall I ever rear them without the tenderness of a mother? And to see them pine away before my face, and not know how to help them, will distract me.

Finding I could neither sleep nor lie still, I rose, intending to search all the woods about, and call to her, that if any accident had prevented sight of her she might at least hear me. But upon opening the door, and just stepping out, how agreeably was I surprised to meet her coming in, with something on her arm. "My dear Youwarkee," says I, "where have you been? What has befallen you to keep you out so long? The poor children have been at their wits' end to find you; and I, my dear, have been inconsolable, and was now, almost distracted, coming in search of you." Youwarkee looked very blank, to think what concern she had given me and the children. "My dearest Peter," says she, kissing me, "pray forgive me the only thing I have ever done to offend you, and the last cause you shall ever have, by my good will, to complain of me; but walk within doors, and I will give you a farther account of my absence. Don't you remember what delight I took the other day to hear you talk of your ship?"—"Yes," says I, "you did so; but what of that?"—"Nay, pray," says she, "forgive me, for I have been to see it."—"That's impossible," says I; and truly this was the first time I ever thought she went about to deceive me.—"I do assure you," says she, "I have; and a wonderful thing it is! But if you distrust me, and what I say, I have brought proof of it; step out with me to the verge of the wood, and satisfy yourself."—"But pray," says I, "who presented you with this upon your arm?"—"I vow," says she, "I had forgot this: yes, this will, I believe, confirm to you what I have said."—I turned it over and over; and looking wistfully upon her, says I, "This waistcoat, indeed, is the very fellow to one that lay in the captain's locker in the cabin"—"Say not the very fellow," says she, "but rather say the very same, for I'll assure you it is so; and had you been with me, we might have got so many things for ourselves and the children, we should never have wanted more, though we had lived these hundred years; but as it is, I have left something without the wood for you to bring up." When we had our talk out, she, hearing the children stir, took them up, and was going, as she always did, to get their breakfasts. "Hold," says I, "this journey must have fatigued you too much already; lay yourself to rest, and leave everything else to me."—"My dear," says she, "you seem to think this flight tiresome, but you are mistaken; I am more weary with walking to the lake and back again, than with all the rest. Oh," says she, "if you had but the graundee, flying would rest you, after the greatest labour; for the parts which are moved with exercise on the earth, are all at rest in flight; as, on the contrary, the parts used in flight are when on earthly travel. The whole trouble of flight is in mounting from the plain ground; but when once you are upon the graundee at a proper height, all the rest is play, a mere trifle; you need only think of your way, and incline to it, your graundee directs you as readily as your feet obey you on the ground, without thinking of every step you take; it does not require labour, as your boat does, to keep you a-going."

After we had composed ourselves, we walked to the verge of the wood, to see what cargo my wife had brought from the ship. I was astonished at the bulk of it; and seeing, by the outside, it consisted of clothes, I took it with much ado upon my shoulders and carried it home. But upon opening it, I found far more treasure than I could have imagined; for there was a hammer, a great many spikes and nails, three spoons, about five plates of pewter, four knives and a fork, a small china punchbowl, two chocolate cups, a paper of needles, and several of pins, a parcel of coarse thread, a pair of shoes, and abundance of such other things as she had heard me wish for and describe; besides as much linen and woollen, of one sort or another, as made a good package for all the other things; with a great tin porridge-pot, of about two gallons, tied to the outside; and all these as nicely stowed as if she had been bred a packer.

When I had viewed the bundle, and poised the weight, "How was it possible, my dear Youwarkee," said I, "for you to bring all this? You could never carry them in your hands."—"No, no," replied she, "I carried them on my back."—"Is it possible," says I, "for your graundee to bear yourself and all this weight too in the air, and to such a height as the top of these rocks?"—"You will always," replies she, "make the height a part of your difficulty in flying; but you are deceived, for as the first stroke (I have heard you say often) in fighting is half the battle, so it is in flying; get but once fairly on the wind, nothing can hurt you afterwards. My method, let me tell you, was this; I climbed to the highest part of the ship, where I could stand clear, having first put up my burden, which you have there; and then getting that on my back near my shoulders, I took the two cords you see hang loose to it in my two hands, and extending my graundee, leaped off flatwise with my face towards the water; when instantly playing two or three good strokes with my graundee, I was out of danger; now, if I had found the bundle too heavy to make my first strokes with, I should directly have turned on my back, dropped my bundle, and floated in my graundee to the ship again, as you once saw me float on the lake." Says I, "You must have flown a prodigious distance to the lake, for I was several days sailing, I believe three weeks, from my ship, before I reached the gulf; and after that could be little less than five weeks (as I accounted for it), and at a great rate of sailing too under the rock, before I reached the lake; so that the ship must be a monstrous way off." "No, no," says she, "your ship lies but over yon cliff, that rises as it were with two points; and as to the rock itself, it is not broader than our lake is long; but what made you so tedious in your passage was many of the windings and turnings in the cavern returning in to themselves again; so that you might have gone round and round till this time, if the tide had not luckily struck you into the direct passage: this," says she, "I have heard from some of my countrymen, who have flown up it, but could never get quite through."

"I wish with all my heart," says I, "fortune had brought me first to light in this country; or (but for your sake I could almost say) had never brought me into it at all; for to be a creature of the least significancy, of the whole race but one, is a melancholy circumstance."—"Fear not," says she, "my love, for you have a wife will hazard all for you, though you are restrained; and as my inclinations and affections are so much yours, that I need but know your desires to execute them as far as my power extends, surely you, who can act by another, may be content to forego the trouble of your own performance. I perceive, indeed," continued she, "you want mightily to go to your ship, and are more uneasy now you know it is safe than you was before; but that being past my skill to assist you in, if you will command your deputy to go backwards and forwards in your stead, I am ready to obey you."

Thus ended our conversation about the ship for that time. But it left not my mind so soon; for a stronger hankering after it pursued me now than ever since my wife's flight, but to no purpose.

We sat us down and sorted out our cargo, piece by piece; and having found several things proper for the children, my wife longed to enter upon some piece of work towards clothing Pedro in the manner she had heard me talk of, and laid hard at me to show her the use of the needles, thread, and other things she had brought. Indeed I must say she proved very tractable; and from the little instruction I was able to give her, soon out-wrought my knowledge; for I could only show her that the thread went through the needle, and both through the cloth to hold it together; but for anything else I was as ignorant as she. In much less time than I could have imagined, she had clothed my son Pedro, and had made a sort of mantle for the youngest. But now seeing us so smart (for I took upon me sometimes to wear the green waistcoat she had brought under my dirty jacket), she began to be ashamed of herself, as she said, in our fine company; and afterwards (as I shall soon acquaint you) got into our fashion.

Seeing the advantages her flight to the ship, and that so many conveniences arose from it, she was frequently at me to let her go again. I should as much have wished for another return of goods as she, but I could by no means think of parting with my factor; for I knew her eagerness to please me, and that she would stick at nothing to perform it. And, thinks I, should any accident happen to her, by over-loading or otherwise, and I should lose her, all the other commodities of the whole world put together would not compensate her loss. But as she so earnestly desired it, and assured me she would run no hazards, I was prevailed on at length, by her incessant importunities, to let her go; though under certain restrictions which she promised me to comply with. As first, I insisted upon it that she should take a tour quite round the rock, setting out the same way I had last gone with my boat; and, if possible, find out the gulf, which I told her she could not mistake, by reason of the noise the fall of the water made; and desired her to remark the place, so as I might know within-side where it was without. And then I told her she might review and search every hole in the ship as she pleased; and if there were any small things she had a mind to bring from it, she was welcome, provided the bundle she should make up was not above a fourth part either of the bulk or weight of the last. All which she having engaged punctually to observe, she bade me not expect her till I saw her, and she would return as soon as possible. I then went with her to the confines of the wood (for I told her I desired to see her mount), and she, after we had embraced, bidding me to stand behind her, took her flight.

XX

I had ever since our marriage been desirous of seeing Youwarkee fly; but this was the first opportunity I had of it; and indeed the sight was worthy of all the attention I paid it; for I desired her slowly to put herself in proper order for it, that I might make my observation the more accurately; and shall now give you an account of the whole apparatus, though several parts of the description were taken from subsequent views; for it would have been impossible to have made just remarks of everything at that once, especially as I only viewed her back parts then.

I told you before, I had seen her graundee open, and quite extended as low as her middle; but that being in the grotto by lamplight, I could not take so just a survey as now, when the sort of light we ever had was at the brightest.

She first threw up two long branches or ribs of the whalebone, as I called it before (and indeed for several of its properties, as toughness, elasticity, and pliableness, nothing I have ever seen can so justly be compared to it), which were jointed behind to the upper bone of the spine, and which, when not extended, lie bent over the shoulders on each side of the neck forwards, from whence, by nearer and nearer approaches, they just meet at the lower rim of the belly in a sort of point; but when extended, they stand their whole length above the shoulders, not perpendicularly, but spreading outwards, with a web of the softest and most pliable and springy membrane that can be imagined, in the interstice between them, reaching from their root or joint on the back up above the hinder part of the head, and near half-way their own length; but when closed, the membrane falls down in the middle upon the neck, like a handkerchief. There are also two other ribs rising as it were from the same root, which, when open, run horizontally, but not so long as the others. These are filled up in the interstice between them and the upper ones with the same membrane; and on the lower side of this is also a deep flap of the membrane, so that the arms can be either above or below it in flight, and are always above it when closed. This last rib, when shut, flaps under the upper one, and also falls down with it before to the waist, but is not joined to the ribs below. Along the whole spine-bone runs a strong, flat, broad, grisly cartilage, to which are joined several other of these ribs; all which open horizontally, and are filled in the interstices with the above membrane, and are jointed to the ribs of the person just where the plane of the back begins to turn towards the breast and belly; and, when shut, wrap the body round to the joints on the contrary side, folding neatly one side over the other. At the lower spine are two more ribs, extended horizontally when open, jointed again to the hips, and long enough to meet the joint on the contrary side cross the belly; and from the hip-joint, which is on the outermost edge of the hip-bone, runs a pliable cartilage quite down the outside of the thigh and leg to the ankle; from which there branch out divers other ribs horizontally also when open, but when closed, they encompass the whole thigh and leg, rolling inwards cross the back of the leg and thigh till they reach and just cover the cartilage. The interstices of these are also filled up with the same membrane. From the two ribs which join to the lower spine-bone, there hangs down a sort of short apron, very full of plaits, from hip-joint to hip-joint, and reaches below the buttocks, half-way or more to the hams. This has also several small limber ribs in it. Just upon the lower spine-joint, and above the apron, as I call it, there are two other long branches, which, when close, extend upon the back from the point they join at below to the shoulders, where each rib has a clasper, which reaching over the shoulders, just under the fold of the uppermost branch or ribs, hold up the two ribs flat to the back like a V, the interstices of which are also filled up with the aforesaid membrane. This last piece, in flight, falls down almost to the ankles, where the two claspers lapping under each leg within-side, hold it very fast; and then also the short apron is drawn up by-the strength of the ribs in it, between the thighs forward, and covers the pudenda and groin as far as the rim of the belly. The whole arms are covered also from the shoulders to the wrist with the same delicate membrane, fastened to ribs of proportionable dimensions, and jointed to a cartilage on the outside in the same manner as on the legs.

It is very surprising to feel the difference of these ribs when open and when closed; for, closed, they are as pliable as the finest whalebone, or more so, but when extended, are as strong and stiff as a bone. They are tapering from the roots, and are broader or narrower as best suits the places they occupy, and the stress they are put to, up to their points, which are almost as small as a hair. The membrane between them is the most elastic thing I ever met with, occupying no more space, when the ribs are closed, than just from rib to rib, as flat and smooth as possible; but when extended in some postures, will dilate itself surprisingly. This will be better comprehend by the plates, where you will see several figures of glumms and gawrys in different attitudes, than can be expressed by words.

As soon as my wife had expanded the whole graundee, being upon plain ground, she stooped forward, moving with a heavy wriggling motion at first, which put me into some pain for her; but after a few strokes, beginning to rise a little, she cut through the air like lightning, and was soon over the edge of the rock and out of my sight.

It is the most amazing thing in the world to observe the large expansion of this graundee when open; and when closed (as it all is in a moment upon the party's descent) to see it sit so close and compact to the body, as no tailor can come up to it; and then the several ribs lie so justly disposed in the several parts, that instead of being, as one would imagine, a disadvantage to the shape, they make the body and limbs look extremely elegant; and by the different adjustment of their lines on the body and limbs, the whole, to my fancy, somewhat resembles the dress of the old Roman warriors in their buskins; and, to appearance, seems much more noble than any fictitious garb I ever saw, or can frame a notion of to myself.

Though these people, in height, shape, and limb, very much resemble the Europeans, there is yet this difference, that their bodies are rather broader and flatter, and their limbs, though as long and well shaped, are seldom as thick as ours. And this I observed generally in all I saw of them during a long time among them afterwards; but their skin, for beauty and fairness, exceeds ours very much.

My wife having now taken her second flight, I went home, and never left my children till her return; this was three days after our parting. I was in bed with my little ones when she knocked at the door. I soon let her in, and we received each other with a glowing welcome. The news she brought me was very agreeable. She told me she first went and pried into every nook in the ship, where she had seen such things, could we get at them, as would make us very happy. Then she set out the way I told her to go, in order to find the gulf. She was much afraid she should not have discovered it, though she flew very slow, that she might be sure to hear the waterfall and not over-shoot it. It was long ere she came at it; but when she did, she perceived she might have spared most of her trouble, had she set out the other way; for, after she had flown almost round the island, and not before, she began to hear the fall, and upon coming up to it, found it to be not above six minutes' flight from the ship. She said the entrance was very narrow, and, she thought, lower than I represented it; for she could scarce discern any space between the surface of the water and the arch-way of the rock. I told her that might happen from the rise or fall of the sea itself. But I was glad to hear the ship was no farther from the gulf; for my head was never free from the thoughts of my ship and cargo. She then told me she had left a small bundle for me without the wood, and went to look after her children. I brought up the bundle, and though it was not near so large as the other, I found several useful things in it, wrapped up in four or five yards of dark blue woollen cloth, which I knew no name for, but which was thin and light, and about a yard wide. I asked her where she met with this stuff; she answered, where there was more of it, under a thing like our bed, in a cloth like our sheet, which she cut open, and took it out of.—"Well," says I, "and what will you do with this?"— "Why, I will make me a coat like yours," says she, "for I don't like to look different from my dear husband and children."—"No, Youwarkee," replied I, "you must not do so; if you make such a jacket as mine, there will be no distinction between glumm and gawry;* the gowren praave,† in my country, would not on any account go dressed like a glumm; for they wear a fine flowing garment called a gown, that sits tight about the waist, and hangs down from thence in folds, like your barras,‡ almost to the ground, so that you can hardly discern their feet, and no other part of their body but their hands and face, and about as much of their neck and breasts as you see in your graundee."

Youwarkee seemed highly delighted with this new-fancied dress, and worked day and night at it against the cold weather. Whilst she employed herself thus, I was busied in providing my winter stores, which I was forced to do alone now, herself and children taking up all my wife's time. About a fortnight after she had begun mantua-making, she presented herself to me one day, as I came from work, in her new gown; and, truly, considering the scanty description I had given her of

---

* Man and woman.
† Modest women.
‡ The back flap of the graundee.

such a garment, it appeared a good comely dress. Though it had not one plait about the body, it sat very tight thereto, and yet hung down full enough for a countess; for she would have put it all in (all the stuff she had) had there been as much more of it. I could see no opening before, so asked her how she got it on. She told me she laid along on the ground, and crept through the plaits at the bottom, and sewed the body round her after she had got her hands and arms through the sleeves. I wondered at her contrivance; and, smiling, showed her how she should put it on, and also how to pin it before: and after she had done that, and I had turned up about half a yard of sleeve, which then hung down to her fingers' ends, I kissed her, and called her my country-woman; of which, and her new gown, she was very proud for a long time.

XXI

THE AUTHOR GETS A BREED OF POULTRY, AND BY WHAT MEANS—BUILDS THEM A HOUSE—HOW HE MANAGED TO KEEP THEM IN WINTER.

One day, as I was traversing the woods to view my bird-traps, looking into the underwood among the great trees on my right hand, I saw a wood-hen (a bird I used to call so, from its resemblance in make to our English poultry) come out of a little thicket. I know not whether my rustling or what had disturbed it; but I let her pass, and she ran away before me. When she was fairly out of sight, I stepped up, and found she had a nest and sixteen eggs there. I exactly marked the place, and taking away one of the eggs, I broke it, at some distance from the nest, to see how forward they were; and I had no sooner broke the shell but out came a young chicken. I then looked into the nest again, and taking up more of the eggs, I found them all just splintered in the shell, and ready for hatching. I had immediately a desire to save them, and bring them up tame; but I was afraid if I took them away before they were hatched, and a little strengthened under the hen, they would all die; so I let them remain till next day. In the meanwhile I prepared some small netting of such a proper size as I conceived would do, and with this I contrived, by fastening it to stakes which I fixed in the ground, to surround the nest, and me on the outside of it. All the while I was doing this, the hen did not stir, so that I thought she had either been absent when I came, or had hatched and gone off with the young ones. As to her being gone I was under no concern; for I had no design to catch her, but only to confine the chickens within my net if they were hatched. But, however, I went nearer, and peeping in, found she sat still, squeezing herself as flat to the ground as she could. I was in twenty minds whether to take her first, and then catch the chickens, or to let her go off, and then clap upon them; but as I proposed to let her go, I thought if she would sit still till I had got the chickens, that would be the best way; so I softly kneeled down before her, and sliding my hand under her, I gently drew out two, and put them in a bag I had in my left hand. I then dipped again and again, taking two every turn; but going a fourth time, as I was bringing out my prize, the hen jumped up, flew out, and made such a noise that, though I the minute before

ROBERT PALTOCK

saw six or seven more chicks in a lump where she had sat, and kept my eye upon them, yet before I could put the last two I had got into my bag, these were all gone, and in three hours' search I could not find one of them, though I was sure they could not pass my net, and must be within the compass of a small room, my toils enclosing no more. After tiring myself with looking for them, I marched home with those eight I had got.

I told Youwarkee what I had done, and how I intended to manage the little brood, and, if I could, to bring them up tame. We kept them some days very warm by the fire, and fed them often, as I had seen my mother do with her early chickens; and in a fortnight's time they were as stout and familiar as common poultry. We kept them a long while in the house; and when I fed them I always used them to a particular whistle, which I also taught my wife, that they might know both us and their feeding-time; and in a very short while they would come running, upon the usual sound, like barn-door fowls to the name of Biddy.

There happened in this brood to be five hens and three cocks; and they were now so tame that, having cut their wings, I let them out, when the weather favoured, at my door, where they would pick about in the wood, and get the best part of their subsistence; and having used them to roost in a corner of my ante-chamber, they all came in very regularly at night and took their places. My hens, at the usual season, laid me abundance of eggs, and hatched me a brood or two each of chickens; so that now I was at a loss to know what to do with them, they were become so numerous. The ante-chamber was no longer a proper receptacle of such a flock, and therefore I built a little house, at a small distance from my own, on purpose for their reception and entertainment. I had by this time cleared a spot of ground on one side of my grotto, by burning up the timber and underwood which had covered it: this I enclosed, and within that enclosure I raised my aviary, and my poultry thrived very well there, seemed to like their habitation, and grew very fat.

My wife and I took much delight in visiting and feeding them, and it was a fine diversion also to my boys; but at the end of summer, when all the other birds took their annual flight, away went everyone of my new-raised brood with them, and one of my old cocks, the rest of the old set remaining very quiet with me all the winter. The next summer, when my chicks of that year grew up a little, I cut their wings, and by that means preserved all but one, which I suppose was either not cut so close as the rest, or his wings had grown again. From this time I found, by long experience, that not two out of a hundred that had once wintered with me would ever go away, though I did not cut their wings; but all of the same season would certainly go off with the wild ones, if they could anyways make a shift to fly. I afterwards got a breed of blacknecks, which was a name I gave them from the peculiar blackness of their necks, let the rest of their bodies be of what colour they would, as they are, indeed, of all colours. These birds were as big, or bigger, than a turkey, of a delicious flavour, and were bred from turkey eggs hatched under my own wood-hens in great plenty. I was forced to clip these as I did the other young fowl, to keep them, and at length they grew very tame, and would return every night during the dark season. The greatest difficulty now was to get meat for all these animals in the winter, when they would sit on the roost two days together if I did not call and feed them, which I was sometimes forced to do by lamp-light, or they would have starved in cloudy weather. But I overcame that want of food by an accidental discovery; for I observed my blacknecks in the woods jump many times together at a sort of little round heads, or pods, very dry, which hung plentifully upon a shrub that grew in great abundance there. I cut several of these heads, and carrying them home with me, broke them, and took out a spoonful or more from each head of small yellow seeds, which giving to my poultry, and finding they greedily devoured them, I soon laid in a stock for twice my number of mouths, so that they never after wanted. I tried several times to raise a breed of water-fowl by hatching their eggs under my hens; but not one in ten of the sorts, when hatched, were fit to eat; and those that were would never live and thrive with me, but go away to the lake, I having no sort of water nearer me; so I dropped my design of water-fowl as impracticable. But by breeding and feeding my land-fowl so constantly in my farmyard, I never wanted of that sort at my table, where we eat abundance of them; for my whole side of the lake in a few years was like a farmyard, so full of poultry that I never knew my stock; and upon the usual whistle they would flock round me from all quarters. I had everything now but cattle, not only for the support, but convenience and pleasure of life; and so happily should I have fared here, if I had had but a cow and bull, a ram and sheep, that I would not have changed my dominions for the crown of England.

ROBERT PALTOCK

XXII

REFLECTIONS ON MANKIND—THE AUTHOR WANTS TO
BE WITH HIS SHIP—PROJECTS GOING, BUT PERCEIVES IT
IMPRACTICABLE—YOUWARKEE OFFERS HER SERVICE, AND
GOES—AN ACCOUNT OF HER TRANSACTIONS ON BOARD—
REMARKS ON HER SAGACITY—SHE DESPATCHES SEVERAL
CHESTS OF GOODS THROUGH THE GULF TO THE LAKE—AN
ACCOUNT OF A DANGER SHE ESCAPED—THE AUTHOR HAS
A FIT OF SICKNESS.

Strange is the temper of mankind, who, the more they enjoy, the more they covet. Before I received any return from my ship, I rested tolerably easy, and but seldom thought upon what I had left behind me in her, thinking myself happy in what I had, and completely so since my union with my dear wife; but after I had got what I could never have expected, I grew more and more perplexed for want of the rest, and thought I should never enjoy true happiness while even a plank of the ship remained. My head, be I where I would, or at what I would, was ever on board. I wished for her in the lake, and could I but have got her thither, I thought I should be an emperor; and though I wanted for nothing to maintain life, and had so good a wife and five children I was very fond of, yet the one thing I had not, reduced the comfort of all the rest to a scanty pattern, even so low as to destroy my whole peace. I was even mad enough to think of venturing up the cavern again, but was restrained from the attempt by the certain impracticableness of it Then I thought Youwarkee should make another trip to the ship. But what can she bring from it, says I to myself, in respect of what must be left behind? Her whole life will not suffice to clear it in, at the rate she can fetch the loading hither in parcels. At last a project started, that as there were so many chests on board, Youwarkee should fill some of them and send them through the gulf to take their chance for the lake. This, at first sight, seemed feasible; but then I considered how they could be got from the ship to the gulf; and again, that they would never keep out the water, and if they filled with a lading in them they would sink; or, if this did not happen, they might be dashed to pieces against the crags in the cavern. These apprehensions stopped me again; till, unwilling to quit the thought, "True," says I, "this may happen to some; but if I get but one in five, it is better than nothing." Thus I turned and wound the affair in my mind; but objections still started too obstinate to be conquered.

In the height of my soliloquy in comes Youwarkee, and seeing my dejected look, would needs know the meaning of it I told her plainly that I could get no rest from day to day ever since she first went to the ship, to think such a number of good things lay there to be a prey to the sea, as the ship wasted, when they might be of such infinite service here; and that, since her last flight, I had suffered the more, when I thought how near the gulf was to the ship; so that could I but get thither myself with my boat, I would contrive to pack up the goods in the chests that were on board, and carrying them in the boat, drop them near the draught of the water, which of itself would suck them under the rock down the gulf; and when they were passed through the cavern, I might take them up in the lake. "Well," says she, "Peter, and why cannot I do this for you?"—"No," says I, "even this has its objections." Then I told her what I feared of their taking water, or dashing against the rock, and twenty other ways of frustrating my views: "But, above all," says I, "how can you get such large and weighty things to the gulf without a boat? There is another impossibility! it won't do."

Youwarkee eyed me attentively. "Pr'ythee, my dear Peter," says she, "set your heart at rest about that. I can only try; if no good is to be done, you shall soon know it, and must rest contented under the disappointment."—I told her if I was there, I could take all the things out of the chests, and then melt some pitch and pour into every crack, to keep out the water when they were set afloat. "Pitch!" says she, "what's that?"—"Why," says I, "that is a nasty, hard, black sticking thing that stands in tubs in the ship, and which being put over the fire in anything to melt will grow liquid, and when it is cold be hard again, and will resist the water and keep it out."—Says she, "How can I put this pitch within-side of the chest-lid when I have tied it up?"—"It is to no manner of purpose," says I, "to talk of it; so there's an end of it."—"But," says she, "suppose yourself there, what things would you bring first?"—I then entered into a long detail of particulars; saying I would have this and that, and so on, till I had scarce left out a thing I either knew of or could suppose to be in the ship; and for fear I had not mentioned all, says I at last, if I was there, I believe I should leave but little portable behind me.

"So, so, my dear," says Youwarkee, "you would roll in riches, I find; but you have mentioned never a new gown for me."—"Why, aye!" says

I, "I would have that too."—"But how would you melt the pitch?" says she.—"Oh," says I, "there is a tinder-box and matches in a room below, upon the side of the fire-hearth." And then I let her see one I had brought with me, and showed her the use of the flint and steel.—"Well, my dear," says she, "will you once more trust me?"—I told her, her going would be of little more use than to get a second gown or some such thing; but if she was desirous, I would let her make another flight, on her promise to be back as soon as possible.

In the evening she set out, and stayed two days, and till the night of the third. I would here observe that though it was much lighter and brighter on the outside of the rock where the ship lay than with us at Graundevolet, yet having always her spectacles with her, I heard no more complaint of the glare of light she used to be so much afraid of: indeed, she always avoided the fire and lamp at home as much as she could, because she generally took off her spectacles within doors; but when at anytime she had them on, she could bear both well enough.

Upon her return again, she told me she had shipped some goods to sea for me, which she hoped would arrive safe (for by this time she had had my seafaring terms so often over, she could apply them very properly), and that they were in six chests, which she had pitched after my directions.—"Aye!" says I, "you have pitched them into the sea perhaps; but after my directions, I am satisfied was beyond your ability."—"You glumms," says she, "think us gawrys very ignorant; but I'll satisfy you we are not so dull of apprehension as you would make us. Did you not show me one day how your boat was tarred and caulked, as you call it?"—"I did," says I; "what then?"—"I'll tell you," says she. "When I had emptied the first chest, and set it properly, I looked about for your pitch, which at last I found by its sticking to my fingers; I then put a good piece into a sort of little kettle, with a long handle, that lay upon the pitch."—"Oh, the pitch-ladle!" says I.—"I know not what you call it," says she; "but then I made a fire, as you told me, and melted that stuff; afterwards turning up the chest side-ways, and then end-ways, I poured it into it, and let it settle in the cracks, and with an old stocking, such as yours, dipped into the pitch, I rubbed every place where the boards joined. I then set the chest on the side of the ship, and when the pitch was cold and hardened in it, filled it top-full of things: but when I had done thus, and shut the lid, I found that would not come so close but I could get the blade of a knife through anywhere between it and the chest; whereupon I cut some long slips of the cloth I was packing up, and fitting them all round the edge of the chest, I dipped them into the pitch, and laid them on hot; and where one slip would not do, I put two; and shutting the lid down close upon them, I nailed it, as I had seen you do somethings, quite round; then tying a rope to the handle, I tipped the chest into the sea, holding the rope. I watched it sometime, and seeing it swim well, I took flight with the rope in my hand, and drew the chest after me to the gulf, when, letting go the rope, away it went. I served five more in the same manner: and now, my dearest, I am here to tell you I hope you will be able to see at least some of them, one time or other, in the lake."

I admired in all this at the sagacity of the gawrys. Alas! thinks I, what narrow-hearted creatures are mankind! Did I not heretofore look upon the poor blacks in Africa as little better than beasts, till my friend Glanlepze convinced me, by disabling the crocodile, the passage of the river, and several other achievements, that my own excellences might have perished in a desert without his genius; and now what could I, or almost any of us masterpieces of the creation (as we think ourselves) and Heaven's peculiar favourites, have done in this present case, that has been omitted by this woman (for I may justly style her so in an eminent degree), and that in a way to which she was bred an utter stranger?

After what I had heard from Youwarkee, I grew much more cheerful; which she, poor creature, was remarkably pleased with. She went with me constantly once, and sometimes twice a day, for several days together, to see what success at the lake; till at length she grew very impatient, for fear, as she afterwards told me, I should either think she had not done what she said, or had done it in an ineffectual manner. But one day, walking by the lake, I thought I saw something floating in the water at a very great distance. "Youwarkee," says I, "I spy a sail!" Then running to my boat and taking her in, away we went, plying my oars with all my might; for I longed to see what it was. At nearer view I perceived it to be one of my wife's fleet. But what added to my satisfaction was to see Youwarkee so pleased, for she could scarcely contain herself.

When we came close to it, up she started: "Now, my dear Peter," says she, "torment yourself no more about your goods on board; for if this will do, all shall be your own."—She then lent me a hand to take it in; but we had both work enough to compass it, the wood had soaked in so much water. We then made the best of our way homewards to my wet-dock; when, just as we had landed our treasure, we saw two more boxes coming down the stream both together, whereupon we launched again, and brought them in one by one; for I did not care to trust them both on one bottom, my boat being in years, and growing somewhat crazy.

We had now made a good day's work of it; so, mooring the boat, we went home, intending to be out next morning early with the cart, to convey our imports to the grotto.

After supper, Youwarkee looking very earnestly at me, with tears just glittering in her eyes, broke out in these words—"What should you have thought, Peter, to have seen me come sailing, drowned, through the cavern, tied to one of your chests?"—"Heaven forbid such a thought, my charmer!" says I. "But as you know I must have been rendered the most miserable of all living creatures by such a sight, or anything else that would deprive me of you, pray tell me how you could possibly have such a thought in your head?"—She saw she had raised my concern, and was very sorry for what she had said. "Nothing, nothing," says she, "my dear! it was only a fancy just come into my head."—"My dear Youwee," says I, "you must let me know what you mean: I am in great pain till you explain yourself; for I am sure there is something more in what you say than fancy; therefore, pray, if you love me, keep me on the rack no longer."—"Ah, Peter!" says she, "there was but a span between me and death not many days ago; and when I saw the line of the last chest we took up just now, it gave so much horror I could scarce keep upon my feet."—"My dear Youwee, proceed," says I; "for I cannot bear my torment till I have heard the worst."—"Why, Peter," says she, "now the danger is over, I shall tell you my escape with as much pleasure as I guess you will take in hearing of it. You must know, my life," says she, "that having cast that chest into the sea, as I was tugging it along by that very line, it being one of the heaviest, and moving but slowly, I twisted the string several times round my hand, one fold upon another, the easier to tow it; when, drawing it rather too quick into the eddy, it pulled so hard against me, towards the gulf, and so quick, that I could in no way loosen or disengage the cord from my fingers, but was dragged thereby to the very rock, against which the chest struck violently. My last thought, as I supposed it, was of you, my dear" (on which she clasped me round the neck, in sense of her past agony); "when taking myself for lost, I forbore further resistance; at which instant the line, slackening by the rebound of the chest, fell from my hand of itself, and the chest returning to the rock, went down the current. I took a turn or two round on my graundee to recollect my past danger, and went back to the ship, fully resolved to avoid the like snare for the future. Indeed I did not easily recover my spirits, and was so terrified with the thought, that I had half a mind to have left the two remaining chests behind me; but as danger overcome gives fresh resolution, I again set to work, and discharged them also down the gulf, as I hope you will see in good time."

My heart bled within me all the while she spoke, and I even felt ten times more than she could have suffered by the gulf. "My dearest Youwee," says I, "why did you not tell me this adventure sooner?" "It is too soon, I fear, now!" says she; for she then saw the colour forsake my lips, my eyes grow languid, and myself dropping into her arms. She screamed out, and ran to the chest, where all was empty; but turning every bottle up, and from the remaining drops in each collecting a small quantity of liquor, and putting it by little and little to my lips, and rubbing my wrists and temples, she brought me to myself again; but I continued so extremely sick for some days after, that it was above a week before I could get down with my cart to fetch up my chests.

When I was able to go down, Youwarkee would not venture me alone, but went herself with me. We then found two more of the chests, which we landed; and I had work sufficient for two or three days in getting them all up to the grotto, they were so heavy, and all the way through the wood being up hill.

We had five in hand, and watched several days for the sixth, when seeing nothing of it we gave it over for lost; but one day, as I was going for water, Youwarkee would go with me, and urged our carrying the net, that we might drag for some fish. Accordingly we did so; and now having taken what we wanted, we went to the rill, and pushing in the head of the boat (as I usually did, for by that means I could fill the vessel as I stood on board), the first thing that appeared was my sixth chest. Youwarkee spied it first, and cried, pointing thereto, "O Peter, what we have long wished for, and almost despaired of, is come at last! let us meet and welcome it." I was pleased with the gaiety of her fancy. I did as she desired; we got it into the boat, after merrily saluting it, and so returned home. It took us up several days time in searching, sorting, and disposing our cargo, and drying the chests; for the goods themselves were so far from being wetted or spoiled, that even those in the last chest, which had lain so long in the water, had not taken the least moisture.

Youwarkee was quite alert at the success of her packing, but left me to ring her praises, which I did not fail of doing more than once at unpacking each chest, and could see her eyes glow with delight to see she had so pleased me.

She had been so curious as to examine almost everything in the ship; and as well of things I had described, and she did know, as of what she did not, brought me something for a sample; but, above all, had not forgot the blue stuff, for the moment she had seen that she destined it to the use of herself and children.

XXIII

The religion of the author's family.

Youwarkee and I having fixed ourselves, by degrees, into a settled rota of action, began to live like Christians, having so great a quantity of most sorts of necessaries about us. But I say we lived like Christians on another account, for you must not think, after what I have said before, that I and my family lived like heathens; no, I will assure you, they by degrees knew all I knew, and that, with a little artificial improvement, and a well-regulated disposition, I hoped, and did not doubt, would carry them all to heaven. I would many a time have given all my interest in the ship's cargo for a Bible; and a hundred times grieved that I was not master of a pocket one, which I might have carried everywhere about me. I never imagined there was one aboard, and if there were, and Youwarkee should find it, I supposed it would be in Portuguese, which I knew little of, so it would be of small service to me if I had it.

Since I am on the topic of religion, it may not be amiss, once for all, to give you a small sketch of my religious proceedings after coming into my new dominions. I have already told you that from my first stop at the rock I had prayed constantly morning and evening, but I cannot say I did it always with the same efficacy. However, my imperfect devotions were not without good effect; and I am confident, wherever this course is pursued with a right view, sooner or later the issue will prove the same to others as I found it to myself; I mean, that mercies will be remembered with more gratitude, and evils be more disregarded, and become less burdensome; and surely the person whose case this is, must necessarily enjoy the truest relish of life. As daily prayer was my practice, in answer to it I obtained the greatest blessing and comfort my solitude was capable of receiving; I mean my wife, whose character I need not farther attempt to blazon in any faint colours of my own after what has been already said, her acts having spoken her virtues beyond all verbal description.

After we were married, as I call it—that is, after we had agreed to become man and wife—I frequently prayed before her, and with her (for by this time she understood a good deal of my language); at which, though contrary to my expectation, she did not seem surprised, but readily kneeled by and joined with me. This I liked very well; and upon

ROBERT PALTOCK

my asking her one day after prayer if she understood what I had been doing (for I had a notion she did not)—"Yes, verily," says she, "you have been making petitions to the image of the great Collwar."*—"Pray," says I (willing gently to lead her into a just sense of a Supreme Being), "who is this Collwar? and where does He dwell?"—"He it is," says she, "that does all good and evil to us."—"Right," says I, "it is in some measure so; but He cannot of Himself do evil, absolutely and properly, as His own act"—"Yes," says she, "He can; for He can do all that can be done; and as evil can be done, He can do it."—So quick a reply startled me. Thinks I, she will run me aground presently; and from being a doctor, as I fancied myself, I shall become but a pupil to my own scholar. I then asked her where the great Collwar dwelt? She told me in heaven, in a charming place.—"And can He know what we do?" says I.—"Yes," replied she, "His image tells Him everything; and I have prayed to His image, which I have often seen, and it is filled with so much virtue that it is His second self; for there is only one of them in the world who is so good: He gives several virtues to other images of Himself, which are brought to Him, and put into His arms to breathe upon; and the only thing I have ever regretted since I knew you is, that I have not one of them here to comfort and bless us and our children."

Though I was sorry for the oddity of her conceptions, I was almost glad to find her so ignorant, and pleased myself with thinking that as she had already a confused notion of a Supreme Power, I should soon have the satisfaction of bringing her to a more rational knowledge of Him.

"Pray, Youwee," says I, "what is your God made of?"—"Why of clay," says she, "finely painted, and looks so terrible he would make you tremble to behold him."—"Do you think," says I, "that is the true Collwar's real shape, if you could see Himself?" She told me yes, for that some of His best servants had seen him, and took the representation from Himself. "And pray, do you think He loves His best servants, as you call them, and is kind to them?"—"You need not doubt it," says she.—"Why, then," replied I, "how came He to look so terrible upon them when they saw Him, as you say they did? for I can see no reason, how terrible soever He looks to others, why He should show Himself so to those He loves. I should rather think, as you say He is kind to them, that He should have two images, a placid one for His good, and

* God.

a terrible one for His bad servants; or else, who by seeing Him can tell whether He is pleased or angry? for even you yourself, Youwee, when anything pleases you, have a different look from that you have when you are angry, and little Pedro can tell whether he does well or ill by your countenance; whereas, if you made no distinction, but looked with the same face on all his actions, he would as readily think he did well as ill in committing a bad action." Youwarkee could not tell what to say to this, the fact seeming against her.

I then asked her if she thought the image itself could hear her petitions. She replied, "Yes."—"And can he," says I, "return you an answer?"—She told me he only did that to his best servants.—"Did you ever hear him do it?" says I. "For unless he can speak too, I should much suspect his hearing; and you being one of his best servants, seeing you love him, and pray heartily to him, why should you not hear him as soon as others?"—"No," says she, "there are a great number of glumms on purpose to serve him, pray for us to him, and receive his answers."—"But to what purpose then," says I, "is your praying to him, if their prayers will serve your turn?"—"Oh," says she, "the image hears them sooner than us, and sends the petitions up to the great Collwar, and lets Him know who makes them, and desires Him to let them have what they want."—"But suppose," says I, for argument sake, "that you could see the great Collwar, or know where He was, and should pray to Himself, without going about to His image first, do you think He could not hear you?"—"I cannot tell that," says she.—"But how then," says I, "can He tell what (if it could speak) His image says, which is as far from Him and then her own zealous application, with God's grace, soon brought her to a firm belief in it, and a suitable temper and conduct with respect to God and man."

After I had begun with my children, I frequently referred their further instruction to their mother; for I have always experienced that a superficial knowledge, with a desire of becoming a teacher, is in some measure equivalent to better knowledge; for it not only excites every principle one has to the utmost, but makes matters more clear and conspicuous even to one's self.

By these means, and the Divine blessing thereon, in a few years, I may fairly say, I had a little Christian church in my own house, and in a flourishing way too, without a schismatic or heretic amongst us.

XXIV

The author's account of his children—Their names—
They are exercised in flying—His boat crazy—
Youwarkee intends a visit to her father, but first
takes another flight to the ship—Sends a boat and
chests through the gulf—Clothes her children—Is
with child again, so her visit is put off—An inventory
of the last freight of goods—The author's method
of treating his children—Youwarkee, her son Tommy,
with her daughters Patty and Hallycarnie, set out
to her father's.

I had now lived here almost fourteen years, and besides the three sons before mentioned, had three girls and one boy. Pedro, my eldest, had the graundee, but too small to be useful; my second son Tommy had it complete, so had my three daughters, but Jemmy and David, the youngest sons, none at all. My eldest daughter I named Patty, because I always called my first wife so. I say my first wife, though I had no other knowledge of her death than my dream; but am from that as verily persuaded, if ever I reach England, I shall find it so, as if I had heard it from her aunt's own mouth. My second daughter my wife desired might be called by her sister's name Hallycarnie, and my youngest I named Sarah, after my mother. I put you to the trouble of writing down the names, for as I shall hereafter have frequent occasion to mention the children severally, it will be pleasanter for myself and you to call them by their several names of distinction, than to call them my second son, or my eldest daughter, and so forth.

My wife now took great delight in exercising Tommy and Patty (who were big enough to be trusted) in flighty and would often skim round the whole island with them before I could walk half through the wood. And she would teach them also to swim or sail, I know not which to call it, for sometimes you should see them dart out of the air as if they would fall on their faces into the lake, when coming near the surface they would stretch their legs in a horizontal posture, and in an instant turn on their backs, and then you could see nothing from the bank, to all appearance, but a boat sailing along, the graundee rising at their head, feet, and sides, so like the sides and ends of a boat that you could not discern the face or any part of the body. I own I often envied them this exercise, which they seemed to perform with more ease than I could only shake my leg or stir an arm.

Though we had perpetually swangeans about us, and the voices, as I used to call them, I could never once prevail on my wife to show herself, or to claim any acquaintance with her country folks. And what is very remarkable in my children is, that my three daughters and Tommy, who had the full graundee, had exactly their mother's sight, Jemmy and David had just my sight, and Pedro's sight was between both, though he was never much affected with any light; but I was obliged to make spectacles for Tommy and all my daughters when they came to go abroad.

I had in this time twice enlarged my dwelling, which the increase of my family had rendered necessary. The last alteration I was enabled to do in a much better manner, and with more ease, than the first, for by the return of my flota I had gotten a large collection of useful tools, several of iron, where the handles or wood-work preponderated the iron; but such as was all, or greatest part of that metal, had got either to the rock, or were so fast fixed to the head of the ship, that it was difficult to remove them, so that my wife could get comparatively few of this latter sort, though some she did. It was well, truly, I had these instruments, which greatly facilitated my labours, for I was forced to work harder now than ever in making provision for us all; and my sons Pedro and Tommy commonly assisted. I had also had another importation of goods through the gulf, which still added to my convenience. But my boat made me shudder everytime I went into her; she had leaked again and again, and I had patched her till I could scarce see a bit of the old wood. She was of unspeakable use to me, and yet I could not venture myself in her, but with the utmost apprehension and trembling. I had been intending a good while, now I had such helps, to build a new one, but had been diverted by one avocation or other.

About this time Youwarkee, who was now upwards of thirty-two years of age, the fondest mother living, and very proud of her children, had formed a project of taking a flight to Arndrumnstake, a town in the kingdom of Doorpt Swangeanti, as I called it, where her father, if living, was a colamb* under Georigetti, the prince of that country. She imparted her desire to me, asking my leave; and she told me, if I pleased,

---

* Governor.

ROBERT PALTOCK

she would take Patty and Tommy along with her. I did not much dislike the proposal, because of the great inclination I had for a long time to a knowledge of, and familiarity with, her countrymen and relations; and now I had so many of her children with me, I could not think she would ever be prevailed on, but by force, to quit me and her offspring, and be contented to lose six for the sake of having two with her, especially as she had showed no more love for them than the rest, so I made no hesitation, but told her she should go.

I expected continually I should hear of her departure, but she saying no more of it, I thought she had dropped her design, and I did not choose to mention it. But one day, as we were at dinner, looking mighty seriously, she said, "My dear, I have considered of the journey you have consented I should take, but in order thereto it is necessary that I prepare several things for the children, especially those who have no graundee, and I am resolved to finish them before I go, that we may appear with decency, both here and at Arndrumn-stake; for I am sure my father, whose temper I am perfectly acquainted with, will, upon sight of me and my little ones, be so overjoyed, that he will forgive my absence and marriage, provided he sees reason to believe I have not matched unworthily, unbecoming my birth; and after keeping me and the children with him, it may be two or three months, will accompany me home again himself with a great retinue of servants and relations; or, at least, if he is either dead or unable for flight, my other relations will come or send a convoy to take care of me and the children; and, my dear, as I shall give them all the encomiums I can of you, and of my situation with you, while I am among them, I would have them a little taken with the elegance of our domestic condition when they come hither, that they may think me happy in you and my children; for I would not only put my family into a condition to appear before them, but to surprise the old gentleman and his company, who never in their lives saw any part of mankind with another covering than the graundee." When she had done, I expressed my approbation of her whole system, as altogether prudent, and she proceeded immediately to put it in execution. To work she went, opened every chest, and examined their contents. But while she was upon the hunt, and selecting such things as she thought fit for her purpose, she recollected several articles she had observed in the ship, which she judged far more for her turn than any she had at home. Hereupon she prayed me to let her take another trip to the vessel, and to carry Tommy with her.

After so many trials, and such happy experience of her wise and fortunate conduct, I consented to her flight, and away went she and her son. Upon their return, which was in a few days, she told me what they had been doing, and said, as she so often heard me complain of the age of my boat, and fear to sail in her, she had fitted me out a little ship, and hoped it would in due time arrive safely. As she passed quickly on to other things, I never once thought of asking her what she meant by the little ship she spoke of; but must own that, like a foolishly fond parent, I was more intent on her telling me how Tommy had found a hoard of playthings, which he had packed up for his own use.

As to this last particular, I learned by the sequel of the story, when the spark, proud of his acquisition, came to me, that he had been peeping about in the cabin whilst his mother was packing the chests, and seeing a small brass knob in the wainscot, took it for a plaything, and pulling to get it out, opened a little door of a cupboard, where he had found some very pretty toys that he positively claimed for himself, among which were a small plain gold ring, and a very fine one set with diamonds, which he showed me upon two of his fingers. I wondered how the child, who had never before seen such things, or the use of them, should happen to apply these so properly; but he told me in playing with this, meaning the diamond ring, about his fingers, it slipped over his middle-finger joint, and he could not get it off again, so he put the other upon another finger to keep it company.

We watched daily, as usual on such occasions, for the arrival of our fleet. It was surprising that none of the chests which Youwarkee shot down the gulf were ever half so long in their passage as I was myself, but some came in a week, some in a few days more, and even some in less, which I attributed to their following directly the course of the water, shooting from shelf to shelf as the tide sat; and I believe my keeping the boat I sailed in so strictly and constantly in the middle of the stream, was the reason of my being detained there so long. In less than a fortnight everything came safe but one chest, which, as we never heard of it, I suppose was either sunk or bulged.

Being one day upon shore, watching to see if anything more was come through the cavern, I spied at a distance somewhat looking very black and very long, and by the colour and shape thereof I took it for a young whale. Having observed it sometime making very little way, I took my old boat and followed it, but was afraid to go near it, lest a stroke with its tail—which I then fancied I saw move—might endanger my boat and myself too; but creeping nearer and nearer, and seeing it did not stir, I believed it to be dead; whereupon, taking courage, I drew so close that at length I plainly perceived it was the ship's second boat turned upside down. It is not easy to express the joy I felt on this discovery. It was the very thing I was now, as I have said, in the greatest want of. I presently laid hold of it and brought it ashore; and it was no small pleasure to find, on examining, that though it had lain so long dry, it was yet quite sound, and all its chinks filled up in its passage; and it proved to me afterwards the most beneficial thing I could have had from the ship.

I got all my goods home from the lake to my grotto, by means of the cart, as usual. My wife and daughters waited with impatience for me to unpack, that they might take possession of such things as would be needful for rigging out the family against the supposed reception of the old glumm, and had set all the chests in the order they desired they might be opened in. But Tommy running to me, with a "Pray, daddy, open my chest first! pray, give me my playthings first!" it was, to satisfy him, concluded in favour of his demand. So, he pointing to the chest which he regarded as his property, I opened it, whilst his eyes were ready to pierce through it, till I came to his treasure. "There, there they are, daddy!" says he, as soon as I had uncovered them. And indeed, when I saw them, I could not but much commend the child for his fancy; for the first things that appeared were a silver punch or wine can and a ladle, then a gold watch, a pair of scissors, a small silver chafing-dish and lamp, a large case of mathematical instruments, a flageolet, a terrella or globular loadstone, a small globe, a dozen of large silver spoons, and a small case of knives and forks and spoons; in short, there was, I believe, the greatest part of the Portuguese captain's valuable effects.

These Tommy claiming as his own proper chattels, I could not help interposing somewhat of my authority in the affair. "Hold, hold, son!" says I, "these things are all mine; but as I have several of you who will all be equally pleased with them, though, as the first finder, you may be entitled to the best share, you are not to grasp the whole, you must all have something like an equality; and as to somethings which may be equally useful to us all, they must be set up to be used upon occasion, and are to be considered as mine and your mother's property." I thereupon gave each of them a large silver spoon, and with a fork I scratched the initials of their names respectively on them, and divided several of the trifles amongst them equally. "And now, Tommy," says I, "you for your pains shall have this more than the rest," offering him the flageolet. Tommy looked very gloomy, and though he durst not find fault, his dissatisfaction was very visible by coolly taking it, tossing it down, and walking gravely off. "I thought," says I, "Tommy, I had made a good choice for you; but, as I find you despise it, here, Pedro, do you take that pretty thing, since your brother slights it" Tommy replied, speaking but half out, and a little surly, more than I ever observed before, "Let him take it if he will, I can get bits of sticks enough in the wood."

My method had always been to avoid either beating or scolding at my children, for preferring their own opinion to mine; but I ever let things turn about so, that from their own reason they should perceive they had erred in opposing my sentiments, by which means they grew so habituated to submit to my advice and direction, that for the most part my will was no sooner known to them than it became their own choice; but then I never willed according to fancy only, but with judgment, to the best of my skill.

Tommy, therefore, as I said before, having shown a disapprobation of my doings; to convince him of his mistake, I took the flageolet from Pedro. "And now, Pedro," says I, "let me teach you how to manage this piece of wood, as Tommy calls it, and then let me see if in all the grove he can cut such another." On this I clapped it to my mouth, and immediately played several country-dances and hornpipes on it; for though my mother had scarce taught me to read, I had learnt music and dancing, being, as she called them, gentlemanlike accomplishments. My wife and children, especially Tommy, all stared as if they were wild, first on me, then on one another, whilst I played a country-dance; but I had no sooner struck up an hornpipe, than their feet, arms, and heads had so many twitching and convulsive motions, that not one quiet limb was to be seen amongst them; till having exercised their members as long as I saw fit, I almost laid them all to sleep with Chevy Chase, and so gave over.

They no sooner found themselves free from this enchantment, than the children all hustled round me in a cluster, all speaking together, and reaching out their little hands to the instrument I gave it Pedro. "There," says I to him, "take this slighted favour as no such contemptible present."

Poor Tommy, who had all this while looked very simple, burst into a flood of tears at my last words, as if his heart would have broke; and running to me, fell on his knees, and begged my pardon, hoping I would forgive him. I took him up, and kissing him, told him he had very little offended me; for, as he knew, I had more children to give anything to which either of the rest despised; it was equal to me who had it, so it was thankfully received. I found that did not satisfy; still in tears, he said, "Might he not have the stick again, as I gave it to him first?" "Tommy," says I, "you know I gave it to you first; but you disapproving my kindness, I have now given it Pedro, who, should I against his will take it from him, would have that reason to complain which you have not, who parted with it by your own consent; and therefore, Tommy, as I am determined to acquaint you as near as I can with the strict rules of justice, there must no more be said to me of this matter." Such as this was my constant practice amongst them; and they having always found me inflexible from this rule, we seldom had any long debates.

Though I say the affair ended so with regard to what I had to do in it, yet it ended not so with Tommy; for though he knew he had no hopes of moving me, he set all his engines at work to recover his stick, as he called it, by his mother's and sisters' interest. These solicited Pedro very strongly to gratify him. At length Pedro—he being a boy of a most humane disposition—granted their desire, if I would give leave; and I having signified, that the cause being now out of my hands, he might do as he pleased, he generously yielded it. And indeed he could not have bestowed it more properly; for Tommy had the best ear for music I ever knew; and in less than a twelvemonth could far outdo me, his instructor, in softness and easiness of finger; and was also master of every tune I knew, which were neither inconsiderable in number, nor of the lowest rate.

Youwarkee, with her daughters, sat close to work, and had but just completed her whole design for the family clothing, when she told me she found herself with child again. As that circumstance ill suited a journey, she deferred her flight for about fifteen months; in which time she was brought to bed, and weaned the infant, which was a boy, whom I named Richard, after my good master at the academy. The little knave thrived amain, and was left to my farther nursing during its mammy's absence; who, still firm to her resolution, after she had equipped herself and companions with whatever was necessary to their travelling, and locked up all the apparel she had made till her return, because she would have it appear new when her father came, set out with her son Tommy and my two daughters Patty and Hallycarnie, the last of which by this time being big enough also to be trusted with her mother.

XXV

Youwarkee's account of the stages to Arndrumstake—
The author uneasy at her flight—His employment
in her absence; and preparations for receiving her
father—How he spent the evenings with the children.

My wife was now upon her journey to her father's; but where that was, or how far off, it was impossible for me to conceive by her description of the way; for she distinguished it not by miles or leagues, but by swan-geans, and names of rocks, seas, and mountains, which I could neither comprehend the distance of from each other, nor from Graundevolet, where I was. I understood by her, indeed, there was a great sea to be passed, which would take her up almost a day and night, having the children with her, before she reached the next arkoe, though she could do it herself she said, and strain hard, in a summer's night; but if the children should flag by the way, as there was no resting-place between us and Battringdrigg, the next arkoe, it might be dangerous to them, so she would take the above time for their sakes. After this, I found by what she said there was a narrow sea to pass, and a prodigious mountain, before she reached her own country; and that her father's was but a little beyond that mountain. This was all I could know in general about it. At their departure she and the children had taken each a small provision for their flight, which hung about their necks in a sort of purse.

I cannot say, notwithstanding this journey was taken with my concurrence and consent, that I was perfectly easy when they were gone, for my affection for them all would work up imaginary fears too potent for my reason to dispel, and which at first sat with no easy pressure upon my mind. This my pretty babies at home perceiving, used all the little winning arts they could to divert and keep up my spirits; and from day to day, by taking them abroad with me, and playing with and amusing them at home, I grew more and more persuaded that all would go right with the absent, and that in due time I should see them return again.

But as the winter set in, I went little abroad, and then we employed ourselves within doors in preparing several things which might not only be useful and ornamental, if the old glumm should come to see us, but might also divert us, and make the time pass less tediously. The first thing I went upon was a table, which, as my family consisted of so many, I intended to make big enough for us all. With that view I broke up a couple of chests, and, taking the two sides of one of them, I nailed them edge to edge by strong thick pieces underneath at each end and in the middle; then I took two chest-lids with their hinges, nailing one to each side of my middle piece, which made two good flaps; after this, with my tools, of which I had now a chest-full, I chopped out of new stuff and planed four strong legs quite square, and nailed them strongly to each corner of my middle board; I then nailed pieces from one leg to the other, and nailed the bed likewise to them; then I fastened a border quite round within six inches from the bottom, from foot to foot, which held all fast together. When all this was done, still my table was imperfect; I could not put up the flaps, having no proper support. To remedy this I sawed out a broad slip from a chest-side, and boring a large hole through the centre, I spiked it up to the under-side of the table's bed, with a spindle I contrived just loose enough to play round the head of the spike, filing down that part of the spindle which passed through the bed of the table, and riveting it close; so that when my flaps were set up I pulled the slip crosswise of the table, and when the flaps were down, the slip turned under the top of the table lengthwise: next, under each flap, I nailed a small slip lengthwise of the flaps, to raise them on a level, when up, with the top of the table. When I had thus completed the several parts of this needful utensil, I spent sometime and pains by scraping and rubbing, to render it all as elegant as could be, and the success so well answered my wish, that I was not a little proud of the performance; and what rendered my work thereon a still more agreeable task, was my pretty infants' company, who stood by, expressing their wonder and approbation at every stroke.

Now I had gotten a table, I wanted chairs to it; for as yet we had only sat round the room upon chests, which formed a bench of the whole circumference, they stood so thick. There was no moving of them without a monstrous trouble everytime I might have occasion to set out my table: besides, if I could have dragged them backwards and forwards, they were too low to be commodious for seats; so I resolved to make some chairs and stools also, that might be manageable. I will not trouble you with the steps I took in the formation of these; only, in general, you must know, that some more chests I broke up to that purpose served me for timber, out of which I framed six sizeable handsome chairs, and a competent number of stools.

But now that I was turned joiner, I had another convenience to provide for. I had nothing wherein to enclose things, and preserve them from dust, except the chests, and they were quite unfit for holding liquors, victuals, and such like matters, but open shells, as most of my vessels were. Wherefore, having several boards now remaining of the boxes I had broken up for chairs and stools, I bethought me of supplying this great deficiency; so of these spare boards, in a workmanlike way (for by this time I was become a tolerable mechanic), I composed a very tight closet, holding half-a-dozen broad shelves, shut up by a good pair of doors, with a lock and key to fasten them. These jobs took me up almost three months, and I thought I had not employed them idly, but for the credit and service of my family. I was now again at leisure for farther projects. I was uncertain as to my wife's return, how soon she might be with me, or how much longer she might stay; but I was sure I could do nothing in the meanwhile more grateful than increasing, by all means in my power, the accommodations of my house, for the more polite as well as convenient reception of her father, or any else who might accompany her home in the way of a retinue, as she talked of. I saw plainly I had not room for lodging them, and that was a circumstance of main importance to be provided for. Hereupon I thought of adding a long apartment to one of my outer-rooms, to range against the side of the rock; but reflecting that such a thing would be quite useless, unless I could finish it in time, so as to be complete when my guests came, and not knowing how soon that might be, I resolved to quit this design; and I fell upon another which might do as well, and required much less labour and fewer days to perfect.

I remembered that amongst those things my wife had packed up on board the ship, and which came home through the gulf, there were two of the largest sails, and a couple of a smaller size. These I carried to the wood, and tried them in several places to see where they might be disposed to most advantage in the nature of a tent, and having found a convenient spot to my purpose, I cut divers poles for supporters, and making straining lines of my matweed, I pitched a noble one, sufficient to cover or entertain a numerous company, and so tight everywhere as to keep out the weather. The front of this new apartment I hung with blue cloth, which had a very genteel effect. I had almost forgotten to tell you that I contrived (by hanging one of the smaller sails across, just in the middle, which I could let down or raise up at pleasure) to divide the tent occasionally into two distinct rooms.

ROBERT PALTOCK

When I had proceeded thus far, there were still wanting seats for this additional building, as I may call it, and though I could spare some chests to sit on, I found they would not half do. For a supplement, then, I took my axe and felled a couple of great trees, one from each side of the tent, sawed off the tops, and cut each of the trunks in two about the middle: these huge cylinders I rolled into the tent with a good deal of toil and difficulty; two of them I thrust into the inner division, and left two in the outer. I placed them as benches on both sides, then, with infinite pains, I shaved the upper face of each smooth and flat, and pared off all the little knots and roughnesses of the front, so that they were fitted to sit on, and their own weight fixed them in the place where I intended them to be. At the upper end of the farther chamber I set three chests lengthwise for seats, or any other use I might see fit to put them to.

During these operations we were all hard at it, and no hand idle but Dicky in arms, and Sally, whom he kept in full employ; but Pedro, being a sturdy lad, could drive a nail, and lift or carry the things I wanted, and Jemmy and David, though so young, could pick up the chips, hold a nail or the lamp, or be some way or other useful; for I always preached to them the necessity of earning their bread before they ate it, and not think to live on mine and their brother's labour.

The nights being pretty long, after work was over, and Sarah had fed her brother and laid him in his hammock, we used to sit all down to enjoy ourselves at a good meal, for we were never regular at that till night; and then after supper, my wife being absent, one or other of the young ones would begin with something they had before heard me speak of, by saying, "Daddy, how did you use to do this or that in England?" Then all ears were immediately open to catch my answer, which certainly brought on something else done either there or elsewhere; and by their little questions and my answers they would sometimes draw me into a story of three hours long, till, perhaps, two or three of my audience were falling asleep, and then we all went to bed.

I verily believe my children would, almost any of them, from the frequent repetition of these stories, have given a sufficient account of England to have gained a belief from almost any Englishman of their being natives there.

I frequently observed, that when we had begun upon Cornwall, and traversed the mines, the sea-coast, or talked of the fine gentlemen's seats, and such things, one would start up, and, if the discourse flagged ever so little, would cry, "Ay; but, daddy, what did you do when the crocodile came after you out of the water?" And another, before that subject was half-ended (and I was forced to enter on everyone they started), would be impatient for the story of the lion; and I always took notice that the part each had made the most reflections on, was always most acceptable to the same person: but poor Sally would never let the conversation drop without some account of the muletto, it was such a pretty, gentle creature, she said.

XXVI

My head, as well as my hands, had now been employed for five
months in adjusting all things in the most suitable manner for
the reception of Youwarkee and her friends; but nobody coming, and
light days getting forward apace, I begin to grow very uneasy, and had
formed divers imaginations of what might occasion her stay. Thought
I, I am afraid all the pains I have been taking will be to no purpose; for
either her father will not let her return, or she has of herself come to
such a resolution; for she knows I cannot follow her, and had rather,
perhaps, live and enjoy the three children she has with her, amidst a
number of her friends and acquaintance, than spend the remainder of
her days with me and all our offspring in this solitude.

But then I reflected she chose it herself, or at least declared herself
perfectly satisfied, yea, delighted therewith. And here are her children
with me, the major part of them; yet, what can I think? since her return
is put off till the swangeans are over this arkoe, she will never bring
her relations now in this unseasonable time for flight; therefore I must
think, if she intended to return at all, it would have been before now;
and as the case is not so, my fear of losing her entirely prevails greatly.
Oh! says I, that we had but a post here as we have in England; there
we can communicate our thoughts at a distance to each other without
any trouble, and for little charge! What a country is this to live in! and
what an improper creature am I to live in it! Had I but the graundee,
I would have found her out by this time, be she where she would; but,
whilst everyone about me can pass, repass, and act as they please, I am
fixed here like one of my trees, bound to the spot, or, upon removal, to
die in the attempt. Alas! why did I beget children here, but to make
them as wretched and inconsolable as myself! Some of them are so
formed, indeed, as to shift for themselves; but they owe it to their
mother, not to me. What! am I a father of children who will be bound

one day to curse me? Severe reflection! Yet I never thought of this till now. But am I the only father in such a case? No, surely! for am not I as much bound to curse my father as my children are to curse me? He might have left me happy if he would; I would them if I could. Again, are there not others who, by improper junction with persons diseased in body or vicious in mind, have entailed greater misery upon their posterity than I have on mine! My children are all healthy, strong, and sound, both in body and mind; and is not that the greatest blessing that can be bestowed on our beings? But they are imprisoned in this arkoe! What then? With industry, here is no want; and as they increase they may settle in communities, and be helpful to each other. I have lived here well nigh sixteen years, and it was God's pleasure I should be here; and can I think I was placed here with an injunction contrary to the great command, "Increase and multiply?" If that were so, can it be possible I should have received the only means of propagating, as it were, from Heaven itself? No, it was certainly as much my Maker's will that I should have posterity here, as that I myself should at first be brought thither. This is a large and plentiful spot, and capable of great improvement, when there shall be hands sufficient. How many petty states are less than these my dominions! I have here a compass of near twenty miles round, and how many thousands grow voluntarily grey in a far less circuit?

I had hardly finished my reflections (for I was sitting by myself in my tent upon one of the trees I had turned into benches), when I heard a musical voice call, "Peter! Peter!" I started. "What's this?" says I. "It is not Youwarkee's voice! What can this mean?" Listening, I heard it again, but at so great a distance I could but just perceive the sound. "Be it where it will," says I, "I will face it!" Thus speaking, I went out of the tent, and hearkened very attentively, but could hear nothing. I then ran for my gun, and walked through the wood as fast as I could to the plain; but still I neither saw nor heard anything. I was then in hopes of seeing somebody on the lake, but no one appeared; for I was fully determined to make myself known to whomsoever I should meet; and, if possible, to gain some intelligence of my wife. But after so much fruitless pains, my hopes being at an end, I was returning when I heard, "Peter! Peter!" again at a great distance, the sound coming from a different quarter than at first. Upon this I stopped, and heard it repeated; and it was as if the speaker approached nearer and nearer. Hereupon I stepped out of the wood (for I had just re-entered it upon my return home), when I saw two persons upon the swangean just over my head. I cried out, "Who's that?" And they immediately called again, "Peter! Peter!"—*Ors clam gee*, says I; that is, Here am I.—On this they directly took a small sweep round (for they had overshot me before they heard me) and alighted just by me; when I perceived them to be my wife's countrymen, being dressed like her, with vol. only broader chaplets about their heads, as she had told me the glumms all wore. After a short obeisance, they asked me if I was the glumm Peter, barkett* to Youwarkee. I answered I was. They then told me they came with a message from Pendlehamby, colamb† of Arndrumn-stake, my goppo,‡ and from Youwarkee his daughter. I was vastly rejoiced to see them, and to hear only the name of my wife. But though I longed to know their message, I trembled to think of their mentioning it, as one of them was just going to do, for fear of hearing something very displeasing; so I begged them to go through the wood with me to the grotto, where we should have more leisure and convenience for talk, and where, at the same time, they might take some refreshment. But though I had thus put off their message, I could not forbear inquiring by the way after the health of my goppo, and my wife and children, how they got to Arndrumnstake, and how they found their relations and friends. They told me all were well; and that Youwarkee, as she did on me, desired I would think on her with true affection. I found this was the phrase of the country. As for the rest, I hoped it would turn out well at last, though I dreaded to hear it.

Being arrived at the grotto, I desired my guests to sit down, and take such refreshment as I could prepare them. When they were seated, I went to work in order to provide them a repast. Seeing my fire piled up very high, and burning fierce, and the children about it, they wondered where they were got, and who they had come to, and turned their faces from it; but I setting some chairs, so that the light might not strike on their eyes, they liked the warmth well enough; though, I remarked, the light did not affect them so much as it had done Youwarkee.

Whilst I was cooking, the poor children got all up in a corner, and stared at the strangers, not being able to conceive where they came from; and by degrees crept all backwards into the bedchamber, and hid themselves; for they had never before seen anybody but my own family.

---

* Husband.
† Governor.
‡ Father-in-law.

I observed that one of my guests paid more than ordinary respect to the other; and though their graundees made no distinction between them, yet there was something I thought much more noble in the address and behaviour of the latter; and taking notice that he was also the chief spokesman, I judged it proper to pay my respects to him in a somewhat more distinguishing manner, though so as not to offend the other if I should happen to be mistaken.

I first presented a can of my Madeira, and took care, as if by accident, to give it to Mr. Uppermost, as I thought him, who drank half of it, and would have given the remainder to his companion, but I begged him to drink it all up, and his friend should be served with some presently: he did so, and thanked me by lifting his hand to his chin. I then gave the other a can of the same liquor, which he drank, and returned thanks as his companion had before. I then took a can myself, and telling them I begged leave to use the ceremony of my own country to them, I drank, wishing their own health, and that of all relations at Arndrumnstake. He that I took for the superior fell a-laughing heartily: "Ha, ha, ha!" says he, "this is the very way my sister does everyday at Arndrumnstake."—"Your sister, sir!" says I, "pray has she ever been in Europe or England?"— "Well!" says he, "I have plainly discovered myself, which I did not intend to do yet; but, truly, brother Peter, I mean none other than your own wife Youwarkee."

The moment I knew who he was, I rose up and taking him by the right hand, lifted it to my lips and kissed it. He likewise immediately stood up, and we embraced each other with great tenderness. I then begged him, as I had so worthy and near a relation of my wife's with me, that he would not delay the happiness I hoped for, in a narrative from his mouth, how it fared with my father, wife, and children, and all their kinsfolks and friends whom I had so often heard mentioned by my dearest Youwarkee, and so earnestly desired to see.

My brother Quangrollart (for that, he told me, was his name) was preparing to gratify my impatience; but seeing I had set the entertainment on the table, which consisted chiefly of bread, several sorts of pickles and preserves, with some cold salted fish, he said that eating would but interrupt the thread of his discourse; and therefore, with my leave, he would defer the relating of what I desired for a little while; which we all thinking most proper, I desired him and his friend (who might be another brother for aught I knew) to refresh themselves with the poor modicum I was able to provide them.

ROBERT PALTOCK

Whilst my brother Quangrollart was looking upon and handling his plate, being what he had never before seen, his friend had got the handle of one of the knives in his mouth, biting it with all his force; but finding he could make nothing of that end he tried the other, and got champing the blade. Perceiving what he was at, though I could not help laughing, I rose, and begging pardon, took the knife from him; telling him I believed he was not acquainted with the use of that instrument, which was one of my country implements; and that the design of it, which was called a knife, and of that other (pointing to it), called a fork, was the one to reduce the food into pieces proper for chewing, and the other to convey it to the mouth without daubing the fingers, which must happen in handling the food itself; and I then showed him what use I put them to, by helping each of them therewith to somewhat, and by cutting a piece for myself, and putting it to my mouth with the fork.

They both smiled and looked very well pleased; and then I told them that the plate was the only thing that need be daubed, and when that was taken away the table remained clean. So, after I had helped each of them for the first time, I desired them to help themselves where they liked best; and, to say the truth, they did so more dexterously than I could have expected.

During our repast we had frequent sketches of the observations they made in their flight, and of the places where they had rested; and I could plainly see that neither of them had ever been at this arkoe before, by hinting that if they had not taken such a course they had missed me.

I took particular notice which part of my entertainment they ate most of, that I might bring a fresh supply of that when wanted; and I found that though they eat heartily of my bread and preserves, and tasted almost of everything else, they never once touched the fish; which put me upon desiring I might help them to some. At this they looked upon each other, which I readily knew the meaning of, and excused themselves, expressing great satisfaction in what they had already gotten. I took, however, a piece of fish on my own plate, and eating very heartily thereof, my brother desired me to give him a bit of it; I did so, taking care to cut it as free from bones as I could, and for greater security cautioning him, in case there should be any, to pick them out, and not swallow them. He had no sooner put a piece in his mouth, but, "Rosig," says he to his friend, "this is padsi."—I thought indeed I had puzzled my brother when I gave him the fish, but by what he said of it, he puzzled me; for I knew not what he meant by padsi, my wife having told me they had no fish, or else I should have taken that word for their name of it. However, I cut Rosig a slice; and he agreeing it was padsi, they both ate heartily of it.

While we were at dinner, my brother told me he thought he saw some of my children just now; for his sister had informed him she had five more at home; and he asked me why they did not appear and eat with us. I excused their coming, as fearing they would only be troublesome; and said, "When we had done they should have some victuals." But he would not be put off, and entreated me to admit them. So I called them by their names, and they came, all but Dicky, who was asleep in his hammock. I told them that Reglumm,* pointing to Quangrollart, was their uncle, their mamma's brother, and ordered them to pay their obeisance to him, which they severally did. I then made them salute Rosig. This last would have had them sit down at table; but I positively forbade that; and giving each of them a little of what we had before us, they carried it to the chests and eat it there.

When we had done, the children helped me to clear the table, and were retiring out of the room; but then I recalled them and desired their uncle to excuse their stay, for as he had promised me news of their mammy and her family, it would be the height of pleasure to them to hear him. He seemed very much pleased with this motion, desiring by all means they might be present while he told his story. Whereupon I ordered them to the chests again, while Quangrollart delivered his narrative.

* Gentleman.

XXVII

H aving set on the table some brandy and Madeira, and each of us taken one glass of both, I showed, by the attentiveness of my aspect and posture, how desirous I was he should proceed to what he had promised. Observing this, he went on in the following manner:— "Brother Peter," says he, "my sister Youwarkee, as I don't doubt you will be glad to hear of her first, arrived very safe at Arndrumnstake the third day after she left you, and after a very severe flight to the dear little Hallycarnie,* who was a full day and a night on her graundee; and at last would not have been able to have reached Battringdrigg but for my sister's assistance, who, taking her sometimes on her back for a short flight, by those little refreshments enabled her to perform it: but from Battringdrigg, after some hours' rest, they came with pleasure to the White Mountains, from whence, after a small stay, they arrived at Arndrumnstake.

"They alighted at our covett,† but were opposed at their entrance by the guards, to whom they did not choose to discover themselves, till notice was given to my father; who, upon hearing that some strangers desired admittance to him, sent me to introduce them, if they were proper persons for his presence, or else give orders for such other reception as was suitable to them.

"When I came to the guard, I found three gawrys and a glumm boss,‡ whose appearance and behaviour, I must own, prejudiced me very much in their favour. I then asked from whence they came, and their business with the colamb. Youwarkee told me they came not about business of public concern, relating to the colamb's office, but out of a dutiful regard, as relations, to kiss his knees.—'My father' said I, 'shall know it immediately; but first, pray inform me of your name?'—'Your father!' replied Youwarkee; 'are you my brother Quangrollart?'—'My name is so,' says I, 'but I have only one sister, now with my father, and how I can

---

* One of Wilkins' daughters.
† Capital Seat.
‡ Youth.

be your brother, I am not able to guess.'—'Have you never had another sister?' says she.—'Yes,' says I, 'but she is long since dead; her name was Youwarkee.' At my mentioning her name, she fell upon my neck in tears, crying, 'My dear brother, I am that dead sister Youwarkee, and these with me are some of my children, for I have five more; but, pray, how does my father and sister?'—I started back at this declaration, to view her and the children, fearing it was some gross imposition, not in the least knowing or remembering anything of her face, after so long an absence; but I desired them to walk in, till I told my father.

"The guard observing the several passages between us, were amazed to think who it could be had so familiarly embraced me; especially as they saw I only played a passive part in it.

"When I went in, I did not think proper directly to inform my father what had happened; but calling my sister Hallycarnie, I let her into the circumstances of this odd affair, and desired her advice what to do: 'For,' says I, 'surely this must be some impostor; and as my father has scarce subdued his sorrow for my sister's loss, if this gawry should prove a deceiver, it will only revive his affliction, and may prove at this time extremely dangerous to him: therefore let us consider what had best be done in the matter.'

"Hallycarnie, who had attentively weighed all I said, seemed to think it was some cheat, as well as I did; for we could neither of us conceive that anything but death, or being slit, could have kept Youwarkee so long from the knowledge of her relations; and that neither of them could be the case was plain, if the person attending was Youwarkee. 'Besides, brother,' says Hallycarnie, 'she cannot surely be so much altered in fifteen years, but you must have known her; and yet, now I think, it is possible, you being so much younger, may have forgot her; but whilst we have been talking of her, I have so well recollected her, that I think I could hardly be imposed upon by any deceiver.' "I then desired her to go with me to the strangers and see if she could make any discovery. She did so, and had no sooner entered the abb,* but Youwarkee called out, 'My dear sister Hally-carnie!' and she as readily recollecting Youwarkee, they in transport embraced each other; and then your wife presenting to us her three children, it proved the tenderest scene, except the following, I ever saw.

"My father having kept his chamber sometime with a fever, and though he was pretty well recovered, having not yet been out of it, we

---

* Room.

consulted how we might introduce our sister and children to him, with as little surprise as might be, for fear of a relapse by too great a hurry of his spirits. At length we concluded I should go tell him that some strangers had arrived desiring to see him; but on inquiry, finding their business was too trifling to trouble him upon, I had despatched them; I was then to say how like one of them was to my sister Youwarkee; and whilst I was speaking, Hallycarnie was to enter, and keep up the discourse till we should find a proper opportunity of discovery. I went in, therefore, as had been agreed; and upon mentioning the name of Youwarkee, my father fetched a deep sigh and turned away from me in tears. At that instant Hallycarnie came in as by accident. 'Sir,' says she, 'what makes you so sad? are you worse today?'—'Oh,' says he, 'I have heard a name that will never be out of my heart, till I am in hoximo.'*— 'What, I suppose my sister?'—''Tis true,' replied he, 'the same.'—Says she, 'I fancied so, for I have just seen a stranger as like her as two dorrs† could be, and would have sworn it was she, if that had been possible. I thought my brother had been so imprudent as to mention her to you; and I think he did not do well to rip up an old sore he knew was almost healed, and make it break out afresh.'—'Ah! no, child,' says my father, 'that sore never has, nor can be healed. O Great Image! why can't it by some means or other be ascertained what end she came to?'

"'Sir,' says my sister, 'I think you are much to blame for these exclamations, after so long absence; for, if she be dead, what use are they of? and if she be not, all may be well, and you may still see her again.'—'Oh, never, never!' says my father; 'but could I be sure she was alive, I would take a swangean and never close my graundee till I found her, or dropt dead in the search.'—'And suppose you could meet with her, sir,' says I, 'the very sight would overcome you, and be dangerous.' 'No, believe me, boy,' says he, 'I should then be fully easy and composed; and were she to come in this moment, I should suffer no surprise, but pleasure.'—'No surprise, sir?' says I.—'Not if she were alive and well,' says he.—'Then, sir,' says Hallycarnie, 'will you excuse me if I introduce her?' and went out directly without staying for an answer.

"When she was gone, 'Quangrollart,' says my father sternly, 'what is the meaning of yours and your sister's playing thus upon my weakness? It is what I can upon no account forgive. It looks as if you were weary

---

* A place where the dead are buried.
† A fruit like an apple.

of me, and wanted to break my heart. To what purpose is all this prelude of yours, to introduce to me somebody, who, by her likeness to my daughter, may expose me to your scoff and raillery? This is a disobedience I never expected from either of you.'

"'The Great Image attend me!' says I; 'sir, you have much mistaken me; but I will not leave you in doubt, even till Hallycarnie's return. You shall see Youwarkee with her; for all our discourse, I'll assure you, has but been concerted to prepare you for her reception, with three of her children.' 'And am I then,' says he, in a transport, 'still to be blessed?'— 'You are, sir,' says I, 'assure yourself you are.'

"By this time we heard them coming, but my poor father had not power to go to meet them: and upon Youwarkee's nearer approach, to fall at his knees, his limbs failing him, he sunk, and without speaking a word, fell backwards on a cught drappec,* which stood behind him; and, being quite motionless, we concluded him to be stone-dead. On this the women became entirely helpless, screaming only, and wringing their hands in extravagant postures. But I, having a little more presence of mind, called for the calentar;† who, by holding his nose, pinching his feet, and other applications, in a little time brought him to his senses again.

"You may more easily conceive than I describe, both the confusion we were all in during my father's disorder, and the congratulations upon his recovery; so, as I can give you but a defective account of these, I shall pass them by, and come to our more serious discourse, after my father and your wife had, without speaking a word, wept themselves quite dry on each other's necks.

"My father, then looking upon the three children (who were also crying to see their mamma cry), 'And who are these?' says he.—'These, sir,' says Youwarkee, 'are three of eight of your grandchildren.'—'And where is your barkett?' says he. 'At home with the rest, sir,' replied she, 'who are some of them too small to come so far yet; but, sir,' says she, 'pray excuse my answering you anymore questions, till you are a little recovered from the commotion I perceive my presence has brought upon your spirits; and as rest, the calentar says, will be exceedingly proper, I will retire with my sister till you are better able to bear company.' My father was with much difficulty prevailed with to part with her out of

---

* A bed or couch covered with a sort of cotton.

† A sort of doctor in all great families.

ROBERT PALTOCK

his sight: but the calentar pressing it, we were all dismissed, and he laid down to rest."

My brother would have gone on, but I told him, as it grew near time for repose, and he and Rosig must needs be fatigued with so long a flight, if they pleased (as I had already heard the most valuable part of all he could say, in that my father had received my wife and children so kindly, and that he left them all well) we could defer his farther relation till the next day; which they both agreeing to, I laid them in my own bed, myself sleeping in a spare hammock.

END OF VOLUME I

VOLUME II

I

A DISCOURSE ON LIGHT—QUANGROLLART EXPLAINS THE
WORD CRASHEE—BELIEVES A FOWL IS A FRUIT—GIVES A
FURTHER ACCOUNT OF YOUWARKEE'S RECEPTION BY HER
FATHER, AND BY THE KING—TOMMY AND HALLYCARNIE
PROVIDED FOR AT COURT—YOUWARKEE AND HER FATHER VISIT
THE COLAMBS, AND ARE VISITED—HER RETURN PUT OFF TILL
NEXT WINTER, WHEN HER FATHER IS TO COME WITH HER.

The next day I prepared again of the best of everything for my new guests. I killed three fowls, and ordered Pedro (who was as good a cook almost as myself) to get them ready for boiling, whilst we took a walk to the lake. Though we went out in the clearest part of the morning, I heard no complaint of the light. I took the liberty to ask my brother if the light did not offend him; for I told him my wife could not bear so much without spectacles.—"What is that spectacle?" says he.— "Something I made your sister," says I, "to prevent the inconvenience of too much light upon her eyes."—He said the light was scarce at all troublesome to him, for he had been in much greater, and was used to it; and that the glumms, who travelled much abroad, could bear more light than the gawrys, who stayed much at home: these stirring but little out unless in large companies, and that of one another, and very rarely admitted glumms amongst them before marriage. For his own part, he said, he had an office at Crashdoorpt,* which, though he executed chiefly by a deputy, obliged him to reside there sometimes for a long season together; that being a more luminous country than Arndrumnstake, light was become familiar to him; for it was very observable that some who had been used to it young, though they might in time overcome it, yet at first it was very uneasy.

I was upon the tenter whilst he spoke, lest, before he had done, a question I had a thousand times thought to have asked my wife, should slip out of my head, as it had so often done before, and was what I had for years desired to be resolved in; viz., what the meaning of the word slit was, when applied to a man. So, on his pausing, I said that his mention of Crashdoorpt reminded me of inquiring what crashee meant,

---

* The country of the Slits.

when applied to a glumm or gawry. "It would be no hard task," he said, "to satisfy me in respect of that, as I already understood the nature of the graundee;" whereupon he went on thus: "Slitting is the only punishment we use to incorrigible criminals: our method is, where anyone has committed a very heinous offence, or, which is the same thing, has multiplied the acts of offence, he has a long string tied round his neck, in the manner of a cravat; and then two glumms, one at each end, take it in their hands, standing side by side with him; two more standing before him, and two behind him; all which in that manner take flight, so that the string keeps the criminal in the middle of them: thus they conduct him to Crashdoorpt, which lies farther on the other side of Arndrumnstake than this arkoe does on this side of it, and is just such an arkoe as ours, but much bigger within the rocks. When they come to the covett they alight, where my deputy immediately orders the malefactor to be slit, so that he can never more return to Normnbdsgrsutt, or indeed by any means get out of that arkoe, but must end his days there. The method of slitting is thus: The criminal is laid on his back with his graundee open, and after a recapitulation of his crimes, and his condemnation, the officer with a sharp stone slits the gume* between each of the filuses† of the graundee, so that he can never fly more. But what is still worse to new-comers, if they are not very young, is the light of the place, which is so strong that it is some years before they can overcome it, if ever they do."

This discourse gave me a great pleasure; thereupon I repeated the dialogue that had passed between me and Youwarkee about my being slit, and how we had held an argument a long time, without being able to come at one another's meaning. "But pray, brother," says I, "how comes that light country to agree so well with you?"—"Why," says he, "the colambat‡ of Crashdoorpt is reckoned one of the most honourable employments in the state, by reason of the hazard of it, and the person accepting it must be young: it was, by my father's interest at court, given to me at nine years of age; my friend Rosig has followed my fortune in it ever since, being much about my age, and has a post under me there: in short, by being obliged to be so much there, and from so tender an age too, I have pretty well inured myself to any light."

---

* The membrane.
† Ribs.
‡ Government.

By this time we had got home again to dinner, which Pedro had set out as elegantly as my country could afford, consisting of pickles and preserves, as usual, a dish of hard eggs, and boiled fowls with spinage.

My guests, as I expected, stared at the fowls, but never offered to touch them, or seemed in the least inclined to do so. I was afraid they would be cold, and begged them to let me help them. I put a wing on each of their plates, and a leg on my own; but perceiving they waited to see how I managed it, I stuck in my fork, cut off a slice, dipped it in the salt, and put it in my mouth. Just as I did they did, and appeared very well pleased with the taste. "I never in my life," says Rosig, "saw a crullmott* of this shape before"; and laid hold of a leg (taking it for a stick I had thrust in, as he told me afterwards), intending to pull it out; but finding it grew there, "Mr. Peter," says he, "you have the oddest-shaped crullmotts that ever I saw; pray what part of the woods do they grow in?"—"Grow in?" says I.—"Aye," says he, "I mean whether your crullmott-trees are like ours or not?"—"Why," says I, "these fowls are about my yard and the wood too."—"What!" says he, "is it a running plant like a bott?"†—"No, no," says I, "a bird that I keep tame about my house; and these (showing him the eggs) are the eggs of these birds, and the birds grow from them."—"Pr'ythee," says Quangrollart, "never let's inquire what they are till we have dined; for my brother Peter will give us nothing we need be afraid of."

It growing into the night by that time we rose from table, I set a bowl of punch before them, made with my treacle and sour ram's-horn juice, which they pulled off plentifully. After some bumpers had gone round, I desired my brother to proceed where he left off, in the account of my wife's reception with her father.

"When my father," says he, "had recovered himself by some hours' repose, the first thing he did was to order my sister Youwarkee to be called; who, coming into his presence, he took her from her knees, kissed her, and ordered all to depart but myself and Hallycarnie. Then bidding us sit down, says he to your wife, 'Daughter, your appearance, whom I have so long lamented as dead, has given me the truest cordial I could have received, and I hope will add both to my health and years. I have heard you suspect my anger for some part of your past conduct (for he had hinted so to her sister and me), which you justly enough

---

* A fruit like a melon.
† A gourd.

imagined may be censured; but, my dear life, I am this day, what I did not expect anymore to be, a father of a new-born child; and not of one only, but of many; and this day, I say, daughter, shall not be spent in sorrow and excuses, or anything to interrupt our mutual felicity; neither will I ever hereafter permit you to forget my forgiveness, or attempt to palliate any of your proceedings; for know, child, that a benevolence freely bestowed is better than twice its value obtained by petition: I, therefore, as in presence of the Great Image, your brother and sister, at this instant erase from my mind forever what thoughts I may have had prejudicial to the love I ever bore you, as I will have you to do all such as may cloud the unreserved complacency you used to appear with before me. And now, Quangrollart,' says he, 'let the guard be drawn out before my covett, and let the whole country be entertained for seven days; proclaim liberty to all persons confined; and let not the least sorrow appear in any face throughout my colambat.'

"I retired immediately, and gave the necessary orders for the speedy despatch of my father's commands, which indeed were performed to the utmost; and nothing for seven days was to be heard through the whole district of Arndrumnstake but joy and the name of Youwarkee.

"My father, so soon as he had despatched the above orders, sent for the children before him, whom he kissed and blessed, frequently lifting up his eyes in gratitude to the Great Image for the unexpected happiness he enjoyed on that occasion; and then he ordered Youwarkee to let him know what had befallen her in her absence, and where she lived, and with whom.

"Youwarkee was setting out with some indirect excuses; but my father absolutely forbid her, and charged her only to mention plain facts, without flourishes. So she began with her swangean, and the accidental fall she had, your taking her in after it, and saving her life. She told him your continued kindness so wrought upon her, that she found herself incapable of disesteeming you, but never showed her affection, till, having examined every particular of your life, and finding you a worthy man, she could not avoid becoming your wife; and she said the reasons why she always declined being seen by her friends in their swangeans, was for fear she should be forced from you, though she longed to see us; and that at last she was to come by your consent, and that, had it rested there only, she might have come much sooner, for that you would often have had her show herself to her friends, when you heard them, having strong desires yourself to be known to them.

"My father, upon hearing this, was so charmed with your tenderness and affection to his daughter, that you already rival his own issue in his esteem, and he is persuaded he can never do enough for you or your children.

"The noise of Youwarkee's return, and my father's rejoicing, soon spread over all Normnbdsgrsutt; and King Georigetti sent express to my father, to command him to attend with your wife and children at Brandleguarp, his capital. Thither accordingly we all went with a grand retinue, and stayed twenty days. The king took great delight, as well as the ladies of the court, to hear Youwarkee and her children talk English, and in being informed of you and your way of life; and so fond was Yaccombourse (who, though not the king's wife, is instead of one) of my nephew Tommy, that, upon my father's return, she took him to herself, and assured my sister he should continue near her person till he was qualified for better preferment. The king's sister Jahamel would also have taken Patty into her service; but she begged to be permitted to attend her mother to Arndrumnstake; so Hallycarnie, her sister, who chose to continue with Jahamel, was received in her room.

"Upon my father's return to Arndrumnstake, he found no less than fifteen expresses from several colambs, desiring to rejoice with him on the return of his daughter, with particular invitations to him and her to spend sometime with them. My father, though he hates more pomp than is necessary to support dignity, could do no less than severally visit them, with Youwarkee, attended by a grand retinue, spending more or less days with each; hoping when that was over, he should have some little time to spend in retirement with his daughter before her departure, who now began to be uneasy for you, who, she said, would suffer the greatest concern in her absence: but upon their return from those visits, at about the end of four months' progress, they found themselves in as little likelihood of retirement as the first day; for the inferior colambs were continually posting away, one after another, to perform their respects to my father, and all the inferior magistrates of smaller districts sending to know when they might be permitted to do the same. Poor Youwarkee, who saw no end of it, expressed her concern for you in so lively a manner to my father, that finding he could by no means put a stop to the goodwill of the people, and not bearing the thoughts of Youwarkee's departure till she had now received all their compliments, he resolved to keep her with him till the next winter set in in these parts, and then to accompany her himself to Graundevolet. In the meanwhile, that you might not remain in an uneasy suspense what was become of my sister, he ordered me to despatch messengers express to inform you of the reasons of her stay; but I told him, if he pleased, I would execute that office myself, with my friend Rosig, with which he was very well pleased, and enjoined me to assure you of his affection, and that he himself was debtor to you for the love and kindness you had shown his daughter.

"Thus, brother," says Quangrollart, "I hope I have acquitted myself of my charge to your satisfaction, and it only now remains that I return you my acknowledgments for your hearty welcome to myself and friend; which (with concern I speak it) I am afraid I shall not have an opportunity to return at Arndrumnstake, the distance being so immensely great and you not having the graundee. Tomorrow morning my friend and I will set out on our return home."

Quangrollart having done, I told him I could not but blush at the load of undeserved praises he had laid on me; but as he had received his notion of my merits from a wife too fond to let my character sink for want of her support, it would be sufficient if himself could conceive of, and also represent me at his return, in no worse a light than other men; and though it gave me pain to think of losing my wife so long, yet his account of her health and the company he assured me she would return in, would doubly compensate my loss; and I begged of him, if it might be with any convenience, he would let some messenger come the day before her, to give me notice of their approach. As to their departure on the morrow, I told them I could by no means think of that, as I had proposed to catch them a dinner of fresh fish in the lake, and to show them my boat, and how and where I came into this arkoe, believing, by what I had observed, it would be no small novelty to them. So, having engaged them one day more, we parted for that night to rest.

II

I was heartily sorry to lose my brother thus quickly, and still more so to find it would be a long time yet ere I should see my wife; however, I was resolved to behave as cheerfully as possible, and to omit nothing I could do, the few remaining hours of Quangrollart's stay with me, to rivet myself thoroughly in his esteem, and to dismiss him with a most cordial affection to me and the rest of my children here with him. I rose early in the morning, to provide a good breakfast for my guests, and considering we should be in the air most part of that day, I treated them with a dish of hot fish-soup, and set before them on the table a jovial bottle of brandy and my silver can; this last piece I chose to show them, as a specimen of the richness of my household furniture, and the grandeur of my living, concealing most of my other curiosities till Pendlehamby my father-in-law's arrival, for I thought it would be imprudent not to have somewhat new of this kind to display at his entertainment.

After a plenteous meal, we set out on our pleasurable expedition, having told Pedro what to get for dinner, and that I believed we should not return till late.

We first took a turn in the wood, but I did not lead them near my tent, because I did not choose my wife should hear of that till she came. I then showed them my farmyard and poultry, which they were strangely surprised at, and wondered to see so many creatures come at my call, and run about my legs only upon a whistle, though before there were only two or three to be seen. They asked me a hundred questions about the fowl, which I answered, and told them these were some such as they had eaten, and called crullmotts, the day before. I afterwards carried them to hear the music of those plants that I call my cream-cheese, which, as there happened to be a small breeze stirring, made their usual melody.

When we had diverted ourselves sometime in the wood, we went to the wet-dock, where I showed them my boat. At first view they wondered what use it was for; to satisfy them in that I stepped in, desiring them to follow me; but seeing the boat's agitation, they did not choose to venture till I assured them they might come with the greatest safety; at length, with some persuasion and repeated assurances, I prevailed on them to trust themselves with me.

We first rowed to the bridge, where I informed them by what accident I was drawn down the stream on the other side of the rock, and after a tedious and dangerous passage, discharged safe in the lake through that opening.

I then told them how surprised I had been, just before I knew Youwarkee, with the sight of her country-folks, first on the lake, and then taking flight from that bridge, and what had been my thoughts, and how great my terrors on that occasion.

After we had viewed the bridge, I took them to my rill (for by this time they were reconciled to the boat, and would help me to row it), and showed them how I got water. I then landed them to see the method of fishing, for which purpose I laid my net in proper order, and fixing it as usual, I brought it round out at the rill, and had a very good haul, with which I desired them to help me up; for though I could easily have done it myself, I had a mind to let them have a hand in the sport, with which they were pleased. I perceived, however, the fish were not agreeable to them, for when anyone came near their hands, they avoided touching it: notwithstanding, having got the net on shore, I laid it open; but to see how they stared at the fish, creeping backwards, and then at me and the net, it made me very merry to myself, though I did not care to show it.

I drew up at that draught twenty-two fishes in all, of which a few were near an ell long, several about two feet, and some smaller. When they saw me take up the large ones in my arms, and tumble them into the boat, they both, unrequested, took up the small ones, and put them in likewise; but dropping them everytime they struck their tails, the fish had commonly two or three falls ere they came to the boat.

I asked them how they liked that sport, and they told me, it was somewhat very surprising that I should know just where the fish were, as they could see none before I pulled them up, and yet they did not hear me whistle. I perceived by this they imagined I could whistle the fish together as well as the fowls, and I did not undeceive them, being well enough pleased they should think me excellent for something, as I really thought they were on account of the graundee.

Upon our return, when I had docked my boat, as there were too many fish to carry up by hand to the grotto, I desired them to take a turn upon the shore till I fetched my cart for them. I made what haste I could, and brought one of my guns with me, which I determined, upon some occasion or other, to fire off; for I took it they would be more surprised at the explosion of that than at anything they had yet seen. Having loaded my fish, and marched backwards, they eyed my cart very much, and wondered what made the wheels move about so, taking them for legs it walked upon, till I explained the reason of it, and then they desired to draw it, which they did with great eagerness, one at a time, the other observing its motions.

As we advanced homewards, there came a large water-fowl, about the size of a goose, flying across us. I bid them look at it, which they did. Says my brother, "I wish I had it!"

"If you have a mind for it," says I, "I'll give it you."

"I wish you would," says he, "for I never saw anything like it in my life!"

"Stand still then," says I; and stepping two or three yards before them, I fired, and down it dropped. I then turned about to observe what impression the gun had made on them, and could not help laughing to see them so terrified. Rosig, before I could well look about, had got fifty paces from me, and my brother was lying behind the cart of fish. I called and asked them what was the matter, and desired them to come to me, telling them they should receive no harm, and offered my brother the gun to handle; but he, thanking me as much as if he had, retired to Rosig.

Finding they made a serious affair of it (for I saw them whispering together), I was under some apprehension for the consequences of my frolic. Thinks I, if under this disgust they take flight, refusing to hear me, and report that I was about to murder them, or tell any other pernicious story to my father of me, I am absolutely undone, and shall never see Youwarkee more. So I laid down the gun by the fish, and moving slowly towards them, expostulated with them upon their disorder; assuring them that though the object before them might surprise them, it was but a common instrument in my country, which every boy used to take birds with; and protested to them that the gun of itself could do nothing without my skill directing it, and that they might be sure I should never employ that but to their service. This, and a great deal more, brought us together again; and when we came to reasoning coolly, they blamed me for not giving them notice. Says I, "There was no room for me to explain the operation of the gun to you whilst the bird was on the wing, for it would have been gone out of my reach before I could have made you sensible of that, and so have escaped me; which, as you desired me to get it you, I was resolved it should not do. But for yourselves, surely you could have no diffidence in me; that is highly unbecoming of man to man, especially relations; and, above all, a relation to whom you have brought the welcomest news upon earth, in the love of my dear father, and his reconciliation to my wife."

At last, by degrees, I brought them to confess that it was only a groundless sudden terror which suppressed their reason for a while, but that what I said was all very true; and as their serious reflection returned, they were satisfied of it. I then stepped for the bird, and brought it to them; it was a very fine-feathered creature, and they were very much delighted with the beauty of it, and desired it might be laid upon the cart and carried home.

All the way we went afterwards to the grotto, nothing was to be heard from them but my praises, and what a great and wise man brother Peter was. "And no wonder now, sister Youwarkee," says Quangrollart, "once knowing him, could never leave him." It was not my business to gainsay this, but only to receive it with so much modesty as might serve to heighten their good opinion of me; and I found, upon my wife's return, that Quangrollart had painted me in no mean colours to his father.

I once more had the pleasure of entertaining them with the old fare, and some of the fresh fish, part boiled and part fried, which last they chose before the boiled. We made a very cheerful supper, talking over that day's adventures, and of their ensuing journey home, after which we retired to rest, mutually pleased. We all arose early the next morning. We took a short breakfast, after which Quangrollart and Rosig stuck their chaplets with the longest and most beautiful feathers of the bird I shot, thinking them a fine ornament. Being now ready for departure, they embraced me and the children, and were just taking flight, when it came into my head, that as the king's mistress had taken Tommy into her protection, it might possibly be a means of ingratiating him in her favour if I sent him the flageolet (for I had, in my wife's absence, made two others near as good, by copying exactly after it). I therefore desired to know if one of them would trouble himself with a small piece of wood I very much wanted to convey to my son. Rosig answered, "With

all his heart; if it was not very long he would put it into his colapet."*
So I stepped in, and fetching the flageolet, presented it to Rosig. My
brother seeing it look oddly, with holes in it, desired (after he had asked
if it was not a little gun) to have the handling of it. It was given him,
and he surveyed it very attentively. Being inquisitive into the use of it,
I told him it was a musical instrument, and played several tunes upon
it; with which he and his companion were in raptures. I doubt not they
would have sat a week to hear me if I would have gone on; but I desiring
the latter to take care of its safety, he put it in his colapet, and away
they went.

---

* A bag they always carry round the neck.

III

The news my late visitors had brought me set my mind quite at
ease; and now having leisure to look into my own affairs, with the
summer before me, I began to consider what preparations I must make
against the return of my wife; for, according to the report I had heard,
I concluded there would be a great number of attendants; and as her
father would no doubt pique himself upon the grandeur of his equipage,
if his followers should see nothing in me but a plain dirty fellow, I
should be contemned, and perhaps my wife, through my means, be
slighted, or at least lose that respect the report of me had in a great
measure procured her.

The first thing therefore that I did, was to look into my chests again,
wherein I knew there were many of the Portuguese captain's clothes,
and take out such as would be most suitable to the occasion, and lay
them all by themselves. I found a blue cloth laced coat, double-breasted,
with very large gold buttons, and very broad gold button-holes, lined
with white silk; a pair of black velvet breeches, a large gold-laced hat,
and a point neckcloth with two or three very good shirts, two pair of
red-heeled shoes, a pair of white and another of scarlet silk stockings,
two silver-hilted swords, and several other good things; but upon
examination of these clothes, and by a letter or two I found in the
pockets of some of them, directed to Captain Jeremiah Vauclaile, in
Thread-needle Street, London, I judged these belonged to the English
captain, taken by the Portuguese ship in Africa. I immediately tried
some of them on, and thought they became me very well, and laid all
those in particular chests, to be ready when the time came, and set them
into one of my inner rooms.

Upon examining the contents of another chest, I found a long scarlet
cloak laced, a case of razors, a pair of scissors, and shaving-glass, a long-
wig and two bob-wigs, and laid them by; for I was determined, as I
might possibly have no other opportunity, to make myself appear as
considerable as I could.

When I had digested in my mind upon what occasions I would appear in either of them, and laid them in proper order, Pedro and I went several days to work with the net, and caught abundance of fish, which I salted and dried; and we cut a great quantity of long grass to dry, and spread in my tent for the lower gentry, and made up a little cock of it; we also cut and piled up a large parcel of firewood; and as I had now about thirty of the best fish-skins, each of which would cover four chairs, I nailed them on for cushions to my chairs, and the rest I sewed together, and made rugs of them.

I had observed that my brother Quangrollart, and Rosig, neither of them had beards, and as they were quite smooth-chinned, I conjectured that none of their countrymen had any: So, says I, if that is the case, as I have now both scissors and razors, I will e'en cut off mine, to be like them. I then set up my glass, taking my scissors in hand; but had not quite closed them for a snip, when I considered that as I was not of their country, and was so different from them in other respects, whether it would not add to my dignity to appear with my beard before them. This I debated sometime, and then determined in favour of my beard; but as this question still ran in my mind, and I wavered sometimes this way, sometimes that, I some days after prepared again for execution, and took a large slip off; when, says I, how can I tell whether I can shave after all? I have not tried yet, and if I can't, how much more ridiculous shall I look with stubbed hair here and there, than with this comely beard? I must say, I never in my life had so long a debate with myself, it holding upwards of two months, varying almost everytime I thought of it; till one day, dressing myself in a suit I had not before tried on, and looking in the glass: It can never be, says I, that this grave beard should suit with these fine clothes; no, I will have it off, I am resolved. I had no sooner given another good snip, than spying the cloak, I had a mind to see how I looked in that. Aye, says I, now I see I must either wear this beard or not this cloak. How majestic does it look! So sage, so grave, it denotes wisdom and solidity; and if they already think well of me, don't let me be fool enough to relinquish my claim to that for a gay coat. I had no sooner fixed on this, than I took up all the implements to put again into the chest; and the last of them being the glass, I would have one more look before I parted with it; but my beard made such a horrid, frightful figure, with the three great cuts in it, that though it grieved me to think I must part with it just when I had come to a resolution to preserve it, I fell to work with my scissors, and off it came; and after two or three trials I became very expert with my razor.

Winter coming on, as I knew I must soon have more occasion than ever for a stock of provision, from the increase of mouths I expected, I laid in a stock for a little army; and when the hurry of that was over, I kept a sharp look-out upon the level, in expectation of my company, and had once a mind to have brought my tent thither to entertain them in; but it was too much trouble for the hands I had, so I dropped the design. I took one or other of the children with me everyday, and grew more and more uneasy at hearing nothing of them; and as uncertain attendance naturally breeds thoughtfulness, and the hours in no employ pass so leisurely as in that, my mind presaged numberless intervening accidents that might, if not entirely prevent their coming, at least postpone it.

Thinks I (and that I fixed for my standard), Youwarkee, I am sure, would come if she could; but then, says I, here is a long flight, and to be undertaken by an old man too (for I thought my father-in-law much older than I afterwards found him), who is now quiet and safe at home; and having his daughter with him, is no doubt desirous of continuing so: now, what cares he for my uneasiness? He can find one pretence or other, no doubt, of drilling on the time till the dark weather is over; and then, forsooth, it will be too late to come; and thus shall I be hung up in suspense for another year. Or what if my brother, as he called himself, for he may be no more a brother of mine than the Pope's, for ought I know, came only on a pretence to see how I went on; and not finding, for all his sham compliments to me, his sister married to his father's liking, should advise him not to send my wife back again; and so all the trouble I have had on their account should only prove a standing monument of my foolish credulity! Nay, it is not impossible, but as I have already had one message to inform me Tommy and Hallycarnie are provided for, as much as to say in plain English I shall see them no more, so I may soon have another by some sneaking puppy or other, whom I suppose I am to treat for the news, to tell me my wife and Patty are provided for too, and I am to thank my kind benefactors for taking so great a charge off my hands. Am I? No! I'll first set my tent, clothes, chairs, and all other mementoes of my stupidity on fire, and by perishing, what's left of us, in the blaze, exterminate at once the wretched remains of a deserted family. I hate to be made a fool of!

I had scarce finished my soliloquy, when I heard a monstrous sort of groan or growl in the air, like thunder at a distance. "What's that, Pedro?" says I.—"I never heard the like before, daddy!" says he.—"Look about, boy," says I, "do you see anything?"—We heard it again. "Hark!" says Pedro, "it comes from that end of the lake."—While we were listening to the third sound, says Pedro, "Daddy, yonder is something black upon the rock, I did not see just now."—"Why, it moves," says I, "Pedro; here is news, good or bad."—"Hope the best, daddy," says Pedro; "I wish it may be mammy."—"No," says I, "Pedro, I don't expect her before I hear from her."—"Why, then," says Pedro, "here they come; I can plainly discern three of them. If my brother Tommy should be there, daddy!"—"No," says I, "Pedro, no such good news; they tell me Tommy's provided for, and that's to suffice for the loss of my child: and yet, Pedro, if I could get you settled in England in some good employ, I should consent to that: but what Tommy's to be I know not."

By this time the three persons were so near that, seeing us, they called out "Peter!" and I making signs for them to alight, they settled just before me, and told me that Pendlehamby and Youwarkee would be with me by light next day.

I had no sooner heard this, but so far was I from firing my tent, that I invited them to my grotto, set the best cheer before them, and with overhaste to do more than one thing at once, I even left undone what I might have done.

I asked them who came with my father; and they told me about two hundred guards: that knocked me up again, as I had but prepared for about sixty; thinks I, My scheme is all untwisted. I then asked them what loud noise it was, and if they heard it just before I saw them over the rock. They told me they heard only the gripsack they brought with them to distinguish them from ordinary messengers; and then one of them showed it me, for I had before only taken it for a long staff in his hand: "but," says he, "you will hear them much louder tomorrow, and longer, before they come to you."

Having entertained them to their content, I sent them to rest, not choosing to ask any questions; for I avoided anticipating the pleasure of hearing all the news from Youwarkee herself. However, the boys and I prepared what provisions of fowl and fish we could in the time, to be ready cold against they came, and then laid down ourselves.

IV

My mind ran so all night upon the settling the formality with which I should receive Pendlehamby, that I got little or no rest. In the morning I spread my table in as neat a manner as I could, and having dressed myself, Pedro, Jemmy, and David, we marched to the plain; myself carrying a chair, and each of them a stool. I was dressed in a cinnamon-coloured gold-button coat, scarlet waistcoat, velvet breeches, white silk stockings, the campaign-wig flowing, a gold-laced hat and feather, point cravat, silver sword, and over all my cloak; as for my sons, they had the clothes my wife made before she went.

When we heard them coming, I marshalled the children in the order they were to sit, and charged them to do as they saw me do, but to keep rather a half-pace backwarder than me; and then sitting down in my chair, I ordered Pedro to his stool on my right hand, and Jemmy to his on my left, and David to the left of Jemmy.

I then sent two of the messengers to meet them, with instructions to let Youwarkee know where I waited for them, that they might alight at a small distance before they came to me. This she having communicated to her father, the order ran through the whole corps immediately when and where to alight.

It will be impossible for me by words to raise your ideas adequate to the grandeur of the appearance this body of men made coming over the rock; but as I perceive your curiosity is on the stretch to comprehend it, I shall faintly aim at gratifying you.

After we had heard for sometime a sound as of distant rumbling thunder, or of a thousand bears in consort, serenading in their hoarsest voices, we could just perceive by the clearness of the dawn gilding on the edge of the rock, a black stream arise above the summit of it, seemingly about forty paces broad; when the noise increasing very much the stream arose broader and broader; and then you might perceive rows of poles, with here and there a streamer; and as soon as ever the main body appeared above the rock, there was such a universal shout as rent the air, and echoing from the opposite rock returned the salute to them again. This was succeeded with a most ravishing sound of voices in song, which continued till they came pretty near me; and then the first line, consisting of all the trumpets, mounting a considerable height, and still blowing, left room for the next ranks, about twenty abreast, to come forward beneath them; each of which dividing in the middle, alighted in ranks at about twenty paces distant from my right and left, making a lane before me, at the farther end of which Pendlehamby and his two daughters alighted with about twenty of his guards behind them, the remainder, consisting of about twenty more, coming forward over my head, and alighting behind me; and during this whole ceremony, the gripsacks sounded with such a din, it was astonishing.

Poor Youwarkee, who knew nothing of my dress, or of the loss of my beard, was thunderstruck when she saw me, not being able to observe any visage I had for my great wig and hat; but putting a good face upon the matter, and not doubting but if the person she saw was not me, she should soon find her husband, for she knew the children by their clothes, she came forward at her father's right hand, I sitting as great as a lord, till they came within about thirty paces of my seat; and then gravely rising, I pulled off my hat and made my obeisance, and again at ten steps forwarder; so that I made my third low bow close at the feet of Pendlehamby, the children all doing the same. I then kneeling with one leg, embraced his right knee; who raising me up, embraced me. Then retiring three steps, and coming forward again, I embraced Youwarkee sometime; during which the children observed my pattern with Pendlehamby, who took them up and kissed them.

I whispered Youwarkee to know if anymore of her relations were in the train, to whom I ought to pay my compliments; she told me only her sister Hallycarnie, just behind her father. I then saluted her, and stepping forward to the old gentleman's left hand, I ushered him through the lines of guards to my chair; where I caused him to sit down with Youwarkee and Hallycarnie on each side, and myself on the left of Hallycarnie.

After expressing the great honour done me by Pendlehamby in this visit, I told him I had a little grotto about half a mile through the wood, to which, if he pleased to command, we would retire; for I had only placed that seat to relieve him immediately upon his descent.

Pendlehamby rose, and all the gripsacks sounded, he leading Youwarkee in his right hand, and I Hallycarnie in mine.

At the grotto, my father being seated, taking Youwarkee in my hand, we paid our obedience to him. I would have asked his pardon for taking his daughter to wife without his leave, and was going on in a set speech I had studied for the purpose; but he refused to hear me, telling me I was mistaken, he had consented. I was replying I knew he had been so good as to pass it over, but that would not excuse—when he again interrupted me by saying, "If I approve it and esteem you, what can you desire more!"—So, finding the subject ungrateful, I desisted.

I then gave each of them a silver can of Madeira, and Youwarkee retired. I soon made an excuse to follow her to learn if she was pleased with what I had done. Says she, "My dearest, what is come to you? I will promise you, but for fear of surprising my father, I had disowned you for my husband."—"Dear Youwee," says I, "do you approve my dress, for this is the English fashion?"—"This, Peter," says she, "I perceived attracted all eyes to you, and indeed is very showy, and I approve it in regard to those we are now to please; but you are not to imagine I esteem you more in this than your old jacket; for it is Peter I love in this and all things else; but step in again, I shall only dress, and come to you."

My wife, being dressed in her English gown, just crossed the room where my father sat, to see Dicky, who was in another side-room. I was then sitting by, and talking with him. "Son," says my father, "I understood you had no other woman in this arkoe but my daughter; for surely you have no child so tall as that," pointing to my wife.—"No, sir," said I, "that is a friend."—"Is she come to you," says he, "in my daughter's absence?"—"Oh, sir," says I, "she is very well known to my wife."

Whilst we were talking in comes Youwarkee with the child in her arms, which she kept covered to the wrists with her gown-sleeve, to hide her graundee; and playing with the child, talked only in English to it. "Is this your youngest son?" says my father.—I told him yes.— "Pray, madam," says I, "bring the child to my father."—"Madam," says he, "you have a fine baby in your arms; has his mother seen him since she came home?" He speaking this in his own tongue, and Youwarkee looking at me as if she could not understand him, I interpreted it to her. My sister then desired to see the child, but I was forced again to interpret there too. In short, they both talked with my wife near half an hour, but neither of them knew her; till at last, saying in her own language, "That is your granddaddy, my dear Dicky!" the old gentleman smoked her out.—"I'll be slit," says he, "if that is not Youwarkee!"—"It's impossible!" says Hallycarnie.—"Indeed, sister," says Youwarkee, "you are mistaken!" and my father protesting he had not the least suspicion of her, till she spoke in his tongue, rose and kissing her and the child, desired her to appear in that habit during his stay.

I asked Pedro what provision had been made for the guards: "Son," says my father, "I bring not this number of people to eat you up; they have their subsistence with them," and he would by no means suffer me to allow them any. I then desired to know if there were any officers or others to whom he would have shown any particular marks of distinction.—"Son," says the old glumm, "you seem to have studied punctilios; and though I should be sorry to incommode you for their sakes, if you could procure some shelter and sleep-room for about twenty of them who are superiors, ten at a time, while the rest are on duty, I should be glad." I told him I had purposely erected a tent, which would with great ease accommodate a greater number; and as they were of distinction, with his leave I insisted upon providing for them; to which, with some reluctance, I procured his consent.

When Pendlehamby was refreshed, he would go with me to see the officers' quarters, and showing him my tent, he having never seen such a thing before, was going to climb up the outside of it, taking it for earth. "Hold, sir," said I, "you cannot do so!" Then taking him to the front of it, I turned aside the blue cloth and desired him to walk in; at which he seemed wonderfully pleased, and asked me how it was made. I told him in as few words as I could; but he understood so little of it, that anything else I had said might have done as well. He mightily approved it; and calling the chief officer, I desired he would command my house, and that provision should be supplied to his quarters daily; at which he hesitating, I assured him I had my father's leave for what I offered; whereupon he stroked his chin.

I then asked him if he had any clever fellows under him to serve them, and dress their provisions; but he hoped, he said, they were ready dressed, as his men knew little of that matter; but for any other piece of service, as many as I pleased should be at my command.

The manner of their dinner—Believe the fish
and fowl to be fruits—Hears his brother and the
colambs are coming—Account of their lying—Peter's
reflections on the want of the graundee—They view
the arkoe—Servants harder to please than their
masters—Reason for different dresses the same day.

Pendlehamby having a mind to view my arkoe, took a long walk with Hallycarnie in the wood till dinner-time; and he having before told me that some of his guards always waited on him at meals, I ordered their dinner before his return, sending a large dish of cold fowls, cut into joints, into the tent, to be spread on clean leaves I had laid on the chests; and setting a sufficient quantity of bread and fish there also, I desired the officers present to refresh themselves now, and the rest when relieved should have a fresh supply. I saw there was an oddity in their countenances, which at first I did not comprehend; but presently turning about to the superior, "Sir," says I, "though this food may look unusual to you, it is what my island affords, and you will be better reconciled to it after tasting." So taking a piece of fowl and dipping it in the salt, I ate a bit myself, and recommended another to him; who, eating it, they all fell to without further scruple, above all things commending the salt as what they had never tasted the like of before, though they thought they had both of the fish and fowl.

I then told them where my supply of water came from, and that they must furnish themselves with that by their own men.

Upon the return of my father and sister, the gripsack sounded for dinner; when four officers on duty entering, desired, as their posts, to have the serving up of the dishes. One of them I perceived, having set on the first dish, never stirred from behind Pendlehamby; but upon his least word or sign, ordered the others what to do or bring, which he only presented to my father; and he frequently gave him a piece from his own plate; but the other officers served at the table promiscuously.

After dinner I brought in a bowl of punch; when begging leave to proceed in my country method, I drank to my father's health. "So, daughter," says he to my wife, "we are at the old game again. Son," says he, "this is no novelty to me, Youwarkee constantly drinking to the health of her dear Peter, and the children at Graundevolet, and obliging us to pledge her, as she called it; but I thank you, and will return your civility;" so taking a glass, "son and daughter," says he, "long life, love, and unity attend you and my grandchildren!" Youwarkee and I both rising till he had done, returned him our thanks.

When we had sat sometime, "Son," says my father, "you and your wife having lived so retired, I fear my company and attendants must put you to an inconvenience; now, as my son intends you a visit also, in company with several of my brother colambs, if we shall be too great a load upon you, declare it, for they will be at Battringdrigg arkoe tomorrow, to know whether it will be agreeable for them to proceed.

"You know, son," says my father, "the mouth is a great devourer, and that the stock your family cannot consume in a year, by multiplying their numbers, may be reduced in a day: now freely let me know (for you say you provided for us) how your stock stands, that you may not only pleasure us, but we not injure you."

I told him, as for dried fish I had a vast quantity, and that my fowls were so numerous I knew not my stock; as to bread, I had a great deal, and might have almost what more I would; and then for fresh fish, the whole province of Arndrumnstake could not soon devour them; but for my pickles and preserves, I had neither such large quantities, nor conveniences to bestow them if I had.

"If this be the case, son," says my father, "I may send your brother word to proceed;" and despatched ten messengers with a gripsack to hasten his son's arrival.

It now began to be time for rest, and the old gentleman growing pretty mellow with the punch, which, by the heavy pulls he took at it, I perceived was no disagreeable entertainment to him, I conducted him to his repose; and disposing of the rest of the family, Youwarkee and I, with great impatience, retired.

You may imagine I was sincerely glad to find myself once more alone with my Youwarkee; when, after a transport of mutual endearments, I desired to know how Pendlehamby first received her; which she told me, with every circumstance, in so affecting a manner that the tears forced passage from mine eyes in perfect streams; and I loved the dear man ever after as my own father.

She told me Tommy was in great favour at court before her brother returned from me; but ever since I sent him the flageolet he had been caressed above measure, and would soon be a great man; that Hallycarnie was a constant attendant on Jahamel both in her diversions and retirement; and, she did not doubt, would in time marry very well; as for Patty, she said her father intended, with my leave, to adopt her as his own child.

My wife slept very sound after her journey; but my hurry of spirits denying me that refreshment, I never so much as now lamented the want of the graundee.—"For," thinks I, "now I have once again tasted the sweets of society, how shall I ever relish a total desertion of it, which in a few days must be the case, when all this company are fled, and myself am reduced to my old jacket and water-cart again! Now, if I was as others here are, I might make a better figure than they by my superior knowledge of things, and have the world my own; nay, I would fly to my own country, or to someother part of the world, where even the strangeness of my appearance would procure me a good subsistence. But," says I, "if with my graundee I should lose my sight, or only be able to live in the dark in England, why, I should be full as bad as I am here! for nobody would be able to keep me company abroad, as my hours for the air would be theirs of retirement; and then, at home, it would be much the same; no one would prefer my company in a dark room in the daytime, when they could enjoy others in the light of the sun; then how should I be the better for the graundee, unless I fixed a resolution of living here, or hereabouts? and then to get into company, I must retire to still darker regions, which my eyes are no ways adapted to: in short, I must be quite new moulded, new made, and new born too, before I can attain my desires. Therefore, Peter," says I, "be content; you have been happy here in your wife and children without these things; then never make yourself so wretched as to hope for a change which can never possibly happen, and which, perhaps, if obtained, might undo you; but intend only what you can compass, by weighing all circumstances, and your felicity will lie in very narrow bounds, free from two of the greatest evils a man can be beset by, hopes and fears; two inseparable companions, and deadly enemies to peace; for a man is destroyed by hope through fear of disappointment."—This brought me a show of peace again.—"Surely," says I, "I am one of the most unaccountable amongst mankind! I never can reflect till I am worn down with vexation. O Glanlepze! Glanlepze!" says I, "I shall never forget thy speech after engaging the crocodile, that everything was to be attained by resolution by him that takes both ends of a thing in his view at once, and fairly deliberates what may be given and taken from end to end. Surely," says I, "this ought to be engraven on brass, as I wish it was on my heart; it would prevent me many painful hours, help me with more ease to compass attainable ends, and to rest contented under difficulties insuperable: and if I live to rise again, I will place it where it shall never be more out of my sight, and will enforce it not only more and more on myself, but on my children."

With this thought I dropped to sleep, and with this I awaked again, and the first thing I did was to find a proper place to write it, which, having fixed for the door of my cupboard, I took a burnt stick for my pencil, and wrote as follows:—"He that is resolved to overcome, must have both ends of an object in view at once, and fairly deliberate what may be given and taken from end to end; and then pursue the dictates of cool reason." This I wrote in English, and then in the Doorpt Swangeantine tongue; and having read it twice or thrice over, I went for water and fish, and returned before the family were up.

I took care today also that the officers should be as well served as possible, and where an accommodation must be wanting, I rather chose to let it fall on my father than on them; for I had ever observed it to be an easier thing to satisfy the master than the man; as the master weighs circumstances, and from a natural complacency in himself, puts a humane construction upon that error or omission which the servant wholly attributes to slight and neglect.

My company being abroad, about the time I expected their return I dressed myself as the day before, only without my cloak, and in a black bob-wig, and took a turn to meet them.

Pendlehamby spying me first among the trees, "Daughter Youwarkee," says he, "you have a husband, I think, for everyday in the week. Who's this? my son Peter! Why, he is not the same man he was yesterday." She told him she had heard me say we changed our apparel almost everyday in England; nay, sometimes twice or thrice the same day.—"What!" says Pendlehamby, "are they so mischievous there they are fearful of being known in the latter by those who saw them in the former part of the day?"

By this time I was come up, and after paying due compliments, says Youwarkee—"My father did not know you, my dear, you are so altered in your other wig; and I told him in your country they not only change wigs, but their whole clothing, two or three times a day sometimes."— "Son," says my father, "if it be so, I cannot guess at the design of a man's making himself unlike himself."—"Oh, sir," says I, "it is owing to the different functions he is to perform that day: as, suppose, in the morning he is to pursue business with his inferiors, or meet at our coffee-houses to hear and chat over the news of the day, he appears in a light easy habit proper for despatch, and comes home dirty; then, perhaps, he is to dine with a friend at mid-day, before whom, for respect's sake, not choosing to be seen in his dirty dress, he puts on something handsomer; and after spending sometime there, he has, it may be, an appointment at court, at play, or with his mistress, in all which last cases, if he has anything better than ordinary, it is a part of good breeding to appear in that; but if the very best was to be used in common, it might soon become the worst, and not fit for a nice man to stir abroad in."—"The different custom of countries you have told me of," says my father, "is surprising: here are we born with our clothes on, which always fit, be we ever so small or large; nay, are never the worse for constant wearing; and you must be eternally altering and changing colour, shape, and habit. But," says he, "where do they get all these things? Does every man make just what he likes?"—"No," says I, "there are a particular set of men whose business it is to make for all the rest."—"What!" says he, "I suppose their lasks make them?"—"No, sir, they are filgays," says I. "It is their trade, they do it for a livelihood, being paid by them they work for. A suit of their clothes," says I, taking up the flap of my coat, "will cost what we call twelve or fourteen pounds in money."—"I don't understand you," says he.—"Why, sir," says I, "that is as much as will provide one moderate man with all the necessary things of life for two months."—"Then," says he, "these nice men must be very rich."—"No, sir," said I, "there you are under a mistake; for if a man, very rich, and who is known to be so, neglects his habit, it is taken to be his choice; but one who is not known to be rich, and is really not so, is, by appearing gay sometimes, thought to be so; for he comes little abroad, and pinches miserably at home, first to get that gay suit, and then acts on the same part to preserve it, till some lucky hit may help him to the means of getting another, as it frequently happens, by a good marriage; for though he is but seldom seen in public, yet always appearing so fine when he is, the ladies, whose fancies are frequently more tickled with show than sense, admitting him only at first as a companion, are at last, if worth anything, taken in the toils he is ever spreading for them; and, becoming his wife, produce a standing fund to make him a rich man in reality, which he but personated before."

ROBERT PALTOCK

Pendlehamby could not well understand all I said; and I found by him that all the riches they possessed were only food and slaves; and as I found afterwards when amongst them, they know the want of nothing else; but I am afraid I have put them upon another way of thinking, though I aimed at what we call civilising of them.

VI

Quangrollart arrives with the colambs—Straitened
for accommodation—Remove to the tent—Youwarkee
not known—Peter relates paid of his travels—Dispute
about the beast-fish skins.

Sleeping longer than usual, I was awakened next morning by a
gripsack from Quangrollart; upon hearing of which I roused
immediately, thinking they were at my door; but the messenger told me
they could not be there in what I understood by his signs to be about
two hours, for they have no such measure for time as hours; so I dressed
at leisure, and then went to Youwarkee and waked her. "Youwee," says
I, "your brother will be here presently, and I having a mind you should
appear as my countrywoman, would have you dress yourself."

We walked down to the level, and but just saved our distance; for the
van of them were within the arkoe before we arrived, and with such a
train after them as seemed to reach the whole length of the arkoe. The
regularity and order of their flight was admirable, and the break of the
trumpets so great, sounding all the way they came (for we had not only
one set of them, but at least thirty, there being so many colambs and
petty princes in the train, each with fifty attendants), that I wondered
how they could bear it. As the principals alighted, which was at least a
hundred paces from me, the gripsacks still kept wing, sounding as long
as we stayed.

This was a very tedious ceremony, for the guards alighting with their
colambs, ranged just as Pendlehamby's had done, but reached as far as
the eye could see. As they moved towards us, Youwarkee and I, having
stood still sometime, moved slowly forward to meet them.

It would have surprised you to have seen the deference they paid us;
and I believe the guards took us for something above the mortal race.
Youwarkee showed no part of her graundee, having on sleeves down to
her wrists, white silk stockings and red-heeled shoes; so that none of
them knew her for one of them.

The first that we met was my brother, to whom we had only an
opportunity of paying our compliments *en passant* before another
graundee came up, who was succeeded by another and another, to the
number of thirty; some out of respect to my father and brother, and

some out of mere curiosity to see me; and as fast as each had paid his salutes, he passed us, till we found we had no more to meet, when we turned about, and fell in with the company.

When we came to the grotto, I was very much put to it for room, we scarce being able to stand upright by each other, much less to sit down; which my father perceiving, "My dear friends," says he, "had my son known in time of so much good company, he would have been better provided with seats for us all; but considering all we see is the labour only of his own hands, we should rather admire at the many conveniences we see here, than be uneasy there are no more. And, son," says he, "as we are now so large a body, I propose we adjourn to the officers' quarters and let them take ours." I returned my father thanks for the hint, and led the way, the rest following, where we found room enough and to spare.

Though Youwarkee was with us all dinner-time helping the guests, we had no sooner done, "But," says Quangrollart aloud, "Brother Peter, are we not to see my sister?" I not hearing perfectly what he said, though I perceived he spoke to me, "Sir," says I.—"My sister Youwarkee!" says he, "why won't she appear? Here are several of her good friends as well as myself will be glad to see her." My father then laughed so heartily that the rest taking notice of it, my poor brother was put to the blush. "Son," says my father, "don't you know your own sister?"—"We have not seen her yet," says one of the colambs, "or any lady but your daughter Hallycarnie and that attendant." My brother then seeing how it was came up to salute my wife; but even then had his scruples, till he saw her smile, and then begged pardon for his oversight, as did all the colambs upon saluting her; my brother declaring that, as she was somewhat behind me on the level, he had only paid her the respect of his chin, taking her for someone attending me. The colamb following my brother, assured her the little regard shown her by Quangrollart, who, he thought, should know best where to bestow his respects, was the reason of his taking no more notice of her; and each confessing his mistake arose from too nearly copying the steps of his immediate predecessor, they all made excuse, and the mistake made us very merry, till they proposed taking a turn in the woods, it being a great novelty to them, they said; but I begged they would leave me behind to prepare for their return.

Having refreshed themselves after they came home, Quangrollart (being put upon it by some of the colambs) told me I could not render a more acceptable favour to the whole company than to relate to them an account of my adventures; "for though," says he, "I told them last night what I remembered to have heard from you, yet the variety was so great I could not deliver the facts in order as I heard them, but was obliged to take here a piece and there another, as they occurred to me, making rather several stories of it than a continued series of facts."

All the colambs immediately seconded the motion, and desired me to begin. I then ordering a clear table and a bowl of punch, and having drank all the company's healths, began my narration, hoping to have finished it before bedtime; but they pressing me to be very particular, and frequently one or other requiring explanations upon particular facts, and then one making a remark upon something which another answered, and a third replied to, they got the talk out of my hands so long that, having lost themselves in the argument, and forgot what I said last, they begged my pardon and desired me to go on; when one, who in contemplation of one fact had lost best part of another, prayed me to go on from such an incident, and another from one before that; so that I was frequently obliged to begin half-way back again. This method not only spun out my story to a very great length, but instead of its being finished that evening, as I had proposed, it was scarce well begun before bedtime drew on; so I just having brought them to Angola, told them, as it grew late, if they pleased, I would finish the remainder next night, which they agreed to.

Quangrollart then asked my father if he had been fishing since he came; but he told him he knew not what he meant. Then all the company desired I would show them what that was. I told them they might command me as they pleased; so we appointed the next morning for that exercise. "But, gentlemen," says I, "your lodging tonight gives me the greatest pain; for I know not what I shall do about that. I have a few beast-fish skins which are very soft and hairy, but not a sufficiency for so many friends as I would at present be proud to oblige; but I can lay them as far as they will go upon as much dry reeds and grass as you please." I then sent a servant to Youwarkee for the skins; after which, they one and all crying out if they had but good dry reeds they desired no better lodging, I despatched hands to bring away a large parcel of them to the tent, which they did in a trice. Then waiting on those few who lay at the grotto to their quarters, and having sent Youwarkee to her sister, I returned to the tent to take up my own lodging with those I had left there.

I had not yet entered the tent when I heard a perfect tumult within, everyone talking so loud, and all together, that I verily thought they had fallen out and were going to handicuffs. However, I resolved to go in amongst them and try to compose their difference; when just entering, and they spying me, several ran to me with each a skin in his hand, the rest following as fast as they could. "Gentlemen," says I, "I hoped to have found you all at rest."—"So we should have been," says one of them, "but for these what you call 'ems."—"It is my unspeakable misfortune," says I, "that I have no more at your service, and am sorry that I should cause them to be brought, since each of you cannot have one." Says one of them, "I don't want one, I have seen enough of it."— "Then, gentlemen," says I, "it is possible there may be so many more of that colamb's mind that there may be sufficient for those who desire them." They neither knew what to make of me nor I of them all this while; till an old colamb perceiving our mistake, "Mr. Peter," says he, "we have only had a dispute."—"I am sorry at my heart for it," says I, "but I perceived you were very warm before I entered, and am in great hopes of compromising matters to all your satisfactions."—"I was going," says the same colamb, "to tell you we had a dispute about what these things were, nothing else." I was then struck on a heap, being quite ashamed they should think I suspected they had been quarrelling for the skins; and how to come off I knew not. "You'll excuse me, sir," says I, "for expressing a concern that you could not each have one to examine into at the same time, that one of you need not have waited to make your remarks till the other had done."—"No occasion, no occasion for that, Mr. Peter," said they all together; "we shall have leisure enough to examine them tomorrow; but we want to know what they are, and where they grow."—"Gentlemen," says I, "each of these is the clothing of a particular fish. And where do they grow?" said they. "In the lake," says I; "they are a living creature, who inhabit that great water; I often catch them when I am fishing, the same exercise we shall go upon tomorrow."

I had much ado to persuade them they did not grow on trees, which I was then much more surprised at than sometime after, that I returned their visit; but having satisfied them, and given them some possible hopes they might see one alive next day, they were very well contented, and we all lay down to rest.

VII

Go a-fishing—Catch a beast-fish—Afraid of the gun—How Peter altered his net—Fish dinner for the guards—Method of dressing and eating it.

I appeared before them in the morning, in my old jacket, and an old hat with brims indented almost to the crown, a flannel nightcap, and chequered shirt. "How now, son!" says my father, "what have we here?"—"Sir," says I, "this will show you the use of our English fashion I mentioned the other day, and the necessity of it. You see me in this indifferent habit, because my next business requires it; but when I come back, and have no further dirty work to do, I shall then dress, as near as I can, to qualify me for your company."

"Are you for moving, gentlemen?" says my brother; "I believe it is time." They then all arising we went to the lake, where getting into my boat, and telling them that any six of them might go with me, they never having seen such a thing before, and not much liking the looks of it, all made excuses, till my brother assuring them it was very safe, and that he had sailed in it the last trip, three or four of them, with my father, and Hallycarnie, who was very desirous of seeing me fish, got in, and we sailed a great way up the lake, taking my gun as usual with me.

It gave me exceeding delight to see the whole body of people then in the arkoe on the graundee; some hovering over our heads, and talking with us; others flying this way, others that, till I had pitched upon a spot to begin my operation; when rowing to shore, and quitting my boat, the whole body of people settled just by me, staring at me and my net, and wondering what I was doing. I then taking a sweep as usual, got some of the soldiers to assist me to shore with it; but when the cod of the net landed, and the fish began to dash with their tails at the water's edge, away ran all my soldiers, frighted out of their wits to think what was coming: but it being a large hale, and a shelving bank, I could not lift it to the level myself; which my brother, who had seen the sport before, perceiving, though not one of the rest stirred, lent me a hand, and we got it up.

You cannot imagine what surprise appeared in every face upon opening the net, and seeing all the fish naked. They drew up by degrees closer and closer, for I let the fish lie sometime for their observation;

ROBERT PALTOCK

but seeing the large fish, upon my handling them, flap their tails, they very expeditiously retired again. I then tossed several of them into the boat; but two of them being very large, and rough-scaled ugly fish, I did not think I could lift them myself, so desired assistance, but nobody stirred. I expected some of the colambs would have ordered their men to have helped me, but they were so terrified with seeing me handle them, that they could not have the conscience to order their men on so severe a duty, till a common man came to me, and taking the tail, and I the head, we tossed them both into the boat.

I went higher up the lake than usual, in hopes of a beast-fish to show them; but though I could not meet with one, I had several very great hauls, and took three or four of my lobsters, very large ones. This was the second trial I had made of my net since I had altered it, and it gave me great satisfaction, for I could now take as many fish at one draught as I could before have done at ten. I had found that though my net was very long, yet for want of a bag, or cod, to enclose the fish, many that were included within its compass would, whilst I drew round, swim to the extremes, and so get out, for want of some inlet to enter at; for which reason I sawed off the top of a tree at about ten feet from the ground, and drawing a circle of six feet diameter round the tree, on the ground, I stuck it round with small pegs, at two inches' distance. Then I drove the like number of nails round the top of the trunk of the tree, and straining a length of mat-line from each peg on the ground to a correspondent nail on the tree, I tied my matline in circles round the strained lines, from top to bottom, about two inches' distance at the bottom, but at a less distance where the strained lines grew nearer to each other towards the top; and having secured all the ends, by some line twisted round them, I cut a hole in the middle of my net, and tied the large ground-end over the hole in the net, and gathered the small end up in a purse, tying it up tight; and by this means I now scarce lost any fish which once were within the sweep of my net.

Having had so good success, I had a design of returning, but thought, as I could now so easily entertain a multitude, I might as well take another haul or two, and make a handsome treat for the soldiery. Then coming up to my drill's mouth, I fixed my implements for a draught there, and beginning to draw up, I found great resistance in the net, and got two or three to help me; but, coming near shore, when the company saw the net tumble and roll, and rise and fall, they all ran as if they were mad, till I called them and told the colambs it was only one of the fish whose skins I had shown them; upon which, by that time I had discharged the fish from the net, they were all round me again; but no sooner had he got loose, than up he rose, whirled his wings, and at the same instant uttered such a groan that my whole company retreated again, thinking me somewhat more than a man, who could face so dreadful an enemy. I entreated them to come and view it; but finding no arguments could bring them nearer, I edged round till I got him between me and the water, and shot him dead.

Upon the report of my gun the whole field was in the air, darting and screaming, as I have often seen a flight of rooks do on the same occasion; and I am apt to believe some of them never returned again, but went directly home.

I was a little concerned to see the confusion I had caused; and laying down my gun, my brother, who though at a distance when I shot, knowing what I was at, and coming up to me, it put the rest upon their consideration; and they alighted one by one, at a distance, till they were all on the level again.

My father and the colambs, who were the first that durst approach, wondered what I had done, and how the fish came to be dead, and whence so much fire and smoke proceeded, for they were sure I brought none with me, and asked me abundance of questions; but as I knew I must have occasion for answering to the same thing twenty times over, had I entered upon an explanation there, I deferred giving them satisfaction till we came home, when all at once might be capable of hearing what was said. So I told them the most necessary thing at present was to stow the fish in the boat; for it was the largest I had ever taken, and I could not wholly do it myself. I made several efforts for help, but in vain, till the same soldier who had helped me with one of the first fish, came to my relief, and desiring my orders what to do, assisted me; and the rest seeing the difficulty we both had to manage it, one or two more of them came up, and we shipped it on board.

I then called the colambs to me, telling them I was sorry I had given such a general disturbance to them, by shooting the fish; but as they kept at too great a distance from me to have notice of my design, and if I had followed them the fish might have escaped before my return, I was obliged to do as I did, which was without any possibility of hurting them. But, as I had given them such a fright, I hoped they would this one day give me an opportunity of complimenting their guards with a fish-dinner, if we could anyway contrive to dress it; for whoever did that must be able to bear the close light of a large fire. They all shook their heads but my brother, who told me he had in his retinue six men from Mount Alkoe, purposely retained for their strong sight, to attend him always to Crashdoorpt, who, he believed, for the benefit of the rest, would undertake the cookery if I would show them how. I desired he would give them orders to attend me on the other side of the lake, and I would instruct them at my landing; and then I crossed over with my booty.

Finding the Mount Alkoe men waiting for my landing, I asked if they could bear the sight of fire. They told me they were used to much greater light and flames than I had ever seen, they believed.—"Very good," said I; "then get into my boat, three of you, and hand out that fish to the shore."—I found they were more afraid of the fish than of the fire, for not one of them stirred till I got in and tossed out several small ones; and then taking up a large one, "Help me, somebody!" says I, they looking a little at one another, till one of them venturing to take it, the rest fell heartily to work, and despatched the whole lading presently. I then laid a small parcel upon my cart, for our own eating and the officers', and sending them to the grotto, I gave the cooks their charge.

"Now," says I, "my lads, do you serve all the rest of the fish as I do this," cutting it open at the same time, and throwing away the guts, "and I will send each of you such an instrument as I use here," pointing to my knife. "I shall order six large heaps of wood to the level, to be piled up there. When you have done the fish, do you set fire to the heaps, and let them burn till the flame is over and the coals are clear; then lay on your fish, and if any are too large to be manageable, cut them in proper pieces, and with sticks, which I will send you, turn them over and over, walking round the fire, and with the forked end of the stick toss the least off first, and afterwards the greater; but be sure throw the fish as far as ever you can from the fire, amongst the men, that they may not be obliged to come too near it: and in this manner go on, till either they have enough, or your fish are gone; and when you have done, come to the grotto for your reward."

I then set abundance of hands to work to carry wood, to be laid in six heaps, two hundred paces from each other, and told them how to pile it. I then prepared six long taper sticks with forked ends, and ordered more hands to divide the fish equally to the piles. I sent others with salt and bread; and I ordered them to let me know when all was ready.

While these preparations were making, my tent-visitors had all dined, and my cart had returned with the beast-fish, which the company desired might be brought in, when everyone passed his judgment upon it, and a long dissertation we had on the marvellous works of Collwar. I let them go on with their show, though I could have disproved most of their conclusions from the little knowledge I had of things; but I never was knight-errant enough to oppose my sentiments to a multitude already prepossessed on the other side of the question; for this reason, because I have ever observed that where several have imbibed the same ridiculous principle in infancy, they never want arguments, though ever so ridiculous, to support it; and as no one of them can desert it without impeaching the judgment of the rest, they encourage each other in their obstinacy, and quite out-vote a single person; and then, the laugh beginning on the strongest side, nothing is so difficult as to get it out of their hands. But when a single man in the wrong hears a just argument from a single antagonist which he cannot contradict, he imbibes its force, and whilst that lasts, as nothing but a better argument, with better reasons, can remove it, he from thenceforth adapts his adversary's reasons for his own, to oppose against his own former opinion.

In the height of our disputations on the beast-fish, came news that the broil was going to begin; and as I expected very good diversion at it, I invited the company to go see it, telling them, in my opinion, it would exceed the sport in taking them. We passed through the wood till we came amongst the shrubs, where I placed them to be out of harm's way; and the fire, which was now nothing but cinders, was of no inconvenience to them. They were pleased with it to perfection; for, first, the six men who walked round the fires, by the glowing light of the embers and the shining of their graundees, looked like men on fire; then, to see each fire surrounded with a circle of men at the diameter of near two hundred paces, as close as they could well stand, by a more distant shine of the fire, had a very pleasing effect; but when the broilers began to throw the fish about (for each man stood with some salt and a cut of bread in his hand), to see a body of a hundred men running for it, and whilst they were stooping and scrambling for that, to see a hot fish fall on the back of one, which was whipped off by another, who, scalding his mouth with it, threw it in the face of a third; when a fourth, fifth, and sixth, pulling it in pieces, ran away with it; and to see the different postures, courses, and groups, during this exercise and running feast, was the most agreeable farce my guests had ever seen in their lives; and, to the great saving of my liquors, kept us in the wood for full three hours, not a soul stirring till the feast was over.

We spent best part of this evening in discourse on the passages of the day, the reflections on which not being concluded till bedtime, my adventures were postponed till the next night; but we had first concluded upon a shooting for the next morning (for they were all extremely desirous of knowing how I did it), at a time they should have opportunity of seeing me and making remarks; and I, being unwilling they should think me a conjuror, agreed to make them masters of part of the mystery of powder and ball.

VIII

This being the fifth morning, I cleaned up my best gun, and prepared my balls, and we all took a walk towards the bridge, everyone admiring my gun as we went; but I could get none of them to carry it, and we had at least five hundred questions proposed about it. I told them they need not be afraid of it, for it was only wood and iron; but they knew nothing of iron. I then showed them how I made it give fire, by snapping the cock; they thought it was very strange. I then put a little powder in the pan, and made it flash, and showing them the empty pan, they would not be persuaded but I had taken away the powder before the flash, or else, they said, it was impossible that should be all gone upon flashing only; for they said it was a little nut, using the same word to express both nut and seed. I then desired one of them to put in some powder and snap it himself; but having prevailed with him to try the experiment, if I had not through caution held my hand upon the barrel, the gun had been on the ground, for the moment it flashed, he let go and ran for it.

I had a great inclination to gain the better of their prejudices, and used abundance of arguments to prove the gun as innocent a thing as a twig I took up; and that it was the powder which, when set on fire, the flame thereof wanting more room than the powder itself did, forced itself, and all that opposed it, out of the mouth of the gun with such fury as to make the noise they heard; and being just come to the rock, "Now," says I, "you shall see that what I tell you is true." They told me they desired nothing more than that I would make them understand it, for it was the strangest thing they had ever seen. "Well, then," says I, "observe; I put in this much powder only, and with this rag I stop it down close. Now," says I, "you see by the length of this stick that the rag and powder take up the space only of a finger's depth on the inside of the gun." They saw that plainly they said; "But how could that kill anything?"—"Now, look again," says I, "I put in a little more powder, as I did before when I made a flash, and you see there is a little hole from this powder through the side of the gun to the powder within. Do you observe that this communicates with that through this hole?"—"Yes," said they, they did.—"Now," says I, "when I put fire to this, it sets fire to that within, which fire turning to flame, and wanting room, bursts out at the mouth of the gun; and to show you with what force it comes out, here handle this round ball," giving them a bullet to handle; "you feel how heavy it is: now, can any of you throw this ball as far as that rock?" for I stood a good hundred paces from it.—They told me No.—"And don't you think," says I, "that if the force of the fire made by this powder can throw this ball to that rock, that force must be very great?"—They said, they thought it must, but believed it to be impossible.—"But," says I, "if it not only throws it to the rock but beats out a piece of the stone, must not that be much more violent?" They agreed it must.—Then putting in the ball, "Now," says I, "we will try." I then ordered one to daub a part of the rock, about breast high, with some mud, and first to observe about it if the rock was anywhere fresh broken, or not; who, returning, reported that the rock was all of a colour and sound, but somewhat ragged all about the mud.—"Did you lay the mud on smooth?" says I. He replied, "Yes."—Then lifting up my gun, I perceived they were creeping off; so I took it down again, and calling, reasoned with them upon their fears. "What mischief," says I, "can you apprehend from this gun in my hand! Should I be able to hurt you with it, are you not all my friends or relations—could I be willing to do it? If the gun of itself could hurt, would I handle it as I do? For shame! be more courageous; rouse your reason, and stand by me; I shall take care not to hurt you. It looks as if you mistrust my love to you, for this gun can do nothing but what I direct it to." By such like persuasions, rough and smooth, I prevailed upon the major part of the colambs and officers to stand near me to see me fire, and then I shot; but though my words had engaged them to stand it, I had no sooner snapped but the graundees flew all open, though they closed again immediately; and then we fell to question and answer again. I desired them to walk to the rock; and sent the person who put up the mark before, to see and show us exactly what alteration there was. He told us there was a round hole in the mud, pointing to it, which he did not leave there, and taking away the mud, a thick shiver of the rock followed it. They then all agreed that the ball must have made both the hole in the mud and also splintered the rock, and stood in amaze at it, not being able to comprehend it: but, by all the art I had, I could not prevail with a man of them to fire the gun himself, till it had been buzzed about a good while, and at last came to my ears, that a common soldier behind said he should not be afraid of it if the gentleman would show him how.

I then ordered the fellow to me, and he told me, with a composed look, that it had always been his way of thinking, that what he saw another do he could do himself, and could not rest till he had tried. "And, sir," says he, "if this gun, as you call it, does not hurt you, why should it hurt me? And if you can make it hit that rock, why should not I, when you have told me how you manage it?"—"Are not you the man that first helped me up with the large fish yesterday?" says I. He told me he was.

I was prodigiously pleased with the fellow's spirit, "And," says I, "my friend, if you will, and I live, you will hit it before you have done." I then showed him the sight of the gun, and how to hold it; and being perfect in that, "Now," says I, "shut your left eye, and observe with your right, till this knob and that notch are exactly even with each other and the middle of that mark; and when they are so, pull this bit with your fore-finger, holding the gun tight to your shoulder." He so exactly pursued my directions that he hit the very middle of the mud; and then, without any emotion, walked up with the gun in his hand, as I had done before; and turning to me very gravely, "Sir," says he, "it is hit." I told him the best marksman on earth could not be sure of coming so near his mark. He stroked his chin, and giving me the gun again, was walking to his place; but I stopped him, and seeing something so modest and sincere in his countenance and behaviour, and so generous in his spirit, I asked him to which colamb he belonged. He told me to colamb Pendlehamby.—"To my father?" says I; "then sure I shall not be denied."

I took him with me to my father, who was not yet come up to the rock. "Sir," says I, "there is a favour I would beg of you."—"Son," says he, "what is it you can ask that I can refuse you?" Says I, "This man belongs to your guards; now there is something so noble and daring in his spirit, and yet so meek and deserving in his deportment, that if you will load me with obligation, it is to make him an officer; he is not deserving of so ill a station as a private man."

My father looking at me, "Son," says he, "there is something to be done before he can be qualified for what you require." This, thinks I, is a put-off. "Pray, sir," says I, "what can a man of courage, sense, and a cool temper, want to qualify him for what I ask?"—"Something," says he, "which none but myself can give; and that, at your desire, I will supply him with." Then, my father calling him, "Lask Nasgig, bonyoe," says he; that is, Slave Nasgig, lie down. Nasgig (for that was his name) immediately fell on his face, with his arms and hands straight by his sides; when my father, setting his left foot on Nasgig's neck, pronounced these words: "Lask, I give thee life, thou art a filgay!" Then Nasgig, raising himself on his knees, made obeisance to my father, and standing up, stroked his chin; and my father taking him by the hand in token of equality, the ceremony ceased.

"Now, son," says my father, "let me hear your request."—"It is only, sir," said I, "preferment for the deserving, equal to his merit." My father asked him if he understood the duty of a gorpell. He did not reply yes, but beginning, gave a compendious sort of history of his whole duty; at which all the colambs were very much surprised, for even his comrades were not apprised, or ever imagined, he knew more of military affairs than themselves. My father then asked him if he knew how to behave as a duff; but he made as little difficulty of that as the other, going through the several parts of duty in all the different branches, in peace and war, at home and abroad. "Son," says my father, "it is a mystery to me you should have found out more in an hour than I myself could in half an age; for this man was born in my palang, of my own lask, and has been mine and my father's these forty years. I shall be glad if you will look on the rest of my lasks, and give me your opinion; I may have more as deserving." I told him such as Nasgig were not to be met with very often; but when they were found, ought to be cherished accordingly.

"Sir," says I, "nature works upon the same sort of materials divers ways; on some in sport, and some in earnest; and if the necessary qualifications of a great man are impressed on our mass, it is odds but we improve regularly into one, though it may never be publicly known, or even to ourselves, till a proper occasion; for as a curious genius will be most inquisitive after, and is most in the end retentive of knowledge, so no man is less ostentatious of it. He covets knowledge, not from the prospect of gain, but merely for its own sake; the very knowing being his recompense: and if I may presume to give you a hint how properly to bestow your favours, let it be on persons like this; for the vain, knowing man, who is always showing it, as he for the most part labours for it, to show out with, and procure his rise by it, were it not for the hopes of that, would not think knowledge worth attaining; and as his rise is his aim, if he could invent anymore expeditious method than that, he would not pretermit any ill act that might advance him according to his lust of rising. But the man who aims at perfection, from his natural inclination, must, to attain his end, avoid all ill courses, as impediments to that perfection he lusts after; and that, by Nasgig's worth being so little known, I'll answer for it is his character. And this being true, yourself will deduce the consequence, which is the fitter man to bear place; for with me it is a maxim, he that labours after truth for truth's sake (and that he surely must who proposes no worldly view in it) can't arrive at his ends by false methods, but is always the truest friend to himself and others, the truest subject to his lord, and the most faithful servant to his God."

My father then turning to me, "Son," says he, "you have enlightened me more than ever I was before, and have put me on a new way of thinking, for which I am to return you many thanks." And the whole company doing the same, says my father, "I lost a brave general officer lately, who was destined to the western wars which are breaking out, and have been long debating in my mind to whom I should commit his corps; and but for the hazard of the enterprise, I would have now given it to Nasgig; but shall be loth to lose him so soon after I am acquainted with his worth, so will think of somesother post nearer my person for him, less dangerous, though perhaps not so honourable."

"Great sir," says Nasgig, "I am too sensible of the honour already done me, to think any post wherein I may continue to serve you either too mean or too hazardous for me; and as valour is nowhere so conspicuous as in the greatest dangers, I shall esteem my blood spent to great advantage in any enterprise where my duty under your command leads me. I therefore rather humbly request this dangerous post, that I may either lose my life in your service, or live to see you justified in your advancement of me by the whole nation. For what can I do, or how can I demonstrate my affection to your person and pleasure, in an inactive state?"

Here the whole level rang with applause to Nasgig.

My father then giving his hand to Nasgig, in token of friendship, and his word for investiture in the command of that vacant post, the whole level again resounded with, "Long live Pendlehamby, and his servant Nasgig!"

This being the last day of my company's stay, for they had agreed to go homewards next morning, some of them moved to return the sooner, that they might have time to hear out my story. So that our stay was very little longer.

In our return home, Nasgig singled me out to return his acknowledgments for my favour; and viewing my gun told me they had no such thing growing in his country. I told him if he had it, it would do no good without my powder. I then, at his request, described what I had heard of our method of fighting in battle in Europe; and mentioning our cannon, he said he supposed they killed every man they hit. "No," says I, "not so bad as that. Sometimes they hit the flesh only, and that is commonly cured; sometimes break a leg or arm, and that may in time be cured—some so well as to be useful again, and others are cut off, and healed up again; but if the ball hits the head or vitals, it is commonly mortal."—"Oh," says he, "give me the head or vitals, then; no broken limbs for me."

After dinner, at their request, I went on with my story, at repairing the castle, and my escape with Glanlepze, and so on to the crocodile; when I repeated his speech to me on that account, and told them it had made such an impression upon me that I had endeavoured to make it the leading thought of my mind, and had set it down upon one of my doors at the grotto that it might the oftener be in my sight when any difficulty arose.

One of the colambs begged pardon for interrupting, but told me, though he understood what Glanlepze meant, he could not tell how I could set what he said down at my grotto, or have it in my sight, and desired me to explain that. I would have told my guest I took it down in writing, if that would not have puzzled the cause more; but to go the nearest way I could, I told him we had a method in my country of conveying to a man at a great distance whatever we have a mind to say to him, and in such a manner that nobody but himself would know what we would have him know. And pausing here a little to consider the easiest method of demonstrating this to their senses, they told me they had gone as far as their conjectures could carry them, but could conclude on nothing so improbable as sending it by a messenger. I told them that in part was my way, but my messenger should not know the message he carried. That gravelled them quite, and they were unanimous that was what could not be done. By this time I had sent for a wood-coal, to write with upon my deal table, and kneeling down to the table, I began to write, "Honoured sir, I send this to gain by your answer to it an account of your arrival at Arndrumnstake." I then called them all to me. "Now," says I, "suppose I want to know how my father gets back to Arndrumnstake, my way is this—I set down so many words as will express my meaning to my father, after the manner you see on this table, and make a little distance between each word, which is the same thing as you do in speaking; for there, if you run one word into another, and don't give each its proper sound, who can understand you? For though you speak what contains all the words, yet without the proper sound and distinction it is only confusion. Do you understand that?" They told me they did. "Then," says I, "these are the words I would have my father know, I being at this arkoe, and he at Arndrumnstake. Honoured sir," and so I read on. "Here," says I, "you must take us to be countrymen, and that he and I understand both the same method. Now look, this word, which ends where you see the gap, stands for *honoured*, and this next for *sir*, the next for *I*, and so on; and we both using the same method, and seeing each other's words, are able to open our minds at a distance." I was now in hopes I had done, and was going on with my story: "But," says one of the colambs, "Mr. Peter, though this is a matter that requires consideration, I plainly see how you do it, by agreeing that all these strokes put into this form shall stand for the word honoured, and so on, as you say, let who will make them; but have not you set down there the word Arndrumnstake?"—"Yes," says I.—"Why then," says he, "none of your countrymen could understand what that means."—"No," says I, smiling; "but they could."—Says he, "You say you agree what strokes shall stand for one word, and what for another; but then how could your countrymen, who never knew what strokes you would set down for Arndrumnstake, know that your strokes meant that very country? for that you could not have agreed upon before either of you knew there was any such place."

I was at a loss, without spending more words than I was willing about it, how to answer this close reasoner; and talking of syllables and letters would only have perplexed the affair more, so I told him the readiest for despatch; that as every word consisted of one or more distinct sounds, and as some of the same sounds happened in different words, we did not agree so much upon making our strokes stand for several words, as for several sounds; and those sounds, more or less of them, added together, made the particular words. "As, for example," says I, "*Arn* is one sound, *drumn* is another sound, and *stake* is another; now, by our knowing how to set down these several sounds by themselves, we can couple them, and apply them to the making up any word, in the manner we please; and therefore he, by seeing those three sounds together, knows I mean *Arndrumnstake*, and can speak it as well, though he never heard the whole word spoken together, as if he heard me speak to him."—"I have some little notion of what you mean," says he, "but not clear enough to express myself upon it; and so go on! go on! And pray what did you do about the reeds?"

I then resuming my discourse where I left off, completed my narration that night; but I could perceive the water in my father's eyes when I came to the account of Youwarkee's fall and the condition I took her up in.

When I had done, they adjusted the order of their flight, for avoiding confusion, one to go so long before another, and the junior colambs to go first.

In the morning nothing was to be heard but the gripsacks: the men were all ranged in order to go off with their respective colambs; and after all compliments passed, the junior colamb arising, walked half-way to the wood, where his gripsack standing to wait for him, preceded him to the level, the next gripsack standing ready to sound as soon as the first removed; and this was the signal for the second colamb to move, so that each colamb was a quarter of a mile before the other.

My father was the last but two; but I shall never forget his tenderness at parting with his daughter and grandchildren, and I may say with myself too; for by this time he had a high opinion of me. Patty went with my father, she so much resembling my wife, that my father said he should still have his two daughters in his sight, having her with him.

At parting, I presented Nasgig with a broadsword; and showing him the use of it, with many expressions of gratitude on his part, and respect on mine, he took flight after the rest.

IX

PETER FINDS HIS STORES LOW—SENDS YOUWARKEE TO THE
SHIP—RECEIVES AN INVITATION TO GEORIGETTI'S COURT.

For the first few days after our company had left us, Youwarkee could
not forbear a tear now and then for the loss of her father and sister;
but I endeavoured not to see it, lest I should, by persuading her to the
contrary, seem to oppose what I really thought was a farther token of
the sweetness of her disposition; but it wore off by degrees, and having
a clear stage again, it cost us several days to settle ourselves and put our
confused affairs in order; and when we had done we blessed ourselves
that we could come and go, and converse with the pleasing tenderness
we had hitherto always done.

She told me nothing in the world but her concern for so tender a
father, and the fear of displeasing me if she disobliged him, should have
kept her so long from me; for her life had never been so sweet and serene
as with me and her children; and if she was to begin it again, and choose
her settlement and company, it should be with me in that arkoe. I told
her though I was entirely of her opinion for avoiding a life of hurry, yet
I loved a little company, if for nothing else but to advance topics for
discourse, to the exercise of our faculties; but I then agreed it was not
from mere judgment I spoke, but from fancy. "But, Youwee," says I, "it
will be proper for us to see what our friends have left us, that we don't
want before the time comes about again." Then she took her part, and
I mine; and having finished, we found they would hold out pretty well,
and that the first thing to be done was to get the oil of the beast-fish.

When we came to examine the brandy and wine, I found they had
suffered greatly; so I told Youwarkee, when she could spare time, she
should make another flight to the ship. "And," says I, "pray look at all
the small casks of wine or brandy, or be they what they will, if they are
not above half-full, or thereabouts, they will swim, and you may send
them down." I desired her to send a fire-shovel and tongs, describing
them to her: "And there are abundance of good ropes between decks,
rolled up, send them," says I, "and anything else you think we want, as
plates, bowls, and all the cutlasses and pistols," says I, "that hang in the
room by the cabin: for I would, me-thinks, have another cargo, as it
may possibly be the last, for the ship can't hold forever."

Youwarkee, who loved a jaunt to the ship mightily, sat very attentive to what I said, and told me, if I pleased, she would go the next day; to which I agreed.

She stayed on this trip till I began to be uneasy for her, being gone almost four days, and I was in great fear of some accident; but she arrived safe, telling me she had sent all she could anyways pack up; and anyone who had seen the arrival of her fleet would had taken it for a good ship's cargo, for it cost me full three weeks to land and draw them up to the grotto; and then we had such a redundancy of things, that we were forced to pile them upon each other to the top of the room.

It began to draw towards long days again, when one morning, in bed, I heard the gripsack. I waked Youvarkee, and told her of it; and we both got up, and were going to the level, when we met six glumms in the wood, with a gripsack before them, coming to the grotto. The trumpeter, it seems, had been there before; but the others, who seemed to be of a better rank, had not. We saluted them, and they us; and Youwarkee knowing one of them, we desired them to walk to the grotto.

They told us they came express from Georigetti's palace, with an invitation to me and Youwarkee to spend sometime at his court. I let them know what a misfortune I lay under in not being born with a graundee, since Providence had pleased to dispose of me in a part of the world where alone it could have been of such infinite service to me, or I should have taken it for the highest honour to have laid myself at their master's feet: and after someother discourse, one of them pressed me to return his master my answer, for they had but a very little time to stay. I told them they saw plainly, by baring my breast to them, that I was under an absolute incapacity for such a journey, and gratifying the highest ambition I could have in the world; for I was pinned down to my arkoe, never more to pass the barrier of that rock. One of them then asking, if I should choose to go if it was possible to convey me thither, I told him he could scarce have the least doubt, was my ability to perform such a journey equal to my inclination to take it, that I should in the least hesitate at obeying his master. "Sir," says he, "you make me very happy in the regard you show my master; and I must beg leave to stay another day with you." I told him they did me great honour; but little thought what it all tended to.

We were very facetious; and they talked of the number of visitors I had had here; and they mentioned several facts which had happened, and, amongst the rest, that of Nasgig, who, they said, since his return, had been introduced by Pendlehamby to the king, and was, for his great prudence and penetration, become Georigetti's great favourite. They told me war was upon the point of breaking out, and several other pieces of news, which, as they did not concern me, I was very easy about.

The next morning they desiring to walk, and view what was most remarkable in my arkoe, and above all to see me fire my gun, which they had heard so much of; I gratified them at a mark, and hit the edge of it, and found them quite staunch, without the least start at the report. I paid them a compliment upon it, and told them how their countrymen had behaved, even at a second firing: "But," says he who was the chief spokesman, and knew, I found, as much as I could tell him, "that second fright was from seeing death the consequence of the first; and though you had then to do mostly with soldiers, you must not think they choose death more than others, though their duty obliges them to shun it less."

The same person then desired me to show him how to fire the gun; which I did, and believe he might hit the rock somewhere or other; but he did not seem to admire the sport, and I, having but few balls left, did not recommend the gun to the rest.

A little before bedtime the strangers told me they believed I should see Nasgig next morning. I presently thought there was somewhat more than ordinary in this visit, but could noways dive to the bottom of it.

Just before they went to rest, they ordered the trumpeter to be early on the rock next morning; and upon the first sight of Nasgig's corps, to sound notice of it, for us to be ready to receive him.

ROBERT PALTOCK

X

Nasgig comes with a guard to fetch Peter—Long
debate about his going—Nasgig's uneasiness at Peter's
refusal—Relates a prediction to him, and proceedings
thereon at Georigetti's court—Peter consents to go—
Prepares a machine for that purpose.

We were waked by the trumpet giving notice of Nasgig's coming;
I did not care to inquire of the strangers into the particulars of
his embassy; "for be it what it will," thinks I, "Nasgig is so much my
friend that I can know the motives of it from him, and, or I am much
deceived, he is too honest to impose upon me." But I had but little time
for thought, for upon our entering the level, we found him and his train,
of at least a hundred persons, just alighting before us.

We embraced, and professed the particular pleasure fortune had done
us in once more meeting together. When we arrived at the grotto, he told
me he was assured I had been informed of the occasion of his visit; and
that it would be the greatest honour done to his country that could be
imagined. He then laid his hand on my beard, which was now of about
five months' growth, having never shaved it since my father went, and
told he was glad to see that.—"And are you not so to see me?" says I.—
"Yes, surely," says he, "for I prize that for your sake."—"But," says I, "pray
be open with me, and tell me what you mean by my being informed of
the occasion of your coming?"—"Why," says he, "of Georigetti's message
to you, as it will be of such infinite service to our country: and," says he,
"if you had not consented to it, the messengers had returned and stopped
me."—"True," says I, "one of the messengers told me the king would be
glad to see me; which as I, so well as he, knew it was impossible he should,
in return to his compliment, I believe I might say what a happiness it
would be to me if I could wait on him. But pray what is your immediate
message? for I hear you are in great favour at court, and would never have
come hither with this retinue in so much ceremony on a trifling account."

"My dear Peter," says Nasgig, "know that your fame has reached
far and near since I saw you before; and our state, though a large
and populous one, and once of mighty power and twice its present
extent, by the revolt of the western part of it, who chose themselves a
king, has been so miserably harassed by wars, that the revolters, who

are ever fomenting discontent and rebellion amongst us, will, by the encroachments they daily make on us, certainly reduce us at last to a province under their government; which will render us all slaves to a usurped power, set up against our lawful sovereign. Now these things were foretold long enough before they actually began to be transacted; but all being then at peace, and no prospect of what has since happened, we looked not out for a remedy, till the disease became stubborn and incurable."—"Pray," says I, "by whom were the things you mention foretold?"—"By a very ancient and grave ragan," says he.—"How long ago?" says I.—"Oh, above four times the age of the oldest man living," says he.—"And when did he say it would happen?" says I.—"That," says he, "was not quite so clear then."—"But how do you know," says I, "that he ever said any such thing?"—"Why, the thing itself was so peculiar," says he, "and the ragan delivered it so positively, that his successors have ever since pronounced it twelve times a year publicly, word for word, to put the people in mind of it, and from whom they must hope for relief; and now the long-expected time being come, we have no hopes but in your destruction of the tyrant-usurper."—"I destroy him!" says I: "if he is not destroyed till I do it, I fear your state is but in a bad case."—"My good friend Peter," says he, "you or nobody can do it."—"Pugh," says I, "Nasgig, I took you for a man of more sense, notwithstanding the prejudices of education, than to think, because you have seen me kill a beast-fish that could not come to hurt me at the distance of twenty paces, that I can kill your usurper at the distance he is from me."— "No, my good friend," says Nasgig, "I know you take me to have more judgment than to think so."—"Why, what else can I do," says I, "unless he will come hither to be killed by me?"—"Dear Peter," says he, "you will not hear me out."—"I will," says I, "say on."—"You, as I said before, being the only person that can, according to our prediction, destroy this usurper and restore peace among us, my master Georigetti, and the whole state of Normnbdsgrsutt, were going to send a splendid embassy to you; but your father advising to repose the commission wholly in me, they all consented to it, and I am come to invite you over to Brandleguarp for that purpose. I know you will tell me you have not the graundee, and cannot get thither: but I am assured you have what is far better; the wisdom you have will help you to surmount that difficulty, which our whole moucheratt cannot get over. And I am sure did you apply half the thought to accomplish it you seem to do to invent excuses against it, you would easily overcome that. And now,

ROBERT PALTOCK

dear friend," continues he, "refuse me not; for as my first rise was owing to your favour, so my downfall as absolutely attends your refusal."

"Dear Nasgig," says I, "you know I love you, and could refuse you nothing in my power; but for me to be mounted in the air, I know not how, over these rocks, and then drowned by a fall into the sea, which is a necessary consequence of such a mad attempt; and all this in prosecution of a project founded upon an old wife's tale, is such a chimera as all men of sense would laugh at; as if there was no way of destroying me, but with a guard of a hundred men to souse me into the wide ocean. A very pretty conqueror of rebels I should prove, truly, kicking for life till the next wave sent me to the bottom."

Nasgig looked then so grave, I almost thought I should have heard no more of it; but after a short pause, "Peter," says he, "I am sorry you make so light of sacred things; a thing foretold so long ago by a holy ragan, kept up by undoubted tradition ever since, in the manner I have told you; in part performed, and now waiting your concurrence for its accomplishment; but if I cannot prevail with you, though I perish at my return, I dread to think you may be forced without thanks to perform what generously to undertake will be your greatest glory."

"Pray," says I, "Nasgig (for now I perceive you are in earnest), what may this famous prediction be?"

"Ah, Peter!" says Nasgig, "to what purpose should I relate so sacred a prediction to one who, though the most concerned in it, makes such a jest of it?"

His mentioning me as concerned in it, raised my curiosity once more to desire a relation of it. "Why should I relate it," says he, "if you are resolved not to fulfil it?"—I told him I had no resolution against anything that related to my own good, or that of my friends. "But the greatest question with me," says I, "is, whether I am at all concerned in it."—"Oh clearly, clearly!" says he, "there is no doubt of it; it must mean you or nobody."—I told him I must judge by the words of it that I was the person intended by it; and till that was apparent to my reason, it would be difficult to procure my consent to so perilous an undertaking.—"And," says he, "will you, upon hearing it, judge impartially, and go with me if you can take the application to yourself?"—"I cannot go quite so far as that," says I; "but this I'll promise you, I'll judge impartially, and if I can so apply it to myself, that it must necessarily mean me, and no other, and if you convince me I may go safely, I will go."

Nasgig was so rejoiced at this, he was at a loss how to express himself. "My dear Peter," says he, "you have given me new life! our state is free! our persons free! we are free! we are free! And, Peter," says he, "now I have given vent to my joy, you shall hear the prediction.

"You must know, this holy ragan lived four ages ago; and from certain dreams and revelations he had had, set himself to overturn our country-worship of the Great Image; and by his sanctity of life, and sound reasonings, had almost effected it under the assistance of Begsurbeck, then our king, who had fully embraced his tenets; but the rest of the ragans opposing him, and finding he could not advance his scheme, he withdrew from the ragans to a close retirement for several years; and just before his death, sending for the king and all the ragans, he told them he should certainly die that day, and that he could not die at peace till he had informed them what had been revealed to him; desiring them to take notice of it, not as a conjecture of his own, but a certain verity which should hereafter come to pass. Says he, 'you know you have rejected the alteration in your religion I proposed to you; and which Begsurbeck, here present, would have advanced; and now I must tell you what you have brought upon yourselves. As for Begsurbeck, he shall reign the longest and most prosperously of all your former and future kings; but in twice his time outrun, the west shall be divided from the east, and bring sorrow, confusion, and slaughter, till the waters of the earth shall produce a glumm, with hair round his head, swimming and flying without the graundee; who, with unknown fire and smoke, shall destroy the traitor of the west, settle the ancient limits of the monarchy, by common consent establish what I would have taught you, change the name of this country, introduce new laws and arts, add kingdoms to this state, and force tributes from the bowels of the earth of such things as this kingdom shall not know till then, and shall never afterwards want; and then shall return to the waters again. Take care,' says he, 'you miss not the opportunity when it may be had; for once lost, it shall never, never more return; and then, woe, woe, woe to my poor country!'— The ragan having said this, expired.

"This prediction made so great an impression on Begsurbeck, that he ordered all the ragans singly before him, and heard them repeat it; which having done, and made himself perfect in it, he ordered it to be pronounced twelve times in the year on particular days, in the moucherait, that the people might learn it by heart; that they and their children being perfect in it, might not fail of applying it, when the man from the waters should appear with proper description.

"Thus, Peter," says he, "has this prediction been kept up in our memories as perfectly as if it had but just been pronounced to us."—:"'Tis very true," says I, "here may have been a prediction, and it may have been, as you say, handed down very exactly from Begsurbeck's days till now; but how does that affect me? how am I concerned in it? Surely, if any marks would have denoted me to be the man, some of the colambs who have so lately left me, and were so long with me, would have found them out in my person, or among the several actions of my life I recounted to them."—"Upon the return of the colambs from you," says Nasgig, "they told his majesty what they had heard and seen at Graundevolet, and the story was conveyed through the whole realm: but every man has not the faculty of distinction. Now, one of the ragans, when he had heard of you, applying you to the prediction, and that to you, soon found our deliverer in you; and at a public moucheratt, after first pronouncing the prediction, declared himself thereon to the following effect:

"'May it please your majesty—and you the honourable colambs—the reverend ragans—and people of this state,' says he, 'you all know that our famous king Begsurbeck, who reigned at the time of this prediction, did live sixty years after it in the greatest splendour, and died at the age of one hundred and twenty years, having reigned full ninety of them; and herein you will all agree with me, no king before or since has done the like. You all likewise know, that within two hundred years after Begsurbeck's death, that is, about twice his reign of ninety years outrun, the rebellion in the west began, which has been carried on ever since; and our strength diminishing as theirs increases, we are now no fair match for them, but are fearful of being undone. So far you will agree matters have tallied with the prediction; and now, to look forward to the time to come, it becomes us to lay hold of the present opportunity for our relief, for that, once slipped, will never return; and if I have any skill in interpretations, now is the time of our deliverance.'

"'Our prediction foretells the past evils, their increase and continuance, till the waters of the earth shall produce a glumm. Here I must appeal to the honourable colambs present, if the waters have not done so in the person of glumm Peter of Graundevolet, as they have received it from his own report.'

"All the colambs then rising, and making reverence to the king, declared it was most true.

"'The next part,' says the ragan, 'is, he is to be hairy round his head; and how his person in this respect agrees with the prediction, I beg leave to be informed by the colambs.'

"The colambs then rising, declared that having seen and conversed with him, they could not observe any hair on the fore part of his head; but I answered that when I left you I well remembered your having short stubs of hair upon your cheeks and chin; which I had no sooner mentioned than your father arose and told the assembly that though he did not mind it whilst he was with you, yet he remembered that his daughter, a year before, had told him that you had hair on your face before as long as that behind.

"This again putting new life into the ragan, he proceeded—'Then let this,' says he, 'be put to the trial by an embassy to glumm Peter; and if it answers, there will be no room to doubt the rest. Then,' says the ragan, 'it is plain by the report of the colambs, that glumm Peter has not the graundee.'

"'As to the next point, he is to swim and fly. Now I am informed he swims daily in a thing he calls a boat.'—To which the colambs all agreed.—'And now,' says he, 'that he flies too, that must be fulfilled; for every word must have a meaning, and that indeed he must do if ever he comes hither.' I therefore advise that a contrivance be somehow found out for conveying glumm Peter through the air to us, and then we shall answer that part of the prediction; and I think, and do not doubt, but that may be done.

"'Now,' says he, 'let us see the benefit predicted to us upon the arrival of glumm Peter.' Our words are: 'Who, with unknown fire and smoke, shall destroy the traitor of the west.' What can be plainer than this? For I again appeal to the colambs for his making unknown fire and smoke.

"'Thus far,' says the ragan, 'we have succeeded happily towards a discovery of the person; but it ends not here with the death of the traitor; but such other benefits are to accrue as are mentioned in the following part of the prediction: they are blessings yet to come, and who knows the end of them?'

"'I hope,' says the ragan, 'I have given satisfaction in what I have said, and shall now leave it to the care of those whose business it is to provide that none of those woes pronounced against us may happen, by missing the time which, when gone, will never return.'

"The assembly were coming to a resolution of sending you a pompous embassy, but your father prevailed for sending me only; 'For,' says he, 'my son thinks better of him than of the rest of our whole race.' So this important affair was committed to me, with orders to prepare a conveyance for you, which I cannot attempt to do; but shall refer myself to your more solid judgment in the contrivance of it."

I had sat very attentive to Nasgig, and from what he had declared, could not say but there was a very great resemblance between myself and the person predicted of. "But then," says I, "they are idolaters: Providence would not interpose in this affair, when all the glory of its success must redound to an idol. But," says I, "has not the same thing often happened from oracular presages, where the glory must redound to the false deity? But what if, as is predicted, their religion is to be changed to the old ragan's plan, and that will be to the abolition of idolatry? I know not what to say; but if I thought my going would gain a single soul to the eternal truth, I would not scruple to hazard my life in the attempt."

I then called in Youwarkee, told her the whole affair of the prediction, which she had often heard, I found, and could have repeated. I told her that the king and states had pitched on me as the person intended by their prediction, and that Nasgig was sent to fetch me over: "And indeed," says I, "Youwee, if this be a true prediction, it seems very applicable to me as far as I can see."—"Yes, truly," says she, "so it does, now I consider it in the light you say the ragan puts it."—

"Why," says I, "prophecies and predictions are never so plain as to mention names; but yet, upon the solution, they become as intelligible as if they did, the circumstances tallying so exactly. But what would you have me do? Shall I, or shall I not, go?"—"Go!" says she, "how can you go?"—"Oh," says I, "never fear that. If this is from above, means will soon be found; Providence never directs effects without means."

Youwarkee, whose head ran only on the dangers of the undertaking, had a violent conflict with herself; the love of me, of her children, and of her country, divided her so, she was not capable of advising. I pressed her opinion again, when she told me to follow the dictates of my own reason; "And but for the dread of losing you, and for my children's sakes," says she, "I should have no choice to make when my country is at stake: but you know best."

I told Youwarkee that I really found the prediction the plainer the more I thought of it; and that, above all, the change of religion was the uppermost; for if I can reduce a State from the misery and bondage of idolatry to a true sense of the Supreme Being, and seemingly by His own direction, shall I fear to risk my own life for it? or, will He suffer me to perish till somewhat at least is done towards it? And how do I know but the whole tendency of my life has been by impulse hither for this very purpose? "My dear Youwee," says I, "fear nothing, I will go."

I called Nasgig, and told him my resolution, and that he had nothing now to do but prepare a means of conveying me.—He said he begged to refer that to me, for my own thoughts would suggest to me both the safest and easiest means.

I wanted to venture on the back of some strong glumm; when Nasgig told me no one could endure my weight so long a flight. But what charmed me most was, the lovely Youwarkee offered to carry me herself if she could: "And if I can't hold out," says she, "my dear, we can but at last drop both together." I kissed the charming creature with tears in my eyes, but declined the experiment.

I told Nasgig I wanted to divide my weight between two or four glumms, which I believed I could easily do; and asked if each could hold out with a fourth part of my weight.—He told me there was no doubt of that; but he was afraid I should drop between their graundees, he imagining I intended to lie along on their backs, part of me on each of them, or should bear so much on them as to prevent their flight. I told him I did not purpose to dispose of myself in the manner he presumed, but if two or four could undoubtedly bear my weight so long a flight, I would order myself without any other inconvenience to my bearers than their burden. He made light of my weight between four, as a trifle, and said he would be one with all his heart.—"Nay," says I, "if four cannot hold out, can eight?" He plainly told me, as he knew not what I meant, he could say nothing to it, nor could imagine how I could divide so small a body as mine into eight different weights, for it seemed impossible, he said, to him; but if I would show him my method, he would then give me his opinion.

I then, leaving him, took out my tools: I pitched upon a strong board my wife had sent me from the ship, about twelve feet long, and a foot and a half broad, upon the middle of which I nailed down one of my chairs; then I took one cord of about thirty-four feet long, making handloops at each end, and nailed it down in the middle to the under-side of my board, as near as I could to the fore-end of it, and I took another cord of the same length and make, and this I nailed within three feet of the farther end of my board. I then took a cord of about twenty feet long, and nailed about three feet before the foremost, and a fourth of the same length, at the farther end of my board; by which means the first and third ropes being the longest and at such a distance from the short ropes, the glumms who held them would fly so much higher and forwarder than the short-rope ones, that they and their ropes would be quite out of the others' way, which would not have happened if either the ropes had been all of one length, or nearer to or farther from one another; and then considering that if I should receive a sudden jerk or twitch, I might possibly be shook off my chair, I took a smaller rope to tie myself with fast to the chair, and then I was sure if I fell into the sea I should at least have the board and chair with me, which might possibly buoy me up till the glumms could descend to my assistance.

Having carried the machine down to the level with the help of two of Nasgig's men, he being out on a walk, and having never seen it, I ordered one of the men to sit upon the chair, and eight more to hold by the loops and rise with him; but, as I found it difficult at their first rising, not being able to mount all equally, to carry the board up even, and the back part rising first, the front pitched against the ground and threw the fellow out of the chair, I therefore bade them stop, and ordering eight others to me, said I, "Hold each of you one of these ropes as high as you can over your heads; then." says I to the eight bearers, "mount on your graundees, and come round behind him in the chair gently, two and two, and take each of you a loop, and hover with it till you are all ready, and then rise together, keeping your eye on the board that it rises neither higher at one end nor one side than the other, and see you all feel your weight alike; then fly across the lake and back again." They did so, and with as much ease, they told me, as if they had nothing in their hands; and the man rode with so much state and composure, he said, that I longed to try it myself; so, shifting places with the glumm, I mounted the chair, and tying myself round, I asked if anyone knew which way Nasgig walked. One of them pointing to where he saw him just before in the wood, I ordered them to take me up as before, and go that way.

Upon coming to the place where I expected Nasgig was, I hallooed and called him; who, knowing my voice, ran to the skirt of the wood; and seeing me mounted in my flying chair, I jokingly told him I was going, if he had any commands; but he mounting immediately came up to me, and viewing me round, and seeing the pleasure the men seemed to carry me with, says he, "Are you all sure you can carry him safe to Battringdrigg?"—They all replied, "Yes, with ease."—"This then," says he, "is your doom: if you perform it not, everyone shall be slit; but if you carry the deliverer safe, you are filgays every man of you!" he verily thinking I was then going off; but I undeceived him, by ordering them to turn about and set me down where I was taken up.

Nasgig alighting and viewing my contrivance, "This, Peter," says he, "is but a very plain thing."—"It is so," says I, "but it is as far as my ingenuity could reach."—"Ah, Peter!" says he "say not so, for if the greatest difficulties, as I and all my nation thought it would be to convey you to them, are so plain and easy to you, what must lesser things be? No, Peter, I did not call it plain because it might be easily done when it was seen, but in respect to the head that formed it; for the nearest way to attain one's end is always the best, and attended for the most part with fewest inconveniences; and I verily think, Peter, though we believe the rise or fall of our State wholly depends on you, you must have stayed at Graundevolet but for your own ingenuity. Well, and when shall we set out?" says he.—I told him it would take up sometime to settle the affairs of my family, and to consider what I had best take with me; and required at least three days, being as little as I could have told him for that purpose.

Nasgig, who as he was an honest man, and for making the best for his patrons, was sorry it was so long, though he, imagining at the same time it was short enough for one who was to go on such an enterprise, was glad it was no longer; and immediately despatched a trumpet express with notice, that on the fourth day he should be at the height of Battringdrigg, and that having myself formed a machine for that purpose, I would accompany him.

I began next to consider what part I had to act at Doorpt Svangeanti (for I neither could nor would call it by any other name when I came thither), and what it was they expected from me. I am, says I, to kill a traitor; good, that may be, but then I must take a gun and ammunition; and why not some pistols and cutlasses? If I cannot use them all, I can teach others who may. I will take several of them, and all my guns but two, and I will leave a pair of pistols; I may return and want them. I will take my two best suits of clothes, and other things suitable; for if I am to perform things according to this prediction, it may be a long time before I get back again. Thinks I, Youwarkee shall stay here with the children, and if I like my settlement I can send for her at anytime. I then began to see the necessity of making at least one more machine to carry my goods on. And says I, as they will be very weighty, I must have more lasks to shift in carrying them, for I will retain sixteen for my own body-machine, in order to relieve each other; and as the distance is so great, I will not be stinted for want of fresh hands.

Being come to this resolution, I called Nasgig, and ordered eight fresh lasks to attend my baggage; these he soon singled out: so, having settled all matters with my wife, and taken leave of her and the children, I charged them not to stir out of the grotto till I was gone; and leaving them all in tears, I set out with a heavy heart for the level, where the whole convoy and my two machines waited for me.

XI

When we came to the level, I desired Nasgig to draw all his men into a circle as near as they could stand. I then asked them who would undertake to carry me: when not a man but proffered his service, and desired to have the post of honour, as they called it. I told them my question was only in case of necessity to know whom I might depend upon, for my bearers were provided, saving accidents. "But, my friends," says I, "as you are equally deserving for the offered service, as if you were accepted, are any of you desirous of being filgays?" They all answering together, "I, I, I!"—"Nasgig," says I, "you and I must come to a capitulation before I go, and your honour must be pledged for performance of articles."

I began with telling them what an enemy I was to slavery: "And," says I to Nasgig, "as I am about to undertake what no man upon earth ever did before: to quit my country, my family, my every conveniency of life, for I know not what, I know not where, and from whence I may never return; I must be indulged, if I am ever so fortunate as to arrive safe in your country, in the satisfaction of seeing all these my fellow-travellers as happy as myself: for which reason I must insist upon every man present alighting with me in safety, being made free the moment we touch the ground; and unless you will engage your honour for this, I will not stir a step farther."

Nasgig paused for an answer, for though my bearers were his own lasks, and he could dispose of them at pleasure, yet as the rest were the king's, he knew not how far he might venture to promise for them; but being desirous to get me over the rock, fearing I might still retract my purpose, he engaged to procure their freedom of the king. And this, I thought, would make the men more zealous in my service.

I then permitting them to take me up, we were over the rock as quick as thought, and when I had a little experienced the flight, I perceived I had nothing to fear; for they were so dexterous on the graundee, that I received not the least shock all the way, or scarce a wry position, though every quarter of an inch at hand made a considerable deflection from the perpendicular. We shifted but twice till we came to Battringdrigg, the manner, of which I directed as I sat in my chair; for I ordered the new man to hover over him he was to relieve, and reaching down his hand to meet the others which were held up with a rope, the old bearer sunk beneath the chair, and the reliever took his course. This we did one by one, till all were changed; but there was one, a stout young fellow, at the first short rope on my right hand, who observing me to eye him more than the rest, in a bravado would not be relieved before we arrived at Battringdrigg arkoe; and I afterwards took him into my family.

As it was now somewhat advanced into the light season, I had hopes of a tolerable good prospect; but had it been quite light, I should have never been the better for it. I had been upon very high mountains in the inland parts of Africa, but was never too high to see what was below me before, though very much contracted; but here, in the highest of our flight, you could not distinguish the globe of the earth but by a sort of mist, for every way looked alike to me; then sometimes on a cue given, from an inexpressible height my bearers would dart as it were sloping like a shooting star, for an incredible distance, almost to the very surface of the sea, still keeping me as upright as a Spaniard on my seat. I asked them the reason of their so vast descent, when I perceived the labour they had afterwards to attain the same height again. They told me they not only eased their graundees by that descent, but could fly half as far again in a day, as by a direct (they meant horizontal) flight; for though it seemed laborious to mount so excessive high, yet they went on at the same time at a great rate; but when they came to descend again, there was no comparison in their speed. And, on my conscience, I believe they spoke true, for in their descents I think no arrow could have reached us.

In about sixteen hours, for I took my watch with me, we alighted on the height of Battringdrigg: when I thought I had returned to my own arkoe, it was so like it, but much larger. Here we rested for hours; I opened my chest, and gave each of my bearers a drop of brandy. Nasgig and I also just wetted our mouths, and ate a piece of preserve to moisten us; the rest of the lasks sitting down, and feeding upon what they had brought with them in their colapets; for their method is, when they take long flights, to carry a number of hard round fruits, flat like my cream-cheeses, but much less, which containing a sort of flour they eat dry; then drinking, which swells, and fills them as much as a good meal of anything else would. Here we met with abundance of delightful pools of water on the vast flat of the rocks. They told me, in that arkoe the young glumms and gawrys came in vast flights separately, to divert themselves on the fine lakes of water, and from thence went sometimes as far as my arkoe for that purpose; but that was but seldom.

When we had sufficiently rested, they shut their colapets, which sometimes hung down from their necks, and were sometimes swung round to their backs, and crossing the arkoe and another large sea, but nothing comparable to the first, arrived in about six hours more to the height of the White Mountains, which Nasgig told me were the confines of Georigetti's territories. But, thinks I, it may belong to whom it will for the value of it; for nothing could be more barren than all the top of it was; but the inside of it made amends for that, by the prodigious tall and large trees it abounded with, full of the strangest kinds of fruits I had ever seen; and these trees, most of them, seemed to grow out of the very stone itself, not a peck of dirt being to be collected near them. Without-side of these mountains, it was scarce darker than at my arkoe; for I made all the observation my time would allow me; when spying at a vast distance several lights, which were unusual things to me in that country, they told me the largest was the burning mountain Alkoe: this I remembered to have heard the name of upon some former occasion, though I could not recollect what; and that the rest were of the same sort, but smaller. I asked if they were in Georigetti's territories. They said no, they belonged to another king formerly, whose subjects were as fond of fire as Georigetti's were of avoiding it; and that many of them worked with it always before them, and made an insufferable noise by it.

At hearing the above relation, an impression struck my fancy, that they might be a sort of smiths or workers in iron, or other metals; and I wished myself with them, for I had a mighty notion of that work, having been frequently at a neighbouring forge when a boy, and knew all their tools, and resolved to get all the information I could of that country someother time; for our company drawing to their posts, and preparing to set forward again, I could have no more talk now; and you must know, I had observed so many idle rascals before I left England, who could neither strike a stroke nor stir a foot whilst you talked with them, that I feared if I asked questions by the way, they should in answering me neglect their duty, and let me drop.

When we came near our journey's end, Nasgig asked me where I would please to alight I told him I thought at my father's; for though I came on a visit to the king, it would not show respect to go before him just off a journey. But I might have spared me the trouble of settling that point; for we were not gone far from the Black Mountain, it going by that name within side, though it is called the White without, before we heard the gripsacks, and a sort of squeaking or screaming music, very loud. Nasgig told me the king was in flight. I asked him how he knew that, for I could see nobody. He knew it, he said, by the gripsack, and the other music, which never played but on that occasion; and presently after, I thought the whole kingdom were on the graundee, and was going to order my bearers back to the mountain, for fear of the concourse. Thinks I, they will jostle me down out of civility, and I shall break my neck to gratify their curiosity. So I told Nasgig if he did not somehow stop the multitude, I would turn back for the mountain, for I would never venture into that crowd of people.

Nasgig sprung away to the king and informed him; but the king, fearing the people should be disgusted at his sending them back, gave orders for the whole body to file off to the right and left, and taking a vast sweep each way, to fall in behind me; but upon no account to come near me, for fear of mischief. This was no sooner said than done, and all spreading into two vast semicircles, met in a train just behind my chair.

Nasgig had also persuaded the king to retreat back to the palace, telling him it was not with me as with them, who could help themselves in case of accident; but as I was under the guidance of others, and on a foundation he should scarce, in my condition, have ventured upon, he was sure I should be better satisfied with his intended respect only, than to receive it there: "But," says he, "that your majesty may see his contrivance, I will cause him to alight in the palace garden, where you may have the pleasure of viewing him in his machine."

The king returning, ordered all the colambs, who waited my arrival, to assemble in council again; and as I went over the city, I was surprised to see all the rock of which it consisted quite covered with people, besides prodigious numbers in the air, all shouting out peals of welcome to me; and as we were then but little above their heads, everyone had something to say of me; one wondering what I had got on; another swearing he saw hair on my face as long as his arm; and in general, everyone calling on the Image for my safety.

The king was present when I alighted in the garden; and himself taking me from my chair, I bent on one knee to kiss his hand; but he took me in his arms, called me his father, and told me he hoped I would make his days equal in glory to his great ancestor Begsurbeck. We complimented sometime before he took me into a small refectory in the garden, and gave me some of his sort of wine, which I found was loaded with ram's-horn, and some dried and moist sweetmeats. He then told me I had a piece of ceremony to go through, after which he hoped to have me to himself. I told him, whatever forms of State were customary, they become necessary, and I should obey him.

His majesty then called one of the persons in waiting, and telling him he was going to the room of audience, ordered him to conduct me thither forthwith.

Following my guide, after a long walk through a sort of piazza, we entered under a stately arch, curiously carved, into a very spacious room, lighted with infinite numbers of globe-lamps, where he desired me to sit down on a round stone pedestal covered with leaves, and all round the sides were running foliages exquisitely wrought; on the walls were carved figures of glumms in several actions, but chiefly in battle, or other warlike exercises, in alto-relievo, very bold, with other devices interspersed. I sat down, having first paid my submission to the throne, and to the several colambs who sat on the king's right and left, down the sides of the room.

The person then who introduced me, going into the middle of the room, spoke to this effect: "Mighty king—and you honourable lords his colambs—here is present the glumm Peter of Graundevolet; I wait your commands where to dispose him."

Then the king and all the colambs arising, another person stepped forth, and looking at me, for I was standing, "Glumm Peter of Graundevolet," says he, "I am to signify to you that the mighty king Georigetti, and all his honourable colambs, congratulate your arrival in Normnbdsgrsutt, and have commanded me to give you rank according to your merit." Then the king and colambs sat down, and I was led to the king's right hand, and placed on the same stone with, but at some small distance from, his majesty.

The king then told me the great pleasure I had done him and his colambs, in my so speedy arrival upon their message; but said he would give me no farther trouble now than to know how I chose to be served; and desired me to give orders to a bash he would send to me, for whatever I wanted; and then giving orders to a bash to show me my lodgings, I was permitted to retire to refresh myself.

I was then conducted to my apartment, up a sloping flight of stone, very long, with a vast arch over my head; I believed it might be fifty paces long at least, but being a very broad easy ascent, and smooth, it was not in the least fatiguing. All the way I went were the same sorts of globe lights as in the audience-room. The staircase, if I may call it so, it answering the same purpose, was most beautifully carved, both sides and top. At length I came into a very large gallery, at least fourscore paces long, and about twenty broad; on each side of which hung the same globes. At the farther end of this gallery I entered by an arch, very narrow, but most neatly wrought, into an oval room; in the middle of this room, on the right hand, was another small neat archway; entering through which about ten paces, there were two smaller arches to the right and left, and within them, with an easy ascent of about three paces, you came to a flat trough of stone, six or seven feet long, and about the same width; these, I understood by my bash, were the beds to lie on.

I asked him if they were used to lie on the bare stone. He told me some did, but he had orders to lay me on doffee; and presently up came four fellows with great mats, as I took them for by my globe light, full of something, which, by their so easily carrying so great bulk, I perceived was very light. They pitched it down upon my stone bedstead, and first with great sticks, and then with small switches having beat it soundly, retired.

Whilst I was looking about at the oddity of the place, I found my bash was gone too. "So," says I, "all gone! I suppose they intend I shall now go to bed." I then went into my bed-chamber, for there were globe lights there too, and observing my bed lay full four feet above the stone, and sloping higher to the sides and head, I went to feel what it was; but laying my hand upon it, it was so soft I could feel no resistance till I had pressed it some way; and it lay so light, that a fly must have sunk upon it.—"Well," thinks I, "what if I never lay thus before, I believe I have lain as bad!"

I then took a turn into my oval room again, and observed the floor, sides, and all was stone, as smooth as possible, but not polished; and the walls and ceiling, and in short every place where they could be ornamented, were as well adorned with carvings as can be conceived.

Though nobody came near me yet, I did not care to be too inquisitive all at once, but I longed to know what they burnt in the globes, which gave so steady a light, and yet seemed to be enclosed quite round, top and sides, without any vent-hole for the smoke to evaporate. Surely, thinks I, they are a dullish glass, for they hung almost above my touch, and must be exceeding hot with the fire so enclosed, and have some small vent-hole though I can't see it. Then standing on tiptoe to feel, it struck quite cold to my finger; but I could only reach to touch that, or any of the rest, being all of one height.

Whilst I was musing thus, I heard the sound of voices coming along the gallery; and presently came a train of servants with as much victuals as a hundred men could eat, and wines proportionable; they set it down at the upper end of the oval room, on a flat of stone, which on making the room had been left in the upper bend of the oval quite across it, about table high, for that purpose. These eatables, such as were liquid, or had sauces to them, were served up in a sort of grey stone bowls; but the dry were brought in neat wooden baskets of twig-work.

The servants all retiring into the gallery, except my bash, I asked him if anybody was to eat with me: he told me no.—"I wonder," says I, "they should send me so much, then." He replied it was the allowance of my apartment by his majesty's orders; which silenced me.

I believe there were twenty different things on the table, insomuch that I did not know where to begin, and heartily wished for an excuse to get rid of my bash, who stood close at my elbow, that I might have smelt and tasted before I helped myself to anything, for I knew not what anyone thing was.

In this perplexity, I asked my bash what post he was in under his majesty. He said, one of the fifty bashes appointed to be near the king's favourites when at court. "And pray," said I, "are you the person to attend me?" He was, he said, the principal to wait on my person; but there were at least sixty others, who had different offices in this apartment. "I would be glad," said I, "to know your name, that I may the more readily speak to you." He told me his name was Quilly. "Then, pray, Quilly," says I, "do you know what is become of my baggage and chair?" I found, though he guessed at my baggage, he was puzzled at the name of chair. "My seat," says I. "Oh, I understand you," says he. "Then, pray, will you go bring me word of them, and see them brought safe up into the gallery?" He tripped away on my errand. So thinks I, now I am fairly rid of you! but I had scarce turned any of my viands over, before I found he had but stepped into the gallery, to send some of the idle fellows-in-waiting there. And this putting me to a nonplus, "Quilly," says I, "you know I am a stranger here; and as different countries have different ways and customs, as well of dressing their eatables as other things, and these dishes being dressed contrary to my custom, I shall be glad if you will name some of them to me, that I may know them when I see them again."

Quilly began with this, and ran on to that, which was a fine dish; and the other few but the king have at their tables. "And here," says he, "is a dish of padsi; and there—"

"Hold, hold," says I, "Quilly, let's try these first before you proceed;" for I remembered, at my grotto, they all eat my fish for padsi, and I cut a slice of it; for I always carried my clasp-knife in my pocket, and they had no such thing there; and laying it on a round cake I took for my trencher, I tasted it, and found it so, to my apprehension, in the palate; but it did not look or flake like fish, as I observed by the slices they had cut it into; for all the victuals were in long slices ready to bite at. I asked him if these things were not all cut, and with what; for I understood they had no knives, showing him mine. He said the cook cut it with a sharp stone. I then asked him the name of several other things, and at last he came to crullmott, which having heard of before, I now tasted, and could have sworn it had been a hashed fowl. I asked him if crullmotts were very common; he told me yes, towards the bottoms of the mountains there were abundance of crullmott-trees.—"No, no," says I, "not trees; I mean fowls, birds."—"I don't know what they are," said he; "but these crullmotts grow on very large trees." Indeed, I did not know yet what I was at. "But," says I, "if your fowls do, sure your fish don't grow on trees too!"—"We have none of them," says he, "in this country."—"Why," says I, "it is but this moment I tasted one."—"I don't know," said he, "where the cook got it."—"Why, here," says I, "what you call padsi I call fish."—"Aye, padsi," says he, "'grows upon a bush in the same woods."—"Well done," says I, "this is the first country I was ever in where the fish and fowl grew on trees. It is ten to one but I meet with an ox growing on some tree by the tail before I leave you."

I had by this time, out of these two and someother pickings, made up a very good meal; and putting my knife into my pocket, desired something to drink. My bash asked me what I pleased to have. I told him, anything to take a good draught of. Then he filled me a bott of wine, very well tasted, though too sweet for meals; but putting some water to it, it did very well.

My messengers being returned, and having set all my things in the gallery, I desired Quilly to let the victuals be taken away; upon which there came more servants than dishes, who took all at once, but some wine and water I desired might remain.

I told Quilly I saw there were two beds. "Who are they for?" says I.—"One for you and one for me," says he; "for we bashes never leave the king's favourites."—"Pray, Quilly," says I, "what is the meaning that to the several rooms I have been in, there is never a door?"—"Door," says he, "I don't know that."—"What!" says I, "don't you shut your rooms at night?"—"No, no. Shut at night! I never heard of that."—"I believe," says I, "Quilly, it is almost bed-time; is it not?"—"No, no," says Quilly, "the gripsack has not sounded."—"How do you know," says I, "in this country, when you shall lie down, and when rise? for my wife has told me you have no clocks."

"No; no clocks," says he.—"Then," says I, "does everyone rise and lie down when they please? or do you all lie down and all rise together about the same time?"—"Oh," says Quilly, "you will hear the gripsack presently. There are several glumms who take it by turns to sound it for the rest, and then we know it is time to lie down; and when they sound it again, we know it is time to rise." And afterwards I found these people guessed the time (being twelve hours between sound and sound) so well, that there were but few minutes' variation at anytime between them and my watch; and I set my watch to go from their soundings at six o'clock.

I found myself pretty much fatigued after my journey; for though I had only to sit still, yet the excessive velocity of such an unusual motion strained every muscle as much as the hardest labour; for you may imagine I could not at first be without my fears upon ever so small a variation of my chair, which, though I could not possibly by my own inclination one way or other rectify, yet a natural propensity to a perpendicular station involuntarily biasses one to incline this or that way, in order to preserve it; and then at first my breath being ready to fail me, in proportion to the celerity of the flight, and to my own apprehensions, and being upon that exercise near thirty hours, and without sleep for almost forty, you may judge I wanted rest; so I told Quilly I would lie down, and ordered him not to disturb me till I waked of myself.

I could not prevent the officiousness of my valet to put me to bed, and cover me with the down, or whatever it was; for having no sheets, I pulled off nothing but my coat, wig, and shoes, and putting on my flannel night-cap, I laid me down.

XII

I Have known some travellers so peculiar in their taste as not to be
able to sleep in a strange lodging. But, thanks to my kind stars, that
did not prove my case; for having looked on my watch when I went to
bed, as I call it, and finding it was down, I wound it up, and observed it
began to go at about three o'clock—whether day or night, matters not;
and when I waked it was past nine, so that I know I had slept eighteen
hours; and finding that a very reasonable refreshment, and myself very
hungry, I called Quilly to get me my breakfast.

Quilly told me his majesty had been to visit me, but would not
have me disturbed. I, begging him to despatch my breakfast as soon
as possible, and let me have some water for my hands, he ordered the
gallery-waiters, and everything came immediately.

My breakfast was a brown liquid, with a sort of seeds or grain in it,
very sweet and good; but the fear of the king's return before I was ready
for him, prevented my inquiring into what it was. So, having finished it,
and washed my hands, Quilly presented me a towel, which looked like
an unbleached coarse linen, but was very soft and spongy; and I found
afterwards was made of threads of bark stripped from some tree. I put
on my brown suit, sword, and long wig, and sent Quilly to know when
it was his majesty's pleasure I should wait upon him.

I had been so much used to lamplight in my grotto, that the lights
of this gloomy mansion did not seem so unusual a thing to me as
they would have done to a stranger. The king sent me word he would
admit me immediately, and Quilly was my conductor to his majesty's
apartment.

We passed through the gallery, at the farther end of which was a
very beautiful arch, even with the staircase, through which Quilly led
me into a large guard-room, wherein were above a hundred glumms,
posted in ranks, with their pikes in hand, some headed with sharp-
pointed stone, others with multangular stone, and others with stone
globes. Passing through these, we entered another gallery as long as
that to my apartment; then under another arch we came into a small

square room, carved exceeding fine; on the right and left of which were two other archways, leading into most noble rooms. But we only saw them, passing quite cross the little room, through an arch that fronted us into a small gallery of prodigious height; at the farther end of which Quilly, turning aside a mat, introduced and left me in the most beautiful place in the universe, where, neither seeing nor hearing anybody stir, I employed myself in examining the magnificence of the place, and could, as I then thought, have feasted my eye with variety for a twelvemonth. I paced it over one hundred and thirty of my paces long, and ninety-six broad. There were arches in the middle of each side, and in the middle of each end; the arch ceiling could not be less than the breadth of the room, and covered with the most delightful carvings, from whence hung globe-lights innumerable, but seemingly without order, which I thought appeared the more beautiful on that account. In the centre of the room hung a prodigious cluster of the same lights, so disposed as to represent one vast light; and there were several rows of the same lights hung round the room, one row above another, at proper distances. These lights represented to me the stars, with the moon in the middle of them; and after I came to be better acquainted with the country, I perceived the lights were to represent the southern constellations. The archways were carved with the finest devices imaginable, gigantic glumms supporting on each side the pediments.

At every ten paces all along the sides and ends, arose columns, each upon a broad square base, admirably carved; these reached to the cornice or base of the arched ceiling quite round the room. On the panels between each column were carved the different battles and most remarkable achievements of Begsurbeck himself. Over the arch I entered at, was the statue of Begsurbeck, and over the opposite arch the old prophetic ragan. In the middle of the room stood a long stone table lengthwise, most exquisitely carved, almost the length of the room, except where it was divided in the middle about the breadth of the archways, in order for a passage from one arch to the other. In short, to describe this one room particularly would make a volume of itself.

I stayed here a full hour and a half, wondering why nobody came to me; at length turning myself about, I saw two glumms coming towards me, and having received their compliments, they desired me to walk in to the king. We passed through another middling room, and taking up a mat at the farther side of it, I was conducted in where his majesty was sitting with another glumm. They both arose at my entrance, and calling me their father, and leading me, one by each hand, obliged me to sit down between them.

After some compliments about my journey, and accommodation since, the king told me I had not waited so long without, but he had some urgent despatches to make; and as he chose to have me in private with him, he imagined, he said, I would be able to divert myself in the boskee. I declared I had never seen anything like it for grandeur and magnificence before; but the beauty of the sculpture, and disposition of the lights, were most exquisite.

All this while I felt the other glumm handling my long wig, and feeling whether it grew to my head, or what it was; for he had by this time got his finger under the caul, and was pulling my hair down; when I turning about my head, "Glumm Peter," says the king, "don't be uneasy, the ragan will do you no hurt, it is only to satisfy his curiosity; and I chose to have the ragan here, that we may more leisurely advise with you what course to take in the present exigencies of my State. I have fully heard the story of your travels from my colambs, and we have returned thanks to the Great Image for bringing you, after so many hazards and deliverances, safe to my dominions for our defence."

The ragan desired to know whether all that hair (meaning my wig) grew upon my head or not. I told him no, it was a covering only, to put on occasionally; but that hair did grow on my head, and pulling off my wig I showed them. The ragan then asked me if I had hair of my own growing under that too (meaning my beard, which he then had in his hand, for their glumms have no beards); but I told him that grew there of itself.—"O parly Puly!" says the ragan, rising up, and smiting his hands together, "It is he! It is he!"

"Pray," says I, "ragan, who is this Puly you speak of?"—"It is the image," says he, "of the great Collwar."—"Who is that?" says I.—"Why, he that made the world," says he.—"And, pray," says I, "what did his image make?"—"Oh," says he, "we made the image."—"And, pray," says I, "can't you break it again?"—"Yes," says he, "if we had a mind to be struck dead, we might; for that would be the immediate consequence of such an attempt; nay, of but holding up a finger against it in contempt."—"Pray," says I, "did ever anybody die that way?"—"No," says he, "no one ever durst presume to do it."—"Then, perhaps," said I, "upon trial, the punishment you speak of might not be the consequence of such an attempt. Pray," says I, "what makes Collwar have so great a kindness for that image?"—"Because," says he, "it is his very likeness, and he gives him all he asks for us; for we only ask him. Why," says he, "it is the image that has brought you amongst us."

I did not then think it a proper time to advance the contrary to the person I then had to do with, as I was sure it would have done no good; for a priest is only to be convinced by the strongest party: so I deferred my argument on that head to a fitter opportunity.

"Most admirable Peter," says the king, "you are the glumm we depend upon to fulfil an ancient prediction delivered by a venerable ragan. If you will, Ragan I. O. shall repeat it to you, and therein you will be able to discern yourself plainly described, in not only similar, but the express words I myself, from your story, should describe you in."

In good earnest, I had from divers circumstances concluded that I might be the person; and resolved, as I thought I had the best handle in the world for it from the prediction, to do what I could in the affair of religion, by fair means or stratagem (for I was sensible my own single force would not do it), before I began to show myself in their cause, or else to desert them; and having had a small hint from Nasgig of what the old ragan's design was in part, and which I approved of, I purposed to add what else was necessary as part of his design, if his proposals had been approved of.

I told the king I would excuse the ragan the repetition of the prediction, as I had partly been informed of it by Nasgig; and that conceiving myself, as he did, to be the person predicted of by the ragan, I had the more readily set out on this expedition, which nothing but the hopes of performing so great a good could have prevailed with me to undertake; and I did not doubt, with God's blessing, to accomplish it.

The king grew exceeding joyous at what I said, and told me he would call a moucheratt, at which all his colambs should attend, to have their advice, and then we would proceed to action; and ordered the ragan to let it be for the sixth day, and in the meantime that he and his brethren should, day and night, implore the Image to guide their deliberations.

The ragan being gone, I told the king I had something to impart to him, in which it was my duty to obtain his majesty's sentiments before I appeared publicly at the moucheratt. He desired me to proceed: I told him I had been sometime considering the old ragan's prediction, with the occasion of it; "and," says I, "it is plain to me that all these mischiefs have befallen you for neglect of the ragan's proposal concerning religion; as I understand your great ancestor would have come into it, and would have had his people done so too, but for the ragans, who hindered it.

"You find," says I, "by your traditional history, that Begsurbeck lived long, and reigned gloriously; and I would aim at making you as prosperous as he was, and infinitely more happy, not only in outward splendour here, but in great glory hereafter."

Perceiving that my discourse had quickened the king's attention, says I, "I must let your majesty know it is the old ragan's plan I must proceed upon in every branch of it."—"Why," says the king, "he would have abolished our worship of the Image."—"And so would I," says I; "nay, not only would, but must and will, before I engage myself in your deliverance; and then, with the only assistance of the great Collwar, whom I adore, and whom you must too, if you expect any service from me, I don't doubt to prevail."

"Your majesty sees," says I, "in few words, I have been very plain with you; and I desire you, in as concise and plain a manner, to answer me, what are your thoughts on this head? for I can say no more till I hear them."

The king seeing me so peremptory: "Glumm Peter," says he, looking about to see no one was near, "I have too much sense to imagine our Image can do either good or hurt; for if it could have done us good, why would it not in our greatest distress, now near two hundred years past? For my own part, I put no trust in it, nor did my famous ancestor the great Begsurbeck; but here is my difficulty, where to choose another object of worship; for I perceive by myself, mankind must, through natural impulse, look to somewhat still above them, as a child does to his father, from whom he hopes for and expects succour in his difficulties; and though the father be not able to assist him, still he looks to him; and therefore, I say, we must have another before we can part with this, or the people, instead of the part who have been in the defection, will all desert me; for they are easy now in hopes of help from the Image, and every little gleam of success is attributed to it; but for the disadvantages we receive, the ragans charge them on the people's not praying and paying sufficiently; which they, poor souls, knowing in their consciences to be true enough, are willing rather, as they are bid, to take the blame upon themselves, than to suffer the least to fall on the Image."

"All this," says the king, "I am sensible of; but should I tell them so, my life must pay for it; for the ragans would bring some message from the Image against me, to desert or murder me; and then happy would be the first man who could begin the mischief, which the rest would soon follow."

This so frank and unexpected declaration gave me great confidence in the king; and I told him, if that was his opinion, he might leave the rest to me. I would so manage it, that the thing should be brought about by my means; and I would then satisfy all his scruples, and make him a flourishing prince. But I could not help reflecting with myself, how nearly this distant prince, and his State, copied some of my neighbours in Europe.

XIII

Having now fully entered into the spirit of the business with my own good liking, I was determined to push it vigorously, or perish in the attempt. "Have I," says I, "so large a field before me now to manifest my Maker in to a whole nation, and under His own call, and to fulfil their own prediction too; and shall I shrink at the possible danger? Or may there not rather be no probability of danger in it? The nation is in distress, the readier therefore to try any remedy for help: their Image has stood idle two hundred years; there has been an old prophecy, or at least if not true, as firmly believed to be true as if it was so; and this, in regard to the people, answers in all respects as well. But why should it not be true? It is better attested by the frequent repetition, from the original delivery to this time, than are many traditions I have heard of amongst us Christians, which have come out spick and span new from the repositories of the learned, of twelve or fifteen hundred years old, little the worse for lying by; though they are not pretended to have seen light all that time, and are undoubted verities the moment they receive the grand sanction. Then if any means but fraud or force can gain so large a territory to the truth, and I am the only person can introduce it, shall not I endeavour it? Yes, surely; but I am not excluded all advantages neither, for all the works of Providence are brought to pass by appointed means: and indeed, were it otherwise, what could we call Providence? For a peremptory fiat, and it is over, may work a miracle, it is true, but will not exhibit the proceedings of Providence. Therefore let me consider, in a prudential way, how to proceed to the execution of what I am to set about—and guide me, Providence! I beseech you, to the end."

Upon the best deliberation I could take, I came to the following resolutions: First, to insist on the abolition of the Image-worship, and to introduce true religion by the fittest means I could find opportunity for.

Secondly, as the revolters had been one people with those I would serve, and had this prediction amongst them too, and were interested in it, in hopes of its distant accomplishment; so if they came properly to the knowledge that the person predicted of had appeared, and was ready for execution of his purposes, it must stagger their fidelity to their new master; and, therefore, I would find means to let them know it.

Thirdly, that I would not march till I was in condition not easily to be repulsed, for that would break both the hopes and hearts of my party, and destroy my religious scheme, and, therefore, I would get some of my cannon.

Fourthly, that I would go to the war in my flying-chair, and train up a guard for my person with pistols and cutlasses.

These resolutions I kept to myself till the moucheratt was over, to see first how matters would turn out there.

Whilst I waited for the approaching moucheratt, my son Tommy, and daughter Hallycarnie, paid their duties to me. It is strange how soon young minds are tainted by bad company. I found them both very glad to see me, for everybody, they said, told them I was to be their deliverer. They had both got the prophecy by heart, and mentioned the Image with all the affection of natural subjects. The moment Tommy spoke of it to me, "Hold," says I, "young man. What's become of those good principles I took so much pains to ground you in? Has all my concern for your salvation been thrown away upon you? Are you become a reprobate? What! an apostate from the faith you inherited by birthright? Is the God I have so often declared to you a wooden one? Answer me, or never see my face more."

The child was extremely confounded to see me look so severe, and hear me speak so harsh to him. "Indeed, father," says he, "I did not willingly offend, or design to show any particular regard to the Image, for, thanks to you, I have none; but what I said was only the common discourse in everybody's mouth; I meant neither good nor harm by it."

"Tommy," says I, "it is a great fault to run into an error, though in company of multitudes; and where a person's principle is sound at bottom, and founded upon reason, no numbers ought to shake it. You are young, therefore hearken to me; and you, Hallycarnie, whatever you shall see done by the people of this country, in the worship of this idol, don't you imitate it, don't you join in it. Keep the sound lessons I have preached to you in mind; and upon every attempt of the ragans, or any other, to draw you aside to their worship, or even to speak or act the least thing in praise of this idol, think of me and my words, pay your adoration to the Supreme Father of spirits only, and to no wooden, stone, or earthen deity whatsoever."

The children wept very heartily, and both promised me to remember and to do as I had taught them.

Being now in my oval chamber, and alone with my children, I had a mind to be informed of somethings I was almost ashamed to ask Quilly. "Tommy," says I, "what sort of fire do they keep in these globes? and what are they made of?"—"Daddy," says he, "yonder is the man shifting them, you may go and see." Being very curious to see how he did it, I went to him. As I came near him, he seemed to have something all fire on his arm. "What has the man got there?" says I. "Only sweecoes," says Tommy. By this time I came up to him; "Friend," says I, "what are you about?"—"Shifting the sweecoes, sir," says he, "to feed them."—"What oil do you feed with?" says I.—"Oil!" says he, "they won't eat oil; that would kill them all."—"Why," says I, "my lamp is fed with oil."

Tommy could scarce forbear laughing himself; but for fear the servant should do so too, pulled me by the sleeve, and desired me to say no more. So turning away with him, "Daddy," says he, "it is not oil that gives this light, but sweecoes, a living creature. He has got his basket full, and is taking the old ones out to feed them, and putting new ones in. They shift every half day and feed them."—"What!" says I, "are all these infinite number of globes I see living creatures?"—"No," says he, "the globes are only the transparent shell of a bott, like our calibashes. The light comes from the sweecoe within."—"Has that man," says I, "got any of them?"—"Yes," says he, "you may see them. The king and the colambs, and indeed every man of note, has a place to breed and feed them in."—"Pray, let us go see them," says I, "for that is a curiosity indeed."

Tommy desired the man to show me the swee-coes; so he set down his basket, which was a very beautiful resemblance of a common higler's basket, with a handle in the middle, and a division under it, with flaps on each side to lift up and down. It was made of straw-coloured small twigs, neatly compacted, but so light as scarce to be of any weight. Opening one of the lids, I could make very little distinction of substances, the bottom seeming all over of a white colour. I looking surprised at the light, the man took out one, and would have put it into my hand, but perceiving me shy of it, he assured me it was one of the most innocent things in the world. I then took it, and surveying it, it felt to my touch as smooth and cold as a piece of ice. It was about as long as a large lobworm, but much thicker. The man seeing me admire the brightness of its colour, told me it had done its duty, and was going to be fed, but those which were going upon duty were much clearer; and then opening the other lid, those appeared far exceeding the others in brightness, and thickness too. I asked what he fed them with. He said, "Leaves and fruit; but grass, when he could get it, which was not often, they were very fond of."

Having dismissed my children, I sent for Nasgig, to gain some intelligences I wanted to be informed of. The moment I saw him it came into my mind to inquire after my new filgays. He said the king granted my request at the first word. I told him then he had saved his honour with me, and I was obliged to him. "But," says I, "you told me my bearers should be free too."—"They are so," says he.—"Then there is one thing I want," says I, "and that is to see the second bearer on my right hand, who came through without shifting. I have a fancy for that fellow," says I, "to be about my person. I like him; and if you can give him a good word, I should be glad to treat with him about it."

"My friend Peter," says he, "you are a man of penetration, though it ill becomes me to say so in regard of persons; but I can say that for him, if he likes you as well as you seem to like him, he is the trustiest fellow in the world; but as he knows his own worth, he would not be so to everybody, I can tell you that."—"I don't fear his disliking me," says I, "for I make it my maxim to do as I would be done by; and if he is a man of honour, as you seem to say, he would do the same, and we shall be soon agreed."—"But," says Nasgig, "it being now the fourth day since he was freed, he may be gone home perhaps, for he is not of our country, but of Mount Alkoe. If Quilly can find him, he will come." So he ordered Quilly to send for Maleck of Mount Alkoe, with orders to come to me.

We descended from one discourse to another, and at length to King Georigetti's affairs, when Nasgig, giving a sigh, "Ah, Peter!" says he, "we shall loiter away our time here till the enemy are upon our backs. There is venom in the grass; I wish my good master is not betrayed."—"By whom?" says I.—"By those he little suspects," says he.—"Why," says I, "they tell me you are much in his favour; if so, why do you suffer it?"—"I believe," says Nasgig, "I am in his favour, and may continue in it, if I will join in measures to ruin him, but else I shall soon be out of it."—"You tell me riddles," says I.—"These things," says he, "a man talks with his

ROBERT PALTOCK

head in his teeth. There is danger in them, Peter; there is danger!"—"You don't suspect me," says I, "do you?"—"No," says he, "I know your soul too well; but there are three persons in these dominions who will never let my master rest till out of his throne, or in hoximo. I am but lately in favour, but have made as many observations, perhaps, as those who have been longer about the king."

"Nasgig," says I, "your concern proceeds from an honest heart. Don't stifle what you have to say; if I can counsel you with safety, I'll do it; if not, I'll tell you so."

"Peter," says he, "Georigetti was the only son of a well-beloved father, and ascended his throne ten years ago on his decease: but Harlokin, the prince of the revolters, whose head is never idle, finding that whispers and base stories spread about did not hurt Georigetti, or withdraw his subjects' affections, has tried a means to make him undo himself."—"As how?" says I.—"Why," said he, "by closely playing his game he has got one of his relations into the king's service, than whom he could never have chosen a fitter instrument. He, by degrees, feeding the king's humour, and promising mountains, has pushed into the best places into the kingdom. His name is Barbarsa, a most insolent man, who has had the assurance to corrupt the king's mistress, and has prevailed and brought her over to his interest."—"Oh perfidy!" says I, "is it possible?"—"Yes," says he; "and more than that, has drawn in, till now, an honest man called Nicor; and it has been agreed between them to protract this war, till by their stratagems in procuring the revolt of Gauingrunt, a very large and populous province, and now the barrier between us and the rebels, and two or three more places, they shall have persuaded Georigetti to fly; and then Barbarsa is to be king, and Yaccom-bourse his queen. A union is then to be struck between him and Harlokin, and peace made, by restoring some of the surrendered provinces; and upon the death of the first of them, or their issue, childless, the survivor, or his issue, is to take the whole. They laugh at your uniting the dominions, and the old prediction."

"These," said I, "Nasgig, are serious things, and, as you say, are not lightly to be talked of; but, Nasgig, know this, he that conceals them is a traitor. Can you prove this?"—"I have heard them say so," says Nasgig.—"How!" says I, "and not discover it!"—"I am as anxious for that as you can be," says he; "but for me to be cashiered, slit, and sent to Crashdoorpt, only for meaning well, without power to perfect my good intentions, where will be the benefit to my master or me?"—"When and where did you hear this?" says I.—"Several and several times," says he, "in my own bed."—"In your own bed?" says I.—"I'll tell you," says he; "it so happens that when I rest at the palace, as I am bound to do when on duty, there is a particular bed for me: now, as the whole palace is cut out of one solid rock, though Yaccom-bourse's apartment at the entrance is at a prodigious distance from the entrance to mine, yet my bed, and one in an inner apartment of hers, stand close together; the partition, indeed, is stone, but either from the thinness of it, or some flaw in it, I have not yet discovered, I can plainly hear every word that is spoken. And there it is, in their hours of dalliance, when they use this bed, that I hear what I have now told you."—"Say nothing of it," says I, "but leave the issue to me."

By this time the messenger returned with Maleck, and he and I soon agreeing, I took him into my service.

I went to bed as usual, but could get no rest, Nasgig's story engrossing my whole attention; I was resolved, however, to be better informed before I acquainted the king of it; but rising pretty early next morning, the king came into my chamber, leaning upon Barbarsa, to tell me that he had received an express that Gauingrunt had revolted. "Peter," says he, "behold a distressed monarch; nay, an undone monarch!"—"Great sir," says Barbarsa, "you afflict yourself too much; here is Mr. Peter come to assist you, and he will settle all your concerns, never fear." I eyed the man, and (though prejudice may hang an honest person) found him a villain in his heart; for even while he was forcing a feeling tone of affliction, he was staring at my laced hat and feather that lay on the seat, by which I was sure nothing could be at a greater distance than his heart and tongue. His sham concern put me within a moment of seizing him in the king's presence; but his majesty, at that instant speaking, diverted me.

Before the king left me, I told him, having certain propositions to make to the moucheratt next day, it was possible they might require time to consider them; wherefore it would be proper, at this critical time, to let them meet every other day, business or none, till this affair was over. The king ordered Barbarsa to see it was so, and then we parted.

XIV

Hold a moucheratt—Speeches of ragans and colambs—
Peter settles religion—Informs the king of a plot—
Sends Nasgig to the ship for cannon.

Attending at the moucheratt today, I happened to be seated within two paces of the idol. There was the most numerous assembly that had ever been seen; and when all was quiet, the king opened with signifying the revolt of Gauingrunt, the approach of the enemy, and no forces in the field to stop them. This he set forth in terms so moving, that the whole assembly were melted into sighs; till one of the colambs rising up, says he: "His majesty has set forth the state of his affairs in such a manner, and I am satisfied a true one, that it becomes us all to be vigilant. We all seem to have, and I believe have, great faith in the remedy this day to be proposed to us, in answer to our ancient prediction; and as I doubt not but glumm Peter is the man, so I doubt not but through his management we shall still receive help; but let us consider if we might not have prevented these pressing evils, and especially this last, by speedier preparations against them. What province, or member of a State, will not revolt to a numerous host just ready to devour them, if they can receive no assistance from their head? for, to my certain knowledge, his majesty had ordered this almost a year ago, and not a man gone yet. Can we expect Peter to go singly to fight an army? Did your prediction say he should go alone? No, he shall slay; that is, he and his army; what is done by them being always attributed to their general. Inquire, therefore, into your past conduct, send Peter, your general, and trust to the Great Image."

His majesty then said, if there had been any remissness in executing his commands, he believed it was done with a view to his service; but a more proper opportunity might be found for an inquiry of that nature. As for the present moucheratt, it was called solely to propose to Peter the execution of the remaining part of the prediction; or, at least, such part of it as seems now, or never, to wait its accomplishment.

Here arose a ragan, and told the assembly, in the name of himself and brethren, that the prediction had never yet been applicable to anyone person till glumm Peter arrived; and that his sagacity of itself was a sufficient recommendation of him to the guidance of the enterprise;

and requested that glumm Peter might forthwith be declared protector of the army, and set forward with it, that the State might receive safety, and the Great Image its proper honour.

I could now hold out no longer; but, standing up, made my speech in the following manner, or very near it: "Mighty king—you, reverend ragans—and honourable colambs—with the good people of this august assembly—I am come hither, led by the force of your own prediction, at the request of his majesty and the states, at the peril of my life, to accomplish things said to be predicted of me, glumm Peter. If, then, you have a prediction, if, then, your prediction describes me, and the circumstances of these times, it consisting of several parts, they ought seriously to be weighed, that I may know when and where I am to begin my operation, and when and where to leave off; for in predictions the whole is to be accomplished as much as any member of it.

"It is said I shall destroy the traitor of the ancient limits of your monarchy. Are you willing, therefore, that should be done? yea, or nay?" Then everyone answered, "Yea."—"And by common consent establish what the old ragan would have taught you?" Here the king rose up; but Barbarsa giving him a touch (for everyone waited to be guided by the voice of the ragans), he sat down again; and no one answering Yea, west; "I am ready to enter upon it and settle the question."

I again put the same question, and told them, as it was their own concern, I would have an answer before I proceeded. One of the ragans then rose, and said that part of the prediction was too loose to be relied on, for it was to settle what he would have taught: "Now, who knows," says he, "what he would have taught?" The assembly paused a considerable time, and just as I was opening my mouth to speak, an ancient and venerable ragan rose: says he, "I am sorry, at my years, to find that truth wants an advocate; my age and infirmities might well have excused me from speaking in this assembly, so many of my brethren being present, younger and better qualified for that purpose than myself; but as we are upon a sacred thing, and lest, as I find none of them care to declare the truth, I should also be thought to consent to its suppression if I sat silent and suffered it to be hid under a quibble, I must beg to be heard a few words. My brother, who spoke last, says the words are too loose which say, 'and by common consent establish what I would have taught'; but I beg leave to think it far otherwise, for we all know what he would have taught, and the memory of that hath been as exactly kept as the prediction; for how could our ancestors have opposed his doctrine, but from hearing and disapproving it? And we all know, not only the prediction, but the doctrine, hath been punctually handed down to us; though, woe be to us! we have not proclaimed it as we have done the prediction; and let me tell you, when you, my brethren, severally come to my years, and have but a single step farther to hoximo, you will wish you had taught it, as I do, who believe and approve it." The poor old man, having spoke as long as his breath and spirits would permit him, sat down, and I again resumed the question, as I now thought, on a much better foundation than before, and was immediately told by another ragan that there would be no end to the assembly if we considered every point at once, for we might next go upon what countries we should conquer, and of whom to demand tribute; which would be debating about the fruit before the seed was sown. But his opinion was, to go on and quell the rebellion, and restore the monarchy, and then go upon the other points.

I told them, if they had made so light of the prediction as not to declare publicly, since they knew it, what the ragan would have taught, it ill became me to be more zealous in their own concerns than they were themselves; and I should imagine there was very little truth in any part of it, and would never hazard my life for their sakes who would not speak the truth to save the kingdom, and desired leave of the states for my departure; for I was not a person, I told them, to be cajoled into anything. I undertook it at first voluntarily; and no man could, or should, compel me to it: my life they might take, but my honour they should never stain, though I was assured I could easily, with their concurrence, complete all that related to them.

The senior colamb immediately rising, desired me to have a little patience, and not to leave the assembly (for I was going out) till I had heard him.

"Here is," says he, "this day a thing started, which, I think, every whit as much concerns us all, and the body, and every member of the people to know, as it does Peter; and I am surprised, unless the present ragans believe what their predecessor would have taught to be better than what they now teach (for nothing else can make us consent to it), that they should scruple to let us know it, and keep us ignorant, who are worshippers as well as themselves, of any matter which so nearly concerns us to know. I am for obliging the ragans to declare the truth. If this be a true prediction, all the relatives to it are true, and I insist that we hear it."

This speech emboldened several others; and all the populace siding with the colambs out of curiosity, cried out to know it.

Perceiving the ragans still hush, I rose; and beckoning the populace to silence, "Mighty king—you, honourable colambs—and you, good people," says I—"for it is to you I now speak, hear me with attention. You think, perhaps, that the suppression of the truth by your ragans (charged to their teeth by the most reverend of their whole body, whose infirmities rendering him unable, though his will is good, to declare this secret to you) will prevent the knowledge of that truth your old ragan would have taught, but you are mistaken; and that you may know I don't come here at a venture to try if I can relieve you, but with an assurance of doing it if you consent, I must let you know from me what the ragan would have taught. The ragan would have demolished this trumpery piece of dirt, this grimalkin, set out with horrid face and colour to fright children; this," I say, "he would have demolished, being assured it could neither do good nor hurt, give joy or grief to any man, or serve any other purpose whatsoever, but to procure a maintenance to a set of men who know much better than they dare to tell you. Can any of you believe this stupid piece of earth hears me?" Some of the ragans cried, "Yes!"—"And that he can revenge any affront I shall give him?" Again, "Yes, to be sure!"—"Let him then, if he dare," says I, whipping out my cutlass, and with the backside of it striking his head off. "This," says I, "O glumms, is what the ragan knew, and what I defy them to deny. Now," says I, "I will further show you to whom the old ragan would have taught you to make your petitions and pay your adorations; and that is to the Supreme Being, Maker of heaven and earth, of us and all things; who provides for us meat and drink, and all things, by causing the earth, which He has made, to produce things necessary for our use; that Being, whom you have heard of by the name of Collwar, and are taught at present to be afraid to speak to. And I appeal to your own hearts if many of you have ever thought of him. Again," says I, "let anything in the shape of man, that gives himself leave to consider at all, only tell me if what he can make, and does make, with his own hands, hath not more occasion to depend on him as its maker than he on that? Why, then, should not we depend upon and pray to our Maker?

"You very greatly mistake me, O glumms," says I, "if you imagine I would have all those reverend men turned out of employment as useless. No, I find they know too much of what is valuable; and therefore those who are willing to continue in the service of the mouch, and faithfully to teach you the old ragan's doctrine, and such farther lights of the great Being as they shall hereafter receive, let them continue your ragans still, and let others be chosen and trained up in that doctrine."

Here the poor old man got up again with much difficulty. "Mr. Peter," says he, "you are the-man predicted of; you have declared the old ragan's mind, and all my brethren know it."

Finding I had the populace on my side (for I did not doubt the king and the colambs), I put the question to the ragans: "Reverend ragans," says I, "you see your prediction this day about to be fulfilled; for if it is a true one, no force of man can withstand it. You see your Image disgraced; you see, and I appeal to you all for the truth of it, that what the ragan would have taught has, without your assistance, been disclosed. I therefore would have you the first to break the bondage of idolatry and turn to the true Collwar, as it will be so much glory to you. Will you, and which of you, from henceforth serve Collwar, and no longer worship an idol? Such of you as will do so, let them continue in the mouch: if none of you will, it shall be my business to qualify a sufficient number of true ragans to form a succession for that purpose. The issue of this great affair depends upon your answers." They waited sometime for a spokesman to begin, and so soon as he was able to get up, the poor old ragan said, "I will continue in it, and do all the good I can: and blessed be the day this prediction is fulfilled to succeeding generations! I have lived long enough to have seen this." Then the rest of the ragans, one by one, followed his example. And thus, with prodigious acclamations, both the ragans and people ended the great affair of religion.

I now more and more believed the truth of the prediction, and told them I should have occasion for seven hundred men before I set out against the rebels; and desired that they might be commanded by Nasgig. This was readily granted. I then told them, as I purposed to act nothing without their concurrence, I desired the colambs would remain in the city till I set out, that they might be readily called together.

I then desired I might be quite private from company till I departed.

I took Nasgig home with me; and when we came there, "My dear friend," says he, "what have you done today! You have crushed a power hitherto immovable; and I shall never more think anything too difficult for you to attempt."—"Nasgig," says I, "I am glad it is over. And now," says I, "you must enter on a new employ: but first, can you provide me fifty honest, faithful glumms for a particular expedition? they must be sensible, close, and temporising." He said he would, and come to me again.

I then desired a private audience with the king; who, on seeing me, began upon my success at the moucheratt. I told his majesty, if I alone, and a stranger, could gain such influence there, I might have had much more if he had joined me, especially as he had told me he gave no credit to the Image; and that I expected he would have appeared on my side. "Ah, Peter!" says he, "monarchs neither see, hear, nor perceive with their own eyes, ears, or understandings. I would willingly have done it; but Barbarsa prevented me, by assuring me it would be my ruin; and as he is my bosom friend, what reproaches must I have suffered if it had gone amiss! Nay, I will tell you that he and Nicor are of opinion that your coming hither, which is looked upon by us all as such a blessing, will one day undo me; 'for,' say they, 'though he may perform what you expect from him, it is not to be supposed he should suffer it to redound to you.' 'No,' say they, 'if he can do these great things, he can soon set you aside.' Thus, though I have no doubt of you, is my spirit wasting within me through perpetual fears and jealousies; and I cannot get these men, who, knowing all my secrets, are feared by me, into my own way of thinking."

"Mighty sir," says I, "don't think I came hither to possess, but redress a kingdom. I lived far more to my ease in my grotto than I can in this palace; but I now desire you," drawing my sword and putting it into his hand, "to pierce this heart's blood and make yourself easy in my death, rather than, suffering me to survive, live in distrust of me. No, great king," says I, "it is not that I would injure you; but though I have been so short a time in your dominions, I find there are those who would, and will too, unless you exert the monarch, and shake off those harpies which, lying always at your ear, are ever buzzing disquiet and mischief to you."—"Peter," says he, "what do you mean? sure I have no more traitors in my State!"—"Your majesty has," says I.—"How can you prove it?" says he. "But pray inform me who they are?"—"I came not hither, great king," says I, "to turn informer, but reformer; and so far as that is necessary in order to this, I will give you satisfaction. I only desire you will wholly guide yourself by my direction for three days, and you shall be able to help yourself to all the information you can require without ray telling you. In the meantime, appear no more thoughtful than usual, or in any other way alter your accustomed habits."

Nasgig having sent me the fifty men, I asked them if they were to be trusted, and if they could carefully and artfully execute a commission I had to charge them with. They assuring me they would, I told them I would let them into my design, which would be the best instructions I could give them, and left the management alone to them.

My confidence in them made them twice as diligent as all the particular directions in the world would have done; so I only told them I had a mind the revolted towns and also the enemy's army should know that the person so long ago predicted of was now at Brandleguarp, and had, as the first step towards reducing them and killing the traitor Harlokin, already altered their religion to the old ragan's plan; and that they had now nothing to expect but destruction to themselves as soon as I appeared against them with my unknown fire and smoke, which I always had with me; and that the thing was looked upon to be as good as done already at Brandleguarp; and then to slip away again unperceived. They all promised me exact performance, and went off.

Nasgig then coming in, I told him he was now under my command, and must take six hundred glumms with him to Graundevolet; tell Youwarkee to show him my ship, and then he must bring me the things I had described to her by the name of cannon. He must bring them by ropes, as I was brought; and bring powder, which she would direct him to, and the heavy balls which lay in the room with the powder. I told him if he thought he should not have men enough he must take more; and must be as expeditious as was consistent with safety. I desired him to tell Youwarkee I hoped in a short time to send for her and all the family over to me. "And now, Nasgig," says I, "my orders are finished; but," says I, "the king! I must assist that good man. I therefore want to know the particular times Barbarsa and Yaccombourse usually meet."— "That," says he, "is every night when she is not with the king; for he is excessively fond of her, and seldom lies without her; but whenever he does, Barbarsa is admitted to her."—"And how can I know," says I, "when she will or will not lie with the king?"

"When she is to lie with him," says he, "the king never sups without her."—"Now," says I, "you must show me your lodging, that I may find it in your absence; and give orders to the guard to let me, and whoever comes with me, enter at anytime." He then took me to his chamber; but I passed through so many rooms, galleries, and passages, that I was sure I should never find it again, so I asked him if Maleck knew the way? and he assuring me he did, I took my leave of him, and he set out for Graundevolet.

XV

The king hears Barbarsa and Yaccombourse discourse
on the plot—They are impeached by Peter at a
moucheratt—Condemned and executed—Nicor
submits, and is released.

I had now several important irons in the fire, and all to be struck
whilst hot; there was the securing religion, sowing sedition amongst
the enemy, tripping up the heels of two ministers and a she-favourite,
and transporting artillery in the air some hundred leagues; either of
which failing might have been of exceeding bad consequence; but as
the affair of the ministers now lay next at hand, I entered upon that in
the following manner.

The king coming to me the next day, as by appointment, and having
assured me he had hinted nothing to anyone, no, not to Barbarsa or
Yaccom-bourse, told me that Barbarsa had given orders for stopping
Nasgig and his men; and had persuaded him not to be in such haste in
suffering me to do as I pleased, but to show his authority and keep me
under. Says I, "Your majesty's safety is so near my heart, that even want
of confidence in me shall not make me decline my endeavours to serve
you. But have you suffered him to stop Nasgig?"—"No," says he, "Nasgig
was gone sometime before he sent."—"Oh, sir!" says I, "you do not half
know the worth of that man! but you shall hereafter, and will reward him
accordingly. But now, sir," says I, "to what we meet upon; if you will, as
I told you, but comply with me for three days, without asking questions,
I will show you the greatest traitors in your dominions, and put them
into your power too." He promised me again he would. "Then, sir," says
I, "you must not send to Yaccombourse to sup with you tonight."—
"Nor lie with me?"—"No," says I.—"Pray, what hurt can arise to my
affairs from her?" says he.—"Sir," says I, "you promised me to ask no
questions."—"Agreed, agreed!" says he.—"Then," says I, "please to meet
me at Nasgig's lodgings without being perceived, if you can; at least
without notice taken."—"Good," says he.—"And when you are there, see
or hear what you will, you must not say a word till you are retired again."
All which the king engaging to perform, we parted till evening.

I called Maleck, and asked if he knew the way to Nasgig's lodging.
He told me, very well: and, the time being come, he conducted me

ROBERT PALTOCK

thither, where I had not waited long before the king came, most of the court being in bed. I desired the king to stay in the outer room till I went into the bedchamber two or three times, and I thought we must have put it off till another night: but listening once again, I found they were come, so I called the king, and led him to the place, entreating him, whatever he heard, to keep his patience or he would ruin all. We first heard much amorous discourse between Barbarsa and Yaccombourse, and then the ensuing dialogue.

YAC.: My dearest Barbarsa, what was all that uproar at the moucheratt the other day?

BAR.: Nothing, my love, but that mad fellow Peter, who sets up for a conjuror, and wants us all to dance to his pipe.

YAC.: I heard he overcame the ragans at an argument about the Image.

BAR.: Why, I don't know how that was, but it was the doating old ragan did their business; and truly the king's fingers itched to be on Peter's side, but I gave him a judicious nod, and you know he durst not displease so dear a friend as I am; ha, ha, ha! Am not I a sad fellow, my love, to talk so of my king?

YAC.: He that wants but one step to a throne, is almost a king's fellow

BAR.: And that but a short one too, my dear Yaccee; but I must get rid of that Nasgig, though I think I have almost spoiled him with the king, too. I don't love your thinking rascals: that fellow thinks more than I do, Yaccee.

YAC.: He'll never think to so good purpose, I believe. But how goes cousin Harlokin on? I find Gauingrunt is gone over.

BAR.: And so shall Bazin, Istell, Pezele, and Ginkatt too, my dear; for I am at work there. And then goodnight, my poor King Georigetti; thou shalt be advised to fly, and I'll keep the throne warm for thee.—I don't see but King Barbarsa and Queen Yaccombourse sound much better than Georigetti. Well, my dear, whenever we come to sovereignty, which now cannot be long, if Nicor has but played his part well, for I have not had an account of his success yet; I say, when we come into power, never let us be above minding our own affairs, or suffer ourselves to be led by the nose, as this poor insignificant king does. For, in short, he may as well be a king of mats, as a king of flesh, if he will not use his faculties, but suffer me to make a fool of him thus; and I should be a fool indeed to neglect it, when he thinks it the greatest piece of service I can do him.

YAC.: Come, come, my dear! let us enjoy ourselves like king and queen till we come to the dignity.

Finding a pause, the king, who had admirably kept his temper, even beyond imagination, stole into the outer room. "Peter," says he, "I thank you; you have shown me myself. What fools are we kings! In endeavouring to make others happy, how miserable do we make ourselves! How easily are we deceived by the designing flattery of those below us!—Ungrateful villain!—Degenerate strumpet!—I hate you both.—Peter," says he, "give me your sword; I'll destroy them both immediately."

"Hold, sir," says I, "your majesty has heard sufficient to found a true judgment upon; but kings should not be executioners, or act by passion or revenge; but as you would punish that in others, so carefully avoid it yourself. You who are in so exalted a station, as always to have it in your power to punish a known crime in individuals, have not that necessity to prompt you to a violent act that private persons have, to whom it may be difficult to obtain justice. Therefore my advice is, that you summon the colambs tomorrow, when Barbarsa and Nicor cannot fail to attend; and I would also desire Yaccombourse to be there, you having great proposals to make to the states which you shall want her to hear. I will in the meantime prepare the servants under Quilly, and order Maleck with another posse to attend, as by your command, to execute your orders given by me, and I myself will impeach those bad persons in public; and Nicor, if he will not ingenuously confess what commission he was charged with from Barbarsa, shall be put to the torture I direct, till he discovers it."

The king was very well pleased with this method; so I ordered Quilly, as from the king, to bring all my servants to the assembly, appointing him his place, and Maleck to select me fifty stout persons and to wait to execute my orders on a signal given. So soon as the assembly met, I told them, since I had concerned myself in their affairs, I had made it my business to search into the cause of their calamities; and finding some of the traitors were now approached, not only near to, but even into the capital city, his majesty had therefore ordered me to ask their advice, what punishment was adequate, in their judgments, to the crime of conspiring against him and the State, and holding treasonable correspondence with his enemies under the show of his greatest friends.

I stopped, and looked at Barbarsa; he turned as pale as ashes and was rising to speak, when the senior colamb declared, if any such thing could be made appear, the common punishment of Crash-doorpt was too trivial; but they deserved to be dropped alive either to hoximo or Mount Alkoe. The several colambs all declaring the same to be their judgment, and even those to be too mild for their deserts, I then stepped up to Barbarsa, who sat at the king's left hand, as did Yaccombourse at his right, and telling them and Nicor they were all prisoners of state, I delivered Barbarsa and Yaccombourse in custody to Quilly and his men, and Nicor to Maleck and his men, ordering them into separate apartments, with strict commands that neither should speak to the other upon pain of the last pronounced judgment.

Barbarsa would have spoke, and called out to the king, begging him not to desert so faithful a servant for the insinuations of so vile a man as Peter; but the king only told him the vile man could be made appear presently, and he hoped he would meet his deserts.

I then stood up and told the assembly the whole of what we heard, how it first came to be discovered, and that the king himself had been an ear-witness of it, which the king confirming, the whole assembly rang with confusion, and revenge and indignation appeared in every face.

I then proposed, as we yet knew not what that secret commission was which Nicor was charged with, having enough against the rest, that Nicor might be brought forth; and upon refusal to answer, be put to the torture.

Nicor appearing before the assembly, I told him I was commanded by the king to ask him what commission he was charged with by Barbarsa, and to whom. I told him the safest way for his life, his honour, and his country, was to make a true confession at first, or I had authority to put him to the torture; for, as for slitting and banishment, as they were too slight to atone for this offence, he might rest satisfied his would be of another sort, if he hesitated at delivering the thing in its full truth.

My prelude terrifying him, he openly confessed that his last commission was to several towns, as from the king, and with his gripsack, to order their submission to Harlokin, the king not being in any condition to relieve them; and that as soon as they had submitted, Harlokin would be let into this city, which could not stand against him.

He also declared that it had been agreed, and the boundaries settled, how far Barbarsa, who was to be declared king and marry Yaccombourse, should govern, and how far Harlokin; that Barbarsa was to be styled King of the East, and Harlokin King of the West; and that either of them, on the other's dying childless, was to inherit the whole monarchy.

The king declaring this to be all true, and that by my procurement he heard it all mentioned but the last night between Barbarsa and Yaccombourse as they were solacing themselves in bed, the whole assembly ordered them to be brought out, carried with cords about their necks, and precipitated into Mount Alkoe.

I then begged they might be suffered to speak for themselves before execution; and acquainting them severally with the evidence, I first asked Barbarsa what he had to say against his sentence. He declared his ambition, and the easiness of his master's temper, had instigated him to attempt what had been charged upon him; having, as he thought, a fair opportunity of so doing.—I then asked Yaccombourse the same question; she answered me, her ambition had been her sole governor from a child, and I had done my worst in preventing the progress of that; and whatever else I could do was not worth her notice; "But to have reigned," says she, with some emotion, "was worth the lives of millions, and overbalanced everything!"

I pleaded hard for Nicor, as I perceived him to be only the favourite's favourite, and not in the scrape for his own views, more than what he might merit from his new master; and as he had declared the truth, and I believed I might make further use of him, I obtained that he might be only committed to me, and that I might have liberty of pardoning or slitting as I saw fit; and, as I expected, he afterwards proved very useful to me and my designs, and I pardoned him.

Before the assembly rose, a party of the natives of Mount Alkoe were ordered to convey Yaccombourse and Barbarsa to the mountain, slip their graundees, and drop them there; and thus ended the lives of these two aspiring persons.

When I came home, I called Nicor before me. "You know," says I, "Nicor, you are obliged to me for this moment of your life; but I don't remind you of it for any return I want to myself; but as you are sensible my endeavours are to serve this State, I offer you life and freedom upon condition you employ your utmost diligence to repair your past conduct, by a free declaration of everything in your power that may be for the benefit of the kingdom, as you know the springs by which all these bad

ROBERT PALTOCK

movements have been set at work; and I desire your opinion how best to counteract the schemes formed, and redress the evils."

Nicor being fully convinced of his error, and having lost his patron, was very submissive; and declared he believed none of the provinces would have gone over to Harlokin, unless they had thought it was the king's order Barbarsa had acted by, which, by bearing his gripsack, they made no doubt of. He advised to send expresses with the king's gripsack to such places as had lately submitted, and to such as were about it, to put a stop to them. I told him I had done that; "But not by the gripsack," says he, "and unless they see and hear that, they will give no credit to the message." He then gave me some particular hints in other affairs of no mean consequence; and seeing him truly under concern, and, to my thinking, sincere in what he said, I told him I was an absolute enemy to confinement, and if any person of repute would engage he should be forthcoming upon all occasions that I might have recourse to him, I would let him have his liberty.

Poor Nicor, as it commonly happens to great men in disgrace, finding himself abandoned by all his friends, after trying everybody, dropping some tears, told me next morning he was highly sensible of what a dye his offences had been, for that not one amongst all his former friends would even look upon him in his present circumstances, wherefore he must submit to fate.

Nicor having borne a good character before seduced by Barbarsa, and knowing that an obliged enemy often becomes the sincerest friend, I pressed him again to try his friends. He told me everybody was shy of engaging in such an affair; and that he had rather suffer himself, than meanly to entreat anyone into an unwilling compliance.—"Come, Nicor," says I, "will you be your own security to me? May I take your own word?"—He said he could not expect that; for as the terror of slitting lay over him, and in my hands too, he could not answer but he might deceive me in case he should conceive I had a design against him; which I myself, too, might have from a mistaken motive.

"Why, then, Nicor," says I, "you are free; now use your own discretion. I think you will never cause my judgment to be impeached for what I have done; but if you do, I can't condemn myself for it, and hope I shall have no reason to repent it."

Nicor fell at my feet, embraced them, and was so overcome with my generosity to him, that I could with difficulty prevail on him to rise again; saying he was now more than ever ashamed to see my face. I told him I had not done with him, but would use him henceforth as my friend, and ordered him to call upon me daily, for I might have several occasions for him; and, truly, next to Nasgig, he proved the usefullest man in the kingdom.

XVI

Nasgig returns with the cannon—Peter informs him
of the execution—Appoints him a guard—Settles
the order of his march against Harlokin—Combat
between Nasgig and the rebel general—The battle—
Peter returning with Harlokids head is met by a
Sweecoan—A public festival—Slavery abolished.

The tenth day Nasgig arrived, whilst I happened to be in the king's
garden; and hearing the trumpet coming before, I called out to
him to give Nasgig notice where I was, and to desire him to alight
there.

After ceremonies past, and I had inquired after my wife and children,
and his answers had informed me of their healths, "Well," says Nasgig,
"my friend, am I to live or die?"—"Explain yourself," says I.—"Nay, I
only mean," says he, "have you discovered me to the king?"—"Pardon
me," says I, "dear Nasgig, I must own the truth, I have."—"Then," says
he, "I suppose his majesty has no more commands for me?"—"No,"
says I, "it is not so bad as that neither."—"But, pray," says he, "what
says Barbarsa to it?"—"Oh, nothing at all!" says I; "quite quiet."—"Nor
Yaccombourse? Did you discover her baseness to the king?"—"Yes," says
I, "and the king behaved like a king upon the occasion."—"And where
are they now?" says he.—"Only in Mount Alkoe," says I.—"Mount
Alkoe!" replies he, "what do you mean by that? How can they be in
Mount Alkoe? Did they go of their own accords?"—"They fled off, I
suppose, with ropes about their necks," says I, "as your criminals go to
Crashdoorpt."—"Are they slit too?" says he.—"No," says I, "but slipt,
I'll assure you. Come, my good friend, I'll let you into the history of it."
And then I told all that had happened, and the king's satisfaction at the
judgment of the moucheratt "And now," says I, "Nasgig, you may call
yourself the favourite, I promise you, for his majesty enjoys himself but
to greet you on your return: but have a care of power; most grow giddy
with it, and the next thing to that is a fall."—"Pray," says he, "what is
become of Nicor? Is he under the same condemnation?"—"No," says I,
"Nicor is now by my means absolutely free, and no two greater than he
and I." I told him then my proceedings with him; he was glad of it; for,
he said, Nicor he believed was honest at bottom.

By this time up came the cannon; and truly had my countrymen but the graundee to convey their cannon at so easy an expense from place to place, the whole world would not stand before us. They brought me five cannon, and three swivel guns, and a larger quantity of ammunition than I had spoken for.

I introduced Nasgig to the king upon his return, as the person to whose conduct the safe arrival of my cannon was owing. His majesty embracing him, told him the service he had done him was so great in the affair of Barbarsa, and his management of it so prudent, he should from thenceforth take him into his peculiar confidence and esteem.

Nasgig thanked his majesty for his acceptance of that act of his duty, and desired to know when he pleased the operations for the campaign should begin.—"Ask my father," says the king; "do you conduct the war, and let him conduct you."

Then Nasgig desired to know what number of troops would be requisite. I asked him what number the enemy had; he said about thirty thousand.—"Then," says I, "take you six only, besides the bearers of me and the artillery; and pick me out fifty of the best men you have, as a guard for my person, and send them to me."

I showed these men my cutlasses and pistols, and showed them the use and management of them: "And," says I, "as our enemies fight with pikes, keep you at a distance first, and when you would assault, toss by the pike with your hand, and closing in, have at the graundee; and this edge" (showing them the sharpness of it) "will strip it down from shoulder to heel; you need strike but once for it, but be sure come near enough; or," says I, "if you find it difficult to turn aside the pike, give it one smart stroke with this; it will cut it in two, and then the point being gone, it will be useless."

"These instructions," says I, "if rightly observed, will make us conquerors."

The next thing was to settle the order of my march, which I did in the following manner; and, taking leave of the king, I set out.

First, ten companies of one hundred men, including officers, with each a gripsack, in ten double lines, fifty abreast.

Secondly, four hundred bearers of the cannon, with two hundred to the right, the like to the left, as relays.

Thirdly, two hundred men with the ammunition, stores, hatchets, and other implements.

Fourthly, fifty body-guards, in two lines.

Fifthly, myself, borne by eight, with twelve on the right, and as many on the left, for relays.

Sixthly, two thousand men in columns, on each side the cannon and me, fifty in a line, double lines.

Seventhly, one thousand men in the rear, fifty in a line, double lines.

I consulted with Nasgig how Harlokin's army lay, that I might avoid the revolted towns, rather choosing to take them in my return; for my design was to encounter Harlokin first, and I did not doubt, if I conquered him, but the towns would surrender of course.

When we arrived within a small flight of his army, I caused a halt at a proper place for my cannon, and having pitched them, which I did by several flat stones, one on another to a proper elevation, I loaded them, and also my small-arms, consisting of six muskets and three brace of pistols, and placing my army, two thousand just behind me, two thousand to my right, and the same number to my left, I gave a strict command for none of them to stir forwards without orders, which Nasgig, who stood just behind me, was to give. I then sent a defiance to Harlokin by a gripsack, who sent me word he fought for a kingdom, and would accept it; and, as I heard afterwards, he was glad I did, for since the intelligence I had scattered in his army, they had in great numbers deserted him, and he was afraid it would have proved general. I then putting the end of a match into a pistol-pan with a little powder, by flashing lighted it; and this I put under my chair, for I sat in that, with my muskets three on each side, a pistol in my right hand, and five more in my girdle. In this manner I waited Harlokin's coming, and in about an hour we saw the van of his army, consisting of about five thousand men, who flew in five layers, one over another. I had not loaded my cannon with ball, but small-sized stones, about sixty in each; and seeing the length of their line, I spread my cannons' mouths somewhat wider than their breeches, and then taking my observation by a bright star, for there was a clear dawn all round the horizon, I observed, as I retired to my chair, how that star answered to the elevation of my cannon; and when the foremost ranks, who, not seeing my men stir, were approaching almost over me, to fall on them, and had come to my pitch, I fired two pieces of my ordnance at once, and so mauled them, that there dropped about ninety upon the first discharge, together with their commander; the rest being in flight and so close together, not being able to turn fast enough to fly, being stopped by those behind them, not only hindered those behind from turning about, but clogged up their own passage. Seeing them in such a prodigious cluster, I so successfully fired two more pieces, that I brought down double the number of the first shot; and then giving the word to fall on, my cutlass-guard and the pikemen did prodigious execution. But fearing the main body should advance before we had got in order again, I commanded them to fall back to their former stations, and to let the remainder of the enemy go off.

This did me more good in the event than if I had killed twice as many; for they not only never returned themselves, but flying some to the right, some to the left, and passing by the two wings of their own army, consisting of six thousand men each, they severally reported that they were all that was left of the whole van of the army; and that the prediction would certainly be fulfilled, for that their companions had died by fire and smoke. This report struck such terror into each wing, that everyone shifted for himself, and never appeared more.

The main battle, consisting of about ten thousand men, knowing nothing of what had happened to the wings—for Harlokin had ordered the wings to take a great compass round to enclose us—hearing we were but a handful, advanced boldly; and as I had ordered my men not to mount too high, the enemy sunk to their pitch. When they came near, I asked Nasgig who led them; if it was Harlokin. He told me no, his general, but that he was behind; and Nasgig begging me to let him try his skill with the general, I consented, they not being yet come to the pitch of my cannon. Nasgig immediately took the graundee, and advancing singly with one of my cutlasses in his hand, challenged the general in single combat. He, like a man of honour, accepting it, ordered a halt, and to it they went, each emulous of glory, and of taking all the advantage he could, so that they suddenly did not strike or push; but sometimes one, then the other was uppermost, and whirling expeditiously round, met almost breast to breast; when the general, who had not a pike, but a pikestaff headed with a large stone, gave Nasgig such a stroke on his head that he reeled, and sunk considerably, and I began to be in pain for him, the general lowering after him. But Nasgig springing forward beneath him, and rising light as air behind the general, had gained his height again before the general could turn about to discern him, and then plunging forward, and receiving a stroke across his left arm, at the same time he gave the general such a blow near the outside of the shoulder as slit the graundee almost down to his hip, and took away part of the flesh of the left arm, upon which the general fell fluttering down in vast pain very near me; but not before Nasgig, in his fall, descending, had taken another severe cut at him.

Immediately upon this defeat Nasgig again took his place behind me, our army shouting to the skies; but no sooner had the general dropped, but on came Harlokin, with majesty and terror mixed in his looks, and seeming to disdain the air he rode on, waved his men to the attack with his hand. When he came near enough to hear me, I called him vile traitor, to oppose the army of his lawful sovereign, telling him, if he would submit, he should be received to mercy. "Base creeping insect," says Harlokin, "if thou hast aught to say to me worth hearing, meet me in the air! This hand shall show thee soon who'll most want mercy; and though I scorn to stoop to thee myself, this messenger shall satisfy the world thou art an impostor, and send thee back lifeless to the fond king that sent thee hither." With that he hurled a javelin pointed with flint, sharp as a needle, at me; but I avoiding it, "This, then," says I, "if words will not do, shall justify the truth of our prediction." And then levelling a musket at him, I shot him through the very heart, that he fell dead within twenty paces of me. But perceiving another to take his room, notwithstanding the confusion my musket made amongst them, I ran to my match, and giving fire to two more pieces of ordnance at the same time, they fell so thick about me, that I had enough to do to escape being crushed to death by them; and the living remainder separating, fled quite away, and put an end to the war. I waited in the field three days, to see if they would make head again; but they were so far from it, that before I could return, as I found afterwards, most of the revolting provinces had sent their deputies, who themselves carried the first news of the defeat, to beg to be received into mercy; all of whom were detained there till my return with Harlokin's head.

At my return to Brandleguarp I was met by the king, the colambs, and almost the whole body of the people; every man, woman, and child, with two sweecoe lights in their hands, which unusual sight in the air gave me great alarm, till I inquired of Nasgig what it meant, who told me it must certainly be a sweecoan, or he knew not what it was. I asking again what he meant by that, he told me it was a particular method of rejoicing he had heard of, but never seen; wherein, if the king goes in triumph, all the people of Brandleguarp, from fifteen to sixty, are obliged to attend him with sweecoes. He said it was reported amongst them that in Begsurbeck's time there were two of them, but there had been none since.

When we met them, I perceived they had opened into two lines or ranks of a prodigious length; at the farther end of which was the king, with innumerable lights about him, the whole looking like a prodigious avenue or vista of lights, bounded at the farther end, where the king was, with a pyramid light. This had the most solemn and magnificent effect on the eye that anything of light could possibly have; but as we passed through the ranks, each of the spectators having two lights, one was given to each soldier of the whole army. And then to look backward, as well as forward, the beauty of the scene was inexpressible. We marched all the way amidst the shouts of people, and the sounds of the gripsacks, going very slowly between the ranks; and at length arriving at the pyramid where the king was, I heard abundance of sweet voices, chanting my actions in triumphal songs; but I could take little notice of these, or of my son with his flageolet amongst them, for the extravagant appearance of the pyramid, which seemed to reach the very sky. For, first, there was a long line of a full half-mile, which hovered at even height with the two side ranks; in the centre of that, and over it, was the king single; over him another line, shorter than the first, and again over that, shorter and shorter lines; till, at a prodigious height, it ended in one single light*These all hovering, kept their stations; while the king darted a little space forward to meet me, and congratulate my success; then turning and preceding me, the whole pyramid turned, and marched before us, singing all the way to the city, the pyramid changing several times into divers forms, as into squares, half-moons, with the horns sometimes erect and again reversed, and various other figures. And yet amongst this infinite number of globes there was not the least glaring or offensive light, but only what was agreeable to the people themselves. As the rear of the army entered the lines, they closed upon it, and followed us into Brandleguarp. While we passed the city to the palace, the whole body of people kept hovering till the king and myself were alighted, and then everyone alighted where he best could. All the streets and avenues to the palace were blocked up with people, crowding to receive the king's beneficence; for he had proclaimed a feast and open housekeeping to the people for six days. The king, the colambs, ragans, and great officers of state, with myself, had a magnificent entertainment prepared us in Begsurbeck's great room; and his majesty, after supper, being very impatient to know how the battle went, I told him the only valorous exploit was performed by my friend Nasgig, who opened the way to victory by the slaughter of Harlokin's general. Nasgig then rose, desiring only that so much might be attributed to him as

ROBERT PALTOCK

fortune had accidentally thrown into his scale; for it might have been equally his fate as the general's to have fallen. "But except that skirmish," says he, "and some flying cuts at the van, we have had no engagement at all, nor have we lost a single man; Peter only sitting in his chair, and commanding victory. He spake aloud but thrice, and whispered once to them, but so powerfully that, having at the two first words laid above three hundred of the enemy at their lengths, and brought Harlokin to his feet, with a whisper, at the third word he concluded the war. The whole time, from the first sight of the enemy to their total defeat, took not up more space than one might fairly spend in traversing his majesty's garden. In short, sir," says Nasgig, "your majesty needs no other defence against public or private enemies, as I can see, than Peter; and my profession, whilst he is with us, can be of little use to the State."

After these compliments from Nasgig, and separate ones from the king and the rest, I told them it was the highest felicity to me to be made an instrument by the great Collwar in freeing so mighty a kingdom and considerable a people from the misery of a tyrannical power. "You live," says I, "so happily under the mild government of Georigetti, that it is shocking but to think into what a distressed state you must have fallen under the power of a usurper, who, claiming all as his own by way of conquest, would have reduced you to a miserable servitude. But," says I, "there is, and I am sorry to see it, still amongst you an evil that you great ones feel not, and yet it cries for redress. Are we not all, from the king to the meanest wretch amongst us, formed with the same members? Do we not all breathe the same air? inhabit the same earth? Are we not all subject to the same disorders? and do we not all feel pain and oppression alike? Have we not all the same senses, the same faculties? and, in short, are we not all equally creatures of, and servants to, the same master, the great Collwar? Would not the king have been a slave but for the accident of being begotten by one who was a king? and would not the poorest creature amongst us have been the king had he been so begotten? Did you great men, by any superior merit before your births, procure a title to the high stations in which you are placed? No, you did not. Therefore give me leave to tell you what I would have done. As every man has equal right to the protection of Collwar, why, when you have no enemy to distress you, will you distress one another? Consider, you great ones, and act upon this disinterested principle; do to another, what you, in his place, would have him do to you; dismiss your slaves, let all men be what Collwar made them, free.

But if this unequal distinction amongst you, of man and man, is still retained, though you are at present free from the late disaster, it shall be succeeded with more, and heavier. And now, that you may know I would not have every man a lord, nor everyone a beggar, remember I would only have every serving-man at liberty to choose his own master, and every master his own man; for he that has property and benefits to bestow will never want dependants, for the sake of those benefits to serve him, as he that has them not must serve for the sake of obtaining them. But then let it be done with free-will; he that then serves you will have an interest in it, and do it, for his own sake, with a willing mind; and you, who are served, will be tenderer and kinder to a good servant, as knowing by a contrary usage you shall lose him. I desire this may now be declared to be so, or your reasons, if any there are, against it."

One of the ragans said he thought I spoke what was very just, and would be highly acceptable to Collwar.

Then two of the colambs rose to speak together, and after a short compliment who should begin, they both declared they only arose to testify their consents.

The king referring it to me, and the colambs consenting, I ordered freedom to be proclaimed through the city; so that everyone appeared at their usual duties, to serve their own masters for a month, and then to be at liberty to come to a fresh agreement with them, or who else they pleased.

"This, sir," says I to the king, "will now be a day of joy indeed to those poor hearts who would have been in no fear of losing before, let who would have reigned; for can any man believe a slave cares who is uppermost? he is but a slave still. But now," says I, "those who were so before may by industry gain property; and then their own interest engages them to defend the State."

"There is but one thing more I will trouble you with now—and that," says I to the ragans, "is, that we all meet at the mouch tomorrow, to render Collwar thanks for the late, and implore future favour." And this passed without any contradiction.

When we met, the poor ragans were at a great loss for want of their image, not knowing what to do or say; for their practice had been to prostrate themselves on the ground, making several odd gestures; but whether they prayed, or only seemed to do so, no one knew.

While the people were gathering, I called to a ragan, seeing him out of character. "Suppose," said I "(for I see you want your image), you and your brethren had received a favour of the king, and you was deputed by them to thank him, you would scarce be at a loss to express your gratitude to him, and tell him how highly you all esteemed his benefits, hoping you should retain a just sense of them, and behave yourselves as dutiful subjects for the future, and then desire him to keep you still in his protection. And this," says I, "as you believe in such a Being as Collwar, who understands what you say, you may with equal courage do to Him, keeping but your mind intent upon Him, as if you saw Him present."—"Indeed," says he, "I believe you are right, we may so; but it is a new thing, and you must excuse us if we do it not so well at first."

I found I had a very apt scholar, for after he had begun, he made a most extraordinary prayer in regular order, the people standing very attentive. It was not long, but he justly observed the points I hinted to him.

When he had done, another and another went on, till we had heard ten of them, and in everyone something new, and very *à propos;* and several of them afterwards confessed they never had the like satisfaction in their lives, for they had new hearts and new thoughts, they said.

We spent the sixth-day feast in every gaiety imaginable, and especially of dancing, of which they were very fond in their way; but it was not so agreeable to me as my own country way, there being too much antic in it. New deputies daily arrived from the revolted towns, and several little republics, not claimed by Georigetti before, begged to be taken under his protection; so that in one week the king saw himself not only released from the dread of being driven from his throne, but courted by some, submitted to by others, and almost at the summit of glory a sovereign can attain to.

XVII

A VISITATION OF THE REVOLTED PROVINCES PROPOSED BY
PETER—HIS NEW NAME OF THE COUNTRY RECEIVED—
RELIGION SETTLED IN THE WEST—SLAVERY ABOLISHED
THERE—LASMEEL RETURNS WITH PETER—PETER
TEACHES HIM LETTERS—THE KING SURPRISED AT WRITTEN
CORRESPONDENCE—PETER DESCRIBES THE MAKE OF
A BEAST TO THE KING.

The festival being over, the colambs begged leave to depart; but the king, who now did nothing without me, consulted with me if it was yet proper. I told him, as things had so long been in confusion in the west, that though the provinces had made their submission, yet the necessity of their circumstances, and the general terror, might have caused them only to dissemble till their affairs were composed again, and that as it was more than probable some relations of the deceased Harlokin, or other popular person, might engage them in another revolt, I thought it would not be improper to advise with his colambs about the establishment of the present tranquillity, and not by too great a security, give way to future commotions; and as all the colambs were then present, it might be proper to summon them once more.

When they were met, the king declared the more particular satisfaction he took in that meeting than he had heretofore done, when they had been put to it for means to secure their lives and properties: "For now," says he, "our deliberations must turn upon securing our new acquisitions, and on settling those provinces which, till now, have never fallen under my power. But," says he, "I shall refer it to Peter to propose to you what at present seems most necessary for you to consider of; and that adjusted, shall dismiss you."

I told them that as the too sudden healing of wounds in the body natural, before the bottom was clean and uncorrupt, made them liable to break out again with greater malignity, so wounds in the body political, if skinned over only, without probing and cleansing the source and spring from whence they arose, would rankle and fret within till a proper opportunity, and then burst forth again with redoubled violence. I would therefore propose a visitation of the several provinces; an inquiry into their conduct; an examination into the lives and principles of the colambs, the

ROBERT PALTOCK

inferior officers, and magistrates; and either to retain the old, or appoint new, as there should be occasion. This visitation I would have performed by his majesty—"and so many of you, the honourable colambs," says I, "as he shall see fit should attend him in royal state, that his new subjects may see his majesty, and hear his most gracious words; and being sensible of his good disposition towards them, may be won, by his equity and justice, to a zealous submission to his government, which nothing but the perception of their own senses can establish in the heart This, I don't doubt, will answer the end I propose, and consolidate the peace and happiness of Norm—Normns—I must say Doorpt Swangeanti."

Hearing me hesitate at the word Normndbsgrsutt, and call it Doorpt Swangeanti, the whole assembly rang with Doorpt Swangeanti! and, at last, came to a resolution that the west being now again united to the east, the whole dominions should be called Sass Doorpt Swangeanti, or the Great Flight Land.

They approved the visitation, and all offered to go with the king, but insisted I should be of the party, which agreeing to do, I chose me out two of the most knowing ragans to teach the new religion amongst them, for in every project I had my view to advance religion.

Some were for having the deputies released, and despatched with notice of the king's intentions; but I objecting that they might disrelish their confinement, and possibly raise reports prejudicial to our proceedings, it was thought better to take them with us, and go ourselves as soon as possible.

We set out with a prodigious retinue, first to the right, in order to sweep round the whole country, and take all the towns in our way, and occasionally enter the middle parts, as the towns lay commodious.

We were met by the magistrates and chief officers of each district, at some distance from each city, with strings about their necks, and the crashee instrument borne before them in much humility. His majesty said but little to them on the way, but ordered them to precede him to the city, and conduct him to the colamb's house; when he was commanded to surrender his employment to his majesty, as did all the other officers who held posts under him. Then an examination was taken of their lives, characters, and behaviour in their stations; and finding most of them had behaved well to the government they had lived under (for their plea was, they had found things under a usurpation, and being so, that government was natural to them, having singly no power to alter it); upon their perfect submission to the king, and solemn engagement to advance and maintain his right, they received their commissions anew from his majesty's own mouth. But where anyone had been cruel or oppressive to the subjects, or committed any notorious crime, or breach of trust (for the meanest persons had liberty to complain), he was rejected, and for the most part sent to Crashdoorpt, to prevent the ill effects of his disgrace.

We having displaced but five colambs and a few inferior officers, the moderation and justice of our proceedings gave the utmost satisfaction both to the magistrates and people.

Having observed at Brandleguarp abundance of the small images my wife had spoken of, and thinking this a proper opportunity to show my resentment against them, I ordered several of the ragans of the west before me, and asked what small images they had amongst them. One, who spoke for the rest, told me, very few, he believed; for he had scarce had any brought to him to be blessed. "Where," says I, "is your Great Image?" He told me, "At Youk."—"And have not the people here many small ones?"—"Very few," says he; "for they have not been forced upon us long."—"How forced upon you!" says I; "don't the people worship them?"—"A small number now do," says he.—"Pray speak out," says I. "When might you not worship them?"—"Never, that I know of," says he, "in our state, till about ten years ago, when Harlokin obliged us to it."—"What! did you worship them before?" says I.—"No," says he, "never since it has been a separate kingdom; for we would follow the old ragan's advice of worshipping Collwar, which they not admitting of, the State was divided between us who would and them who would not come into the ragan's doctrine: and though Harlokin was a zealous image-worshipper, yet all he could do would not bring the people heartily into it, for Collwar never wanted a greater majority." This pleased me prodigiously, being what was never hinted to me before; and I resolved not to let my scheme be a loser by it.

As we were to visit Youk in about eight days, I summoned the ragans and people to meet at the mouch; there recounting the great things done by Collwar in all nations. "This I could make appear," says I, "by many examples; but as you have one even at your own towns, I need go no farther."

"I must begin in ancient times, when, I presume, you all worshipped an idol; have you any tradition before this?"—They said, "No."—"This image," says I, "was worshipped in Begsurbeck's days, when an old ragan, whose mind Collwar had enlightened with the truth, would

ROBERT PALTOCK

have withdrawn your reverence from the image to the original Collwar himself; you would not consent: he threatens you, but promises success to Begsurbeck, who did consent; and he had it to an old age. Then those who would also consent, were so far encouraged as to be able to form an independent kingdom. Could nobody yet see the cause? was it not apparent Collwar was angry with the east, that would not follow the old ragan, and cherished the west, who would?

"But, to be short, let us apply the present instance, and sure it will convince us who is right, who wrong.

"So long as the west followed Collwar, they flourished, and the east declined; but no sooner had the west degenerated under the command of Harlokin, and the east by my means had embraced Collwar, but the tables were turned: the east is found weighty, and the west kicks the beam. These things whoso sees not, is blind indeed: therefore let publication be made for the destruction of all small images, and let the harbourers of them, contrary to this order, be slit; and for myself, I will destroy this mother-monster. Take you, holy ragans, care to destroy the brood." And having said this, I hacked the new idol to pieces.

I ordered proclamation for abolishing slavery, under the restrictions used at Brandleguarp: and thus having composed the west, and given a general satisfaction, we returned, almost the whole west accompanying us, till the east received us; and never was so happy a union, or more present to testify it, since the creation, I believe.

I ordered several of the principal men's sons to court, in order for employments, and to furnish our future colambs; and this I did, as knowing each country would rather approve of a member of their own body for their head than a stranger; and, in my opinion, it is the most natural union. And then breeding them under the eye of the king eight or ten years, or more, they are, as it were, naturalised to him too, and in better capacity to serve both king and country.

As my head was constantly at work for the good of this people, I turned the most trifling incidents into some use or other; and made the narrowest prospects extend to the vastest distances. I shall here instance in one only. There was at Youk a private man's son, whom by mere accident I happened to ask some slight question of; and he giving me, with a profound respect and graceful assurance, a most pertinent answer; that, and the manner of its delivery, gave me a pleasure, which upon farther discourse with him, was, contrary to custom, very much increased; for I found in him an extensive genius, and a desire for my conversation. I desired his father to put him under my care, which the old man, as I was then in so great repute, readily agreed to; and his son desiring nothing more, I took him with me to Brandleguarp. I soon procured him a pretty post but of small duty, for I had purposed other employment for him, but of sufficient significancy to procure him respect. I took great delight in talking with him on different subjects, and observed by his questions upon them, which often puzzled me, or his answers to them, he had a most pregnant fancy and surprising solidity, joined to a continual and unwearied application. I frequently mentioning books, writing, and letters to him, and telling him what great things might be attained that way, his inquisitive temper, and the schemes he had formed thereon, put me upon thinking of several things I should never have hit upon without him. I considered all the ways I could contrive to teach him letters; and letting him into my design, he asked me how I did to make a letter. I described a pen to him, and told him I put a black liquor into it, and as I drew that along upon a flat white thing we made use of, called paper, it would make marks which way ever I drew it, into what shape I pleased. "Why then," says he, "anything that will make a mark upon another thing as I please, will do."—"True," says I, "but what shall we get that will make a black mark?"—We were entering further into this debate; but the king sending for me, I left him unsatisfied. I stayed late with the king that night, so did not see Lasmeel (for that was his name) till next night, wondering what was become of him. I asked him then where he had been all the day. He told me he had been looking for a pen and paper. I laughed, and asked him if he had found them.—"Yes," says he, "or something that will do as well:" so he opened one side of his graundee, and showed me a large flat leaf, smooth and pulpy, very long and wide, and about a quarter of an inch thick, almost like an Indian fig-leaf.—"And what am I to do with this?" says I.—"To mark it," says he, "and see where you mark."—"With what?" says I.—"With this," says he, putting his hand again into his graundee, and taking out three or four strong sharp prickles. I looked at them both; and clapping him on the head, "Lasmeel," says I, "if you and I were in England, you should be made a privy-councillor."—"What! won't it do, then?" says he.—I told him we would try.—"I thought," says he, "it would have done very well; for I marked one all about, and though I could not see much at first, by that time I had made an end, that I did first was quite of a different colour from the leaf, and I could see it as plain as could be." I told him as he was of an age to comprehend what I meant, I would take another method

ROBERT PALTOCK

with him than with a child; so I reasoned from sentences backwards to words, and from them to syllables, and so on to letters. I then made one, the vowel A, told him its sound, and added a consonant to it, and told him that part of the sound of each distinct letter put together, as the two letters themselves were, made another sound, which I called a syllable; and that joining two or more of them together made a word, by putting the same letters together as made the sounds of those syllables which made that word. Then setting him a copy of letters, which with very little difficulty were to be drawn upon the leaf, and telling him their sounds, I left him to himself; and when he had done, though I named them but twice over, his memory was so strong as to retain the sounds, as he called them, of everyone but F, L, and Q.

In two months' time I made him master of anything I wrote to him; and as he delighted in it, he wrote a great deal himself, so that we kept an epistolary correspondence, and he would set down all the common occurrences of the day, as what he heard and saw, with his remarks on divers things.

One day, as the king and I were walking in the gardens, and talking of the customs of my country, and about our wars, telling him how our soldiers fought on horseback, the king could not conceive what I meant by a horse. I told him my wife had said there were neither beasts nor fishes in the country; which I was very much surprised at, considering how we abounded with both: "And therefore," says I, "to tell your majesty that a horse is a creature with four legs, you must naturally believe it to be somewhat like a man with four legs."—"Why, truly," says he, "I believe it is; but has it the graundee?" I could not forbear smiling, even at his majesty, and wanted to find some similitude to compare it to, to carry the king's mind that way; for else he would sooner, I thought, conceive it like a tree or a mountain than what it really was; and as I was musing, it came into my head I had given Lasmeel a small print of a horse, which I found in one of the captain's pockets at Graundevolet, and believing it to be the stamp of a tobacco-paper, had kept it to please the children with; so I told the king I believed I could show him the figure of a horse. He told me it would much oblige him.

Seeing several of the guards waiting at the garden arch, I looked, and at last found one of Lasmeel's leaves in the garden, and cutting one of them up with my knife, I took the point of that, and wrote to Lasmeel to send me by the bearer the picture of a horse I gave him, that I might show it the king. And calling one of the guards, "Carry that to

Lasmeel," says I; "he is, I believe, in my apartment, and bring me an answer directly." Then falling into discourse again with the king, and presently turning at the end of the walk, I saw the same guard again. Says I "You cannot have brought me an answer already."—"You have not told me," says he, "what to bring you an answer to."—"Nor shall I," says I; "do as you are bid;" for I perceived then what the fellow stuck at. He walked off with the leaf, but very discontentedly. The king said he wondered how I could act such a contradiction. "This, father," says he, "is not what I expected from you; to order a man to bring an answer without giving him a message." I desired his patience only till the man came back. Presently says the king, "Here he comes!—Well," says he, "what answer?"—"Sir," says the fellow, "I have only had the walk for my pains: for he sent it back again, and a little white thing with it."—"Ha, ha!" says the king, "I thought so.—Come, father, own you have once been in the wrong; for I am sure you intended to give him a message, but having forgot it, would not submit to be told of your mistake by a guard." I looked very grave, reading what Lasmeel had wrote; which was to tell me he had obeyed my orders by sending the horse, for he was just then drawing it out upon a leaf.

"Come, come," says the king, "give the man his message, father, and let him go again."—"Sir," says I, "there is no need of that, he has punctually obeyed me; and Lasmeel was then at the table in my oval chamber with a leaf, and this picture in my hand, before him."

The king was ready to sink when I said so, and showed the print. "Truly, father," says he, "I have been to blame to question you; for though these things are above my comprehension, I am not to think anything beyond your skill." I made no reply to it; but showing the king the picture, the guard sneaked off; and glad he was, I believe, he could do so.

I went then upon the explanation of my horse, and answering fifty questions about him, at last he asked what his inside was: "Exactly the same as your majesty's," said I.—"And can he eat and breathe too?" says he.—"Just as you can," says I.—"Well," says he, "I would never have believed there had been such a creature: what would I give for one of them!"—I set forth the divers other uses we put them to, besides the wars; and by the picture, with some supposed alterations, I described a cow, a sheep, and numberless other quadrupeds; my account of which gave him great pleasure.

ROBERT PALTOCK

XVIII

PETER SENDS FOR HIS FAMILY—A RISING OF
FORMER SLAVES ON THAT ACCOUNT—TAKES A VIEW OF
THE CITY—DESCRIPTION OF IT, AND OF THE COUNTRY—
HOT AND COLD SPRINGS.

Having now some leisure time on my hands to consider over my own affairs, I had thoughts of transporting my family, with all my effects, to Sass Doorpt Swangeanti, but yet had no mind to relinquish all thought of my ship and cargo; for the greatest part of this was still remaining, I having had but the pickings through the gulf. I once had a mind to have gone myself; but considering the immense distance over sea, though I had once come safe, I thought I ought not to tempt Providence, where my presence was not absolutely necessary.

Nasgig, to whose care and conduct any enterprise might be trusted, offered his service to go and execute any commands I should give him. His only difficulty, he said, was that it would be impossible for him to remember the different names of many things, which he had no idea of, to convey the knowledge of them to his mind when he saw them; but barring that, he doubted not to give me satisfaction. I told him I would send an assistant with him, who could remember whatever I once told him; and that I might not burden his memory with names only, Lasmeel should carry his memory with him, and that he, Nasgig, should only have the executive part.

Lasmeel, who had sat waiting an opportunity to put in for a share in the adventure, having a longing desire to see the ship, told Nasgig he had a peculiar art of memory, so as to remember whatever he would as long as he pleased, and that if he carried that with him, they need fear no mistakes.

The king having granted me as many of his guards as I pleased, for the carriage of my things, we appointed them to be ready on the fourth day; when Nasgig and Lasmeel set out with them.

I ordered Lasmeel, however, to be with me the next morning, that we might set down proper instructions; which I told him would be very long, and that he must bring a good number of leaves with him.

When Lasmeel entered my chamber next morning, he informed me that the whole city was in an uproar, especially those who had been freed by me. "What!" says I, "have they so soon forgot their subjection, to misapply their liberty already? But step and bring me word what's the matter, and order some of the ringleaders hither to me." Lasmeel upon inquiry found that it had been given out I was going to leave the country, and they all said, wherever I went they were determined to go and settle with me; for if I left them, they should be reduced to slavery again. However, he brought some of them to me, and upon my telling them I thanked them for their affection to me, but blamed them for showing it in so tumultuous a manner, and that I was so far from intending to leave them, that I was sending for my family and effects in order to settle amongst them, they rejoiced very much, and told me they would carry the good news to their companions, and disperse immediately. But I was now in more perplexity than before, for they having signified my designs to the rest, they rushed into the gallery in such numbers that they forced me up to my very chamber. I told them this was an unprecedented manner of using a person they pretended a kindness for; and told them if they made use of such risings to express their gratitude to me, it would be the direct means to oblige me to leave them: "For," says I, "do you think I can be safe in a kingdom where greater deference is paid to me than to the crown?" They begged my pardon, they said, and would obey me in anything; but the present trouble was only to offer their services to fetch my family and goods, or to do anything else I should want them for; and if I would favour them in that, they would retire directly. I told them when I had considered of it they should hear from me; and this again quieted them.

This disturbance not only took up much of my time, which I could have better employed, but put me to a non-plus how to come off with them; till I sent Maleck to tell them though I set a great value upon their esteem, yet after what had passed, it would be the most unadvisable thing in nature for me to accept their kindness; for having before requested a body of men of the king, as he had graciously granted them, it would be preferring them to the king, should I now relinquish his grant and make use of their offer; and after this I heard no more of it.

I had scarce met with a more difficult task than to fix exact rules for the conduct of my present undertaking, there being so many things to be expressed, wherein the least perplexity arising, might have caused both delay and damage; for I was not only forced to set down the things I would have brought, but the manner and method of packing and securing them; but as Lasmeel could read my writing to Pedro at

ROBERT PALTOCK

home, and Youwarkee on board, it would be a means, though far from an expeditious one, of bringing matters into some order; and after I had done as I thought, I could have enumerated many more things, and was obliged to add an *et cætera* to the end of my catalogue; and while they were ready for flight, I added divers other particulars and circumstances. Nay, when they were even upon the graundee, I recollected the most material thing of all; for my greatest concern was, having broke up so many of my chests, to find package for the things; I say, even so late as that, I bethought me of the several great water-casks I had on board, that would hold an infinite number of small things, and would be slung easily; so I stopped them and set down that, and they were no sooner out of sight and hearing, but remembering twenty more, I was then forced to trust them to my *et cætera*.

I had sent my own flying-chair to bring the boys who had not the graundee, with orders for Pedro to sit tied in the chair, with Dicky tied in his arms; Jemmy to sit tied to the board before the chair, and David behind: so I hoped they would come safe enough; and then my wife and Sally were able to help themselves.

Having despatched my caravan, and being all alone, I called Quilly the next morning, and telling him I had thoughts of viewing the country, I bade him prepare to go with me.

I had now been here above six months, and yet upon coming to walk gravely about the city, I found myself as much a stranger to the knowledge of the place as if that had been the first day of my arrival, though I had been over it several times in my chair.

This city is not only one of, but actually the most curious piece of work in the world, and consists of one immense entire stone of a considerable height, and it may be seven miles in length, and near as broad as it is long. The streets and habitable part of it are scooped, as it were, out of the solid stone, to the level with the rest of the country, very flat and smooth at bottom, the rock rising perpendicular from the streets on each side.

The figure of the city is a direct square; each side about six miles long, with a large open circle in the centre of the square, about a mile in diameter, and from each of the sides of the outer streets to the opposite side runs another street, cutting the centre of the circle as in the figure.

Along the whole face of the rock, bounding the streets and the circle, there are archways; those in the circle, and the four cross streets, for the gentry and better people; and those in the outer streets, for the meaner; and it is as easy to know as by a sign where a great man lives, by the grandeur of his entrance, and lavish distribution of the pillars, carving, and statues about his portico, within and without: for as they have no doors, you may look in, and are not forbid entrance; and though it should look odd to an English reader, that an Englishman should speak with pleasure of a land of darkness, as that almost was, yet I am satisfied whoever shall see it after me will be persuaded, that for the real grandeur of their entrances, and for the magnificence of the apartments and sculpture, no part of the universe can produce the like; and though within doors there is no other manner of light than the sweecoes, yet that, when you are once used to it, is so agreeable and free from all noisome savour, that I never once regretted the loss of the sun within doors, though I often have when abroad; but then that would be injurious to the proper inhabitants, though they can no more see in total darkness than myself.

I have been over some of these private houses, which contain, it may be, thirty rooms, great and small, some higher, some lower, full of sweecoe-lights, and extremely well proportioned and beautiful.

The king's palace, with all the apartments, stands in, and takes up, one full fourth part of the square of the whole city; and is, indeed, of itself a perfect city.

There is no great man's house without one or more long galleries for the ladies to divert themselves at divers sports in, particularly at one like our bowls on a bowling-green, and at somewhat like nine-holes, at which they play for wines, and drink a great deal, for none of them will intoxicate.

In my walk and survey of the city, one of the colambs being making a house to reside in when at Brandleguarp, I had the curiosity to go in. I saw there abundance of botts stand filled with a greenish liquor, and asked Quilly what that was. He said it was what the stone-men used in making houses. I proceeded farther in, where I saw several men at work, and stayed a good while to observe them. Each man had a bott of this liquor in his left hand, and stood before a large bank of stone, it may be 30 feet high, reaching forward up to the ceiling of the place, and ascending by steps from bottom to top; the workmen standing some on one step, some on another, pouring on this liquor with their left hands, and with their right holding a wooden tool, shaped like a little spade. I observed wherever they poured on this water, a smoke arose for a little space of time, and then the place turned white, which was scraped off like fine powder with the spade-handle; and then pouring new liquor, he scraped again, working all the while by sweecoe-lights.

Having my watch in my pocket, I measured a spot of a yard long, about a foot high, and a foot and a half on the upper flat, to see how long he would be fetching down that piece; and he got it away in little above two hours. By this means I came to know how they made their houses; for I had neither seen any tool I thought proper, nor even iron itself, except my own, since I came into the country. Upon inquiry, I found that the scrapings of this stone, and a portion of common earth, mixed with a water they have, will cement like plaster; and they use it in the small ornamental work of their buildings. I then went farther into this house, where I saw one making the figure of a glumm by the same method; but it standing upright in the solid rock against the wall, the workman held his liquor in an open shell, and dipping such stuff as my bed was made of, bound up in short rolls, some larger, some less, into the liquor, he touched the figure, and then scraped till he had reduced it into a perfect piece.

It is impossible to imagine how this work rids away; for in ten months' time after I saw it, this house was completed, having a great number of fine, large, and lofty rooms in it, exquisitely carved to all appearance.

My wonder ceased as to the palace, when I saw how easily this work was done; but sure there is no other such room in the world as Begsurbeck's, that I described above.

The palace, as I said before, taking up one quarter of the city, opens into four streets by four different arches; and before one of the sides, which I call the front, is a large triangle, formed by the entrance out of one of the cross streets, and the two ends of the front of the palace. Along the lower front of it, all the way runs a piazza of considerable height, supported by vast round columns, which seemed to bear up the whole front of the rock, over which was a gallery of equal length, with balustrades along it, supported with pillars of a yet finer make, and over that a pediment with divers figures, and other work, to the top of the rock, which being there quite even for its whole length, was enclosed with balustrades between pedestals all the way, on which stood the statues of their ancient kings, so large as to appear equal to the life. The other two sides of the triangle were dwellings for divers officers belonging to the palace. Under the middle arch of the piazza was the way into the palace, through a long, spacious arched passage, whose farther end opened into a large square; on each side of this passage were large staircases, if I may so call them, by which you ascend gradually, and without steps, into the upper apartments.

The next morning we took another walk, for I told Quilly I had a mind to take a prospect of the country. We then went out at the back arch of the palace, as we had the day before at one of the sides, there being a like passage through the rock from that we went out at, to an opposite arch leading into the garden. I say, we went out at the back arch, and after passing a large quadrangle with lodgings all round it, we ascended through a cut in the rock to a large flat, where we plainly saw the Black Mountain with its top in the very sky, the sides of which afforded numberless trees, though the ground within view afforded very little verdure, or even shrubs. But the most beautiful sight from the rock was to see the people come home loaded from the mountain, and from the woods, with, it may be, forty pound weight each on their backs; and mounting over the rock, to see them dart along the streets to their several dwellings, over the heads of thousands of others walking in all parts of the streets, while others were flying other ways. It was very pleasant to see a man walking gravely in one street, and as quick as thought to see him over the rock, settled in another, perhaps two miles distant.

The near view of the country seeming so barren, naturally led me to ask Quilly from whence they got provision for so many people as the city contained, which, to be sure, could not be less than three hundred thousand. He told me that they had nothing but what came from the Great Forest on the skirts of the mountain. "But for the grain of it, and some few outward marks," says I, "I could have sworn I had eaten some of my country beef the other day at the king's table."—"I don't know what your beef, as you call it, is; but I am sure we have nothing here but the fruit of some tree or shrub, that ever I heard of."—"I wonder," says I, "Quilly, how your cooks dress their victuals. I have eaten many things boiled, and otherwise dressed hot, but have seen no rivers, or water, since I came into this country, except for drinking, or washing my hands, and I don't know where that comes from. And another thing," says I, "surprises me, though I see no sun as we have to warm the air, you are very temperate in the town, and it is seldom cold here; but I neither see fire nor smoke."—"We have," says Quilly, "several very good springs under the palace, both of hot water and cold, and I don't know what we should do with fires; we see the dread of them sufficiently at Mount Alkoe. Our cooks dress their fruits at the hot springs."—"That is a fancy," said I; "they cannot boil them there."—"I am sure we have no other dressing," says he.—"Well, Quilly," says I, "we will go home the way you told me of, and tomorrow you shall show me the springs; but, pray, how come you to be so much afraid of Mount Alkoe? I suppose your eyes won't bear the light; is not that all?"—"No, no," says Quilly, "that is the country of bad men. Some of us have flown over there accidentally, when the mountain has been cool, as it is sometimes for a good while together, and have heard such noises as would frighten any honest man out of his senses, for there they beat and punish bad men." I could not make much of his story, nor did I inquire further, for I had before determined, if possible, to get over thither. As we were now come into the garden, I ordered Quilly to get ready my dinner, and I would come in presently.

We went next morning to view the springs, and indeed it was a sight well worth considering. We were in divers offices under the rock (Quilly carrying two globe-lights before me), in which were springs of very clear water, some of hot, and some of cold, rising within two or three inches of the surface of the floor. We then went into the kitchen, which was bigger than I ever saw one of our churches, and where were a great number of these springs, the hot all boiling full speed day and night, and smoking like a caldron, the water rising through very small chinks in the stone into basons, some bigger, some less; and they had several deep stone jars to set anything to boil in. But what was the most surprising was, you should see a spring of very cold water within a few feet of one of hot, and they never rise higher or sink lower than they are. I talked with the master cook, an ingenious man, about them; and he told me they lie in this manner all over the rocky part of the country, and that the first thing anyone does in looking out for a house, is to see for the water, whether both hot and cold may be found within the compass he designs to make use of; and finding that, he goes on, or else searches another place. And he told me where this convenience was not in great plenty the people did not inhabit, which made the towns all so very populous. He said, too, that those warm springs made the air more wholesome about the towns than in other parts where there were none of them. I thanked him for his information, which finished my search for that time.

XIX

P ETER SENDS FOR HIS FAMILY—P ENDLEHAMBY GIVES A
FABULOUS ACCOUNT OF THE PEOPLING OF THAT COUNTRY—
T HEIR POLICY AND GOVERNMENT—P ETER'S DISCOURSE ON
TRADE—Y OUWARKEE ARRIVES—I NVITES THE KING AND
NOBLES TO A TREAT—S ENDS TO G RAUNDEVOLET FOR FOWLS.

T he days hanging heavy on my hands till the arrival of my family,
I sent Pendlehamby word that as I had sent for my family and
effects in order to settle in this country, and expected them very soon,
I should be glad of his, my brother, and sister's company, to welcome
them on their arrival.

My father came alone, which gave me an opportunity of informing
myself in the rise and policy of the State, as I purposed to take several
farther steps in their affairs, if they might prove agreeable and consistent;
for hitherto, having had only slight sketches or hints of things, I could
form no just idea of the whole of their laws, customs, and government.
Explaining myself, therefore, to him, I begged his instructions in those
particulars.

"Son Peter," says my father, "you have already done too much in a short
time to leave any room to think you can do no more: and as you have
hitherto directed your own proceedings with such incredible success,
neither the king nor colambs will interpose against your inclination, but
give you all the advices in our powers; and I shall esteem your selecting
me for that purpose no small honour.

"Know, then, that this State, by the tradition of our ragans, has
subsisted eleven thousand years; for, before that time, the great mountain
Emina, then not far from the Black Mountain, but now fallen and sunk
in the sea, roaring and raging in its own bowels for many ages, at last
burst asunder with great violence, and threw up numberless unformed
fleshy masses to the very stars; two of which happening in their passage
to touch the side of the Black Mountain (for all the rest fell into the
sea and were lost) lodged there, and lying close together as they grew,
united to each other till they were joined in one; and, in process of time,
by the dews of heaven, became a glumm and a gawry; but being so
linked together by the adhesion of their flesh, they were obliged both to
move which way either would. Living thus a long time in great love and

fondness for each other, they had but one inclination, lest both should be sufferers upon the least disagreement.

"In process of time they grew tired of each other's constant society, and one willing to go here and the other there, bred perpetual disorders between them; for prevention whereof for the future they agreed to cut themselves asunder with sharp stones. The pain indeed was intolerable during the operation; but, however, they effected it, and the wounds each received were very dangerous, and a long time before they were perfectly healed; but at length, sometimes agreeing, sometimes not, they begat a son, whom they called Perigen, and a daughter they called Philella. These two, as they grew up, despising their parents, who lived on the top of the mountain, ventured to descend into the plains, and living upon the fruits they found there, sheltered themselves in this very rock. Meantime, the old glumm and gawry, having lived to a great age, were so infirm that neither of them was able to walk for a long time; till one day, being near each other, and trying to rise by the assistance of each other, they both got up, and leaning upon and supporting each other, they also walked commodiously. This mutual assistance kept them in good humour a great while, till one day, passing along near hoximo, they both fell in.

"Perigen and Philella had several children in the plains; who, as they grew up, increasing, spread into remote parts, and peopled the country. At last, one of them being a very passionate man, at the instigation of his wife, became the first murderer, by slaying his father. This so enraged the people, that the murderer and his wife, in abhorrence of the fact, were conveyed to Mount Alkoe, where was then only a very narrow deep pit, into which they were both thrown headlong; but the persons who carried them thither, had scarce retired from the mouth of the pit, when it burst out with fire, raging prodigiously, and has kept burning ever since. Arco and Telamine (the murderer and his wife) lived seven thousand years in the flames; till having with their teeth wrought a passage through the side of the mountain, they begat a new generation about the foot of the mountain; and having brought fire with them, resolved to keep it burning ever after in memory of their escape; and power being given them over bad men, they and their progeny are now wholly employed in beating and tormenting them.

"A great while after Arco and Telamine were thus disposed of, the people of this country multiplying, it happened one year that all the fruits were so dry that the people, not able to live any longer upon the moisture of them only, as they had always done before, and fearing all to be consumed with drought, one of their ragans praying very much, and promising to make an image to Collwar and preserve it forever, if he would send them but moisture, in one night's time the earth cast up such a flood that they were forced to mount on the rocks for fear of drowning. But the next day it all sunk away again, except several little bubbles which remained in many places for a long time, and the people lived only on the moisture they sucked from the stone where those bubbles settled for many years; for they found that the water arose to the height of the surface, and no higher; and where they found most of those chinks and bubbles they settled and formed cities, living altogether in holes of the rock; till one Lallio, having found out the art of crumbling the rock to dust by a liquor he got from the trees, and working himself a noble house in the rock, in the place where our palace now stands, he told them if they would make him their king, they should each have such a house as his own. To this they agreed, and then he discovered the secret to them.

"This Lallio directed the cutting out this whole city, divided the people into colonies where the waters were most plenty; and while half the people worked at the streets and houses, the other half brought them provisions. In short, he grew so powerful that no one durst dispute his commands; all which authority he transmitted to his successors, who, finding by the increase of the people and the many divisions of them that they grew insolent and ungovernable, they appointed a colamb in every province, as a vice-king, with absolute authority over all causes, except murder and treason, which are referred to the king and colambs in moucheratt.

"As we had no want but of victuals and habitations, the king, when he gave a colambat, gave also the lands and the fruits thereof, together with all the hot and cold springs, to the colamb, who again distributed parcels to the great officers under him, and they part of theirs to the meaner officers under them, for their subsistence, with such a number of the common people as was necessary in respect to the dignity of the post each enjoyed, who for their services are fed by their masters.

"In all cases of war, the king lays before the moucheratt the number of his own troops he designs to send; when each colamb's quota being settled at such a proportion of the whole, he forthwith sends his number from out of his own lasks, and also from the several officers under him; so that every man, let the number be ever so great, can be at the rendezvous in a very few days.

"We have but three professions, besides the ragans and soldiery, amongst us, and these are cooks, house-makers, and pike-makers, of which every colamb has several among his lasks; and these, upon the new regulations, will be the only gainers, as they may work where they please, and according to their skill will be their provision; but how the poor labourers will be the better for it, I cannot see."

"Dear sir," says I, "there are, you see, amongst lasks, some of such parts, that it is great pity they should be confined from showing them; and my meaning in giving liberty is in order for what is to follow; that is, for the introduction of arts amongst you. Now, every man who has natural parts will exert them when any art is laid before him; and he will find so much delight in making new discoveries that, did no profit attend it, the satisfaction of the discovery to a prying genius would compensate the pains; but I propose a profit also to the artificer."— "Why, what profit," says my father, "can arise but food, and perhaps a servant of their own to provide it for them?"

"Sir," says I, "the man who has nothing to hope loses the use of one of his faculties; and if I guess right, and you live ten years longer, you shall see this State as much altered as the difference has been between a lask and a tree he feeds on. You shall all be possessed of that which will bring you fruits from the woods without a lask to fetch it. Those who were before your slaves shall then take it as an honour to be employed by you, and at the same time shall employ others dependent on them; so as the great and small shall be under mutual obligations to each other, and both to the truly industrious artificer; and yet everyone content only with what he merits."

"Dear son," says my father, "these will be glorious days indeed! But, come, come, you have played a good part already; don't, by attempting what you can't master, eclipse the glory so justly due to you."—"No, sir," says I, "nothing shall be attempted by me to my dishonour; for I shall ever remember my friend Glanepze. Sir," says I, "see here." (showing him my watch).—"Why, this," says he, "hung by my daughter's side at Graundevolet."—"It did so," says I; "and, pray, what did you take it for?"—"A bott," says he.—"I thought so," says I; "but as you asked no questions, I did not then force the knowledge of it upon you. But put it to your ear."—He did so. "What noise is that?" says he. "Is it alive?"— "No," says I, "it is not; but it is as significant. If I ask it what time of the day it is, or how long I have been going from this place to that, I look but in its face, and it tells me presently."

My father, looking upon it a good while, and perceiving that the minute hand had got farther than it was at first, was just dropping it out of his hand, had I not caught it. "Why, it is alive," says he; "it moves!"—"Sir," says I, "if you had dropped it, you had done me an inexpressible injury."—"Oh ho," says he, "I find now how you do your wonders; it is something you have shut up here that assists you; it is an evil spirit!" I laughing heartily, he was sorry for what he had said, believing he had shown some ignorance. "No, sir," says I, "it is no spirit, good or evil, but a machine made by some of my countrymen, to measure time with."—"I have heard," says he, "of measuring an abb, or the ground, or a rock; but never yet heard of measuring time."—"Why, sir," says I, "don't you say three days hence I will do so; or such a one is three years old? Is not that a measuring of time by so many days or years?"—"Truly," says he, "in one sense I think it is."—"Now, sir," says I, "how do you measure a day?"—"Why, by rising and lying down," says he.—"But suppose I say I will go now, and come again, and have a particular time in my head when I will return, how shall I do to make you know that time?"—"Why, that will be afterwards, another time," says he; "or I can think how long it will be."—"But," says I, "how can you make me know when you think it will be?"—"You must think too," says he.—"But then," says I, "we may deceive each other, by thinking differently. Now this will set us to rights:" then I described the figures to him, telling him how many parts they divided the day into, and that by looking on it I could tell how many of such parts were passed; and that if he went from me, and said he would come one, or two, or three parts hence, I should know when to expect him. I then showed him the wheels, and explained where the force lay, and why it went no faster or slower, as well as I could; and from my desire of teaching, insensibly perfected myself more and more in it. So that beginning to have a little idea of it, he wished he had one. "And," says he, "will you teach all our people to make such things?"—"Then they would be disregarded, sir," says I.—"It is impossible," says he.—"I'll tell you, sir, how I mean," said I. "I can, hereafter, show you a hundred things as useful as this; now, if everybody was to make these, how would other things be made? Besides, if everybody made them, nobody would want them; and then what would anybody get by them, besides the pleasing their own fancy? But if only twenty men make them in one town, all the rest must come to them; and they who make these, must go to one of twenty others, who make another thing that these men want, and so on; by which means, every man wanting something he does not make, it will be the better for every maker of everything."

"Son," says my father, "excuse me; I am really ashamed, now you have better informed me, I asked so foolish a question." I told him we had a saying in my country, that everything is easy when it is known. "I think," says he, "a man might find everything in your country."

Two days after, my wife and daughter Sally came very early; but sure no joy could be greater than ours at sight of each other. I embraced them both over and over, as did my father, especially Sally, who was a charming child. They told me I might expect everything that evening, for they left them alighting at the height of Battringdrigg; for though they came out the last, yet the body of the people with their baggage could not come so fast as they did. And little Sally said, "We stayed and rested ourselves, purely, daddy, at Battringdrigg, before the crowd came; but as soon as mammy had seen all my brothers safe, who came before the rest, and kissed Dicky, we set out again."

About seven hours after arrived the second convoy from abroad, that ever entered that country. I had too much to do with my wife and children that night, to spare a thought to my cargo; so I only set a guard over them; for though I had now been married about sixteen years, Youwarkee was ever new to me.

I was now obliged to the king again, for some additional conveniences to my former apartment; and the young ones were mightily pleased to have so much more room than we had at home, and to see the sweecoes; but finding themselves waited upon in so elegant a manner, and by so many servants (for with our new rooms, we had all the servants belonging to them), they thought themselves in a paradise to the grotto, where all we wanted we were forced to help ourselves to.

The next day Tommy came to see us, the king having given him a very pretty post, since the death of Yaccombourse; and Hallycarnie, with the Princess Jahamel, her mistress, who was mightily pleased to see Youwarkee in her English dress, and invited her and the children to her apartment.

It was but a few months since my wife saw the children; yet she scarce knew them, they were so altered; for the two courtiers behaved with so much politeness, that their brothers and Sally looked but with an ill eye upon them, finding all the fault, and dropping as many little invidious expressions on them as possible. But I sharply rebuked them: "We were all made chiefly," I told them, "to please our Maker, and that could be done only by the goodness of the heart; and if their hearts were more pure, they were the best children; but if they liked their brothers' and sisters' outward behaviour better than their own, they might so far imitate them."

When we were settled in our new apartment, I unpacked my chairs and tables, and set out my side-board, and made such a figure as had never before been seen in that part of the world. I wanted now some shoes for Pedro, his own being almost past wear, for the young ones never had worn any, but could find none; till applying to Lasmeel, and showing him what I wanted, he pointed to one of the great water-casks; but as there were eleven of them, big and little, I knew not where to begin; till, having invited the king and several of the ministers to dine with me, I was forced to look over my goods for several other things I should want.

In my search, I found half a ream of paper, a leathern ink-bottle, but no ink in it, some quills, and books of accounts, and several other things relative to writing. The prize gave me courage to attempt the other casks; but I found little more that I immediately wanted. In the last cask were several books, two of them romances, six volumes of English plays, two of devotion; the next were either Spanish or Portuguese, and the last looked like a Bible; but just opening it, and taking it to be of the same language, I put them all in again, thinking to divert myself with them someother time. I here found some more paper, and so many shoes, as, when I had fellowed them, served me as long as I stayed in the country.

Having, as I said before, invited the king to eat with me, I was sorry I had not ordered my fowls to be brought; and Youwarkee said she thought to have done it, but I had not wrote for them. I told her I would send Maleck for some of them, I was resolved; for I should pique myself on giving the king a dish he had never before tasted. So I called Maleck, telling him he must take thirty men with him to Graundevolet: "And carry six empty chests with you," says I, "and put eight of my fowls in each chest, and bring them with all expedition."— "Where do they lie, sir?" says he.—"You will find them at roost," says I, "when it is dark."—"I never was there," says he, "and don't know the way."—"What," says I, "never at Graundevolet!"—"Yes," says he, "but not at roost."—I laughed, saying, "Maleck, did not you see fowls when you was there?" He said he did not know; what were they like?—"They are a bird," says I.—"And what sort of a thing is that?" says he. Youwee hearing us in this debate, "Maleck," says she, "did not you see me toss down little nuts to something that you stared at? you saw them eat the nuts."—"Oh dear," says he, "I know it very well, with two legs and no arms."—"The same," says I, "Maleck; do you go look for a little house, almost by my grotto, and at night you will find these things stand on sticks in that house. Take them down gently, and come away with them in the chests." Maleck performed his business to a hair; but instead of forty-eight, brought me sixty, telling me he found the chests would hold them very well; and I kept them afterwards in the king's garden.

XX

PETER GOES TO HIS FATHER'S—TRAVERSES THE BLACK
MOUNTAIN—TAKES A FLIGHT TO MOUNT ALKOE—GAINS
THE MINERS—OVERCOMES THE GOVERNOR'S TROOPS—
PROCLAIMS GEORIGETTI KING—SEIZES THE GOVERNOR—
RETURNS HIM THE GOVERNMENT—PETER MAKES LAWS
WITH THE CONSENT OF THE PEOPLE, AND RETURNS TO
BRANDLEGUARP WITH DEPUTIES.

No further project being ripe for execution, I took a journey home
with my father to Arndrumnstake, and he would take all the
children with him. Youwarkee and I stayed about six weeks, leaving all
the children with my father.

Upon my return, I frequently talked with Maleck about his country;
who they originally were, and how long it had been inhabited, and
what other countries bordered thereon, and how they lay. He told me
his countrymen looked upon themselves to be very ancient, but they
were not very numerous; for the old stock was almost worn out by the
hardships they had undergone; that about three hundred years before,
he said, as he had it from good report, there were a people from beyond
the sea, or, as they called themselves, from the Little Lands, had
strangely overrun them; and he had heard say they would have overrun
this country too, but they thought it would not answer. He said, "when
those people first came, they began to turn up the earth to a prodigious
depth; and now," says he, "bringing some nasty hard earth of several
sorts, they put it into great fires till it runs about like water, and then
beat it about with great heavy things into several shapes; and some of
it, sir," says he, "looks just like that stuff that lay at the bottom of your
ship, and some almost white, and some red; for when I was a boy I was
to have been sent to work amongst them, as my father did; but it having
killed him, I came hither, as many more have done, to avoid it."—"And
what do they do with it," says I, "when they have beat it about as you
say?"—"Then," says he, "they carry it a long way to the sea."—"What
then?" says I.—"Why, then the Little-landers take it, and swim over
the sea with it."—"And what do they do with it?" says I.—"Why," says
he, "there are other people who take it from them, and go away with
it."—"Why do they let them take it?" says I.—"Because," says he, "they

give them clothes for it."—"Do they want clothes," says I, "more than you?" He told me they had no graundee.—"And what other countries have you hereabout?"—"There is one country," says he, "north of Alkoe, where they say there is just such another people as the Little-landers, and they get some of the things from Mount Alkoe."—"What do they do with them?" says I.—"I don't know," says he; "they fetch a great deal; but they won't let anybody come into their country."—"Is there nobody inhabits between the Mountain Alkoe and the sea?" He told me no, the Little-landers would not let them.

Having got what information I could from Maleck, and also from a countryman or two of his he had brought to me, I considered it all over; And, thinks I, if I could but get Mount Alkoe to submit (for they had told me they were only governed by a deputy from the Little Lands) to see the work done, I might, by intercepting the trade to the sea, turn the profit of the country my own way, and make it pass through our hands.

I next inquired of those who brought the fruits from the Great Forest, what sort of land they had there, and found, by their description, it was a light mould, and in many places well covered with grass and herbs; and by all the report I could hear, must be a fruitful country, well managed; and being a flat country and not encompassed on that side with the Black Mountain, was much higher than Doorpt Swangeanti. This news put me upon searching the truth of it; and I made the tour of the Black Mountain and the Great Forest, alighting often to make my observations.

The forest is a little world of wood without end, with here and there a fine lawn very grassy; and indeed the wood-grounds bear it very well, the trees not standing in crowds, but at a healthy distance from each other. I went abundantly farther than anyone had before been, but saw no variation in the woody scene; and coming round westward home, I had a view of hoximo; which is nothing but a narrow cleft in the earth, on the top of the Black Mountain, of a most extraordinary depth; for upon dropping a stone down, you shall hear it strike and hum for a long time before all is quiet again; and laying my ear over the cleft, whilst I ordered one of my attendants to throw a large stone down, after the usual thumps and humming, I imagined I heard it dash in water, so that it is not impossible it may reach to the sea; which is at least six or seven miles below it. Into this hole all dead bodies are precipitated, from the king to the beggar; for four glumms holding by the ankles and wrists of the deceased, fly with them to hoximo and throw them down, whilst the air is filled with the lamentations of the relations of the deceased, and of such others as are induced to follow the corpse for the sake of the wines, on such occasions plentifully distributed to all comers by the gentry, and in the best proportion they are able by even the meanest amongst them.

After a stay of about fourteen days at home, I fixed my next trip for Mount Alkoe; and having told Maleck my design, he said he would go with me with all his heart, but feared I should get no Brandleguarpine to bear me; for he told me they had an old tradition that Mindrack lived there, and would not go for all the world; which has been the greatest security that country has had, for this would have devoured them else, says he.

I spoke to the king, to Nasgig, and the ragans, and found them all unanimous that the mountain Alkoe was the habitation of Mindrack, and that the noises which had been heard there were his servants beating bad men. Says I to myself, Here is one of the usefullest projects upon earth spoiled by an unaccountable prepossession; what must be done to overcome this prejudice?

I told Maleck I found what he said to be too true, as to the people of Brandleguarp: "But," says I, "are there not enough of your countrymen here to carry me thither?" He believing there were, I ordered him to contract with them; but it vexed me very much to be obliged to take these men. However, though I resolved to go, yet I chose to reason the ragans into the project if I could; thinking they would soon bring the people over.

I called several of the ragans together, and said: "Because you are a wiser and more thinking people than the vulgar, I have applied myself to your judgments in the affair of Mount Alkoe. Now, consider with yourselves whether you have any real reason beyond a prepossession, for thinking these people fiends, or devil's servants, as you call them, without further examination; for according to my comprehension, they only, understanding the nature of several sorts of earth, reduce them by labour and fire to solid substances for the use of mankind; and the want of these things is the reason of your living as you do, without a hundredth part of the benefits of life. These sort of people, these noises and these operations, which you hear and see carried on at Alkoe, are to be heard and seen in my country; and we deal and traffic with their labours, from one end of the world to the other; and we who are with them the happiest, without them should be the most miserable of people. Did not some of you see, at my entertainment, what I called my knives and forks and spoons, my pistols, cutlasses, and silver cup? All these, and infinitely more, are the produce of these poor men's industry. Now," says I, "if we settle a communication with these people, your dues will be all paid in these curious things; you will have your people employed in working them, and have strangers applying to you to serve them with what they want; who in return will give you what you want; and you will find yourselves known and respected in the world." Finding some of these arguments applied to the men had staggered them a little, I applied to their senses. Says I, "It still appears to me that you have your prejudices hanging on you; but what will you say if I go thither and return safe? will you be afraid to follow me another time?" They persuaded me from it, as a dangerous experiment; but said, if I did return, they would not think there was so much in it as they suspected.

Maleck having chose me out fourscore of his countrymen, in about a month's time I trained them up to the knowledge of my pistols and cutlasses, and the management of them; and taking a chest with me for the arms and other necessaries, we sallied up to the Black Mountain. I rested there; and there Nasgig and Lasmeel overtook me, saying that when they found me obstinate to go, they could not in their hearts leave me, happen what would. This put new spirits into me, and we consulted how the noises lay, and agreed to engage first upon the skirts of them, where the smokes were most straggling. I charged six guns and all my pistols, which I kept in my chest, and ordered them to alight with me about a hundred paces from the first smoke they saw; then ordered three of them to carry my guns after me, and twelve of them to take pistols and follow me; but not to fire till I gave orders. The remainder I left with the baggage.

We marched up to the smoke, which issued out of a low archway just at the foot of the mountain. It was very light there with the flames of the volcano; and entering the arch, a fellow ran at me with a red-hot iron bar; him I shot dead: and seeing two more and a woman there, who stood with their faces to the wall of the hut or room, as unwilling to be seen, I ordered Maleck to speak to them in a known tongue, and tell them we were no enemies, nor intended them any hurt; and that their companion's fate was owing to his own rashness in running first at me with the hot bar; and that if they would show themselves good-natured and civil to us, we should be so to them; but if they offered to resist openly, or use any manner of treachery towards us, they might depend upon the same fate their companion had just suffered.

Upon hearing this, they approached us; and showing great tokens of submission, I delivered my gun to Maleck, and bade them go on with their work, ordering all the guns out of the shop for fear of a spark. I then perceived they were direct forges, but made after another manner from ours, their wind being made by a great wheel, like a wheel of a water-mill, which worked with the fans or wings in a large trough, and caused a prodigious issue of air through a small hole in the back of the fireplace. They were then drawing out iron bars.

I gave each of these men, and also to the woman, a dram of brandy; which they swallowed down very greedily, and looked for more, and seemed very pleasant. I then inquired into the trade—by whom and how it was carried on; and they told me just as Maleck had done. I then asked where the mines lay; and one of them looking full at me said, "Then you know what we are about."—"Yes," says I, "very well."—He told me the mine was (in his language as Maleck interpreted it) about a quarter of a mile off, and directed me to it. I ordered them to go on with their work, telling them, though I left a guard over them, it was only that they might not raise their neighbours to disturb me; though if they did, I should serve them all as I had done their companion; and left four men with pistols at the archway.

I proceeded to the iron mine, but supposed the men were all within, for I saw nobody; but there were many large heaps of ore lying, which I felt of; and, being vastly heavy, I supposed it might be rich in metal.

I returned to my men at the arch, and asked them what other mines there might be in that country, and of what other metals; but Maleck not knowing the metals themselves, was not able to interpret the names they called them by. I then showed them an English halfpenny, a Portuguese piece of silver money, and my gold watch; and asking if they had any of those, they pointed to the halfpenny and silver piece, but shook their heads at the watch. I then showed them a musket-ball, and they said they had a great deal of that.

I desired them to show me the way to the copper-mine (pointing my finger to the halfpenny), and told them if they would go with me, they should have some more (pointing to my brandy); and they readily agreed, if I would stand by them for leaving their work. I believe it might be two miles farther on the right to the copper-mine; and as these men had the graundee, I expected they would have flown by me; but I found they had a light chain round their graundee which prevented them; so I walked too, and having made them my friends by being familiar with them, I desired they would go in, and let the headman of the works know that a stranger desired to speak with him and view his works, and to inform him how peaceable I was if he used me civilly, but that I could strike him dead at once if he did not.

I do not know how they managed, or what report they made; but the man came to me very courteously, and I bade Maleck ask if he came in friendship, as I did to him; and he giving me that assurance, I went in with him, taking Nasgig and Maleck with me, and leaving our firearms without. I ordered them both, as I did myself, to carry their cutlasses, sheathed in their hands, for fear of a surprise. We saw a great quantity of copper ore and several melting-vats, being just at the mouth of the mine, the mine running horizontally into the side of the mountain, and, as they said, was very rich. I gave the headman a little brandy, and two or three more of them, who had been industrious in showing and explaining things to me.

I desired the foreman to walk out with me; and asking how long he had been in that employ, he told me he was a native of the Born Isles, and was brought thither young, where he first wrought in the iron, then in the silver, and now in this mine: that he had been there twenty years, and never expected to be delivered from his miserable slavery; but as he was now overseer of that work, he did pretty well, though nothing like freedom. He told me they expected several new slaves quickly, for the mines killed those they did not agree with so fast they were very thinly wrought at present, and that the governor was gone to the isles to get more men. I was glad to hear this. "And, pray," says I, "where does the governor reside?" He (pointing to the place) told me. "And what guard," says I, "may he keep?"—"About four hundred men; but nobody durst molest him," says he; "for he tortures them in such a manner, never killing them, that not the least thing can be done against his will."

After we had talked a good while on the misery of slavery, and finding him a man fit for my purpose, I asked him if he would go with me to Brandle-guarp: "For," said I, "there are certainly good mines in those mountains; and if you will overlook them, you shall be free, and have whatever you desire." He shook his head, saying, how could he expect to be free where all the rest were slaves. "And besides," says he, "they are in such commotions among themselves, that it is said the State will be torn to pieces."—"You are mistaken," says I, "very much; I myself have settled peace amongst them, and killed the usurper."—"Is it possible?" says he; "and are you the man it was said they expected to come out of the sea?"—"The very same," says I: "and as to slavery, there is not a slave in the kingdom; nor shall be here, if you will hearken to me."—"That would be a good time indeed," says he.—"Well," says I, "my friend, I promise you it shall be so; only observe this, that when I come to reduce the governor, do none of you miners assist him." He promised he would let the other miners secretly know it, and all should be as I wished; but desired me to be expeditious, for the governor was expected everyday.

I went from him to the other mines, and my guides with me; who seeing me so well received at the copper-mine and reporting it to the others, it caused my proceedings to go on smoothly, and my offers to be readily embraced wherever I came.

Having prepared matters thus, I set Maleck and his countrymen upon the natives, to treat with them about submission to Georigetti, on promise of freedom; who being assured of what I had done at Brandleguarp, and in hopes of like liberty, readily came into it; so that the only thing remaining was, before the governor's return, to attack the soldiery. Having, therefore, renewed my engagements with the miners, and believing myself upon as good terms with the natives as I could wish, I was advised by Nasgig and Lasmeel to return for cannon and a large army before I attacked the soldiery: but I, who had all my life rode upon the spur, having considered that an opportunity once lost is never to be regained; and though I could have wished for some cannon, I valued the men but for show: I therefore formed my resolves to march with the force I had next morning, and pitch upon a plain just by the governor's garrison, in order, if I could, to draw his men out. I did so, and it answered; for upon the first news of my coming, they appeared with a sort of heavy-headed weapons, which hurling round, they threw upwards aslope, in order to light upon the backs of their enemies in flight, and beat them down; but they could not throw them above thirty paces.

I sat still in my chair, with a gun in my hand, and Maleck with another at my elbow, with four more lying by me, ready to be presented; Lasmeel standing by to charge again as fast as we fired. I ordered a party of twenty of my men with cutlasses to attack the van of the enemy, by rushing impetuously upon them, they coming but thin against me; for I was not willing to employ my pieces till I could do more execution. They began the attack about a hundred yards before me, not very high in the air; and my cutlass-men having avoided the first flight of their weapons, fell upon them with such fury, that chopping here a limb and there a graundee, which, disabling their flight, was equally pernicious, they fell by scores before me: but I seeing those in the rear, which made a body of near three hundred, coming very swift and close in treble ranks, one above the other, hoping to bear down my handful of men with their numbers, I ordered my men all to retire behind me, and not till the enemy were passed over my head to fall on them. Maleck and I, as they came near, each firing a piece together, and whipping up another, and then another, in an instant they fell round us roaring and making a horrid yell. This the rest seeing, went over our men's heads, not without many falling from the cuts of my men; and those who escaped were never heard of more.

The miners, who from their several stations had beheld the action, came singing and dancing from every quarter round me, and if I had not drawn my men close in a circle about me, would probably, out of affection, have done me more hurt than two of the governor's armies; for against these common gratitude denied the use of force; and they crowding everyone but to touch me, they said, for fear of being pressed to death myself, as some of them almost were, I ordered them to be let in through my men at one side of the ring, and, passing by and touching me, to be let out on the other side; and this quieted them, but kept me in penance a long time.

We then marched in a body all into the town, where we were going to proclaim Georigetti King of Mount Alkoe, when a surly fellow, much wiser than the rest, as he thought, being about to harangue the people against being too hasty in it, was knocked down and trod to death for his pains; and we went on with the proclamation, giving general liberty to all persons without exception.

The next thing to be considered was how to oppose the governor when he came; and for that purpose I inquired into the manner of his coming, the road he came, and his attendants; and being informed that a hundred of his guards who had not the graundee waited for him at the sea-side, and that he had got no other guard, except a few friends and the slaves he went for, and that the slaves always came first, six in a rank tied together, under convoy of a few of his guards, I went in person to view the route he came, and seeing a very convenient post in a thick wood through which they were to pass, from whence we might see them before they came near us, I posted a watch on the sea side of the wood, and myself and men lay on the hither side of it, just where the governor's party must come out of it again: so that my watch giving notice of their approach, we might be ready to fall on at their coming out of our side of the wood.

When we had waited three days, our watch brought word they were coming; so we kept as close as possible, letting the slaves and guards march on, who came by about two hours' march before the governor: but so soon as he approached I drew up my men on the plain within the wood in ranks, ordering them to lie close on their bellies till they saw me rise, and then to rise, follow me, and obey orders.

Several of the first ranks having passed the wood, just as the governor had entered the open country, I rose and bade Maleck call aloud that if any of them stirred or lifted up a weapon he was a dead man; and then seeing one of the foremost running, I fetched him down with a musket-shot, bidding Maleck tell the rest that if they submitted and laid down their weapons they were safe; but if they refused, I would serve them all as I had done him who fled. This speech, with the terror of the gun, fixed every man to his place like a statue.

I then went forward to the governor, and by Maleck, my interpreter, asked him who they all were with him: he told me his slaves. I then made him call every man before him and give him freedom; which finding no way to avoid (for I looked very stern), he did, and I had enough to do to quiet my new freemen, who I thought would have devoured me for joy. I asked him whither he was going; he said to his government.—"Under whom do you hold it?" says I.—"Under the zaps of the isles," says he. I then told him that whoever held that government for the future, must receive it from the hands of Georigetti, the king of that country, to whom all the natives and miners had already engaged their fidelity. I told him both natives and foreigners had been all declared free.

The governor seemed much dejected, and told me he hoped I would not use him or his company ill. I told him that depended entirely on his own and their good behaviour. I asked him who his friends were that were with him; he said they were some of the zap's relations, who were come to see the method of the government and inspect the mines.

Ordering all the governor's guards and friends to go before, and all my own, but Maleck, to keep backwards some paces, I entered into discourse with him about the state of the isles, and the country of Alkoe; and finding him a judicious person, and not a native of the isles, I thought, with some management, he might prove a useful person to me, but did not like the character I had heard of his severity: so

I plainly told him that only one thing prevented my making him a greater man than ever he was; which was, I had been informed he had a roughness in his nature which drove him to extremities with the poor slaves, which I could not bear. "Sir," says he, "whatever a man is in his natural temper, where slavery abounds it is necessary to act, or at least be thought to do so, in a merciless manner. I am intrusted with the government of a land of only slaves; who have no more love, nor are they capable of any, for me, than the herbs of the ground have. I am to render an account to my masters of their labours; they work by force, and would not stir a step without it, or the fear of correction; for which reason the rod must be ever held over them; and though I seldom let it fall, when I do the suffering of one is too long remembered to permit others quickly to subject themselves to the like punishment: and this method I judged to be the most mild, as the death or sufferings of one but seldom, must, though ever so severe, be milder than the frequent execution of numbers. And as to my appearing severe to them, my post required it; for mercy to slaves being interpreted into fear, arms them with violence against you."

I could not gainsay this, especially as he told me he was glad that I had freed them all: "For no man," says he, "but if he were to choose, would rather reign by love (which he may in a free country, but it is impracticable in one of slaves) than by fear, which alone will keep the latter in subjection."

I asked him whether, as he knew the nature of the country, and the business of the governor, he could become faithful to my master Georigetti. He told me he had ever been faithful to his masters the zaps, and would till he was sure (without suspecting in the least my veracity) all was true that I was pleased to tell him; for nothing could satisfy his conscience but being an eye-witness of it, and then being discharged from any further capacity of serving them in an open way, he should be free to choose his own master; of all whom, Georigetti should to him be most preferable; but begged me not to interpret his desire of retaining fidelity to his old masters till he could no longer serve them, into an implication of assisting them by either open or concealed practices; for, wherever he engaged, he would be true to the utmost.

At the end of six days (for I travelled on foot with them) we arrived at the governor's palace, which we found without a guard, and all the slaves he had sent before him at liberty; so I ordered my men to supply the usual guard, and took my lodging in the governor's apartment.

As Gadsi (for that was the governor's name) was not confined, or any of his friends, he came into my apartment, and told me since he had found all things answered my report, if I pleased, he would quit the palace to me, and everything belonging to the government. I told him he said well. He did so, taking with him only some few things, his own property. So soon as he was without the territory of the palace, I sent for him and his friends back again. He could not help being dejected at his return, fearing some mischief. "Gadsi," says I, "this palace and this country, which I now hold for my master Georigetti, I deliver in custody to you as his governor; and now charge you to make acknowledgment of your fidelity to him." Then taking it from him in terms of my own proposing, I delivered him the regalia, of his government, charging him to maintain freedom: "But," says I, "let no man eat who will not work, as the country and the produce are the king's."

I then summoned an assembly of the people, and sent notice to all the miners to attend me. I told them all that the king desired of them was to make themselves happy: "And as the mines at present," says I, "are the only employment of this country, I would have it agreed by your own consent—for I will force nothing upon you—that every man amongst you, from sixteen to sixty, shall work every third week at the mines and other duties of the government; and two weeks out of three shall be your own to provide in for your families: and if I live to come back again, you shall each man have so much land of his own as shall be sufficient for his family; and I will make it my business to see for seeds to improve it with. And this week's work in three, and if afterwards it can be done with less in four, shall be an acknowledgment to the king for his bounty to you. Do you agree to this?" They all, with one voice, cried out, "We do!"—"Then," says I, "agree amongst yourselves, and part into proper divisions for carrying on the work; that is, into four parts, one for each sort of metal; and then again, each of those four into three parts; and on every seventh day in the morning, let those who are to begin meet those who are leaving off work; so that there be clear six days' work, and one of going and returning. Do you all agree to this?"—All cried, "We do!"—"Then," says I, "whoever neglects his duty, unless through sickness, or by leave of the governor, shall work a double week. Do you agree to this?"—"We do!"—"Then all matters of difference between you shall be decided by the governor; and in case of any injury or injustice, or wrong judgment in the governor, by Georigetti. Do you agree?"—"We do!"—"Then," says I, "agree upon ten men, two for the natives, and two for each mineral work, to send with me to Brandleguarp, to petition Georigetti to confirm these laws, till you shall make others yourselves, and to acknowledge his sovereignty. Do you agree?"—"We do!"

I then told them that as those who had been slaves were now free, they might, if they pleased, return home; but as I should make it my endeavour to provide so well for them in all the comforts of life, I believed most of them would be of opinion their interests would keep them where they were. And, above all things, recommending a hearty union between the new freemen and the natives, and to marry amongst each other, and to continue in love amongst themselves, and duty to the king and his governor; and promising speedily to return and settle what was wanting, I dismissed the assembly and set out for Brandleguarp with the ten deputies; but I left Lasmeel behind with the governor, and two servants with him, to give me immediate notice in case any disturbance should happen in my absence.

XXI

As we alighted at the palace late at night, I kept the deputies with me till next morning, when I went to the king, desiring them to stay in my apartment till I had received his majesty's orders for their admission.

The king was but just up when I came in; and seeing me, embraced me, saying: "Dear father, I am glad to meet you again alive; your stay has given me the utmost perplexity; and could I have prevailed with any of my servants to have followed you, I had sent before this time to have known what was become of you."

I told his majesty, the greatest pleasure of my life consisted in the knowledge of his majesty's esteem for me; and he might depend upon it, I would take care of myself from a double motive whilst I was in his dominions; the one, from the natural obligation of my own preservation, and the other, equally compulsive, of continuing serviceable to his majesty, till I had made him more famous than his ancestor, the great Begsurbeck.

I told his majesty, as a small token of my duty and affection to him, I was come to make him a tender of the additional title of King of Mount Alkoe.—"Father," says he, "we shall never be able to get a sufficient number of my subjects to go thither; for though your safe return may be some encouragement, yet whilst their old apprehensions subsist (and I know not what will alter them) we can do no good; and indeed were they free to go, and under no suspicion of danger, it would cost abundance of men to conquer Mount Alkoe."

"Great sir," said I, "you mistake me: I told you I came to make you a tender of it; I have proclaimed you king there, and freedom to the people; I have held an assembly of the kingdom, placed a governor, taken the engagement of himself and subjects to you, settled laws amongst them for your benefit, the full third part of all their labour; have brought ten deputies, two from each denomination of people among them; and they only wait your command to be admitted, to beg your acceptance of their submission, and pray your royal protection."

"Father," says the king, "you amaze me! but as it is your doing, let them come in."

The deputies being received, and heard by Maleck, their interpreter, very graciously, the king told them, in a very favourable speech, that whatever his father had done, or should do, they might accept as done by himself; and commanded them to remind the governor, for whom he had the highest esteem, to observe the laws, without the least deviation, till his father should make such further additions as were consistent with his own honour and their future freedom; and having feasted them in a most magnificent manner, they returned, highly satisfied with the honours they had received.

This transaction being immediately noised abroad, all the colambs came themselves; and the great cities, by their deputies, sent his majesty their compliments upon the occasion; and there was nothing but mirth and rejoicing throughout the whole kingdom. And those who had refused going with me, as Maleck told me, hung their heads for shame and sorrow that they had missed the opportunity of bearing a part in the expedition.

I demonstrated to the king that the only way to preserve that kingdom was to settle a large colony on the plains, between the mountain and the sea, to intercept clandestine trade, and make a stand against any force that might be sent from the Little Lands to recover the mines. And I promised to be present at the settlement, and an assistant in it.

Most of the colambs, as I said, being at court upon this complimentary affair, the king summoned them for their advice on my proposals, and told them he had ordered me to lay before them my thoughts on the affairs of that kingdom; and after many compliments and encomiums had passed on me, I told them the necessity of the colony, the commodity that would arise from it, how I intended to manage it, and what prospect I had of introducing amongst them several extraordinary conveniences they had never before had.

The colambs, who, for want of practice this way, knew but little of the matter, thinking, nevertheless, that in the general turn of things they must somehow come in for a share, approved of all I said. I desired them then to settle out of what part of the people, and how to be nominated, such choice of the colony as should be made for the new settlement; but found them much at a loss to fix on any method of doing it. So I told them I believed it would be the best way to issue an order for such as would willingly go, to repair to a particular rendezvous; and in case sufficient should not appear voluntarily, to issue another order that the colambs, out of their several districts, should complete the number, so as to make a body of 12,000 men of arms, besides women and children; and that such a territory should be allotted to each, with so much wood-grounds, in common to all, as would suffice for their subsistence; all which passed the vote.

I then told them that this large people must have a head, or governor, to keep them to their duties, and to determine matters of property, and all disputes amongst them. Here they one and all nominated me; but I told them I apprehended I could be more useful other ways, having too many things in my head for the general good, to confine myself to any particular province; but if they would excuse me in presuming to recommend a person, it should be Nasgig. And immediately Nasgig being sent for, and accepting it, they conferred it upon him.

All things, as I judged, went on in so smooth a way, in reference to the new colony, that I was preparing, with the assistance of the proper officer, expresses to be sent with the king's gripsacks into the several provinces, with notice of these orders, and an appointment for a rendezvous. But while this was doing, abundance of people came crowding about me to be informed whether I thought it safe for them to go; and I believe I had fully satisfied all their scruples, when by some management of the ragans, who, having so long declared Mount Alkoe to be inhabited by Mindrack, did not care the people should all of a sudden find out they had deceived them, there was a report ran current, that though I and my bearers, who were all Mount Alkoe men, returned safe, yet if any of the Brandleguarpines had gone, they would never have come back again. This rumour coming to my ears, and fearing whitherto it might grow, I had no small prospect of a disappointment, and I thereupon stopped issuing the orders till I had considered what farther to do in the affair. At length, being persuaded I had already satisfied abundance of their scruples, and in order to dissipate the doubts of others, and to familiarise them in some measure to the country and people of Mount Alkoe, I proposed a prize to be flown for, and gave notice of it for six days all about the country, both to those of Mount Alkoe, and those of Sass Doorpt Swangeanti, that whoever, except those who were with me in the late expedition, should make the most speedy flight to the governor's of Mount Alkoe, to carry a message and bring me an answer

ROBERT PALTOCK

from Lasmeel, should have one of my pistols, with a quantity of powder, and so many balls; and the person who should be second, should have a cutlass and belt. The time being fixed, very few had entered in the first two or three days; but on the third day came several over from Alkoe to enter, which the Brandleguarpines seeing, and having equal inclination to the prize, after half a dozen of them had entered on the fourth morning, before noon on the fifth I had near sixty of them on my list, besides the Alkoe men, making in all about one hundred.

The time of starting was fixed for the sixth morning, from off the rock on the back-side of the palace, upon my firing a pistol.

This unusual diversion occasioned a prodigious confluence of spectators; for scarce a person in Brandleguarp, except those who were either too young or too old for flight, but were upon one or other of the rocks; even the king himself and all his court were there, with infinite numbers from all distant parts.

I had despatched a letter by one of my old bearers to Lasmeel some days before, to inform him of it, that he might get two letters ready wrote, one to deliver to the first, and another to the second messenger, but not to take farther notice of the rest. Now, my flight-race being for the equal benefit of both the kingdoms, it happened, as I was in hopes it would, that so many of the Mount Alkoans coming over to me to be entered, and staying with me till the flight began, and such vast numbers of persons meeting of both nations upon the Black Mountain, to see them go and return, and several of the Swangeantines going, out of bravado, quite through with the flyers; the intercourse of the two nations was that day so great, and the discourse they had with the natives and miners so stripped the Swangeantines of their old apprehensions of danger from Mount Alkoe, that in three days after the whole dread of the place was vanished, and he would then have been thought mad who had attempted to revive it.

The time being come, I set my flyers in a row on the outer edge of the rock; and having given notice that no one should presume to rise till the flyers were on the graundee, and at such a distance, I then let the flyers know I should soon give fire; which I had no sooner done but down they all dropped as one man, as it were, headlong from the edge of the mountain, and presently the whole field were after them. They skimmed with incredible swiftness across the face of the plain, between the rock and the mountain; the force of which descent swung them as it were up the mountain's side in an almost upright posture, till seeming to sweep the edge of the mountain with their bellies, they slid over its surface till they were lost in the body of the Swangean, our rocks echoing the shouts of the mountaineers. I fired my pistol, by my watch, at nine o'clock in the morning, but had no occasion to inquire when it was thought they would return, for everyone was passing his opinion upon it. Some said it could not be till midnight, or very near it; and others, that it would be almost next morning. However, we went to dinner, and coming again about six o'clock by my watch, I was told by the people on the rock, as the general opinion (for it was then topfull), that they could not yet be expected for a long time; and the major part concluded they could not be half-way home yet; when, on a sudden, we heard a prodigious shout from the mountain, which growing nearer and nearer to us, and louder and louder, in a few moments came a slim young fellow, and nimbly alighting on the rock, tripped briskly forward, as not being able to stop himself at once from the violence of the force he came with, and delivered me a letter from Lasmeel as I was sitting in my chair. I gave him joy of the prize, and ordered him to come to my apartment so soon as I got home, and he should have it. I then asked him where he had left the other flyers; he told me he knew nothing of them since he came past the forges in his return; for there he met them going to Lasmeel.— "Why that," says I, "must be a great way on this side the governor's." He told me about an hour's flight. I then told him, as he must be strained with so hard a flight, it would be better if he lay down, and called on me in the morning. He thanked me, and after he had told me his name was Walsi, he said he would take my advice, and springing up as light as air, went off, the rock being quite thronged with those who had followed from the mountain to see the victor.

When Walsi came in, it was just seven o'clock by my watch; so that, according to the best computation by miles I could make from their descriptions of things, I judged he had flown at little more or less than at the rate of a mile a minute.

I stayed till near nine o'clock upon the rock, where it being cold and the time tedious, I was taking Quilly home with me, and designed that Maleck should wait for the coming of the second; but hearing again a shout from the mountain I resolved to see the second come in myself. The noise increasing, I presently saw the whole air full of people very near me, for I had retired near two hundred paces from the edge of the rock to give room to the flyers to alight, and expected nothing less than to be borne down by them; when I spied two competitors, one just over

ROBERT PALTOCK

the back of the other, the uppermost bearing down upon the other's graundee, their heads being just equal; so that the under man perceiving it impossible to sink lower for the rock, or to mount higher for the man above him, and as darting side-ways would lose time, and fearing to brush his belly against the rock, he slackened, just to job up his head in his antagonist's stomach; which giving the upper man a smart check with the pain, and the under one striking at that instant one bold stroke with his graundee, he fell just with his head at my feet, and the other man upon him, with his head in the under man's neck.

Thus they lay for a considerable time, breathless and motionless, save the working of their lungs, and heaving of their breasts; when each asked me if he was not the first, and the under man giving me a letter, I told them "No, Walsi had been in almost two hours ago." They both said it was impossible; they were sure no glumm in the Doorpt could outfly either of them. I ordered them both to call on me in the morning, and I would see they should have right done to their pretensions. The under man had but just told me his name was Naggitt, when another arrived, who, seeing Naggitt before him, told me he was sure he was second; but on seeing the other also he gave it up.

I would stay no longer, it being now so late; but the next morning I was informed that all the rest had stopped at the mountain but two, who were obliged to give out before, being overstrained, and unable to hold it.

The next morning Walsi was the first at my apartment, when I happened to be with the king; and speaking of his business to Quilly, he ordered him to stay in my gallery till I came back; and Quilly presently after seeing Youwarkee, told her the victor at the flight-race was waiting for me in the gallery. Youwarkee, who had great curiosity to see him, having heard how long he came in before the rest, stepped into the gallery, and taking a turn or two there, fell into discourse with him about his flight. And as women are very inquisitive, she distinguished, by the flyer's answers, speech, shape, and manner of address, that it was certainly a gawry she was talking with; though she had endeavoured to disguise herself by rolling in her hair, and tying it round her head with a broad chaplet, like a man; and by the thinness of her body, and flatness of her breasts, might fairly enough have passed for one, to a less penetrating eye than Youwarkee's. But Youwarkee putting some questions to her, and saying she was more like a gawry than a glumm, she put the poor girl—for so it was—to the blush, and at last she confessed the deceit; but upon her knees begged Youwarkee not to mention it, for it would be her undoing.

This confession gave Youwarkee a fair opportunity of asking how she came to be an adventurer for this sort of prize. The girl, finding there was no remedy, frankly confessed she had a strong affection for a glumboss, who was a very stout glumm, she said, but somewhat too corpulent for speedy flight; who ever since the prize had been proposed, could rest neither night nor day, to think he was not so well qualified to put in for it as others, especially one Naggitt, who he well knew made his addresses to her, and also was an adventurer. "Had it been a matter of strength, valour, or manhood," says he, "I had had the best of chances for it; but to be under a natural incapacity of obtaining so glorious a prize, as even the king himself is not master of such another, I cannot bear it." She then said he had told her he was resolved to give in his name and do his utmost, though he died in the flight. "What!" said he, "shall I see Naggitt run away with it, and perhaps with you too, when he has that to lay at your feet which no glumm else can boast of? No; I'll overcome, or never come home without it!"—"I must confess, madam," says Walsi, "as I knew his high spirit could never bear to be vanquished, I was afraid he would be as good as his word, and come to some unlucky end; and told him that though he need not have feared being conqueror in anything else, had it been proposed, yet in flight there were so many, half glumms as they were, who from their effeminate make and size, and little value for anything else, would certainly be in before him; that it was unworthy of a thorough glumm to contend with them for what could be obtained only by those who had no right to or share in anything more excellent; and that he must therefore not think of more than his fatigue for his pains. But as he had set his heart so much upon it, I would enter, and try to get it for him, as from my size and make, I believed few would have a better chance for it than myself. And, thanks to Collwar, madam," says she, "I hope to make him easy in it, if you will but please to conceal your knowledge of who and what I am."

Youwarkee was mightily pleased with her story, and promised she would; but engaged her to come again to her apartment so soon as she was possessed of the prize.

When I returned, hearing Walsi waited for me, I called him in, read the letter he brought, and finding it Lasmeel's, I looked over my list for Walsi's name, for I set them all down as they entered; and finding it the very last name of all, and that it was entered but on the morning the race was flown: "So," says I, "Walsi, I find the last at entering is the first at returning; but I see you have been there, by what Lasmeel has sent me; though there were some last night who questioned it, by your so speedy return. Here," says I, "take the prize, and see they are only used in the service of your country;" and then I dismissed her.

My two competitors appeared next for the cutlass, and had each of them many arguments to prevail with me in favour of him; but I told them I must do justice, and that though the difference was so small between them, yet certainly Naggitt was the nearest me at the time they both ceased flight, his face lying on my foot; so that as they both complained of foul play, and were therefore equal in that respect, Naggitt in justice must have it. And I gave it him with these words, however: "Take it, Naggitt, as certainly yours by the law of the race, but with a diffidence in myself who best deserves it."

I own I pitied the other man's case very much, as I should Naggitt's, had the other won it; but seeing the other turning away, and hearing him say, "But by half a head; when I had strove so hard!" as in a sort of dejection, I told them they were both brave glumms, and of intrepid resolution; and gave him also one, with the like instruction as to Walsi.

Walsi went from me, as she had promised, to Youwarkee, who wanted more discourse with her; for in an affair of love her gentle heart could have dwelt all day upon the repetition of any circumstances which would create delight in the enamoured. Walsi sat on thorns, wanting to be gone; but Youwarkee asking question upon question, Walsi got up and begged she would excuse her, she would come and stay at any other time. "But," says she, "madam, when the man one loves is in pain—for I am sure he is on the rack for fear of a discovery, till he sees me—if you ever loved yourself, you can't blame me for pressing to relieve him."

When she was gone, Youwarkee finding me alone, was so full of Walsi's adventure she could not be silent; but after twenty roundabout speeches and promises that I was to make, not to be angry with anybody, or undo anything I had done that day, and I know not what, out came the story. I was prodigiously pleased with it, and wished I had taken more notice of her. Says Youwarkee, "I endeavoured to keep her till you had done, that you might have seen her."—"And why did not you?" says I.—"My dear," says Youwarkee, "had you seen the poor creature's uneasiness till she got off with it, yourself could not have had the heart to have deferred that pleasure you would have perceived she expected when she came home; nor could you in conscience have detained her."

XXII

This race, notwithstanding all that the ragans could say to keep up their credit, and to prevent the people's perceiving what fools they had made of them, had so good and sudden an effect on the people's prejudices, that upon issuing the first proclamation, there was no occasion for the second; for at least twenty-five thousand men appeared voluntarily at the rendezvous of the old slaves, whose masters, though they were declared free, had used divers devices to oppress them, and render even their freedom a sort of slavery, besides women and children; so that we had now only to pick and choose those who would be likeliest to be of service to the new colony.

Nasgig and I differed now about the choice of persons. He, as a soldier, was for taking mostly single young men, and I for taking whole families, though some were either too old or too young for war. And upon farther consideration he agreed with me; for I told him young men would leave a father, mother, or mistress, behind them, which would either cause a hankering after home, and consequently the bad example of desertion, or else create an uneasy spirit, and perhaps a general distaste to the settlement. So we chose those whole families where they offered, which had the most young men in them, first; then others in like order; after that, man by man, asking them severally if any woman they liked would go with them, and if so, we took her, till we had about thirteen thousand fighting men, besides old men, women, and children; and then, marching by the palace, the king ordered ten days' stores for every mouth, and with this we took our flight; but as I was always fearful of a concourse in the air, Nasgig led them, and I brought up the rear.

Besides the above number of people, I believe we could not have less than ten thousand volunteers to the Black Mountain; some to take leave of their friends, and others out of curiosity, to see our flight. I took three pieces of cannon with me, and proper stores.

Our first stage, after a short halt on the Black Mountain, was to the governor's palace, where Gadsi received us with great respect. I told him my errand, which he approved: "For," says he, "countryman, it is now as much my interest to keep my old masters out, as ever it was to serve them when in; and you have taken the only method in the world to do it effectually." I consulted him where I should fix my colony; and, by his advice, fixed it on this side the wood, with some scattering habitations behind the wood, as watch-houses, to give notice of an enemy, having the wood for shelter, before they could reach the town, and, at the worst, the town for a retreat.

I found by Gadsi, that the ships from the Little Lands were soon expected, for that he said the zaps knew nothing yet of the change of government, nor could, till the ships returned. He asked me, as there was now a good lading, whether I thought fit to let them have it upon proper terms. I told him I would not hinder their having the metals, or endeavour to stop their trade in the least, but should be glad to treat with them about it myself.

I gave the forgemen descriptions for making shovels, spades, pickaxes, hammers, and abundance of other iron implements I should want in the building the new town: all which we got ready and carried with us. We then took flight, and alighted on the spot of our intended city; and having viewed the ground some miles each way, we drew the outlines, and set a great number of hands to cutting down trees, digging holes, and making trenches for the foundations. In short, we were all hands at it, and the women fetched the provisions; but I was obliged to show them every single step they were to take, towards the new erections; and, I must say, it was with great pleasure I did it, they seldom wanting to be told twice, having as quick an apprehension of what they heard or saw, as any people I had ever met with.

The whole city, according to our plan, was to consist of several long straight streets, parallel to each other, with gardens backwards each way, and traverse-passages at proper distances, to cross each street, from one to the other, quite through the whole city.

While this work was in hand, I took a progress to view the other country Maleck had told me of. We had not taken a very long flight, before we saw at a distance several persons of that country travelling to Mount Alkoe for metals. I had a great mind to have some talk with them about their kingdom, and ordered my bearers to go to them; they told me they durst not, for one of them would kill ten men. I did not choose to force them to it, for fear of some mischief; but observing which way they came, and that they came in several small bodies, of six or eight together, and that there was a little wood and some bushes between me and them, I ordered my bearers to sink beneath the trees out of their sight, and to ground me just at the foot of the wood; for I resolved to know something more of them before we parted.

I lay perdue till they arrived within sixty paces of me; then asking Maleck if he knew their language, and he telling me he did, having often conversed with them at the mines, I bid him greet them, and tell them I was a friend, and be sure to stand by me. There were seven of them, and many more at different distances. I showed myself, and Maleck spoke to them, when two or three of the hindermost ran quite away; one stood and looked very surly, but the rest, who had stood with him, turning to run, I bid Maleck tell him if he did not call them back I would kill them. He that stood then called to them, but they mending their pace upon it, I let fly, and shot one in the shoulder, who dropping, I was afraid I had killed him. I then went up to the other, who had not stirred even at the report of the gun, seeming quite terrified. I took him by the hand and kissed it, which made him recover himself a little, and he took mine and kissed it.

I bid Maleck tell him I was a great traveller, and only wanted to talk with him; but seeing the man I had shot stir, I went to him, and told him I was sorry I had hurt him, which I should not have attempted had he not shown a mistrust of me by running away, for I could not bear that: this I said to keep the other with me. I saw I had hurt his shoulder, but being at a great distance, the ball had not entered the blade-bone, but stopping there, had fallen out; so tying my handkerchief over it, I told him I hoped it would soon be well.

I inquired into their country, its name, the intent of their journey this way, their trades, the fruits, birds, and beasts of the country.

The man I had shot, I found, was in pain, which gave me no little concern; so I chiefly applied myself to the other, who told me the name of his country was Norbon, a large kingdom, and very populous, he said, in some parts of it, and was governed by Oniwheske, an old and good king. "He has only one daughter," says he, "named Stygee; so that I am afraid when he dies it will go to a good-for-nothing nephew of his, a desperate debauched man, who will probably ruin us, and destroy that kingdom which has been in the Oniwheske family these fifteen hundred years."—"Won't his daughter have the kingdom," says I, "after his death, or her children?"—"Children," says he, "no, that's the pity; all would be well if she had but children, and the state continue fifteen hundred years longer in the same good family."—"How is it possible for anyone to know that?" says I. "You may know how long it has, but how long it will last, is mere guess-work."—"No," says he, "this very time, and the present circumstances of our kingdom, were foretold at the birth of the first king we ever had, who was of the present royal family."—"How so?" says I.—"Why," says he, "before we had any king, we had a very good old man, who lived retired in a cave by the sea; and to him everybody under their difficulties repaired for advice. This old man happening to be very ill, everybody was under great affliction for fear they should lose him; when flocking to his assistance, he told them they need not fear his death till the birth of a king who should reign fifteen hundred years. At hearing this all persons then present apprehended that his disorder had turned his brain; but he persisted in it, and recovered.

"After a few years, a great number of persons being about him, he told them he must now depart, for that their king was born, and pointed to a sucking child a poor woman had then in her arms. It caused a great wonder in his audience at the thoughts of that poor child ever becoming a king; but he told them it was so decreed, and farther, that as he was to die the next day, if they would gather all together, he would let them know what was to come in future times.

"When they were met, the woman and child being amongst them, he told them that child was their king, and that his loins should produce them a race of kings for fifteen hundred years, during which time they should be happily governed; but then a female inhabitant of the skies should claim the dominion, and, together with the kingdom, be utterly destroyed, unless a messenger from above, with a crown in each hand, should procure her a male of her own kind; and then the kingdom should remain for the like number of years to her posterity. Now," says he, "the time will expire very soon, and as no one has been, or it is believed will ever come, with two such crowns, the princess Stygee, though she undoubtedly will try for it, has little hopes of succeeding her father; for her cousin Felbamko pretends, as no woman ever reigned with us, he is the right heir, and will have the kingdom."—"Pray," says I, "what do you mean by an inhabitant of the air?"—"Oh," says he, "she flies."—"And do most of your country folks fly?" says I; "for I perceive you don't."—"No," says he, "no one but the princess Stygee."—"How comes that about?" says I.—"Her mother, when she was with child with her," says he, "being one day in a wood near the palace, and having straggled from her company, was attacked by a man with a graundee, who, not knowing her, clasped her within his graundee, and would have debauched her; but perceiving her cries had brought some of her servants to her assistance, he quitted her and went off: this accident threw her into such a fright, that it was a long time before she recovered; and then was delivered of a daughter with a graundee."—"My friend," says I, "your meeting with me will be a very happy affair for your kingdom. I am the man the princess expects: go back to the princess and let her and her father know I will be with them in six days, and establish his dominions in the princess."

The fellow looked at me, thinking I joked, but never offered to stir a foot. "Why don't you go?" says I. "And for the good news you bear to the princess, I'll see you shall be made one of the greatest men in Norbon." The man smiled still, but could not conceive I was in earnest. I asked him then how long he should be in going to the palace; he said, "Three days at soonest."—"Deliver but your message right," says I, "and I'll assure you it shall be the better for you." The man seeing me look serious, did at length believe me, and promised he would obey me punctually; but he had not seen how I came to the place he met me at, for I had ordered my bearers into the wood with my chair before I showed myself.

He arrived, as I afterwards found, at the palace, the fourth morning very early; and passing the guard in a great heat, with much ado was introduced to the king, and discharged himself of my message. His majesty, giving no credit to him, thought he had been mad; but he affirming it to be true, and telling the king at what a distance I had knocked down his companion, and made a great hole in his back, only holding up a thing I had in my hand, which made a great noise, Oniwheske ordered his daughter to come before him, who having herself heard the man's report, and being very willing to believe it, with the king's leave, desired that the messenger might be detained till the appointed day, and taken care of; and that preparation should be made for the reception of the stranger, in case it should be true.

The noise of my coming, and my errand, excited everyone's curiosity to see me arrive; and the day being come, I hovered over the city a considerable time, to be sure of grounding right. The king and his daughter, on the rumour of my appearing, came forth to view me and receive me at my alighting. The people were collected into a large square, on one side of the palace, and standing in several clusters at different places, I judged where the king might seem most likely to be, and ordered my bearers to alight there; but I happened upon the most unlucky post, as it might have proved, and at the same time the most lucky I could have found there; for I had scarce raised myself from my chair, but Felbamko pushing up to me through the throng, and lifting up a large club he had in his hand, had certainly despatched me, if I had not at the instant drawn a pistol from my girdle, and shot him dead upon the spot; insomuch that the club, which was then over my head, fell gently down on my shoulder.

I did not then know who it was I had killed, but for fear of a fresh attempt, I drew out another pistol and my cutlass, and inquiring at which part of the square the king was, I walked directly up to him, he not as yet knowing what had happened. His majesty and his daughter met me, and welcomed me into his dominions. I fell at the king's feet, telling him I brought a message, which I hoped would excuse my entering his majesty's dominions without the formality of obtaining his leave.

When we came to the palace, the king ordered some refreshments to be given me and my servants; and then that I should be conducted to the room of audience.

The report of Felbamko's death had reached the palace before us, and that it was by my hand; this greatly surprised the whole court, but proved agreeable news to Stygee.

At my entrance into the room of audience, the king was sitting at the farther end of it against the wall, with his daughter on his right hand; and a seat was placed for me at his left, but nearer to the middle of the room side-ways, on which I was ordered to sit down. There were abundance of the courtiers present, and above me was a seat ordered for one of them, who I found afterwards was one of the religious.

His majesty asked me aloud how it happened that the first moment of my entering his dominions I should dip my hands in blood, and that, too, of one of his nearest relations.

I then got up to make my answer, but his majesty ordering me to my seat again, I told him that as it was most certain I knew no one person in his kingdom, so it could not be supposed I could have an ill design against anyone, especially against that royal blood, into whose hands I then came to render myself; but the truth was that what I had done was in preservation of my own life, for that the person slain had rushed through the crowd upon me with a great club, intending to murder me, and that whilst the blow was over my head, I killed him in such position, that by his fall the club rested on my shoulder, but was then too weak to hurt me.

The king asking if that was the real case, several from the lower end of the room said they were informed it was, and one in particular said he saw the transaction, and I had declared it faithfully. "Then," says the king, "you are acquitted; and, now, what brings you hither? relate your business."

"Great sir," says I, "it is my peculiar happiness to be appointed by Providence as the proposer of a marriage for the princess Stygee your daughter, with a potent neighbouring monarch, having already been enabled to perform things past belief for his honour. Know then, great sir, I am a native of the north, and through infinite perils and hardships at last arrived in the dominions of Georigetti, where I have given peace to his State by the death of the usurper Harlokin. I have also just conquered the kingdom of Mount Alkoe for my master, and am here come to make your daughter an offer of both crowns, and also of all that is my master's, with his person in marriage."

The old priest then rose, and said: "May it please your majesty, we are almost right; but what has always staggered me is, how the person should come, for the messenger to us on this errand is to come from above. Now this person has not the graundee, and therefore could not come from thence. As for the rest, I understand the prince from whom he brings this offer to your daughter has the graundee, and so is a male of her own kind; and I understand the two kingdoms in his possession to be the two crowns in the messenger's hands; but, I say, what I stick at is his coming from above."

"What!" says Stygee, "did not you see him come?"—"No," says he.— "Oh," says she, "he came in the air, and was a long time over the city before he descended."—"That's impossible," says the old priest, "for he is smooth like us."—"Indeed, sir," says she, "I saw him, and so did most of the court." The king and nobles then attesting this truth: "Sir," says the priest to the king, "it is completed, and your majesty must do the rest."

"I little expected," says the king, "to see this day; and now, daughter, as this message was designed for you, you only can answer it. But still I must say it surpasses my comprehension, that in the decree of Providence it should be so ordered that the very hand which brings the accomplishment of what has been so long since foretold us, should, without design, have first destroyed all that could have rendered the marriage state uncomfortable to you."

Stygee then declared she submitted to fate and her father's will.

I stayed here a week to view the country and the sea, which I heard was not far off. Here were many useful beasts for food and burden, fowls also in plenty, and fish near the sea-coasts, and the people eat flesh, so that I thought myself amongst mankind again. I made all the remarks the shortness of the time would allow, and then taking my leave departed.

I returned to the colony, where I heard that the Little-landers had been on the coast; but I not being there, or any lading ready, they were gone away again; however, they had detained two of them. I was pleased with that, but sorry they were returned empty.

I examined the prisoners, and by giving them liberty and good usage they settled amongst us; and the next fleet that came, the sailors to a man were all my own the moment they could get to shore. This, though I thought it would have spoiled our trade at first, brought the islanders and me to the following compromise, and upon this occasion. Their ships having laid on our coasts one whole season for want of hands to carry them back, I came to an agreement with their commanders (for they were all willing to return), that such a number of them should be left as hostages with me till the return of a number of my own men, which I should lend them to navigate their ships home; and I sent word to the zaps that as it might be beneficial to us both to keep the trade still on foot, to prevent the like inconveniences for the future, I would buy their shipping, paying for them in metals, and agree to furnish them yearly with such a quantity of my goods at a stated price, and would send them by my own people; which they approving, the trade went on in a very agreeable and profitable manner, and we in time built several new vessels of our own, and employed abundance of hands in the trade, and had plenty of handicraftsmen of different occupations, each of whom I obliged to keep three natives under him, to be trained up in his business.

XXIII

A DISCOURSE ON MARRIAGE BETWEEN PETER AND
GEORIGETTI—PETER PROPOSES STYGEE—THE KING ACCEPTS
IT—RELATES HIS TRANSACTIONS AT NORBON—THE MARRIAGE
IS CONSUMMATED—ACCOUNT OF THE MARRIAGE-CEREMONY—
PETER GOES TO NORBON—OPENS A FREE TRADE TO MOUNT
ALKOE—GETS TRADERS TO SETTLE AT NORBON—CONVOYS
CATTLE TO MOUNT ALKOE.

At my return to Sass Doorpt Swangeanti, I went directly to the king, and giving him an account of the settlement, and my proceedings thereon, he told me his whole kingdom would not be an equivalent for the services I had done him. I begged of him to look on them in no other light than as flowing from my duty; but if, when I should be no more, he or his children would be gracious to my family, it was all I desired.

"This, father," says the king, "I can undertake for myself; but who's to come after me, nobody knows, for I shall never marry. No! Yaccombourse has given me a surfeit of womankind; and unless the states will settle the kingdom on you, to which I will consent, it will probably be torn to pieces again by different competitors, for I am the last of the line of Begsurbeck, and of all the blood-royals; and indeed who is so proper to maintain it flourishing as he who has brought it to the present perfection?"

"Great sir," says I, "my ambition rises no higher than to abound in good deeds whilst I live, and to perfect my children in the same principle; and this, I hope, will entitle them to a support when I am gone. But," says I, "why is your majesty so averse from marriage, merely on account of a woman you could not expect to be true to you?"—"Not expect it!" says he; "what stronger tie upon earth could she have had to be true than my affection, and all that my kingdom could afford her?"— "Weak things all, sir," says I.—"Why, what could she have had?" said he, in some warmth.—"Honour, sir," says I, "and virtue, both which she abandoned to become yours; and those once lost, how could you expect her to be true?"—"You are too hard for me, father," says he; "but they are all alike, and I don't believe there's a grain of honour in any of them."—"In any of them like Yaccombourse, I admit, sir," says I; "but think not so of others, for no part of our species abounds more with it, or is more tender of it, than a good woman; and take my word for it, sir, there is more real sincerity in an ordinary wife than in the most extraordinary mistress. We are all biassed naturally by interest, and as there can be but one real interest between the man and wife, so the interest of a mistress is, and ever will be, to accommodate herself; for 'tis all one to her with whom she engages, so she can raise but the market by a change. Now if your majesty could find an agreeable and virtuous wife, one deserving of your royal person and bed, and perhaps with a kingdom for her dowry, a partner fit to share your cares as well as glory, would it not be a great pleasure to you to be possessed of' such a mate, and to see heirs arising under your joint tuition, to convey down your royal blood to the latest posterity? Would not this, I say, be a grateful reflection to you in your declining years?"

"Truly, father," says the king, "as you have painted it, the prospect could not fail to please, and under the circumstances you have put it, it would meet my approbation; but where is such a thing as a woman of this character to be found? I fear only in the imagination."

"Sir," says I, after a seeming muse for sometime, "what should you think of Oniwheske, the king of Norbon's daughter? he has but that one child, I hear."—"Dear father, have done," says his majesty; "to what purpose should you mention her? We but barely know that there is such a State, we have never had any intercourse; and, besides, as you say he has but one child, can you suppose she will ever marry, to leave so fine a kingdom, and live here?"—"But, sir," says I, "now we are supposing, suppose she should, with her father's consent, be willing to marry you, would you have her for your queen?"—"To make any doubt of that, father," says he, "is almost to suppose me a fool."—"Then, sir," says I, "her father has consented, and she too; and if I durst have presumed so far, or had known your mind sooner, she would I believe have ventured with me to have become yours, but you might have slighted her, and crowned heads are not to be trifled with; but since you are pleased to show your approbation of it, I can assure you, sir, her person will yield to none in your majesty's dominions; for, sir, I have been there, and have seen her, and she is your own, and her kingdom too, upon demand."

"Father," says the king, looking earnestly at me, "I have been frequently, since I knew you first, in doubt of my own existence. My life seems a dream to me; for if existence is to be judged of by one's faculties only, I have been in such a delusion of them ever since, that as

I find myself unable to judge with certainty of any other thing, so I am subject to doubt whether I really exist. Are these things possible that you tell me, father?"

I then told him the whole affair, and advised him by all means to accept the offer, and marry the princess out of hand.

His majesty, when I had brought him thoroughly to believe me, was as eager to consummate the marriage, as I was to have him; but then, whether he should go to her, or she come to him, was the question. I told him it was a thing unusual for a sovereign to quit his own dominions for a wife; but would advise an embassy to her father, with notice that his majesty would meet and espouse her on the frontiers of the two kingdoms.

The ambassadors returning with an appointment of time and place, it was not above a month before I had settled Stygee on the thrones of Sass Doorpt Swangeanti and Mount Alkoe, with the reversion of the kingdom of Norbon, without a competitor.

I shall here give you an account of the marriage ceremony. The king being arrived on the borders, Stygee, who had waited but a few hours at the last village in Norbon, advanced to his majesty on the very division, as they called it, of the two kingdoms, a line being drawn to express the bounds of each. The king and Stygee having talked apart from the company a little space, each standing hand in hand, on their own respective ground, the chief ragan advanced, and began the ceremony.

He first asked each party aloud, if he and she were willing to be united in body and affections, and would engage to continue so their whole lives to which each party having answered aloud in the affirmative, "Show me then a token!" says he; and immediately each expanding the right side of their graundees, laid it upon the other's left side, so that they appeared then but as one body, standing hand in hand, encased round with the graundee. The ragan then having descanted upon the duties of marriage, concluded the ceremony with wishing them as fruitful as Perigen and Philella. So soon as it was over, and the gripsacks and voices had finished an epithalamium, the bride and bridegroom taking wing, were conducted to Brandleguarp, amidst the acclamations of an infinite number of Georigetti's subjects.

The king had made vast preparations for the reception of the princess Stygee; and nothing was to be heard or seen but feastings and rejoicing for many days; and his majesty afterwards assured me of his entire satisfaction in my choice of his bride, without whom he confessed, that notwithstanding the many other blessings I had procured him, his happiness must have been incomplete.

Intending another flight to Norbon, I was charged with the king and queen's compliments to Oniwheske; which having executed, I opened a free trade to Mount Alkoe; and hearing that small vessels came frequently on the Norbonese coast, to carry off the iron and other metal from thence unwrought, and paid part of their return in wrought metals, I ordered some of the next that came to be stopped and brought to me; and the day before I had fixed for my departure, notice was sent that twelve of those traders were stopped, and in custody at the sea-side. I longed to see them, but then considering that it would take up more time to bring them to Apsilo the capital, where I was, than I should take in going to them and returning, I resolved to go and examine them myself.

They told me they traded with small vessels to Norbon for metals, which they carried home, and wrought great part of it themselves, sending it to and dispersing it in several islands at a distance; and also sold the unwrought to several people who carried it they knew not whither in great ships. They said they kept abundance of hands at work in the trade. I asked if their artificers wrought it for their own profit, or their masters'. They told me for masters, themselves being all slaves.—"And are you all slaves?" says I.—They told me "Yes, all but one," pointing to him. I then ordered him to be secured and removed; and told them if they would procure some hands to settle at Norbon and Mount Alkoe, they should all be made free, have lands assigned them, and have other privileges, and I did not doubt in time would become the richest men in the country; for I understood by them they were acquainted with the use of money. I asked them what other commodities they brought to Norbon in exchange.

They said clothes for the people, both what they received in exchange from others who bought their iron, and some of a coarser sort of their own making. I found in my discourse I had with them, that out of my eleven men there were persons of four different occupations; so I promised those who would stay with me their freedoms, good houses, and other rewards: and sending three hands home with the vessel, and a full freight, according to the value of the cargo they brought, I ordered them to engage as many as they could of their countrymen of distinct trades, to come and settle with me; and to be sure, if they had any grain, corn, roots, plants, or seeds, usually eaten for food, to bring all they could get with them, and they should have good returns for them; and as to those good hands that settled here, they should be allowed all materials to work for their own profit the first year, and after that they should also work for themselves, allowing the king one-tenth of the clear profit. This took so far with them, that it was with the utmost difficulty I got any of them to carry the ship back, for fear they should not be able to return.

Before I parted from them, I assigned the eight who were left all proper conveniences, and recommended them to the king's protection; and I ordered the owner, then in custody, to be conducted to Mount Alkoe, and from thence to Brandleguarp; where, treating him kindly and giving him liberty, I made my proper use of him.

The king having lent me a convoy to conduct my prisoner, and given me a license for as many cattle of the sorts I chose as I pleased to drive to Georigetti's dominions, I made them drive a great number of sheep of the finest wool I ever saw, and very large also; a great number of creatures not unlike an ass for shape, but with two upright horns and short ears, which gave abundance of rich milk; and also some swine. All these were drove to, and distributed at my new colony, where I let them remain till I had provided a proper receptacle for them at Doorpt Swangeanti, near the woods; when I brought many over the Black Mountain, and distributed there, with directions how to manage them; and in about seven years' time we held a little beast-market near Brandle-guarp twice a year, where the spare cattle were brought up, and preserved in salt till the next market; for I had some years before made large salt-works near the sea at Mount Alkoe, which employed abundance of hands, and was now become a considerable trade.

We had iron, copper, and silver money, which went very current; and had butter and cheese from the farms near the woods, as plenty as we had the fruits before, great numbers of families having settled there; and there was scarce a family but was of some occupation or other.

By the accounts I received from the mines, from time to time, it was prodigious to hear what vast quantities of metals were prepared in one year now, by little above one-third of the hands that were usually employed in them before; for now the men's ambition was to leave a good week's work done at their return, for an example to those who were coming; and the overseers told me they would sing and work with the greatest delight imaginable, whilst they pleased themselves with telling one another how they intended to spend the next fourteen days.

　　　　　　　　　　　　　　　　　　　　ROBERT PALTOCK

XXIV

PETER LOOKING OVER HIS BOOKS FINDS HE HAS GOT A LATIN
BIBLE—SETS ABOUT A TRANSLATION—TEACHES SOME OF
THE RAGANS LETTERS—SETS UP A PAPER MANUFACTURE—
MAKES THE RAGANS READ THE BIBLE—THE RAGANS TEACH
OTHERS TO READ AND WRITE—A FAIR KEPT AT THE BLACK
MOUNTAIN—PETER'S REFLECTION ON THE SWANGEANTINES.

All things being now so settled that they would go on of themselves,
and having no further direct view in my head, I spent my time
with my wife; and looking over my books one day to divert myself, with
the greatest joy imaginable I found that the Bible I had taken to be
in the Portuguese tongue was a Latin one. It was many years since I
had thought of that language; but on this occasion, by force of memory
and recollection, and with some attention, consideration, and practice,
I found it return to me in so plentiful a manner that I fully resolved to
translate my Bible into the Swangeantine tongue.

I sent directly for Lasmeel to be my amanuensis, and to work we
went upon the translation.

We began at the creation, and descending to the flood, went on to
the Jewish captivity in Egypt and deliverance by Moses, leaving out
the genealogies and all the Jewish ceremonies and laws, except the Ten
Commandments. I translated the books of Samuel and Kings, down to
the Babylonish captivity. I then translated such parts of the Prophets as
were necessary to introduce the Messiah, and discover Him; the books
of Psalms, Job, and the Proverbs, and with the utmost impatience
hasted to the New Testament. But then considering that when I had
done, as only Lasmeel and myself could read it, in case of our deaths,
the translation must die with us, I chose out six of the junior ragans,
and two of the elder, to learn letters; and in less than twelve months I
had brought them all to read mine and Lasmeel's writings perfectly well.

I instructed these ragans at spare hours, whilst I went on with my
translation; but finding my paper grow low, having had a great supply
of coarse linen, and a sort of calicoes from the isles, in return for our
metals, I set up a manufactory from that, and some gums of the trees,
which we boiled with it to a pulp in iron pans, and beating it to pieces,
made a useful paper which would bear ink tolerably. But I could find

nothing to make ink of, though I sent over all the country to search for every herb and fruit not commonly used; till at last I found an herb and flower on it, which, if taken before the flower faded, would, by boiling thoroughly, become blue; this, by still more boiling in a copper pan till it was dry and burnt hard to the bottom, in some measure answered my purpose, and I fixed upon it as the best I could obtain from all my experiments.

When the ragans were masters of their pens, I set six of them to copy what Lasmeel had finished, and the other two to teach their brethren; and in two years' time, by a pretty constant application (for I made them transcribe it perfectly fair and intelligible), we finished our translation, and two fair copies.

I then ordered the ragans to read a portion of it to the people constantly, in the mouch; they, from the novelty of the story, at first grew so exceeding fond of it, that upon the proper expositions of it I taught the ragans afterwards to make, they began to apply it seriously to religious purposes.

My writing ragans were very fond of their knowledge of letters; and trade and commerce now increasing, which put everyone more or less in want of the same knowledge, they made a great profit of it, by instructing all who applied to them. This increase of writing necessarily provided a maintenance for several persons who travelled to Norbon for quills, and sold them to the Swangeantines at extravagant rates; till the Norbonese hearing that, brought them themselves to the foot of the mountain, where the Swangeantines bought them, as they did several other commodities which one country had and the other wanted, especially iron wares of almost every denomination: so that the mountain, being so excessively high, was the barrier; for the Norbonese finding that difficulty in ascending and descending which the Swangeantines with their graundees did not, there was a constant market of buyers and sellers on the Mount Alkoe side of the Black Mountain, which by degrees grew the general mart of the three kingdoms.

I have often reflected with myself, and have been amazed to think, that so ingenious and industrious a people as the Swangeantines have since appeared to be, and who, till I came amongst them, had nothing more than bare food, and a hole to lie in, in a barren rocky country, and then seemed to desire only what they had, should in ten years' time be supplied not only with the conveniences, but superfluities of life; and that they should then become so fond of them, as rather willingly to part with life itself than be reduced to the state I found them in. And I have as often, on this occasion, reflected on the goodness of Providence, in rendering one part of mankind easy under the absence of such comforts as others could not rest without; and have made it a great argument for my assent to well-attested truths above my comprehension. "For," says I, "to have affirmed, at my first coming, either that these things could have been made at all, or when done could have been of any additional benefit to these people, would have been so far beyond their imaginations, that the reporter of so plain a truth, as they now find it, would have been looked upon as a madman or an impostor; but by opening their views by little and little, and showing them the dependence of one thing upon another, he that should now affirm the inutility of them, would be observed in a much worse light." And yet, without any embellishments of art, how did this so great a people live under the protection of Providence? Let us first view them at a vast distance from any sort of sustenance, yet from the help of the graundee that distance was but a step to them. They were forced to inhabit the rocks, from an utter incapacity of providing shelter elsewhere, having no tool that would either cut down timber for a habitation, or dig up the earth for a fence, or materials to make one; but they had a liquor that would dissolve the rock itself into habitations. They had neither beast nor fish, for food or burthen; but they had fruits equivalent to both, of the same relish, and as wholesome, without shedding blood. Their fruits were dangerous till they had fermented in a boiling heat; and they had neither the sun, nor any fire, nor the knowledge how to propagate or continue it. But they had their hot springs always boiling, without their care or concern. They had neither the skins of beasts, the original clothing, nor any other artificial covering from the weather; but they were born with that warm clothing the graundee, which being of a considerable density, and full of veins flowing with warm blood, not only defended their flesh from all outward injuries, but was a most soft, comely, and warm dress to the body. They lived mostly in the dark rock, having less difference of light with the change of seasons than other people have; but either by custom or make, more light than what Providence has sent them in the sweecoe is disagreeable: so that where little is to be obtained, Providence, by confining the capacity, can give content with that; and where apparent wants are, we may see, by these people, how careful Providence is to supply them; for neither the graundee, the sweecoes, nor their springs, are to be found where those necessaries can be supplied by other means.

Amongst my other considerations, I have often thought that if I had gone to the top of the Black Mountains northward of Brandleguarp, in the very lightest time, I might have seen the sun; but these mountains were so elevated, that our lightest time was only the gilded glimmering of their tops, having never seen so much light on them as totally to eclipse all the stars, of which we had always the same in view, but in different positions.

XXV

Peter's children provided for—Youwarkee's death—
How the king and queen spent their time—Peter
grows melancholy—Wants to get to England—
Contrives means—Is taken up at sea.

I Had now been at Brandleguarp ten years, and my children were all provided for by the king but Dickey, as fast as they were qualified for employment, and such as were fit for it were married off to the best alliances in the country; so that I had only to sit down and see everything I had put my hand to prosper, and not an evil eye in the three kingdoms cast at me: but about my eleventh or twelfth year, my wife falling into a lingering disorder, at the end of two years it carried her off. This was the first real affliction I had suffered for many years, and so soured my temper, that I became fit for nothing, and it was painful to me even to think of business.

The king's marriage had produced four children, three sons and a daughter, which he would frequently tell me were mine.

Old Oniwheske was dead, and the king and queen divided their whole time equally between Brandleguarp and Apsillo; but he was building a palace at my new colony, which by this time was grown to a vast city, and was called Stygena, in compliment to the queen; and this new palace was designed to receive the court one-third of the year, as it lay almost at equal distance between both his other palaces. This method, which his majesty took, at my persuasion, on the death of Oniwheske, though it went against the grain at first, was now grown so habitual to him, and he saw his own interest so much in it in the love and esteem it procured him from the people, that at last he wanted no spur to it.

My melancholy for the death of my wife, which I hoped time would wear off, rather gained ground upon me; and though I was as much regarded as ever by the whole court, yet it grew troublesome to me even to be asked my advice; and it not only surprised those about me, but even myself, to see the same genius, without any visible natural decay, in so short a time, from the most sprightly and enterprising, become the most phlegmatic and inactive.

My longings after my native country, ever since my wife's death, redoubled upon me, and I had formed several schemes of getting thither;

as first, I had formed a project of going off by the islands, as I had so many small vessels at command there, and to get into the main ocean and try my fortune that way; but upon inquiry I found that my vessels could not get to sea, or elsewhere, but to the zaps' islands, by reason of the many rocks and sandbanks which would oppose me, unless I went through the zaps' country, which, in the light they had reason to view me, I was afraid to do. Then I had thoughts of going from the coast of Norbon; but that must have been in one of the foreign vessels, and they coming from a quite different quarter than I must go, in all probability if I had put to sea anyway they were unacquainted with, they having no compass, we must have perished; for the more I grew by degrees acquainted with the situation of Doorpt Swangeanti, the stronger were my conjectures that my nearest continent must be the southern coast of America; but still it was only conjecture. At length, being tired and uneasy, I resolved, as I was accustomed to flight, and loved it, I would take a turn for some days; carry me where it would, I should certainly light on some land, whence at first I could but come back again. I then went to see if my chair, board, and ropes, were sound, for I had not used them for several years past; but I found them all so crazy, I durst not venture in them, which disappointment put off my journey for sometime. However, as I had still the thought remaining, it put me on seeking someother method to put it in practice; so I contrived the poles from which you took me, being a sort of hollow cane the Swangeantines make their spears of, but exceeding strong and springy, which, interwoven with small cords, were my seat, and were much lighter than my chair; and these buoyed me up when your goodness relieved me. I had taken Mount Alkoe bearers, as I knew I must come to a country of more light; and I now find, if I had not fallen, I must soon have reached land, if we could have held out, for we were come too far to think of returning, without a resting-place: and what will become of my poor bearers, I dread to think; if they attempted to return, they must have dropt, for they had complained all the last day and night, and had shifted very often. If in your history you think fit to carry down the life of a poor old man any farther, you will as well know what to say of me as I can tell you; and I hope what I have hitherto said will in some measure recompense both your expense and labour.

FINIS

A Note About the Author

Robert Paltock (1697–1767) was an English novelist and attorney. Born in Westminster, Robert was the son of Thomas Paltock. He became an attorney as a young man and was called to the Bar at Clement's Inn, where he lived until 1759. That year, he moved to Lambeth and married Anna Skinner, with whom he would raise one son. His novel *The Life and Adventures of Peter Wilkins* (1751) is regarded as a fictional travelogue in the tradition of *Robinson Crusoe* (1719) and has influenced generations of writers, including Walter Scott, Robert Southey, Samuel Taylor Coleridge, and Charles Lamb. Despite the novel's success, Paltock's name has been largely forgotten by today's critics and readers. Regardless, *The Life and Adventures of Peter Wilkins* remains an important early adventure novel that capitalized on the growth of the colonial imagination among readers in England and abroad.

A Note from the Publisher

Spanning many genres, from non-fiction essays to literature classics to children's books and lyric poetry, Mint Edition books showcase the master works of our time in a modern new package. The text is freshly typeset, is clean and easy to read, and features a new note about the author in each volume. Many books also include exclusive new introductory material. Every book boasts a striking new cover, which makes it as appropriate for collecting as it is for gift giving. Mint Edition books are only printed when a reader orders them, so natural resources are not wasted. We're proud that our books are never manufactured in excess and exist only in the exact quantity they need to be read and enjoyed.

bookfinity™

Discover more of your favorite classics with Bookfinity™.

- Track your reading with custom book lists.
- Get great book recommendations for your personalized Reader Type.
- Add reviews for your favorite books.
- AND MUCH MORE!

Visit **bookfinity.com** and take the fun Reader Type quiz to get started.

Enjoy our classic and modern companion pairings!

Classic & Modern

Bookfinity is a registered trademark of Ingram Book Group LLC. © 2023 Bookfinity. All rights reserved.